LORD DAMNUS – CONQUEROR OF THE WORLD

Gerry Woodhouse

Best wishes

Gerry Woodhouse

ARTHUR H. STOCKWELL LTD
Torrs Park, Ilfracombe, Devon, EX34 8BA
Established 1898
www.ahstockwell.co.uk

ISBN 978-0-7223-4816-1
Printed in Great Britain by
Arthur H. Stockwell Ltd
Torrs Park   Ilfracombe
Devon EX34 8BA

FOREWORD

As I tell my story, law-abiding twenty-first-century people are concerned at the mushrooming rise in serious crime in the United Kingdom, and the incidents of violence breaking out throughout the world. You only have to watch television, or read the newspapers, to see that crime, bombings and warfare are escalating beyond control.

The world is also being turned upside down by the hundreds of thousands of refugees who are fleeing their war-torn homelands, and settling in far-flung countries.

It isn't by chance that law and order are being flushed down the pan. The deteriorating behaviour in our society is being orchestrated by Damnus, a powerful despot from another dimension in time, who is inciting different factions to fight each other, and turning more and more people to a life of crime. Not only is he feeding on the misery he is creating, but he has other plans for Planet Earth.

He has summoned the sixth-century sorcerer Merlin to the twenty-first century, where he will use his sorcery to provide Damnus with what he desires, which is to conquer the world. The citizens of the world will be powerless to fight against the Damnus takeover, as weapons can never defeat the powerful sorcery at Merlin's disposal.

Every religious sect will be wiped out, and replaced by Damnus's own brand of malevolent worship. This will result in his yet unborn son, Sammael, governing every country in the world on behalf of his father. England will be chosen as the country in which Sammael is to be crowned King of the World.

You had better believe me, because I've seen his son's coronation with my own eyes. Our monarch will crown him on a 25th of December in years to come. That date will forever be known as Damnus Day. The world population will watch the coronation in their billions, and will pledge themselves to him for all time.

You're bound to write me off as a madman, in the same league as those people who predict the end of the world. Don't knock them, because the evil that Damnus creates will result in an apocalypse on the day of reckoning. Every person on earth will die in the process.

CHAPTER ONE

I came to my senses with the images of mutilated and dying people in my mind, all because of the whim of Damnus in his bid to govern the world. I looked around me, and sighed with relief. My sixth-century horrors were behind me. I was back in twenty-first-century Wales, standing in the ruins of Merlin's castle.

My girlfriend should have been with me, but she's no longer a part of my life. I pictured her auburn hair, hanging in ringlets about her shoulders, and her jade-green eyes, which, with one look, had turned my body into warm jelly. The love we shared has been stripped from her mind. She's forgotten me as though I had never existed. Our three-week relationship was blighted by a string of evil events. I'll never forgive Merlin for what he put me through.

I'm getting ahead of myself. You need to hear my story from the very beginning, to understand how Merlin managed to convert mankind to the Damnus creed. To begin with, you have to appreciate that hundreds of parallel worlds exist in another dimension of time, far beyond our eyes. Damnus rules over some of those parallel worlds, while his brother, a powerful ruler called Magnus, governs the remaining worlds. The Damnus conspiracy first came to light on one of Magnus's worlds.

Azurina, a pretty petite lady with long blond hair and stunning cornflower-blue eyes, was walking in her garden. She had hoped to ease the worries that threatened to blow her mind apart. It was a wasted effort. The demons still rode roughshod in her head. It hadn't helped that her husband, Michael, had been summoned to an unexpected meeting with Magnus.

She heard the front door open and, moments later, Michael strolled into the garden. The tall well-built bearded man looked every inch the governor of a parallel-world earth. She couldn't hide her tetchiness.

"You're here at last, are you? Don't just stand there, man! How did the meeting go?"

He shrugged his shoulders. "Reasonably well. Magnus did most of the talking, as usual. Are you sure you want to hear what he said? It can wait, if you'd rather."

"I have to know sometime." She snapped at him. "Come on, then. What have you let us in for?"

"It's not as bad as you think. Magnus has set the two of us a task, but we'll be taking a back seat for the time being," he grunted. "That's just as well, seeing you're pregnant."

She flared at him, "Trust you to mention that! I didn't want this baby, but Magnus ordered us to produce a son for him." She sighed in frustration. "What's he up to?"

Michael rolled his blue eyes at her.

She screamed at him. "Don't look at me like that! I'm only speaking how I feel." The grumpy look didn't suit her. "Well? Are you going to tell me, then?"

"Just calm down and I will. He's worried about Planet Earth. There are signs of ominous changes down there. When he said that Damnus was involved, I asked if his brand of worship was taking over. He slapped me down. This is more than a religious crusade, he said. Damnus is plotting to set up his yet unborn son, in years to come, as a worldwide despot, controlling every nation on earth.

"His right-hand man is the sixth-century sorcerer Merlin, who's totally committed to the Damnus cause. Our all-knowing leader told me that Merlin has been ordered to sire a son, to help Damnus achieve his domination of the world."

"They're all at it, are they, spouting out their orders for children to be spawned?" She pouted. "I'm not thrilled with the idea of mixing with Damnus. Like Magnus, he's a powerful supernatural entity. What chance do we stand against him?"

"Magnus insists he will crush his brother's plans. He's ordered us to travel to earth to set things up for him. I'll tell you what he has in mind when we get there."

She yelled at him, "Don't fob me off like that! You're treating me like a complete idiot. Why are you being so damned evasive? I am a part of this, remember. I've every right to know what he's up to."

"Don't let's fall out. I'll tell you what I can. I said that Merlin has to sire a child. That presents him with an immediate problem. His wife's barren."

Azurina chipped in. "So, another woman will bear his child. Right?"

"Exactly. That's where we come into the picture."

She shuddered. "Magnus isn't expecting me to be that woman, is he?"

He laughed out loud. "What's the point of Merlin taking your body? You're already pregnant. That's all I can tell you for now. The missing pieces will fall into place when we visit earth. Let's be off, then, shall we?"

"You mean, like now?"

"I'm afraid so. Timing is crucial." He pulled her to her feet. "Put some warm clothing on, then we'll be on our way."

A cold March wind swept across the forest clearing. The water in a small pool rippled as the gusting breeze rode across its surface. Dead leaves danced in the air like whirling dervishes. A crude hut stood on the edge of the clearing. Built from branches and rocks, and covered with grass sods, it was a makeshift form of shelter. A huge gnarled rock towered above the forest canopy on the other side of the clearing.

Michael and Azurina materialised on sixth-century earth. She shivered.

"I didn't expect you to bring me to a forsaken hole like this. Why are we here?"

He pointed through the trees. "You see that clearing? Our

twins will soon be walking across there on their way to Merlin's castle. It's not far away."

She smiled knowingly. "You're talking about the brother and sister we don't have. I'm on to your little game, Mister. You're going to create . . ."

She stopped talking and rubbed her stomach. Her face turned red with anger.

He looked worried. "Are you all right, darling?"

"As right as I ever can be, you swine. I've twigged why Magnus wanted a son of us." Her fists beat against his chest. "You lying bastard! I'm not stupid. Our baby will end up as the child that Merlin wants, won't he?" she yelled at him through her tears. "Why didn't you have the guts to tell me!"

He sighed. "I'm sorry. I would have told you when the time was right. Yes. Our leader is counting on our son to snuff out Damnus's dreams, so we have to let him go. Does that make sense to you?"

"No, it doesn't!" She shrugged her shoulders. "What does it matter? The decision's been made, whether I like it or not."

"Stop beating yourself up." He looked her in the eyes. "There's something else you should know. You're expecting twin boys. Our firstborn will live on earth, working for our leader. Our other boy will live with us."

She spluttered in disbelief before her sarcasm showed itself. "Oh, how wonderful! I *will* have a baby to fuss over." Her anger bubbled over. "If he thinks I'm grateful, well, I'm not. This is ridiculous. While I'm caring for one son, my other son is being thrown in at the deep end against Damnus. What is he thinking of? How can our son fight Damnus's plans with Merlin feeding warped thoughts into his mind? Can't the leader use his clout against earth? He's done it before."

"I asked the same question. He wasn't amused. 'I don't intend to get involved straight away,' he said. Magnus insists his plan is the best way of defeating evil. Merlin will send our son to the twentieth century, where he'll guide his footsteps by setting ideas in his head. Merlin will also influence the people around our son, like his surrogate parents. Don't worry yourself about our son doing what Merlin tells him to do, because it won't pan out that way. I'll make certain of that by planting some of my thoughts in his mind when he's born. Merlin will try to take over our son's body, to control what he does, but he will find that he can't, because our son will inherit all of my powers of sorcery. They will stop Merlin from getting inside our son's body and mind. I know it's not making sense, but our son will face Damnus one day. Magnus fell out with his brother centuries ago. When the time is right, he wants him out of the way forever." He shrugged his shoulders. "Don't ask me when that will happen, because I've no idea. That's the way it is. Our son is on his own."

"I've never heard anything so ridiculous. What happens if he fails in his task?"

Michael grunted. "Magnus said he won't succeed at first. It will take years, but 'triumph will blossom out of failure' were the words he used. He wants Damnus to bask in the belief that he's achieved everything he ever dreamt of, and only then will Magnus get our son to pull the carpet from under his feet. He's going to give him a scroll, which will be the key to bringing Damnus down." He pulled a face. "That's it. He told me the meeting was over, and took off."

A faint smile played around her lips. "He's clever, that one, but he's lost the plot," – she thought about what she'd said – "or has he? So, why are we here?"

"Magnus has ordered me to make replicas of the two of us. They'll meet up with Merlin later today. Before they do, I have to pay Merlin a visit to plant some thoughts in his mind. I will persuade him to give our twins a job in his castle, and let them live in that hut over there. I'll also make sure he rapes your twin sister, to produce his male heir." He grinned. "With her body, he'd have raped her anyhow, but I can't leave it to chance."

"Won't Merlin know you're planting thoughts in his mind?"

"Of course not! I'll be invisible. That's why you shouldn't worry about number-one son. As well as being immortal like us, the powers of sorcery that he possesses will keep him out of harm's way."

She looked sheepish. "I'm sorry I doubted you, darling. Is there anything else to tell me?"

He nodded. "In the next few days, Merlin will rape your twin sister. His sorcery will make sure she produces a son. He'll make her forget that he raped her." He roared with laughter. "What a waste of time that is. Our replicas will know what's going to happen to them before it happens. We'll meet up with them, just before our sons are born, and take their place. That's when Merlin will have number-one son snatched from us."

"I'm glad the truth's out. There's one thing that worries me. Will your replicas deceive him?"

"Of course they will. They're as human as we are. Merlin won't realise he's ravishing a make-believe woman. And, before you ask, yes, she can make babies."

"That's amazing. Can Merlin create replica human beings?"

"Our leader says he can, but they don't have blood in their veins, nor beating hearts, like our replicas do."

"If my replica is a copy of me, won't she be carrying twins?"

Michael couldn't hide his amusement. "No. She'll be a virgin. Have faith in my sorcery. I asked the leader if we could listen in on Merlin's conversations, so we know what's going on down on earth over the next few years. He's given me the go-ahead. While Merlin's under my spell, I'll plant two of my hairs into his eyebrows. We'll be able to watch him, and listen to him, on one of our mirrors back home. The leader says I can plant my hairs into number-one son's eyebrows when he's born, so we can see what he's up to and listen to him."

"That's great. We might be able to help him out."

"Only if Magnus gives us the OK. Right. It's time we met our twins."

He muttered a few words, and two naked replicas appeared. They stood with their eyes shut.

Azurina put her hand on the man's chest. She pulled it away and giggled. "His heart's beating, and I felt his breath on my face."

Michael looked pleased. "Not bad, eh?"

"It's like looking at ourselves in a mirror. Can they really mimic what we do?"

"Of course they can. They're living images of us. Everything we've done in our lives and every word we've spoken is stored in their minds. Our memories are their memories."

"You'd better clothe them, or they'll catch their death of cold."

"They can't die. They're immortal, like us." He shouted a few words at them, and their bodies became clothed.

Azurina gasped. "Their clothes are different from what we're wearing."

Michael laughed. "I've given them the clothes that are worn on sixth-century earth." He touched the man's arm. "Your name is Paulus. Your wife is Coruline. You know what I expect of you when I wake you."

He clapped his hands. The replicas showed no sign of emotion, or surprise, as they awoke. The woman kissed Azurina's cheeks while the man shook Michael's hand.

Paulus grinned. "It's an interesting agenda you've set us. We'll meet up with you just before your children are born." He slapped Michael on the back. "I'll give you enough time to call on Merlin before we turn up at his castle. We'll see you in a few months from now."

They walked hand in hand through the clearing before disappearing into the forest.

Michael put his arm around Azurina's waist. "Look at them. They're as much in love as we are."

"What will happen to them when we take their place?"

"The leader says they can live on one of our worlds. Because their child is Merlin's son, I'll remove anything that's evil from his mind. That'll make him one of us. Now, return to our world. I'll join you later."

He embraced her before they both disappeared.

CHAPTER TWO

Sunlight streamed through the windows of Azurina's bedroom, filling the room in its warm yellow glow. Her eyelids fluttered, then she woke up. She reached out for Michael's body. He wasn't there. Her concern ebbed away as her thoughts came alive. He'd left, earlier, to meet up with his deputy governors.

She struggled out of bed and looked at herself in the mirror. The sight of her swollen body made her sigh. Pregnancy had put her busy life on hold.

The bedroom door opened and Michael came in. He took her in his arms and kissed her. She trembled with expectancy, but her body couldn't cope with the erotic thoughts that played havoc with her emotions.

"How are my sons this morning?"

She rubbed at her body. "It won't be long before they're born."

"Good. One of them belongs to Merlin, remember." His unfeeling words came back to haunt him. "Sorry, darling. That sounds as if I don't love him. That's not true. I can't wait to meet up with him when this business is over."

She stared eagerly into his eyes. "When will that be?"

"The leader said about thirty-two years, in earth time. It'll fly by."

The tears trickled down her face.

He cuddled her. "Listen. Magnus wants you to keep an eye on our son from time to time, down on earth."

Her face broke into a broad smile.

Michael frowned. "You're not to make contact with him unless the leader gives the go-ahead." He relaxed. "What are you going to call our boys?"

"How about Raphael and Sariel?"

"Mmm. I like those names."

She winced with pain. "That hurt. I think we had better leave for earth."

"I'll let you get dressed. Merlin's bound to be watching the clearing, so we'll materialise inside that hut our twins live in. Put some warm clothing on."

Paulus and Coruline weren't surprised when Michael and Azurina appeared in the hut.

Michael took charge. "Our babies are due at any moment. After we've delivered them, return to our world and take our other son with you. I'm sure Merlin will be listening for the cries of his newborn son." He laughed. "He mustn't hear two babies crying. I'll use my sorcery to keep one of them quiet after he's born. Swap your clothes with ours. I don't want Merlin getting suspicious at the way we're dressed."

No sooner had they changed than Azurina started to give birth.

Fifteen minutes later, Raphael lay asleep in a cot while Sariel fed at his mother's breast. Michael gently pulled him away and handed him to Coruline.

"Off you go." He allowed himself a smile. "You two will be going through this soon. Thank your lucky stars it won't be twins."

After they had gone, Michael took Raphael in his arms and planted two of his hairs into the sleeping child's eyebrows. "The hairs will keep us in touch with what's going on during his life on earth – which reminds me, I have to set some thoughts in his mind." He placed his hands on the baby's head. "You have inherited my powers of sorcery, but I won't let you use them immediately, unless you have need of them. As a descendant of my line, you are immortal, so no one can harm you. You'll be afraid of no one, and that includes a tyrant called Damnus and his yet unborn son. You will accept situations that seem impossible, without question, fear or consequence, and you will never lose heart when things go against you. You will come into contact with a magician called Merlin, who thinks you're his son. He will try to convince you to help Damnus take over the world and convert mankind to his form of religion. You will fight against the evil that Damnus is creating."

Azurina and Michael huddled together inside the hut. Raphael lay asleep in his cot.

Michael whispered to her, "Merlin's child-snatchers are on their way. We must act out what Merlin expects of us. He thinks we're two unsuspecting mortals." He pulled a face. "I read his mind when we were last here. His men have been ordered to kill us." He paused to let his words sink in. "Don't be afraid. It'll be different from when you died on earth. You'll feel no pain. Think your orders to your spirit, so that when it leaves your body it will take refuge in one of those crows, in the clearing, until we're ready to shape-change. Take Raphael outside."

"Don't worry. I'm not frightened."

She carried the cot outside and placed it in front of a blazing wood fire. Raphael woke up and smiled at her. She picked him up and kissed him, then sat on the trunk of a fallen tree, where she sang a lullaby to him.

Merlin stood in front of a large mirror in his castle, watching the living images in the forest clearing. He roared with laughter as his two men charged into the clearing, shouting at the tops of their voices and brandishing their swords. One of them snatched the child from Azurina. Raphael screamed with fright.

She pleaded with the man, "Give him back to me. He wants his mother."

The man kicked her to the ground.

"Shut your mouth, woman. Merlin wants the child." His pitiless grin showed the rotting, blackened teeth in his mouth.

She shrieked with make-believe pain as he plunged his sword into her heart. The other man ran into the hut. Michael's dagger was no match for the kidnapper's blade. One thrust from the sword killed him.

Merlin beamed his thoughts into the screaming child's mind: 'Stop your crying until you rest in my arms.'

The child fell asleep. One man ripped Azurina's cloak from her body and wrapped it around the child, hiding it from view. His accomplice picked up another of Merlin's thoughts. He dragged Michael's corpse into the clearing and dumped it next to Azurina's body. Their task completed, they hurried to where their horses were tethered and galloped away towards Merlin's castle.

Sweat ran down Merlin's face, from his deep concentration as he stared into the mirror. His thoughts lifted the two dead bodies into the air. He murmured a spell. The bodies broke down into dust, which blew across the clearing. He wiped the images from the mirror with a wave of his hand.

Two crows flew above the clearing, calling to each other with raucous sounds. They landed on the ground.

One of them spoke Michael's words. "Are you all right, darling?"

Azurina answered him. "That's it, then? Merlin has Raphael, and our leader's got his way. I won't ever forget today." The tone in her voice softened. "I'm sorry, Michael. The leader must think I'm a right bitch. If it wasn't for his gift of immortality, I wouldn't be here."

"There's no time for chit-chat. Let's shape-change. Follow me."

They flew under the canopy of the trees and landed on the forest floor. Within seconds, naked replicas of them appeared from nowhere.

Michael spoke from inside his crow. "Move your spirit into your replica body."

As their souls left the crow hosts, the startled birds squawked in terror before beating a hasty retreat. The replicas came to life.

Michael clothed the pair of them using his sorcery. Azurina put her head on his chest and sobbed.

He stroked her hair. "Don't feel bad about giving up Raphael. You can watch him grow up until we meet him one day." His mood changed. "I've had enough of this place. Let's get home."

An anxious Merlin paced the floor of his hall, waiting for his men to arrive. At last the main doors opened and the men walked in. One of them handed the child to him.

He hissed at the man. "Are you certain no one saw the child on your way here?"

The man shook his head. "No, sire. I hid him in the woman's cloak, as you bid me."

He beckoned to them. "Come closer and hear what your reward will be."

They grinned as they moved towards him.

He whispered in their ears, then dismissed them from his presence. As they left the hall, he cried out at them, "Fools. Your reward will be to live on one of Damnus's parallel worlds."

The two men walked into the castle courtyard. Not a word was spoken as they climbed the steps leading to the battlements. They each drew a dagger from their belt and plunged it into their hearts. Two lifeless bodies plummeted into the moat. Their bodies disintegrated as they sank beneath the water.

Merlin woke the child from its sleep. Large cornflower-blue eyes opened wide and stared at him in fascination. Merlin's face broke into a smile as its chubby fingers played with his beard.

His mood changed abruptly. "I have to prepare you for your future life. Sleep until you are born again."

The baby closed its eyes.

He pulled a hair from his beard and planted it in the child's scalp. "My hair will grow with yours, for the rest of your life. I will have a use for it one day." The sorcerer placed his hand on the child's head as he buried a few thoughts into its mind. "I have given you the gift of time travel, which you will discover when you are older. You will have need of it one day. In the meantime, I grant you the gift of living in a dreamworld when you are asleep. You will control your dreams without realising that you are time-travelling. Your dreams will keep your mind sane, to overcome the cruelty which you will suffer at the hands of the parents I have selected for you. Their cruelty will prepare you for helping me in the future. You will forget me. It is time to meet your new parents, in the twentieth century."

Their bodies briefly shimmered before the two of them vanished from sight.

A young couple were watching television in their Christmas-decorated lounge when Merlin appeared. The woman screamed and the man grabbed a poker from the fireplace. He rushed at Merlin.

"How the bloody hell did you get in here? And what are you doing with that baby?"

They both fell silent as Merlin captured their minds. The man dropped the poker and sat down on the sofa next to his wife.

The heavily pregnant woman walked upstairs to her bedroom, under Merlin's influence. He made her lie on the bed, where he removed her skirt and panties before parting her legs. He mumbled more words of magic. Her stomach shrank as a dribble of dark-red vapour seeped from the top of her legs.

He laid his son between her thighs. More words dripped from his mouth. The child's body broke down into a jelly-like substance, which slid up between the woman's legs, and into her body. Her stomach swelled. She was pregnant again.

He spoke to her. "You will have your baby tomorrow."

She got off the bed and dressed herself. They returned to the lounge. Merlin's cheeks moved around as he gathered saliva in his mouth. He spat it on to the carpet. Static electricity crackled in the air as the saliva grew into a globular ball. It bubbled away, letting off spurts of steam before breaking down into two smaller balls. The balls kept changing shape, as if something was trying to escape from them. After a few minutes of shape-shifting, the balls formed themselves into two squat midgets.

Their charcoal-grey skin was covered in wart-like growths, from which long tufts of red hair sprouted. A pair of horns and oversized pointed ears protruded from their goat-like heads. Their eyes glowed red, and small leathery wings flapped on their backs.

They skulked around the room on their stumpy legs, growling menacingly.

Merlin silenced them. "Listen to me, you Damnus-devils. You will live inside the bodies of these two humans, where you will poison their minds so they show no love for my son as he grows up."

They jabbered excitedly as they flew around the living room, before exploding into clouds of red vapour, which flowed up the couple's nostrils.

Merlin laughed as he willed himself back to the sixth century. He reappeared inside a small stone building, hidden away in the forest that surrounded his castle. His mistress, Emeralda, lay naked on a bed of straw. The auburn-haired, green-eyed lady was in the throes of giving birth. An old crone pulled a baby girl from between Emeralda's legs. She slapped it on the back, then washed and dressed the screaming child before nestling her in her mother's arms.

The crone's reward wasn't the few coins she expected. Merlin bundled her outside and cast a spell on her. Her screams went unheard as her head, arms and legs were sucked into her body before she broke down into nothingness.

He returned and sat on the floor beside his mistress. He was a slimly built man. A pair of intense sky-blue eyes sat in a pale, handsome face. His nose was slightly hooked. Long, dark curly hair hung around his shoulders, and his beard flowed to his chest. He kissed her hand.

"I bow to your sorcery, My Lady. Your husband will never know I fathered your child. It was only this morning that we made love."

Emeralda looked worried. "What about the old hag who

delivered the child? She will tell everyone."

"I have done away with her." He pulled a face. "My wife must never learn about us."

She bit at her lip. "Neither must my husband."

"Do not worry about Lord Madrog. I can take care of him," he chided her. "We must hurry. Feed our daughter, then I will take her to her new parents. Before I do, I have to place a thought in her mind which will stop her from having relationships with men as she grows older. I have placed the same thought in my son's mind, so he will show no interest in women. They must both be virgins when we arrange for their paths to cross."

He placed his hand on the baby's head, muttered a few words, then pulled a hair from his arm and planted it in the child's scalp.

She looked puzzled. "What are you doing?"

"My hair will tell me wherever she might be, and where she is travelling to. I have done the same with my son."

"I am impressed. What have you got planned for our daughter?"

"She is a vital part of a mission that my son will undertake when he grows older. Wait here for me. I will tell you more when I return from the twentieth century."

Seconds later, Merlin appeared in the master bedroom of Lovington Rectory. He switched the light on. The Reverend Julius Milner and his wife were asleep. Merlin put them into a deep trance. He pulled the bedclothes back and smiled. Nine months ago he had travelled to their time and had influenced the Reverend's wife, as well as his son's foster-mother, into conceiving a child of their own. He used the same sorcery as he'd done with his son, and placed his daughter in the woman's womb.

He looked down at the reverend gentleman. "Your wife will give birth to my daughter tomorrow. In my son's older years I will use your body to guide him into uncovering the gifts of magic that lie in some stones of mine, which you will pass to him when he is older." He took a pouch from his pocket. "These are the stones that I speak of. Come with me."

The rector got out of bed and followed Merlin downstairs. They walked into the lounge and paused in front of the Reverend's davenport desk. The sorcerer knelt on the floor.

"Watch everything I do, and store it in your mind."

He removed the bottom drawer, put his hand into the recess and pulled out a small wooden box, into which he placed the pouch. He looked up at the rector.

"Remember where the pouch is hidden. I will tell you when I want you to remove it, so you may wear it around your neck, to use the magic of the stones. Forget about the pouch until I tell you. Now return to your bed and sleep."

Merlin switched the light off and was gone.

Emeralda was waiting when he returned. She looked stunning in her green dress, with her auburn locks hanging in ringlets over her bare shoulders. He sat beside her.

"We need to talk about our children's future. I intend to influence their lives, so they follow the path that has been chosen for them. They will be ready to carry out my mission when they are twenty-seven years old."

She shook her head and laughed. "Twenty-seven years? That is a long time to wait, Merlin."

"Your words are ill-chosen, woman. I do not intend to wait twenty-seven years."

She pulled a face.

"You must understand that, as well as having a past and a present life, we have a future life that is already mapped out for us. During the next three weeks we will travel into different parts of our children's lives, to sway them into what I want them to do. They will visit us, in our time, four weeks from now, to carry out my mission. I have granted my son the gift of dream-weaving, which means he will be capable of creating whatever fantasy he wishes in his sleeping hours. I will use his dreamworld to weave a chain of deception that will lead him into learning what the purpose of this mission is all about." He roared with laughter. "In one of his dreams he will watch you imprison me inside a rock."

She laughed. "Really? Tell me more. What is this mission about?"

"My son and our daughter will produce two things which are vital in helping Damnus to conquer the world. I will not tell you what they are, yet. You will enjoy the moment all the more if you wait until they return to our time. I want to surprise you."

"What about your wife? If we are to spend the next few weeks together, she is bound to ask awkward questions. And what am I going to tell my husband?"

A sadistic smile creased his face. "I am the bearer of sad news. My wife will fall down the tower staircase this evening and break her neck."

Her sarcasm showed itself. "I am so sorry to hear that. What about my husband?"

"Make an excuse to bring him here tomorrow. I will put him into a deep trance whilst we travel into the twentieth century to prepare our children's lives for this mission. I have something planned for him when our children join us in the sixth century."

CHAPTER THREE

My name is Christopher Milner, better known as Kit. I first saw the light of day on Christmas Day in the mid-1980s in the market town of Grinton, which nestles in rural Hertfordshire. Some wag once described the town as a cemetery with street lights.

I have a clear image of being born. From a point of darkness I passed into light, with the soft moaning of the wind wafting in my ears. The smell of woodsmoke filled the air. A beautiful lady held me in her arms. She planted a kiss on my cheek, and rocked me from side to side as she sang a lullaby. This loving moment was shattered when I was snatched from her arms by a strange man. That's all I remember.

She wasn't the woman who brought me up as my mother. I used to think it was my first dream. Perhaps that's where my dreamworld started. Let me explain. I didn't enjoy a happy home life, so to compensate for my enduring misery, I managed to harness the unearthly powers of my dreamworld as an escape route from the unhappiness of my waking hours.

I taught myself incredible gifts. When I woke up I could recall every action, and every word, from my dream. I trained my mind to choose the dream I wanted. I even controlled what happened in every fantasy, even to waking up when it suited me. Laugh if you like, but I used to bring back small souvenirs from my dreamworld. I always hid them away from my parents.

My mother was a pretty lady, with jet black hair and large brown eyes. Looking at the five-foot-nothing, bald-headed tub of lard who was my stepfather, I couldn't understand what she had ever seen in him, to want to marry him after my father died in a hit-and-run accident. William Grodam was his name. He was a perpetual moaner, and as work-shy as benefits skivers are.

There were genuine reasons why he couldn't earn an honest living. He hadn't got the time. His days were spent ogling television, or checking whether his horses had won. He was an avid worshipper of anything made from hops, grapes or barley. He'd have given Bacchus a run for his money.

My parents never showed a smidgen of love for me. When I was at home I spent all of my time in my bedroom, out of their way. I was subjected to slaps around the head from my mother. Mr Grodam hated me. I lost count of the number of times he beat me. I knew when a beating was on the cards. The stomping of his club foot on the stairs heralded my punishment time. My mother could never bring herself to come upstairs and comfort me. One strange trait always followed my beatings. I'd wake up the next day with no pain or bruises. Who could blame me for developing hang-ups and fixations, considering my way of life? I ended up with an attitude problem towards adults, and members of the opposite sex in particular.

There was one chink of light. My home problems didn't affect my school life. I treated the teachers with respect, without getting too close to them. School reports spoke of a bright child, in both academic and sporting fields, who was blessed with a vivid imagination. I was popular with my male schoolmates, but found it impossible to bond with the girls.

I left school at sixteen, with no clue as to where my job prospects lay. Mr Grodam called me into the kitchen the day after I left school. Mother was wiping up the breakfast things. With a cigarette dangling from his bottom lip, and a glass of beer in his hand, he put his twopenny-worth in on my future.

"If you think you're loafing around the house now you've left school, you've got another think coming. Get out and find a bloody job." He flicked his ash into the sink. "You can't expect me to keep you fed and watered."

My mother sided with him, as ever. "He's right. I happen to

know there's a job going at the Brook Street auctioneers. You'd better get down there."

I'm not sure where it came from, but a bullish feeling of boldness hit me. I'd had my fill of them, and I thumped the table.

"You've both had your say. Now it's my turn. Listen carefully. Things are going to change in this house, from today. You'll both start showing me some respect. My name's Kit, not 'you little sod', or the other names you call me." My juices were in full flow. "I've had enough of spending all of my time in my bedroom while you two swan around in the lounge. I'll have my meals served in the lounge from now on, so I can watch television," I snorted. "That'll make a change. I never want to see the pair of you sitting in the same room as me, ever. Do you understand?"

A common look of fear showed in their eyes.

My stepfather's reply was short and sweet. "Whatever you say, Kit."

My mother nodded her agreement.

"Good. That's sorted, then. I'm off to find a job. Make sure my dinner's on the table, in the lounge, when I get back."

Grinton is a pleasant Georgian market town, blessed with the usual trappings: a fish-and-chip shop, a church, three chapels, two Chinese takeaways and more than its fair share of public houses. One other landmark mustn't be overlooked. It was to play a major part in my life. The town had once boasted a bustling cattle market. The only reminder of those bygone days was the rusting metal pens, memorials to the animals that had passed through the market on their way to the slaughterhouse. These premises now housed the auctioneering business of Brine & Cherry.

As I walked by their premises, a lady was pinning a piece of paper on their noticeboard. I stopped and read it: 'Intelligent young man wanted to work in the business.'

I went inside and offered myself for the job. A grey-haired lady took me to see a Mr Heaslip, who told me he was the assistant auctioneer. He must have seen something he liked in me, because he offered me the job. It was the first time in my life that I'd felt good about myself.

I learned all about the company during my first few months there. Mr Brine and Mr Cherry were no longer on this earth. The owner was a Martin Henderson. As well as pulling the business strings, he was the head auctioneer. He sold all manner of flotsam and jetsam. It didn't matter that most of the stuff was crap. Mr Henderson applied the well-established principle that mugs will buy anything so long as the hype is pitched at the right level and the auctioneer is under-generous with the truth.

He came over as an affable man. Standing at just under six feet tall, he would have been in his sixties. A shock of curly grey hair sat comfortably with his glowing complexion and twinkling blue eyes. He'd have been handsome in his younger days, but his looks had been squandered on an overindulgence of fatty foods and alcohol. The double chin and bulging stomach were dead giveaways.

In those early years our paths rarely crossed. That suited me fine. My time was spent in the auction rooms under the beady eyes of Arthur Horne, the head porter. Arthur was a sparsely haired, medium-sized bloke of indefinable age. As thin as a broom handle, he knew everything worth knowing about the business. The first day he took me under his wing, he told me he was a director. That was true. He directed, and I did the spadework. Most of the time he could be found in the Robin Hood hostelry, next door, whilst I sweated my guts out. I needed to learn the ropes quickly if I was to survive in his company. The first two years were routine, even boring. More than once I was tempted to leave. I could have earned much more elsewhere, but it never happened.

Arthur told me that Martin Henderson enjoyed a cosy working relationship with several solicitors. His tempting backhanders ensured that the effects from the estates of deceased persons found their way into our salerooms.

My duties centred around the preparation of sale entries.

I had to position each item in its rightful place in the various salerooms. Being a big lad, I clicked for the job of carting the heaviest furniture around.

Arthur had this habit of whining as he wiped his nose on his sleeve, "You're a growing lad, young Kit. You need the exercise to toughen you up. You'll thank me when you're older."

What a load of cobblers! This humping around could only lead to hernia problems, as well as ruining my non-existent sex life. Arthur was the living testimony of my forward thinking. He was the proud owner of a huge double hernia. The bulging truss under his trousers was testament to that.

Mind you, what am I blabbering on about? Here I was, eighteen years old, and I'd never been out with a girl. Life took on a monotonous routine. I was stuck in an ever deepening rut. It didn't take me long to realise that the rut would soon become too deep to climb out of. When that happened I'd be trapped forever, a prisoner of my own manic disbelief in myself.

Thankfully, life would kick me up the backside in years to come.

My first four years at Brine & Cherry flew by. I'd grown a moustache and beard, and stood well over six feet tall. It hadn't helped me find a girlfriend, even though I knew that girls found me handsome, with my dark curly hair and cornflower-blue eyes. I did my best to respond to the female overtures that frequently came my way, but, no matter how hard I tried, a mental barrier stopped me from dallying with their affections – or anything else of theirs for that matter. More worrying were the admiring glances I received from some men. I certainly wasn't gay, no matter what that other genre might have thought.

Just after my twentieth birthday, my parents died. Even though I felt no love for them, the manner of their deaths both disturbed and horrified me. A police investigation found that my stepfather had cut my mother's throat, then made love to her. Before she took her last breath, she had managed to grab the knife he had used, and stabbed him in the back. The police forensic team had found my mother's blood in his stomach.

I was humping a brute of a seventeenth-century coffer around the saleroom, a few days after their deaths, when Arthur put his head around the door. "Martin wants to see you. Now, Kit, not tomorrow."

I made my way to his office. He was sat at his desk with a cup of coffee in his hand. He nodded towards the coffee machine and invited me to help myself, which I did. He motioned me to sit down.

"It's about time I showed some appreciation for the good work you're putting in for me. It hasn't gone unnoticed. I know he shouldn't tittle-tattle, but Arthur tells me you are unhappy at the thought of living in your parents house now that they are gone." He smiled at me. "I might have an answer to your problem. How would you fancy living in the flat above the saleroom? If so, I'll get it decorated, and I'm prepared to furnish it as well. What do you say?"

I'd have been a fool not to accept. "Your offer is much appreciated, Martin. Living on the premises will give me the chance to get more involved in the business and put my parents' deaths behind me."

"Excellent. It'll take about two weeks to sort the flat out, then you can move in."

I was floating on air as I left his office.

Martin was true to his word. A fortnight later I moved into the flat.

The years passed quickly, and before I knew it my twenty-seventh birthday was approaching. I'd spent those years toiling for Martin Henderson. I didn't lug heavy pieces of furniture around any more. I had risen in the ranks to operations manager, on a fairly decent salary.

Socialising still didn't figure in my life. I wasn't hanging out with people at weekends, and certainly didn't find a girlfriend. I could best be described as dull, boring, isolated, workaholic and definitely virginal.

I didn't have the inclination, or the know-how, when it came to chatting up the opposite sex. I've lost count of the number of times I tried to buck this trend. Life delighted in throwing the buck back at me. The fault didn't lie in my body, it lay in my mind.

My failure in socialising was compensated by further improvements in my working life. Martin called me into his office one afternoon and said he wanted me to take over the duties of the assistant auctioneer, who was retiring at the end of the year. "I'm offering you the chance of a lifetime." He threw his head back and laughed. "At the rate of knots you're going, you'll be after my bloody job next year."

How could I refuse? I began understudying the retiring auctioneer.

Martin's auction house boasted three salerooms, where auctions were held every Saturday. Two of the rooms sold what I politely term rubbish. That left the third room, affectionately known as the posh-room. In this inner sanctum we sold the best wares. On certain Saturdays we held our Fine Art Sale in the posh-room, where we sold the very best antiques and collectables. These sales attracted dealers from all over the country, lured on to our premises by the captivating narrative in our glossy, overpriced catalogue.

The months sped by to late August as I learned the special skills and craftiness that every good auctioneer needs at his fingertips. September came and went, and October was upon us. It's a month I shall never forget. Friday and Saturday the 26th and 27th of October are imprinted on my mind. They were the viewing and sale days of our Fine Art Sale. Those two days triggered a chain of events that I could do nothing to prevent.

When I woke up on that fateful Friday morning I was in a buoyant mood. I strolled into Martin's office and parked my backside on the radiator next to his. He couldn't hide his delight at the unusually high quality of goods in the sale. I asked where they had come from.

He smiled like a Cheshire cat. "We have to thank the late Reverend Julius Milner. Most of his effects have found their way here, thanks to a solicitor friend who's handling his estate. It was a bad day for your namesake when he died, but it's going to be one hell of a sale for us." He gave me a funny look. "I don't suppose the old boy was related to you, was he? If so, he might have left you something in his will. Perhaps his favourite commode, with toilet paper, slops and all."

I shook my head. "Reverend Milner certainly isn't a part of my family tree. What do you know about him?"

The radiator creaked as he removed his backside from it. He plonked himself behind his desk.

"My solicitor friend tells me he was the Rector of Lovington."

"Didn't he have any family to leave his things to?"

"A daughter was mentioned, but his wife died some years ago." We nattered for another five minutes before he excused himself. "I have to go out. I'll be back later this afternoon. See you then."

Hundreds of people turned out, to see what we had to sell, but by a quarter to five the last of them had gone. I told Arthur he could clock off, and I'd lock up at five.

Sod's law prevailed. Three people walked in at five to five. One of them caught my eye. He didn't so much attract my attention as demand it. He was just over five feet tall. What he lacked in height he made up for in bulk. He must have weighed in at twenty stone or more. As square as a Centurion tank, he had short black hair and sported a moustache. His podgy, pasty-coloured face wasn't helped by the folds of surplus flesh hanging under his chin. The extra chins were draped over his shirt collar. A dark overcoat struggled to hide his obesity. He was also sporting the worst wig I've ever seen.

I shivered. It had nothing to do with the temperature in the room. Evil wafted from him, filling his airspace with an aura of malevolence. The other two dodgy-looking characters shared the same sinister expression on their faces. They were dressed in mandatory dark overcoats. They towered above the fat man. My gut feeling was to steer clear of them.

Fat-man became visibly agitated when he spotted a davenport desk. He waddled across to it as fast as his stumpy legs would allow. He removed all four drawers, then squatted on the floor and peered inside. Not content with that, he pulled a torch from his overcoat pocket and shone it inside the interior. He pushed the drawers back into place and broke wind as he struggled to his feet. He pointed at the desk, patted it and muttered a few words to his henchmen. Cheesy smirks spread across their faces. Fat-man nodded towards the door. They sauntered out of the saleroom in close convoy.

The davenport was a beautiful desk, made during the 1870s and named after a certain Captain Davenport, who wanted a portable writing desk to take on his military campaigns. It had a hinged lid, very much like a school desk, with four drawers down one side and four matching dummy drawers on the opposite side.

I checked the desk out on my list. It had a reserve tag of £400. I ran my fingers across the polished walnut, feeling the patina that can only build up with age. Fat-man had got to me. I removed the drawers and peered into the dark recess. I wasn't sure what he had expected to find, but if he knew his davenports he could have been looking for a secret hidey-hole. My brief search revealed nothing. I wasn't surprised. Some hidey-holes are harder to find than others, and many desks don't have one.

As I got back on my feet, I had a feeling I was being watched. I turned around. Fat-man and his two henchmen stood staring at me. He waddled across to me. His breath floated up and settled on my face. It smelt as if something had died in his throat and was slowly decomposing. I looked down at the wig and wondered if the white specks were artificial dandruff.

He poked me in the chest with a finger. "Keep your hands off that bloody desk. If you're thinking of buying it, forget it."

The goons stared at me with unsmiling eyes. I kept my cool and ignored his disrespect.

"I don't want to buy the desk. I work here."

His weepy eyes bored into mine. "That's just as well, you twat, because I'm buying it." As he laughed, his chins swung from side to side.

By rights, I should have told the obnoxious little sod his fortune, but I held back. "You can cut that language out, for a start. The auctioneer will take your bid along with that of anyone else who wants to buy it."

Smelly-breath stood his ground. He turned to his lapdogs and attempted a larger-than-life impression of me. "I say, old chaps, the auctioneer is prepared to take my bid tomorrow." He snarled his words out. "Is he putting us in our place or is he taking the piss?" He glared at me.

It made me feel as if he was staring at a piece of shit. He nodded to the thug on his left. For his size, he moved quickly. He grabbed the lapels of my jacket and tugged me towards him. The thug's face was barely an inch from mine. His breath smelt of second-hand curry.

With bloodied eyes bulging from their sockets, and his spittle raining on my face, he told me my fortune. "Listen, knobhead. Billy Grodam's buying that desk. Got it? If I have any more trouble from you, I'll cut your bollocks off."

The guy let go of my jacket. He smoothed his hair, pulled his tie straight and grinned for the benefit of Fat-man.

I felt light-headed with anger. This obnoxious little fat man shared the same name as my late stepfather.

I waggled a finger at my mouth. "Watch my lips, Fat-man. If there's any trouble at the auction tomorrow, I'll call the police. Now get out of here."

The two henchmen moved menacingly towards me.

Grodam growled at them. "Not now, boys." He threw a murderous look at me. It was like looking into a fortune teller's ball and witnessing my own death.

They turned on their heels and walked out of the room.

I should have called the police there and then, but Martin would never have forgiven me, especially with the auction being the next day. I decided to make a clean breast of what had happened when he returned.

He rolled up at a quarter past five. I was in his office within minutes. The happy look on his face clouded over as I told him what had gone on in the posh-room. He sat at his desk, strumming his fingers on the arm of his chair.

"What happens if that lot turn up, tomorrow?"

"Don't worry. I warned them I'll call the police if they cause any trouble."

He seemed satisfied. I was positive that once Fat-man bought the desk, that would be the end of the matter. I didn't realise how naive I could be.

I got stuck into my last two tasks before clocking off. I checked that Dick and Jeff were in the posh-room. Martin had gone against his habit of not spending the pounds by splashing out on two night-security guys to guard the posh-room, because of the unusually high value of goods in there. I found them drinking coffee and reading girly magazines. We traded our usual banter about not falling asleep on the job, or inviting their mates in for an all-night rave. I wished them goodnight and they locked themselves in.

My last chore was to padlock the main gates. I pulled my collar up against the cold night air and strode across the car park with my torch in hand. The quietness of the evening was shattered by the security guys' radio as it blasted out some noisy garbage. As I pulled the first gate across, a car engine roared into life on the far side of the posh-room.

One of our dozy dealers had probably been chatting on his mobile phone and lost track of time. In the light shining through the posh-room windows I saw a car moving slowly towards me. I swore under my breath. The silly sod hadn't got his lights on.

Pulling the gate back open, I waved my torch around to hurry him along, hoping he'd switch his lights on. As the car crawled closer to where I stood, its engine suddenly roared into life as the accelerator was pushed to the floor. The car's tyres screeched on the loose gravel. As the vehicle hurtled towards me, the driver switched his lights on to full beam, blinding me in the process. His intention became obvious. I was his target. The car was almost upon me before my brain engaged first gear. I tried to throw myself out of its path. It was a wasted effort. The front of the car thudded into my lower back. I flew through the air and slid across the gravel. The car raced through the gates before stopping in the road.

In my painful, half-conscious state, my head was full of trivia. I made a mental note to tell Martin that we could do with another load of stones on the car park. And what about having some security lights installed, so that I could see a potential assailant in future?

My whole body was hurting like hell. Then, to add to my state of mind, a hand touched me on the head and a man's voice whispered in my ear. I smelt chocolate on his breath.

"Don't be alarmed, Kit. Things will get better. You possess the gift to change what has just happened."

I ignored the voice. My overactive imagination was playing tricks on me. I heard the crunching of running feet. The next moment someone kicked me in the chest and stomach, and a foot smashed into my face. I momentarily forgot the pain as my lungs gasped for life-giving air. Panic took over. I knew how a fish out of water must feel as I found it impossible to breathe. My life flashed before my eyes. I accepted I was dying, and suffered a single poignant moment of regret. What a way to die, and I was still a virgin!

I opened my eyes for what I thought was the last time. The shadowy outline of my attacker towered over me. It was one of Fat-man's henchmen.

"Take that, you little arsehole." His foot thumped into my chest.

I gasped from the newly inflicted pain and gulped air into my empty lungs. The pain hurt like buggery, but I was breathing.

The bastard beat a hasty retreat. I heard a car door open and the goon's shouted words. "The little prick won't be at the bloody auction tomorrow, Billy." A door slammed shut and the car sped off down the road.

My first attempt to move was a mistake. I fainted from the spasms of pain coursing through my body.

When I came to, Dick and Jeff were fussing over me. One of them shone a torch in my face. It hurt like hell. My head felt as if it was stuffed with cotton wool, muffling the words they shouted at me. I shook my head and regretted it.

Dick's words filtered through the fuzziness. "Bloody hell, Kit. You look a right mess."

I tried to speak and wondered why my mouth wasn't working. It took an effort to raise a hand to my face. I ran my fingers over my swollen lips while my tongue explored the inside of my mouth. Where teeth had once nestled snugly in my gums, only gaps remained. I started to count how many teeth were missing, but gave up after five. In my semi-conscious state, I scraped my fingers through the gravel in a vain attempt to find the missing teeth.

The guys wanted to call an ambulance. I managed to get my mouth working and told them I didn't want one. Goodness knows why, but they agreed without any argument. Between spitting blood and howling with pain, I told them to get me back to my flat.

My slurred words must have been convincing. "Whatever you say, Kit," said Dick. They pulled me into a sitting position. I surprised myself by getting to my feet. From the rasping pain hammering at my chest, I knew some of my ribs were broken.

The lads helped me upstairs and plonked me on the sofa. They didn't say a word as they left me.

My brain pleaded with me to check out the stabbing pains in my chest. I managed to take my shirt off. My body was covered in angry-looking red welts and cuts where the toerag had kicked me. For a moment I was tempted to call an ambulance. An inner part of me turned the idea down. I couldn't believe what I was playing at, as I was in need of urgent medical attention.

I staggered across to the wall mirror to check out my facial injuries. The mirror played a cruel game with me. My reflection showed no sign of the injuries that were causing such excruciating pain. One of my eyes winked and a full set of teeth flashed back at me.

I couldn't believe my ears when my reflection spoke to me. "From where I'm standing, you look a right bloody mess. Don't worry. It won't last. Go and sit down. You'll find a way of making the pain go away."

I let my legs carry me to the sofa. I'd no sooner sat down when the kitchen door creaked open behind me. I tried to turn around, but the pain made it impossible. For one moment I thought Fat-man's hoodlums had come back to finish me off, except it couldn't be them. The only way into the room was up the staircase. I was on my own. The voice that I'd heard in the car park proved me wrong.

"The mirror wasn't lying, Kit. I know you're hurting, but there's an easy way of making the pain go away. You've had plenty of practice in controlling your dream plots, over the years, so why don't you turn the clock back to when that car ran you down and change what happened, in your dreamworld? Get your brain working. It's all about tinkering with time."

Delirium had taken control of my mind. How else could I explain the mystery voice and a talking reflection? I heard the wailing of an emergency vehicle in the distance, and wondered if the two dozy sods had called an ambulance after all.

Tomorrow's sale worried me. I wouldn't be there, that was for sure. It could be months before I was fit enough for work. The words of the mystery voice came to mind. Was there anything to be gained in reliving what had happened in the car park, in my dreamworld? It suddenly made sense. I allowed myself to be drawn into a state of sleep. My pain receded as I set my dream-spinning thoughts into motion.

My dream pattern followed a well-trodden path. The wind wafted around me as I slid down a tunnel of intense white light. In my fantasy world, I was walking across the auction-house car park to lock the main gates. My ears strained for the sound of Fat-man's car above the noise of the posh-room radio. Right on cue, an engine burst into life. Move for move, my dream followed the earlier pattern of events. Knowing what was about to happen, as the vehicle bore down on me I sprang clear of its path and the car sped past me. There was a loud crunching noise as it hit one of the gates. The car didn't stop. It roared off down the road.

I heard the security guys running towards me.

Dick gripped my arm. "Are you all right, chap? We heard a horrible din. What the hell happened?"

I couldn't help laughing out loud at the reality of my dreamscape. "Don't worry, lads. A car hit the gate."

Jeff frowned. "I don't think it's funny. Who was driving it?"

I had the right to lie. This was my dream. "I didn't get the chance to eyeball them. Thanks for your concern, lads, but you'd better get back to the posh-room."

For a fleeting moment I wanted to prolong the dream, if only to enjoy more pain-free time. As I ordered my dream to end, I passed back down that tunnel of light and ended up in my flat. I gritted my teeth against the waves of pain that would soon be hammering at my body. The seconds ticked by, and no intense pain surged through me. I played the tooth-counting game with my tongue. Every molar was nestling in its rightful place.

I got up and looked in the mirror. A healthy face stared back at me. I unbuttoned my shirt. What I saw didn't make sense. The cuts and welts had gone. Childhood memories stirred in my mind. Daytime aches and pains, after my stepfather had beaten me, had always vanished when I woke up the next morning. I shook my head. That was all very well, but how the hell can a dream replace missing teeth and repair broken ribs? On an impulse, I went out and checked the gates. The right hand one was a sorry mess. That presented me with another problem. A gate can't get damaged in a dream and stay that way. As I walked back to the flat, I toyed with the idea that the first cycle of events had been a dream, warning me of what was going to happen. I rubbished the thought. Dreams don't offer a fortune-telling service. In an instant I managed to put everything behind me. What's the point of worrying about something when you don't have an answer?

I was sidetracked by the telephone ringing. I answered it. A man's voice wished me good evening. I was totally bemused. It was the same voice that I'd heard in the car park and in my lounge.

I shouted down the line, "Who is this?"

The man laughed. "It doesn't matter who I am. Let's just say I'm a good friend."

I bridled. "Stop playing silly buggers. What do you want?"

"Calm down, my boy. It's about what happened in the car park this evening."

I was tempted to slam the phone down, but didn't. The soft timbre of his voice was calming me.

"What do you know about this evening?"

"You know I was there. I whispered in your ear, and spoke to you in your lounge. There is a rational answer to what happened. You have to accept that neither of the incidents was one of your dreams, no matter how ridiculous that may sound. You travelled through time and changed what happened the first time round. Think about it, Kit. You'll understand what it's all about soon. I'll be in touch. Goodnight."

I put the phone down, feeling agreeably soothed by the stranger, even though his words made no sense. He'd mentioned time. I checked my watch. It was ten past six. That threw me. I'd gone out to lock the gates just after six. By the time the lads had brought me back to the flat it would have been a quarter past six. I'd been in the flat for about five minutes before I started my dream-weaving, which had lasted just over five minutes. Give or take a minute or two, the time should have been about twenty-five past six. Somehow I'd lost fifteen minutes. The answer was beyond me. I surprised myself by shoving everything to the back of my mind and forgetting it.

CHAPTER FOUR

Sunshine was streaming through the bedroom window when I woke up. I felt totally stress-free after last night's excitement. A shower, a change of clothing and a fried breakfast completed my self-prescribed therapy. Sod last night. I was fit and well, and had other things on my mind. I made my way to Martin's office. The auction wasn't due to start until eleven, but the car park was already filling up. I made a mental note to keep out of Fat-man's way.

Martin told me to pour us a coffee. He believed the caffeine settled his nerves. He stared at me.

"Is there something you should be telling me about the damaged gate?"

I told him what had happened, but didn't mention Fat-man.

"I hope it's nothing to do with yesterday's nonsense in the posh-room."

A necessary lie dropped out. "No, it wasn't. I caught sight of some toerag youngsters in the car. I didn't manage to get their registration number. I'll get the gate repaired."

He visibly relaxed. Perhaps the caffeine was working.

"What about the posh-room? Is everything ready for me?"

I nodded.

He put his cup down and rubbed his hands together. "It's going to be a good day, money-wise. We can't go wrong with the gear we're selling."

I drained my cup and excused myself. There were things to

attend to in the posh-room before Martin started knocking hell out of his gavel. The place was packed out. There was no sign of Grodam.

The usual gaggle of dealers were there. Traffy Evans, a bald, tubby Welshman, was on the other side of the room. I made a mental note to avoid him. He wasn't called Traffy for nothing. He suffered from permanent flatulence, and wasn't fussy where he dropped his soundless time bombs. He was the original bumboy, before that other genre rewrote the English language.

Doris Goring-Hart was checking out the silver lots. A small elderly lady with dyed black hair, she wasn't popular with the other dealers. Her self-assumed haughtiness had prompted them to change her name behind her back. She was affectionately known to them as Doris Boring-Fart.

Out of the corner of my eye, I saw Rick Adams shuffling around the tables displaying the smaller ceramic lots. Rick was a walking scarecrow. His creased black overcoat had once prided itself on being a light fawn colour. A ragged scarf covered the collar of a dirty threadbare shirt. Rick never wore shoes, preferring a pair of cut-down wellington boots. Some dodgy-looking trousers were tucked into them. The dealers called him Dirty Rick. The nickname had nothing to do with his state of dress, but the smell that sometimes wafted in his slipstream. I preferred Traffy's silent bombs to Rick's odours, and that's saying something. Martin had considered banning Rick from our sales, until the human rights issue had raised its head.

Not for the first time, I checked my watch. The sale was due to start in half an hour. I re-donned my porter's smock. Martin had asked me to step in because the usual posh-room porter was ill. Eleven o'clock arrived, and right on cue he mounted the rostrum. A stickler for tradition, he sported a red bow tie, with a sprig of lucky heather pinned to his jacket lapel. Every auctioneer has a pre-sale ritual. Martin was no exception. He blew a kiss to the ladies and bowed to the crowd, earning himself a round of ribald applause.

The auction started. I was kept busy locating and displaying each lot. Martin raced through the books, prints, paintings, metalware and small ceramics. He galloped through the gold and silver lots, and followed them with the larger ceramics. Before I knew it, the furniture came up for sale. My heart fluttered when he offered up the davenport. I sauntered across to where it stood and pointed to it for the benefit of the punters. Two dealers quickly ran the price up to £400.

I relaxed. It had reached its reserve price, and Martin would knock it down at any moment. That's when the door at the back of the posh-room creaked open. Billy Grodam strolled in. He was backed up by four muscled gorillas. Fat-man stood at the back while his sidekicks spread themselves around the room. He stared at me, and drew a finger across his throat. Uncannily, the unease that I'd felt all morning washed away. A sense of calmness oozed through me. He and his hoodlums didn't scare me one bit.

Martin sensed the enthusiasm of the last few minutes had slipped away. "I'm selling the davenport. It dates to about 1870. I have a bid of £400. Do I hear £450? This is silly money for such a fine desk. I'm tempted to buy it myself if another bid isn't forthcoming."

For his health's sake, I hoped he was joking.

A dealer moved the price up to £450, at which point the bidding ran out of steam. I stroked the surface of the desk. A sharp feeling of pins and needles shot up my arm. I rubbed my elbow. The discomfort vanished as quickly as it had started.

Martin was close to knocking the desk down. "I'm bid £450. Do I hear £500? If not, make no mistake, I'm selling the desk."

He raised his gavel, but wasn't given the chance of bringing it down. Billy Grodam came to life. "£500," he shouted.

Martin glared at him. "I have a late bid."

Fat-man looked at me, raised the middle finger of his right hand and rotated it. I willed Martin to bring the gavel down. Grodam could have the bloody desk.

Martin went for the final countdown. "Are there any further bids? If not, I'm selling to the gentleman standing at the back of the room." He raised the gavel. "Going for the first time, going for the second time . . ."

Before the gavel could drop, someone shouted out: "Over here, Martin."

Some twat had raised the price to £550. Whoever it was stood the risk of a right good thumping from Fat-man's henchmen. I felt sorry for the silly bugger. My eyes swivelled round the room. Who'd been so bloody stupid as to up the ante? Everybody's eyes were on me. I was the only one who hadn't noticed it was my arm sticking up in the air. I pulled it down and wondered what the hell I was playing at. Martin turned to me, an incredulous look on his face. He wasn't as surprised as me.

He accepted my bid. I use the expression 'bid' in the loosest sense of the word, on the basis I hadn't consciously made it.

"Well, folks, we have another late bidder." He glared at me before turning his attention to Billy Grodam. "The bid's against you."

Grodam nodded, and raised the price.

God knows what was working my arm. It rose in the air, countering his bid.

Martin looked at Fat-man, as did everyone else in the room. "I have £650. Do I hear £700?"

He moved the bid to £700 and nodded to one of his goons. The gorilla sidled around behind me. Out of the corner of my eye I saw him brush his fingers across the top of the davenport as if he was interested in it.

He put his mouth close to my ear and explained the facts of life to me in a soft, menacing voice. "Listen, arsehole. If you know what's good for you, don't make another bloody bid, or else." He let out a loud laugh for the benefit of the crowd, as if the two of us were sharing a joke, and moved away.

Billy Grodam shot a threatening look at me. I thought of leaving, on the pretext of using the little boy's room. When I tried to move my feet they refused to budge. The only part of me in working order was my arm. The price for the davenport rose to £950, in my favour.

It wasn't me controlling my bidding, but that didn't bother me any more. I'd no idea what was happening, but I was enjoying the moment. I looked across the room at Fat-man. He was working up a sweat, and his wig had slipped over his forehead. He frantically pushed it back with both hands. As our eyes met, I winked at him.

"I have a bid of £950 from Kit Milner." He stared at Fat-man. "Do I hear a further bid from you?"

Billy Grodam glared at me and mouthed an obscenity.

Martin broke the silence. "In the absence of any other bid, I intend to sell the desk."

Fat-man raised two fingers at Martin and walked out of the room followed by his menagerie of goons.

Martin brought the gavel down with an almighty thud. "Sold to Kit Milner."

Everyone broke into applause. One person was yelling at the top of his voice. He was stood at the back of the room, partially obscured by a large wardrobe. All I could see of him was a generous nose and a grey beard peeping out from beneath the confines of his anorak hood. He waved at me. I had no idea who he was. I turned away. When I looked back he'd gone.

Martin's impatient voice brought me back to reality. "What's the buyer's bidding number, Kit?"

I gave him my personal number. He frowned as he wrote it on his sheet. He carried on selling the remaining lots before bringing his gavel down for the last time. He collected his papers, gave me a funny look and swept out of the room.

Most of the crowd melted away to pay for their purchases.

Doris Goring-Hart tapped me on the arm. "Who's the mug who's paid that sort of money for that desk? He must have wanted it badly. Is there a wad of money hidden away in it?"

The other dealers had a good laugh at my expense before wandering away. They'd have laughed even louder if they'd known Kit Milner was the twat who'd bid that kind of money.

The premises emptied during the next half-hour. Martin walked into the saleroom as I was about to lock up. The sour look on his face didn't bode well for me.

"What's going on, Kit? Who were you bidding for?"

He didn't give me the chance to answer. "Whoever it is has paid well over the top. I hope you carried your client's instructions out. When will I get my money?"

I was getting a dab hand at lying. "Don't worry. You'll be paid. Does my client have the usual seven days to pay?"

"He does, but the desk stays in the saleroom until I get my money. And I want cash." He wasn't finished with me. "I saw that nonsense between you and that obnoxious mountain of flesh you were bidding against. What was that big bastard doing standing behind you? I'm not daft. This is to do with yesterday's trouble, isn't it? What really got up my nose was the fat one giving me a two-fingered salute."

Without another word, he walked out.

I locked up and made my way back to the flat. I'd bought a desk that I didn't want, because something was working my arm; yet, for some unknown reason, I didn't care a toss.

If only I'd known that I was about to cram more living into the next few days than I'd done during the last twenty-seven years of my life. After a spot of supper I crept into bed.

As much as I tried, I couldn't sleep. My mind wouldn't let me forget the strange goings-on at the auction. I'd no idea how it had happened, but I'd accepted it. Something had changed inside of me. It felt as if some outside influence had prised my mind open, without any conscious help from me. Strangely, it didn't worry me. I was too busy basking in the warmth of my new-found esteem.

Up to now, my childhood and teenage paths had left their mark on me. My spirit had been ground down to a level where I didn't care a toss as to which direction my path led me. I'd never once looked at life's signposts. My eyes were always set on the ground, not even noticing what lay on the surface. Today, at the auction, a ray of sunshine had burst through my clouds of doubt and uncertainty. I sighed to myself. Would my social life change for the better?

I recall, with a mixture of amusement and horror, the one and only occasion I'd had the temerity to ask a girl out on a date. I was twenty-one at the time. Yours truly was in a state of great agitation as I stood on the threshold of my first close encounter with the opposite sex. I asked her if she would like to go to the local cinema. With a fluttering of eyelids she cooed and wiggled her enthusiastic agreement.

Don't get the wrong impression of me. I have a good rapport with people so long as it's not in my face. Had I been an outgoing chap, I could have pulled any bird I fancied. Whatever the young lady was expecting from me, by the time our date finished she hadn't got it.

I'm getting ahead of myself. This girl was a fluffy, petite natural blonde, with blue eyes. I'll never forget her figure. There was a built-in abundance of it, with everything in the right place.

We sat in the back row, munching popcorn and drinking coffee. I thought I'd cracked the social barrier. But once the popcorn and coffee were finished, what was I supposed to do? I only had to look around me to find the answer, by watching the antics of other young people. They hadn't come to watch the film. Every couple was snogging like mad. But not the two of us. We sat with space between us, watching the screen. My social chinks were beginning to show.

Halfway through the film, she let out a sigh of frustration. Her hand slid along my thigh. During the next few minutes, her hand fondled every part of my lower anatomy. Sadly, I lacked the confidence and knowledge to react to her advances by putting my hand and brain into tandem.

I took the coward's way out and told her I was popping to the toilet. She laughed and squeezed my groin, expecting me to react to her fondling when I returned. I didn't bother to come back. That was my one and only taste of socialising. I resolved never to go down that road again.

These thoughts clouded over, and the grotesque Grodam came to mind. I accepted that our paths were bound to cross another day. My new-found confidence kicked in. I welcomed another run-in with him.

My roving thoughts turned to Martin. I owed him a lot of money. My instinct told me something would turn up. As it happened, destiny solved that problem for me. After an hour of tossing and turning, clouds of tiredness invaded my brain, driving all thoughts away. I beamed in an instruction for no dreams to disturb me. That was a big mistake. My dreams were about to become nightmares, and I could do nothing to stop them.

My years of mind-training flew out of the window as I passed into my dreamworld. The bedroom wall exploded into shapes and images before forming themselves into a forest clearing. The ground was covered in the brown debris of fallen leaves. A hut stood at the forest edge, beside a small pool of water. On the opposite side of the clearing, beyond the pool, stood a huge rock. A feeling of peacefulness bathed the scene. Birds twittered as the breeze played a soothing tune on the few autumn leaves left clinging to the trees.

The calm was shattered as two scantily dressed people ran out of the hut, shouting at the tops of their voices. One was a slim, good-looking chap with long, dark curly hair hanging to his shoulders and a full-length beard. The other, a girl, was a class act. Blessed with delicate pale skin and flowing auburn hair, she was simply beautiful. My feelings for her were heightened at the sight of her bare breasts.

He shouted at her, "You have betrayed me, and toyed with my emotions! All you wanted were my stones. You shall never have them."

The words she screamed at him were tinged with disdain. "Do you really believe I could have fallen in love with someone like you? I hate everything about you, especially your lovemaking. You disgust me, Merlin."

My ears pricked up at the mention of his name. Who hasn't heard of Merlin?

"You poisonous wench. You will feel the power of my sorcery."

The woman's reaction was immediate. She pointed her fingers at him. He was stunned by the fierce torrent of words that spewed from her mouth. Merlin cried out in terror and tried to run into the forest. He managed four steps before stopping.

He turned towards her and shook his head in bewilderment. "I did not know you possessed magical powers. My sorcery is powerful, but I cannot undo the spell you have cast on me." He fell to his knees. "I really love you. Please remove your spell."

She tossed her head and sneered, "Go to your prison, Merlin."

He screamed at her, "This is not the end of me! I will return!" He tugged a pouch from around his neck that was hidden under his clothing. "This is what you were after. My powers of sorcery are contained in the stones that lie in this pouch. You shall never have them."

She tried, in vain, to snatch the pouch from his hand. He flung it at the rock, where it clattered against the surface and disappeared inside the rock. Her witchcraft took a swift course. His body twitched and his clothes fell away, leaving him naked. Small cracks appeared in his flesh, and streams of red vapour seeped from the fissures. His body broke down until he disappeared. On the spot where he'd stood, a cloud of red vapour floated above the ground. It drifted towards the rock, kissed its surface and seeped into the rock face.

The woman shook her fist at the rock. "Damn you. You will never escape from your prison. My force field will make sure of that."

A bolt of lightning flew from her fingertips. As it struck the rock's surface, it crackled, then disappeared.

Three horsemen appeared from out of the forest and clattered into the clearing. They wore light chain mail and metal helmets. Each was armed with a sword and carried a small round shield on his left arm. One of them dismounted. He was a giant of a man, and would have been handsome had it not been for an empty eye socket and a disfiguring scar that ran the length of his face.

He grabbed the woman and yelled at her, "Did our scheme work, wife? Do you have Merlin's magic stones?"

"No, I do not. I am sorry, Lord Madrog. I was forced to imprison him in that rock."

The man lost his temper. "I was unhappy in letting another man take your body. I only allowed it because you swore you could get your hands on those stones."

He slapped her around the head.

Anger flashed in her eyes. "You have gone too far, Madrog! With one word I could take your life away." Her voice was full of scorn. "Of course I did what we planned. I fed him a love potion, thinking it would overwhelm his senses so I could search him for the stones. He realised what I was up to and threatened me with his sorcery."

His manner changed abruptly. He embraced her and planted a lingering kiss on her lips. "I am sorry, Emeralda. I acted in haste. At least we have him imprisoned. We will think of a way to release him and get what we want." He shouted to the other two horsemen. "Collect wood and light a fire."

A huge fire soon burned in front of the hut.

Madrog shouted at the two men, "Your mother and I are staying here. Leave us and return to our camp."

They mounted their horses and galloped into the forest.

He put his hand on his wife's arm. "We must think of a way to get hold of Merlin's stones. Can you not use your magic to remove them from the rock?"

She shook her head, smiled knowingly, then whispered in his ear, but I could hear every word. "Merlin must not hear what I have to tell you. There is another way of getting our hands on his stones."

Madrog couldn't hide the excitement in his voice. "Tell me how."

"He has written a manuscript which will help you to release him from that rock."

"Where is this manuscript?"

"He told me it was hidden somewhere in the forest, around the edge of this clearing."

His softly spoken words were full of menace. "I will send

47

my warriors here tomorrow to search for this manuscript. Your work has not been in vain, my dear." He took hold of her waist. "It has been a long time since I pleasured your body."

She smiled as he pulled her into the hut.

I thought the dream had ended until I heard the woman scream, followed by the raucous sound of her husband's laughter. He walked out of the hut, waving a bloodied sword above his head and dragging the headless body of his wife by her legs. He pulled her corpse close to the fire and let her legs clatter to the ground. He ran his finger along the bloodied blade and licked the blood. He looked down at his wife's body.

"You stupid witch. You have paid the price of your failure, but I have inherited your powers of sorcery by swallowing your blood."

He pointed at her. A powerful blue ray leapt from his fingers. Her body vanished from sight.

He walked over to the rock and shouted at it, "Your sanctuary will be a brief one, Merlin, until the means of releasing you is in my hands. Then I will snuff your life out and take on your powers of sorcery."

Madrog mounted his horse and rode off.

I ordered my mind to leave this nightmare. Nothing happened.

I heard Merlin's voice shout from inside the rock, "Can anyone hear me?"

The sound of whistling drifted from out of the forest. A young fellow strolled into the clearing.

Merlin bellowed at him, "Young man! Young man! Do not be afraid. Draw near the rock. I will reward you if you come closer."

The youth scratched at his head. "Is this some kind of witchcraft?"

"There is no trickery. Come closer and learn how I can make you rich."

His words had the desired effect. The man walked over to the rock.

"Tell me how I can make my fortune."

"I have been trapped in this rock by a witch. Do not touch it.

She placed a force field around it to stop me from escaping."

The young chap's voice took on a note of caution. "I am not getting involved in witchcraft." He gave it some thought and relented. "What must I do to become rich?"

The rock trembled with the sorcerer's laughter. "If my task appeals to you, pick up four rock fragments from the ground."

The man started to walk away.

"This is a trick to imprison me in the rock."

Merlin's voice took on a wheedling tone. "Pick up the fragments, I implore you, and you will become a very wealthy man."

The tempting promise swayed the youth's misgivings. He did as Merlin had asked.

"I will fill your rock fragments with my magical powers. Open your hand that holds the pieces of rock."

The young man did as he was told. The sorcerer recited a string of words. The fragments moved about in the man's palm until they changed into four perfectly rounded stones.

Merlin spoke to him. "Place the stones in a leather bag and wear them around your neck at all times. No one can harm you while you wear them. I will now reward you with the riches that I promised."

The magician chanted a spell. The rock fragments on the ground moved frantically around before coming to rest.

"I have changed these pieces of rock into gold. Gather them up."

The young man picked up a fragment, examined it, then cried out with delight. "It is gold!" He spent the next few minutes picking up every piece before turning to the rock. "Thank you, whoever you are. I will be on my way."

"Before you go, what is your name?"

"I am Gerard de Milner."

"Well, Gerard, one day I will call on a descendant of yours to carry out a mission for me. Do not forget to wear my stones around your neck and never remove them. Make sure you pass the stones to one of your descendants on your death. Tell him what I have told you. Now go."

"I will carry out your wishes."

With a friendly wave to the rock, he started to whistle and strode out of the clearing.

The dreamscape faded away. This fantasy had been too real for comfort. I glanced at my watch. It was just after two o'clock. I lost the battle with my eyelids and fell asleep. Before I knew it, I was in my dreamworld again.

The bloody bedroom wall started to glow. I sighed with relief. What I saw didn't have the semblance of a nightmare about it. A red-brick house with inlaid knapped flintstones showed itself. A sign hung in the porch telling all and sundry that this was Lovington Rectory.

The house faded away, and a brightly lit lounge replaced it. The room oozed good taste, from the quality of the furnishings to the exquisite watercolours and oil paintings adorning the walls.

A fire burned in the Adam fireplace, which was straddled by a mouth-watering mahogany overmantle. Most of the furniture was Georgian, set off by choice pieces from the Victorian period. A Canterbury, stuffed full of sheet music, sat by the piano, and a Victorian barley-twist whatnot, full of silver knick-knacks, reclined in another corner of the room. A davenport stood in the bay window. I walked across to the wall and took a closer look. I could have sworn it was the very same desk that I'd bought at auction. I chuckled to myself for being a complete arse. The furniture and fittings in the room had been offered up for sale at Saturday's Fine Art Sale. This dream was based on figments from my imagination. I sat back on the bed and waited for the rest of the dream to unfold.

The door opened and a grey-haired chap wearing a cleric's dog collar came in. The poor bloke had a deformed back, giving him the appearance of a hunchback. His fine aquiline nose sat in a gentle and kindly-looking bearded face. My dream was still feeding on my world of reality. This was the unknown man who'd shown such delight when I'd bought the davenport.

He moved across to the fire and presented his ample posterior to the flames. Agreeably warmed, he ambled across to the davenport, and knelt down at its right-hand side. He removed the bottom drawer. His head swivelled around and he pointed a gnarled finger at the recess.

He mouthed his words at me – 'Watch what I'm doing' – before sliding his arm inside. As he pulled it out, his shaking hand was holding a small wooden box. He opened it and removed a brown envelope.

I nearly fell off the bed when he spoke to me. It was the same voice that had twice whispered words of comfort after Grodam's car had knocked me down. I pulled myself together. This was old hat. I was still drawing on figments of my subconscious.

He waggled a finger at me. "Remember how I found the box. It's above the bottom dummy drawer. Make sure you find it." He pulled a face and clicked his tongue. "You're an impatient young man who takes a lot of convincing. For goodness sake get a grip of yourself and find this box. It's in my davenport that you bought." He placed the envelope back in the box and put it inside the desk. He struggled to his feet and tapped a finger on the side of his head. "Start using your brain." He shrugged his shoulders. "I can't blame you. I was the same. I'll see you soon."

As he left the room, the wall picture faded away and I woke up.

Was there a secret box in the davenport? Is that why Fat-man had wanted the desk? If so, how did he know? Nothing else was in the offing at this unearthly hour, especially sleep, so what harm could there be in popping down to the posh-room and satisfying the curiosity of a dream-spinner?

I picked up the posh-room keys on my way out. Within minutes I was squatting by the davenport. I removed the bottom drawer and slid my hand inside the cavity. My fingers felt a piece of wood standing proud of the surface. I tried everything I could think of to shift it. My fingers probed, pushed and pulled, but the damned thing wouldn't budge. I was convinced it was an old repair, and cussed myself for being taken in by a dream.

I'd had enough. What in heaven's name was I doing down here at two o'clock on a cold, frosty morning, trying to find a secret compartment that didn't exist? A cup of tea was a far better option than this banal attempt to create a miracle from a state of unreality, all created by a dream.

On their parallel world, Michael and Azurina were watching Kit struggling with the desk.

He shook his head. "Our son's having no luck in finding the secret recess. You've seen more of him than me. Is he coping with the way his life has been turned upside down?"

She smiled. "Some incredible things have been thrown at him these past few days, but he's taken everything on board without a whimper. Anyone else would have gone mad, but not our Raphael."

"Thank goodness I planted my ideas in his head, that he shouldn't worry about anything out of the ordinary that he came across." He pointed at the picture on the mirror. "He's giving up. The sooner he finds the hidden box, the better it will be for our leader's plan. It's vital that Raphael goes on Merlin's mission."

"How long will it be before this mission starts?"

"It will be a few weeks yet. He has more surprises coming his way before that happens." He shook his head. "I think you'd better get down there to make sure he finds what he's looking for."

She gave him a mock salute. "I'm on my way, sir."

As I opened the saleroom door, a fierce gust of wind blew in. It swept around the saleroom, rattling the windows and threatening to blow them out. The force of the wind pushed the davenport across the floor. As it thudded against the far wall, the bottom drawer shot out. I heard something clatter inside the desk. The door slammed shut as the wind swept out of the room.

I didn't allow myself to get carried away, even though I realised that something, or someone, had lent a helping hand. Miracles were becoming commonplace. Accepting that reality situations are the very essence of dream-weaving, it couldn't explain how a dream-man had shown me where the box was hidden. This was stretching incredulity to the limits. The excitement of the hunt became more important than the inconsistency of reasoning. My life was turning upside down, and I couldn't have cared a toss.

I picked a box from out of the desk and opened the hinged lid. Lying inside was a bulging brown envelope. Spidery words were written on it. My heart missed a beat when I saw it was addressed to me. The doubting Thomas in me kicked into gear, sinking the euphoria that had taken me over a moment ago. This was plain silly, and I knew it. I was being asked to accept the impossible suggestion that one of my dreams had been the means of finding this envelope. Dreams can't solve life's problems, full stop. Yet the envelope flew in the face of that argument. The lack of a common-sense factor homed in on me. What was the point of getting an envelope to me in such a complicated manner? Sending it by first-class post would have been a damned sight easier, and certainly less expensive. What if Grodam had bought the desk? The whole thing smelt of silly buggers.

I replaced the desk drawer, locked the saleroom and retraced my steps to the flat. I laid the envelope on the coffee table. It was willing me to open it, but I resisted the urge. Enough was enough. The last twenty-four hours had provided more than its fair share of shocks and surprises, with no answers. Whatever was in the envelope would have to wait. My body gave up on me. I slumped on the sofa and fell into a deep sleep.

It was half past nine when I woke up. A quick shower blew the cobwebs out of my head. I prepared myself for opening the envelope. It felt like the proverbial birthday and Christmas rolled into one.

I tore it open. A letter and a small leather pouch tumbled on to the table. I unfolded the letter. A key was taped to the bottom of the second sheet. I took a peep at who had written it. The scrawled signature of the Reverend Julius Milner spread itself across the bottom of the page.

Martin's sarcasm about the reverend gentleman came to mind. Supposing we were related! He might have left me something in his will. I hoped it wasn't the commode and its contents. The letter was undated:

Dear Kit,

I know you sufficiently well to be on first-name terms. You'll be puzzled by my words, seeing you have never knowingly met me. No matter. By the time you read this letter, I'll be dead. Don't worry. We'll meet up with each other in another period of time. In fact, we'll become acquainted in the near future. Being more precise, we will meet up in the past. Confusing, isn't it? Don't worry. Things will become clearer, I promise. Please trust me.

You have to accept that anything in life is possible for you, especially those things that seem entirely unrealistic. So, what's this all about? You're being groomed to fulfil a mission in the next few weeks. I was given the same chance, but my mind and flesh were too weak. I'm yesterday's man, a failure to the Milner clan.

You'll know what's involved in this mission, from your recent vision about Merlin. Look in the leather pouch. It contains the stones that Merlin gave to the young feller. Take care of them. There are people who would kill you to get their hands on them. Wear the pouch around your neck, and never ever remove it, even when you sleep. It will protect you from the likes of Billy Grodam. The stones also hold special powers. I'll help you to unlock some of them during the next few days.

You must be wondering why I went through all this palaver in getting this letter to you in such a complicated manner. I hid the envelope in my davenport quite deliberately, instead of using conventional means. You know from the vision what the stones are all about. You had to be aware of their existence, instead of just offloading them on to you without you having any idea as to what they were about. That's why you witnessed that vision. You are entering the final stages of your training for your mission to rescue Merlin. In passing my pouch to you, I knowingly signed my own death warrant. It was a deliberate act, which goes some way towards atoning for something I did many years ago that strongly conflicted with my religious beliefs.

More strange things will happen to you in the next few weeks. Don't be concerned about these intrusions into your life, even though they defy logic. Whatever you do, don't ever try and justify what's happening to you. Concentrate on your mission. That's all that is asked of you.

Take the key to my bank manager. He'll give you something you sorely need. The bank's address is written at the foot of this letter. I know you'll be contacting him. Don't be concerned for me. You might even resurrect me one day.

Your friend,
JULIUS MILNER

The letter made no sense, and wouldn't have done so in a month of Sundays. No matter. My mind accepted the Reverend Milner's outrageous statements without a hint of concern. I undid the pouch. Three stones, the shape and size of small marbles, fell into the palm of my hand. This didn't make sense. The young dream-man had been given four stones. Was I really descended from him?

I held one stone between my fingers, and was justified in believing that some special power would make itself known. I was disappointed. An envelope containing Martin's davenport money didn't appear when I made the wish. I put the stones back in the pouch and hung it around my neck.

Was I expected to believe that these stones were connected with my dream about Merlin? The very idea that they'd been handed down over fourteen centuries, before ending up with me, was absurd.

The Reverend Milner hadn't needed to draw a veil of intrigue around this so-called mission. Was it really about Merlin being trapped in that rock? The idea was outrageous. He would have died many centuries ago.

Whatever the rector's key unlocked might make things clearer. I couldn't call at the bank until Monday, but there were other things to occupy my mind. For a start, I wanted to check out Lovington Rectory, which had figured in my dream, if only to satisfy myself that I hadn't gone off my rocker. After that I felt the need, at long last, to satisfy a long-standing urge, which was to spend my first evening mixing with other people, although I had no clear idea where.

CHAPTER FIVE

I set off for Lovington, and two hours later I reached the outskirts of the town. I drove towards the steeple, peeping above the town skyline. Within minutes I had parked outside St Leonard's Church and was walking towards the rectory. It was the same Georgian house that I'd seen in my dream. I should have been shocked, but wasn't. I kidded myself that my dream patterns were changing, moving more towards the reality of life, leaving the brittle and meaningless unrealities of mind games behind me.

A brass plate on the front wall told me that a Reverend Sandra Gardner was the new rector. I got back in the car and drove into the town marketplace, where I parked up.

I chanced on a tea shop in the High Street, and went inside. The interior left no doubt as to what this place dispensed. Endless shelves covered the walls, each one crammed full of decorative teapots, all sitting to attention, their phallic spouts waiting for the day when they would perform their man-made task. They were virgin teapots, destined never to conceive an infusion of tea leaves, or hold a teabag in the womb of their body.

A grey-haired lady welcomed me. She turned out to be the owner. As I was her only customer, she lavished her attention on me. I asked if she'd heard of the late Julius Milner.

She threw her hands up in mock horror. "Heard of him? Of course I have. I'm a regular worshipper at St Leonard's." My question had touched a sensitive memory. "He was a lovely man. Wouldn't hurt a fly. He did a beautiful sermon, always going on about our duty to help those less fortunate than ourselves." She blew her nose, and wiped a tear from her eye. The woman rambled on, sharing stories of her wonderful man. "He was our rector for years. Julius was popular with everyone, inside the church and out. We all loved him. His wife, bless her, died some years ago in a hit-and-run accident. The car driver was never found." Her face took on a cheerless look. "Then we lost him. It was so sad." Her voice fell to a deep whisper. "The coroner said he committed suicide. We couldn't understand why he'd ever do such a thing. Mind you, we noticed a huge change in him during his last few months. The poor man seemed to have the weight of the world on his shoulders. He never let on what was bothering him." Her face screwed up like a dried prune. "We've got a new rector. She's a woman." Her flow of words trailed off.

I felt sorry for the new incumbent. Would she ever achieve the popularity that the Reverend Milner had enjoyed?

"What did he look like?"

"You want to know a lot about him. Why do you ask?" She didn't give me the chance to answer. "Julius had flowing grey hair and a beard, and what you might call a gentle, happy face." She sat down at the table. "I never married, but, had I felt the inclination to do so, he was the man I'd have chosen for my husband." Her face glazed over. She patted her grey locks into place, as if she expected the reverend gentleman to walk through the door.

"Did he have any particular distinctive features?"

"You're asking a lot of questions. But not to worry, eh? We're not being disrespectful to him." The glassy-eyed look reappeared. "Special features, you say? He had the most magnificent nose. It made me shiver just to look at it." From the intense look of delight etched on her face, I thought she was about to have an orgasm, probably for the first time in her life. She recovered her composure. "It was kind of hooked, almost Fagin-like. And the poor man had a hunched back and piercing green eyes." Her eyes moistened over. "I do miss him."

I sat there in my own self-contained stupor. Her description of Julius Milner fitted the man in my dream to a T. Wishing the lady goodbye, I left the cosiness of the tea house and plunged into the darkness of a cold late-October afternoon. I walked back to the car, knowing where my evening pleasures lay. It didn't take me long to reach the outskirts of town, where I'd passed a public house called The Rising Sun, earlier in the day. Don't ask me why, but its rustic quaintness had appealed to me. I pushed the door open and walked into the dimly lit interior. A vocation of vicars and assorted ladies turned their heads and stared at me. For one moment I thought I'd strayed into an Anglican synod convention. My short-lived enthusiasm was quickly dampened. I was about to make a quick exit when I noticed that most of the ladies were sporting stubble on their faces, and three of them had beards.

One of the ladies shouted at me in a beautiful bass voice, "Come on in. Who have you come as? Are you the Bishop of Ely in plain clothes?"

Everyone dissolved into laughter.

One of the vicars walked across and shook my hand. Her feminine voice welcomed me. "Ignore him. The landlord's arranged a 'Vicars and Tarts Night' to drum up some extra trade. Don't worry about your garb. Come and join the fun."

I did my best to swagger up to the bar, as the bishop would have done. This led to cries of laughter. I assumed that the person behind the bar was the barmaid.

"What will it be?" she asked.

Her voice made me go weak at the knees, even though I couldn't see much of her face – or anything else of her, for that matter. She was wearing nun's clothing, with an oversized wimple on her head. For some reason that was beyond me, a thin white veil covered her lower face. Only a stunning pair of green eyes were visible. She pulled me a pint of best bitter, and I asked what her gear was all about.

She nodded towards the most startling tart of all, sporting big breasts, a reasonable pair of legs and a ginger beard and moustache. "Blame him. He's the landlord. We've got a monk coming, he said, so you can dress as a nun and wear a veil." The girl sounded peeved. She turned away to serve someone else.

I wandered across the room. One of the tarts invited me to sit at his table. He introduced his assorted friends. It didn't take long for their infectious banter to seep into me. It had taken me twenty-seven years to socialise with people, and less than ten minutes to discover how much I was enjoying it. I was gutted when the landlord called time. After much back-slapping and shaking of hands I strolled into the cold night air, shouting my last farewells. I pulled my overcoat tightly about me and walked to where the car was parked.

A female shouted goodnight to someone back at the pub. I recognised the voice. It was the barmaid. She was dressed in her normal attire and wearing a headscarf. If I had met her, I wouldn't have known her, except for the giveaway voice and her green eyes. The pub door closed behind her and the bolts were drawn. Her heels clicked on the pavement as she hurried off in the opposite direction.

As I sat in the car, the quietness of the night was shattered by a woman's screams. The shrill sounds floated from down the road, where the barmaid had walked. In the light of a street light I saw two men struggling with her. One had his arm around her neck, while he pulled at her clothing with his other hand. The second guy snatched her handbag and started to rifle through it. The thug put a hand over her mouth to stop her from screaming.

My first reaction was to ring the police on my mobile. I swore, for being so dim. By the time they arrived, the girl could be injured, or something worse. It was two of them against me, but that didn't stop me from tearing towards them. My feet barely touched the ground. The scumbag who was manhandling the girl hit her across the face and dragged her into the bushes. The other guy was too intent on throwing bits and pieces out of her handbag to see me coming. My clenched fist thumped into the back of his head. He grunted, and slumped to the ground in an unconscious heap.

I scrambled through the bushes, where the yob had dragged the girl. The gloom was lightened by the street light shining through the leafless hedge branches. He was sat astride her. Her coat and most of her clothing lay on the ground. She was putting up a fight, but it wasn't enough.

She pleaded with him. "Please let me go. You can have my money and credit cards. They're in my handbag with my mobile phone."

His throaty laugh filled the clearing. "You can keep them, sweetheart. I'm not after your money or your phone. Shut the chat. Lie back and enjoy a shafting from me." The tone of his voice softened. "I'm not going to hurt you. A good-looking girl like you must have done this dozens of times. After I've shagged you, I'll take what we came for and leave you alone."

He wasn't making sense. What were they after? I crept across to where they lay and tapped him on the shoulder. He turned and looked up at me with a grin on his face, expecting to see his mate. The grin vanished as my right foot caught him on the chin. He collapsed in a heap beside the girl.

The girl lay there, her legs stretched apart, naked except for the remnants of her tights hanging around her ankles. The shoes on her feet, and her headscarf, mocked her nakedness.

I knelt by her side and tried to put her at ease. "I'm here to help you. We met at The Rising Sun this evening. I was the one who wasn't in drag."

My words hit home. She let me sit her up, then draped her hands across her chest in a futile attempt to hide her breasts. Her modesty was soon forgotten as she held a hand out to me. I eased her to her feet and picked her coat up. She put it on and draped her arms around me. Her body shook as she clung to me. She stared down at the unconscious yob and started to cry. I guided her through the bushes on to the pavement. The second scumbag was still out cold. I took a tissue from my pocket and pushed it into her hand.

She dabbed at her eyes, then touched my face. "I remember you now." She burst into verbal overdrive. "Thank goodness you were around. This wouldn't have happened if my car hadn't broken down this afternoon. Why the hell did I decide to walk home? I should have got a taxi." She screamed at herself, "What a bloody stupid cow I am!" She put her arms around me and snuggled into my chest.

I gave her a squeeze. "It's all over now. Nobody will hurt you while I'm around. I'll protect you."

She went quiet on me. Perhaps I'd overdone the chivalry.

I broke the silence. "Let's get out of here."

There was no response.

"Are you all right?"

My words got through to her at last. She shook her head. "This can't be right. A bloke's just tried to rape me and I've got my arms around a total stranger. It's not making sense. Yet when I spoke to you in the pub I had this feeling that I'd known you for years." She giggled nervously. "Will you really protect me?"

We were distracted by the sound of her attacker crashing through the hedge. He started yelling filthy expletives at us. The girl screamed as I turned to face him. His language didn't bother me. What he was clutching in his right hand did. The knife blade glinted in the street light as he tossed it from hand to hand.

I stretched my hand out as he rushed towards me. I use the word 'rushed' in the slowest sense of the word. The thug was hell-bent on ripping me apart. As he moved towards me in slow motion I waved a hand in front of my face. It moved at the speed I intended it to. The girl was screaming, but the decibel level of her screams sounded like a foghorn, as the sounds translated themselves into the language of slow motion. Any sense of surprise was lost on me. It was another twist in my changing lifestyle.

The thug's knife moved leisurely towards my chest. At the rate it was moving, I could have walked to the pub and back. With a feeling of malice, I grabbed the hand that held the knife and twisted it sharply. I heard his wrist bone snap. The weapon slipped from his grasp and floated like a feather towards the ground. My other hand moved to his crotch, where his flies were still unzipped. I nestled his family jewels in the palm of my hand. It was too easy. As I lifted him, I squeezed and twisted his tackle in one movement. He floated to the ground, his foghorn sounds of pain showing the hurt he was going through.

The other guy came to life. He got up, put a hand in his pocket and pulled out a gun. I thought my days on earth were over as he pulled the trigger. I couldn't believe my eyes as the bullet pushed its way out of the barrel in slow motion, leisurely winging its way towards my chest. I plucked it out of the air with my fingers and threw it into the bushes. I walked across to the guy at normal speed, and treated him to the same painful treatment that I'd handed out to his mate.

The girl touched my arm at normal speed. She showed no sign of distress at what she'd seen. "Are you all right?"

"Don't worry about me. I'm fine." I dragged my phone out of my pocket. "I'm going to call the police, to pick these scumbags up. After that I'll take you to hospital."

She shoved her face into mine. "You can forget about the hospital, and I don't want the police involved! I'll be fine after a good night's sleep." She calmed down as quickly as she'd blown up. "Don't try and make me change my mind. I want to go home."

"Whatever you say."

I dragged the two yobs across the pavement and plonked them behind the bushes, then picked her clothing up from the clearing and put her scattered belongings back in her handbag. The girl hadn't moved. She looked like a waif and stray. I took hold of her hand and walked her back to the car.

Five minutes later we were parked outside a smart-looking block of flats. We walked up the steps to the front entrance.

I looked her in the eyes. "Here are your clothes and handbag. I'd better be on my way."

I drowned in my own guilt. I'd promised to look after her, yet here I was abandoning the girl on her own doorstep. She pulled a face at the soiled clothing.

"Will you see me to my flat before you go?"

How could I refuse? She keyed a number into the security box. The door swung open and we walked into a well-lit entrance hall. Her smudged mascara and lipstick did nothing to hide her beauty. I melted at the sight of her jade-green eyes topped by long, curving eyelashes. The porcelain whiteness of her face, and her prominent high cheekbones, gave an added dimension to her looks. My libido floundered in the bottomless depths of her beauty.

She took her headscarf off. A mass of auburn hair cascaded around her face and hung in ringlets on her shoulders. I shivered. She bore an uncanny likeness to the Emeralda woman, who I'd seen in my nightmare.

I ushered her into the lift. It moved smoothly up to the top floor. She rummaged in her handbag for a key and unlocked the door of her flat.

I wished her goodnight for a second time. She didn't say a word. Words weren't necessary. Her pleading eyes spoke volumes.

Her tongue licked nervously at her lips. "Don't go yet. How about a coffee?" Her voice took on an imploring tone. "Please."

She stood there, her hands held out in silent invitation, willing me to accept her offer. If she needed my company that badly, who was I to argue?

"All right. I won't stay long, though. You need your rest."

I was rewarded with a huge hug. She switched the lights on and pulled me into the flat. "I feel safer with you around."

This was unreal. I was alone with a beautiful girl for the first time in my life, and didn't even know her name.

I held my hand out. "It's a bit late in the day, but I'm Kit Milner."

She frowned, then took hold of my hand. "I'm Anne Wood." She twigged I was fondling her hand, and let out a nervous laugh. "We can't stand here holding hands all night, can we?" Anne pointed to a sofa. "Make yourself at home. I'll have a quick shower before I make the coffee."

She took her coat off. My eyebrows hit the ceiling at the sight of her nakedness. The girl was a mass of confusion. She ran out of the room, slamming the door behind her. A shrill apology floated from the other room, followed by the noisy banging of drawers, then complete silence.

After a while Anne walked back into the lounge wearing a dressing gown. Her moment of discomfort had passed.

She smiled. "Thanks for being so understanding. I'll have that shower now. I won't be long."

She disappeared into the bathroom. The sound of running water drifted to my ears. After ten minutes the bathroom door opened and she scampered into the bedroom. When she reappeared she looked gorgeous. Her choice of garment was a long wide-sleeved green robe, drawn together with a black sash. I heard myself spluttering inadequate words. Something I said must have hit the target. She tossed her head and blushed.

"I'll always be grateful for what you did this evening. If you hadn't been around . . ." She pulled a face and ran out of words.

I managed to unravel the knot in my tongue. "That's all right. How are you feeling?"

"Much better. Thanks for staying with me." Her face started to flush. "I'll make that coffee."

I followed her into the kitchen. "Show me where the things are. I'll make it. Go and rest on the sofa."

"OK. Coffee and sugar are in that cupboard, milk is in the fridge and spoons are in that drawer. I'll get the cups for you."

When I carried our coffees through, she was asleep. I didn't wake her, but made her more comfortable with a pillow and duvet from her bedroom. In the short time that I'd known her she'd had a devastating effect on me. For the first time in my life a woman had made me feel like someone who mattered. I settled down on the sofa beside her. She slid towards me. I eased an arm around her shoulders, and covered my legs with the duvet. I felt awash with happiness. Was this what love feels like?

It was weird how our paths had crossed. But, there again, the last couple of days had been just as bizarre. I'd watched strange dreams on my bedroom wall, bought a desk that I didn't want, been shown in a dream where to find a hidden box, and inherited some apparently powerful stones as well as a key which opened goodness knows what at a bank.

Were those stones really a passport to great powers, as well as protecting me? I was convinced they'd allowed me to slow down time and saved me from being stabbed and shot by the yobs.

I backtracked on the evening. Of all the places I could have visited, what had taken me to Anne's pub? Had she got a boyfriend? She wasn't wearing a ring, but that meant nothing. I was pushing the boat out too far, too quickly, to even think we might end up as an item. My busy day caught up with me. My eyelids began to flutter and I fell asleep.

CHAPTER SIX

I should have dreamed about Anne, but I didn't. As I travelled down that tunnel of light into my dreamworld I found myself outside St Leonard's Church. The dilapidated noticeboard had one piece of paper pinned to it, reminding people that the churchwardens were appealing for monies to boost the restoration fund. I hoped a new noticeboard was top of their list.

A man dressed in a black cassock walked out of the church and strolled towards me. He was a younger version of the man I'd seen in my dream last night.

"Hello, Kit. I told you we'd be meeting soon."

"Why do I keep on dreaming about you?"

I scolded myself as soon as the words left my lips. This dream was nourished on what had happened during the last twenty-four hours.

"Things will hopefully become clearer by the time I've finished with you. Your world has been turned upside down these last few days, has it not?" He laughed. "That's putting it mildly."

"You can say that again."

"As you know, I'm Julius Milner, rector of the parish of Lovington, and you are Kit Milner, who works at an auction house in Grinton." He took my hand in a firm grip and shook it vigorously. "I know you've found my letter in the davenport. Are you wearing the stones?"

My hand instinctively moved to the pouch hanging under my shirt.

He nodded his head. "Good. Take the contents of my letter seriously, no matter what you might think." He shook his head. "Let's get one thing straight. This isn't one of your fabricated dreams. You've travelled back in time to be here. I know you won't believe me. I recall my own stubbornness to accept the truth about time travel."

I laughed out loud at the impossibility of what he was suggesting, then calmed down. "I'll stick to my own belief if you don't mind."

He shrugged his shoulders and pointed towards the church door. "Come inside, Kit. It's warmer in there."

The church boasted a breathtaking interior, with an angel ceiling and a beautifully crafted wooden altar screen that had somehow managed to escape the ravages of the Victorians.

He guided me to a pew. "Let's sit here. Now, how can I convince you that you're not dreaming?" He fell silent for a few seconds. "I know."

He got up, and returned with a sheet of paper clutched in his hand. "This is a bulletin of this month's services." He shoved it in my face. "As you can see, it's dated February 1999. When you return to your own time, look at it. It will prove that you time-travelled to be here."

His voice took on a serious tone. "I was in the auction house car park when that car did its best to run you down. It wasn't your dream-spinning that changed the attempt on your life." He let out another of his expansive sighs. "It's so simple. You went back in time and changed what had happened. I was at the auction when you bought my davenport. Your arm was being controlled, as well you know, to make sure you bought it."

I was warming to this newfangled dream experience.

"How did you manage to be at the auction? By that time you were . . ." I stopped. A dream wasn't the place to tell him he was dead.

I heard the rustling of paper as he took a half-eaten bar of chocolate from his pocket. I refused the piece that was offered. He popped it into his mouth and chewed noisily on it.

"You were about to say I was dead. So be it. We all have to die one day." He sucked on his teeth to savour the last particles of his treat. "I time-travelled into the future to be there."

I pulled a face.

He glared at me. "Of course I knew I was dead. It was my possessions you were selling off. That was a dead giveaway.

"I don't wish to know how I died, or when it's going to happen. I was never tempted to use the stones to travel into my future and prevent my death. They never sat easily with my religious beliefs."

I started to speak. He shoved his hand across my mouth.

"Listen to me first. I have some important things to tell you before you go. Lovington will play a major part in your future life." He became exasperated. "Get a grip of yourself. There is so much you have to achieve. Don't throw it all away by doubting what the future holds for you." He shook his head. "You're not the only one who is experiencing life changes. My life has been turned upside down these past few weeks by a family who moved into the village a few months ago. They've made my life a living hell." He grunted. "That's putting it mildly. One member of that family has already made your life a misery."

My imagination was caught by this man. I was even prepared to forget I was dreaming.

"You're talking about Grodam, aren't you?"

He nodded. "The unpleasantness started a few weeks ago, when I found the church door had been covered with graffiti. 'Deceased 10th December 1998' was sprayed across the door." He took a tissue from his pocket and blew his nose. "Matters went from bad to worse. Our rectory windows were smashed three times, then we were burgled." His face screwed up in anger. "Burgled is a polite term. The sofa was urinated on, and human faeces smeared over the walls. I knew the Grodams were responsible, but I couldn't go to the police. I had nothing to prove it was them. It was obvious what they were after."

I humoured my dream-reverend. "What were they after?"

"That's the first sensible thing you've said." He undid the top of his cassock and nestled a pouch in the palm of his hand. "They were after my stones." He poked me in the chest. "If they ever get their hands on them, God help us. These stones provide powers that are way beyond your imagination. With their help, you can control people, travel through the pages of time and change what has already happened." He smiled. "The stones saved you from those two yobs this evening. I thought you were a bit hard on them." He flapped his arms about. "You're a novice and have so much to learn." A tear trickled down his face. "I was telling you about the Grodams. They—"

Without warning, his whole body stiffened, and his hands clutched at his throat. His face turned a deep purple, and he couldn't form his words properly. His fingers dragged at the front of my shirt as he finally managed to gasp out a few words: "Walk . . . before . . . too . . . late." His lips continued moving, but no more words came out.

The strange turn ceased as quickly as it had started. His whole body relaxed and his face returned to its normal colour.

He grasped my arm. "Forgive me, my boy. I've suffered several turns like this of late. Ignore my ramblings. My doctor says it's down to the pressures I've been put under these past few weeks." He took a deep breath. "Meg and I were blessed with a daughter, Carin. She was the most beautiful thing in our lives."

"You talk as if your daughter's no longer with you."

His hands clenched and unclenched. "Carin was murdered on the date that was sprayed on the church door. The 10th of December 1998 will be etched in my mind until the day I die. Carin was always home from school by four o'clock. It was gone five when Meg and I got back from a meeting at Ely Cathedral. There was no sign of Carin." He moved his backside around in the pew. "I sensed something dreadful had happened to her. An image of the church altar kept flashing in my mind. I asked Meg to ring the police whilst I slipped across to the church. The main door should have been unlocked, but it was bolted. I walked around the church to the chancel door. It was wide open. When I walked in I found my daughter's naked body on the altar."

This fantasy was getting under my skin. I had enough problems in my own life without taking on someone else's dream-grief.

"Look. I've got other things to worry about. I'm pulling the plug on this dream."

He grabbed my arm. "Please stay, Kit. I don't care whether you think this is a dream or not. Hear me out, I beg you."

Don't ask me why I changed my mind, but I did. "OK. But I have to be going soon."

He squeezed my arm and raised a token smile. "My daughter was dead. Her killer had slit her throat and shoved a wax candle between the top of her legs. You have to know what kind of people you're dealing with. I'm certain that one of the Grodam family killed her." He tapped my pouch. "That's why you're wearing those stones. They'll protect you from the likes of the Grodams." He shook his head. "It's no good telling the police what I've told you. I've got no evidence to point a finger at them. I shouldn't have gone to Ely on that day."

What does one say in a fantasy? I went along with him. "Don't blame yourself."

He snapped at me. "It's all right for you to say that. I'm protected by the stones, but my daughter wasn't. I broke the news to Meg as gently as I could. She suffered a mental breakdown. The Bishop told me to take a few weeks off. During that time Meg and I did nothing else but talk about Carin. It helped to convince us that our future still lay in Lovington."

His story didn't make sense. I snarled at him, "If you can time-travel, why the hell don't you go back in time and save your daughter from being murdered?"

His eyes bulged as he shouted at me, "Don't you think I thought about that! If I had, it would have been a betrayal of my religious beliefs!" He calmed down. "No one has the right of resurrection or killing, even for my own daughter. I will never go down that road."

His reasoning was rubbish thinking. I yelled back at him, "For Christ's sake! You don't need to kill anyone! It's as simple as cancelling your trip to Ely and collecting your daughter from school on the day she was killed."

"Don't you shout at me! If I had done, the Grodams would have found another way of getting back at me. Let me finish my story, then you can bugger off. My first service on returning from holiday went better than I expected. I finished my sermon and processed to the altar to dispense the elements. I glanced up at the stained-glass window behind the altar. My eyes chanced on one of the children in the window." A wistful smile flirted with his face. "The child smiling down at me was my daughter. I was shocked, but I kept my thoughts and feelings under control and completed the service. I didn't let on to Meg about our daughter's image in the stained-glass window. She was already under enough stress as it was." He got up from the pew. "Come with me." We walked up to the altar, and he pointed at the stained-glass window. "That child leaning on the Christ figure's left knee is my daughter."

She was a stunningly beautiful child. Not for the first time I knew my waking life was fuelling this dream. The child looked uncannily like a young Anne Wood. The rector led me out of the church to the far side of the graveyard. He pointed at a new headstone. I peered at the engraved words:

'Carin Anne Milner.
Died 10th December 1998, aged thirteen years.
She fell to earth before she had learned to fly.'

"The Grodam family have moved away. That's not to say I won't meet up with them again." His green eyes bored into mine. "You'd better be off. Think about what I've said, and start believing in yourself. We'll meet again."

I urged my mind to end the images of this manic dream and woke up on Anne's sofa. She lay asleep beside me. I briefly flirted with the dream journey that I'd just vacated. I felt a touch of guilt at becoming emotionally involved in the imaginary capers of Julius Milner. My dreams don't matter any more. Anne is more important. I didn't need to be told that I'd fallen in love with her. I can't make Anne feel the same way about me; but so long as she's prepared to throw a few crumbs of comfort my way, I'll be happy. I can't expect more. With these pleasant thoughts drifting through my mind, I fell into dreamless, unbroken sleep.

CHAPTER SEVEN

Anne's crying woke me. I reached out for her. She wasn't there. I found her in the bathroom, stretched out on the floor. Beads of sweat were running down her face.

I shook her gently. "What's the matter?"

Her eyelids fluttered open. Those breathtaking eyes were filled with pain.

She clawed at my arm. "Help me. I'm hurting like buggery, all over."

I felt angry with her. She should have gone to hospital last night.

"I'll call an ambulance."

I swept her up in my arms and carried her into her bedroom. Within ten minutes the ambulance rolled up. Five minutes later Anne was on her way to King's Lynn Hospital. I telephoned Martin Henderson, telling him I was taking the day off work. He told me in a toneless voice that it was OK.

I made my way to the hospital. When I walked into A & E, a woman behind the enquiry desk directed me to an examination room. A weary-looking nurse took me in to see Anne. She smiled and briefly held my hand before her eyes closed. The nurse said they'd given her something to make her sleep, and I was to ring back that afternoon to see how she was.

I pushed her to the back of my mind. I wasn't being a callous sod. There were other things that needed sorting. I drove back to Lovington Church and went inside. I couldn't explain why the church interior was exactly the same as I'd seen it in my dream.

It reminded me that the rector had given me a service bulletin. I rummaged through my pockets. The search revealed nothing. Some strange things had happened these past few days, but time travel wasn't going to be one of them.

I walked down to the altar to check out the stained-glass window. The rector's daughter wasn't one of the children in the window. I made my way into the churchyard, knowing what I wouldn't find. Carin Milner wasn't buried there. I was right. The dream had been a fantasy and nothing more.

I drove into Lovington and parked in the marketplace. It was a short walk to the teashop that I'd found yesterday. The same friendly old dear welcomed me. The steaming cup of coffee and a toasted sandwich went down well.

I ferreted in my pocket for some change to pay her. The motley collection of coins in my hand wouldn't have paid for the coffee. As I delved into my wallet for a £10 note, a piece of paper fell on to the table. With a feeling of intense unease, I picked it up. The dates of the February services at St Leonard's Church, for 1999, burned into the back of my eyes. Utter confusion hammered at my brain. The coins in my hand fell to the floor and rolled in all directions. I was sweating like a pig as I scrambled on my hands and knees to pick them up. I sat down and ordered another coffee, ignoring the puzzled glances from the other customers.

What was Reverend Milner's piece of paper doing in my wallet? The answer hit me. I let out a sigh of relief, which attracted more funny looks. There was a very good reason. In my childhood dreamworld I'd often brought back real objects to my waking world. The bulletin was just another dream souvenir.

As I sipped my coffee, I knew Julian Milner's assertion about time travel didn't stand up in the light of day. I'd seen the evidence with my own eyes. Where was the likeness of his daughter in the stained-glass window? And what about her non-existent grave?

I paid the bill and strolled down the busy High Street to

Barclays Bank. A friendly young female smiled at me when I reached the counter.

"Good afternoon, sir. How can I help?"

I passed her the key that I'd found in Reverend Milner's envelope. She checked it and inputted some details into her computer. She handed the key back.

"Please wait outside the manager's office, over there. He wants to see you personally."

I didn't get the chance to sit down. The manager's door burst open, and a man fitting my mental image of a bank manager beckoned me into his office. He was tall and skinny, with a shiny bald dome of a head. He peered at me through thick, black-framed glasses. A warm smile creased his face as he shook hands with me.

"Hello, Mr Milner. I'm Kevin King. It's a pleasure to meet you at long last. Please take a seat."

The profuseness of his welcome intrigued me. "You're acting as if you were expecting me today."

He smirked. "Indeed, I am. Indeed, I am." He squirmed in his chair. "Your circumstances have filled me with a feeling of expectancy, ever since your file came to my attention some twelve months ago."

I sighed. Where, oh where, had my organised life gone? This smug-looking man had welcomed me like a long-lost brother. He'd better have a good reason. If so, it would be the first one in the last few days.

He scratched at his bald dome and shrugged his thin shoulders. "Now, where shall I start? In all honesty, Mr Milner, I'm rather confused."

"Join the club. I was hoping you could throw some light on what's going on."

He rubbed his hands together. Composing himself, he opened a desk drawer. With all the aplomb of a magician, he produced a red folder and threw it on the desk.

"Don't worry, Mr Milner. All will be revealed. First things first. I need some form of identification to make sure you are who you say you are." He balanced his glasses on the end of his bulbous nose, and that annoying smirk covered his face. He took a piece of paper out of the folder. "Happily, on this occasion, I know you are indeed Kit Milner. I have your photograph on this copy of your driving licence."

I got to my feet and thumped my fist on his desk. My voice rose by several decibels. "You've got a copy of my driving licence! That's bloody impossible! Where did you get it from? Let me see that piece of paper!"

The fierce look on my face worried him. He got up and edged towards the door. A change of heart later, he sat down again.

His hands placated me. "Please sit down."

He passed the piece of paper to me. It *was* a copy of my driving licence. This latest weird twist in my life consigned me into a state of resigned silence. I passed it back to him and slumped into my chair. Relief showed in his face.

"Let's start at the beginning. Just over twelve months ago I was contacted by a firm of solicitors acting on behalf of a Reverend Julius Milner. Does the name mean anything to you?"

I nodded.

His fingers drummed a rapid tattoo on the top of his desk. His ill-disguised excitement was getting the better of him.

"They informed me that Julius Milner had asked my bank to act as intermediary between him and yourself after his death. They passed this file to me, which includes a copy of your driving licence" – he gave me an old-fashioned look – "no matter where it might have come from." He was growing bolder by the minute. "The solicitors knew nothing about you, or what relationship, if any, you shared with the Reverend Milner. Their client furnished none of this information. His solicitors were under strict instructions not to make direct contact with you." He grunted. "That would have proved difficult, because they had no idea who you were or where you lived." Mr King was getting into his stride. His bald head sparkled with beads of sweat. "The reverend gentleman assured them that you would make contact with my bank." He eyeballed me. "The Reverend even provided them with the exact time and date when you would call on me." He laughed. "We all thought the old boy was off his rocker." He glanced at his watch and swelled with delight. "I'm pleased to say he was of sound mind. You haven't let him down. Your timing today, in seeing me, is as he predicted."

I should have been stunned by what he said, but I wasn't. Out-of-the ordinary events were becoming so commonplace, I was accepting them. Thank goodness I'd learned how to cope with them.

"His solicitor contacted me recently, confirming that Julius Milner had died. Their original letter reminds me that you have a key. May I see it, please?"

I fumbled in my pocket and passed it to him.

"This key opens one of our security boxes." He glanced at another piece of paper. "The security box is registered in your name. The rental on that box expires at midnight tonight." He pushed his chair back and stood up. "I'm satisfied that you have a genuine claim on whatever the security box contains."

He pressed a button, nestling on the corner of his desk. His office door opened and a young man walked in. The manager nodded to him.

"This is Jake Smith-Adams. He'll take you to our security room." He handed the key to the young man and shook my hand. "It's been a pleasure meeting you. If I can be of any further assistance, please let me know. I hope you find the answer to your dreams in the box." He laughed. "The solicitor's letter said you would."

Mr Smith-Adams took me in tow. Several passages later, we halted in front of a metal door. With light-fingered precision, young Smith-Adams punched some numbers into the security pad. The door swung open under his touch, and he led me into the room. The walls were covered in banks of metal drawers.

He rechecked the key number and strode across to one of the drawers. With a deft flourish of his wrist he unlocked it. He handed the metal box to me and waved me towards a table and chair.

"Take the contents of the box away with you when you've

finished. We'll ask you to sign our security register before you leave, to confirm that it was you who emptied the box. Take as long as you like. When you're ready to leave, push the button at the side of the door. Someone will let you out."

I sat down and opened the box. Two brown envelopes lay in the bottom. Both were addressed to me in that spidery handwriting I'd come to know. One was bulky; the other was a smaller envelope. I opened the smaller envelope because it was marked 'Read this first'. It was sealed with wax. I broke the seal and found a letter inside:

Dear Kit,

I've rented a security box at Barclays Bank, Lovington, in your name, knowing you'd be calling today. You still don't believe in time travel, do you? For goodness' sake wake up, man. How did I know you'd be here today, at this particular time? It certainly wasn't guesswork. I travelled forward in time, many months ago. I saw you go into the manager's office and made a note of the time and date.

You certainly take some convincing. When we met back in 1999 I gave you a service sheet. You found that sheet today, didn't you? I saw it drop out of your wallet in the teashop. Today's date in your time is Monday the 29th of October 2012. Doesn't this reinforce my point about time travel?

A cold sweat covered my body, even though the room was as warm as toast. My self-assessed thought processes had been totally destroyed. Did I really hold the key to travelling through time? I put the thought on hold until my brain was in a more receptive mood. I read through the rest of the letter:

Your stones provide the gift of moving through time. Use that gift, for heaven's sake, and stop shilly-shallying around. There's no difficulty involved. All you need do is to concentrate on the date and time, and where you want to travel to.

There is a price to pay for possessing the stones. They don't come for nothing. You are duty-bound to undertake this mission to rescue Merlin from that rock before Madrog gets his hands on him.

I found it impossible to accept the mission. Because of this, I surrendered the stones to you. Now that you have them, get off your butt and be ready for your mission when you're called upon to carry it through.

There's another envelope in the security box. It contains enough money to pay for my davenport. I never dreamt it would fetch £950! You have to blame that dreadful man Grodam for pushing the price up. The money will cover the cost, together with your boss's commission, with a bit left over. All good wishes, Kit. We'll bump into each other again, even though I lie in my grave as you read this letter.

Your sincere friend,

Julius Milner.

PS: You were puzzled as to how the bank manager had a copy of your driving licence. I time-travelled into your flat whilst you were asleep. I borrowed your driving licence and copied it. I'm sorry this made you lose your rag with the bank manager. He got really worried about your behaviour, didn't he?

I read the letter three times. It was full of weird nonsense, yet it made sense. Julius Milner was dead, and buried, yet he'd seen me find the service sheet in the tea shop and watched me turn up at the bank. Either the reverend gentleman had the services of a good soothsayer or he could time-travel. I finally accepted that he was telling the truth. Even so, one factor refused to gel with me. His daughter must be alive, because her face wasn't in the stained-glass window and I hadn't found her grave. I came up with the only possible answer. It meant visiting St Leonard's Church on the day she was murdered, to test my theory – always assuming I possessed the gift of time travel.

The bulky envelope sat staring at me. I tore it open and stifled a gasp. It contained a profusion of £50 notes. Within minutes I'd counted out £1,500.

I locked the box and stuffed the letters and cash into my coat pockets. The manager let me out when I rang the bell. With a self-satisfied look, he took the key and guided me back to the banking chamber, where I signed the security register. I shook his hand and bade him goodbye.

Once I was back in my car, I rang the hospital. A pleasant lady told me that Anne was making good progress. I asked her to tell Anne that I'd visit her later in the day.

I made myself comfortable in readiness to test Julius Milner's premise on time travel. My icy calmness surprised me. I was on the verge of achieving the impossible, yet I felt as cool as a cucumber. I mentally repeated the instructions that I hoped would get me space-bound: 'Lovington Marketplace, the 10th of December 1998, at half past two in the afternoon.'

I ceased the mantra as a current of air ruffled my hair. The next moment I was rushing down that same white tunnel of light that I'd always experienced in what I'd thought were my dreamworld journeys. I found myself standing outside my High Street teashop. The folk walking by showed no surprise at my sudden appearance. When I looked down at myself I could see why they were treating me as if I didn't exist.

In their eyes, I didn't. I was invisible. A fleeting feeling of panic passed. I walked down to the public toilets, where I locked myself in a cubicle. It didn't take me long to find out how to make myself visible. It was as simple as placing the command in my mind. A warm feeling filtered through me. I felt on a high at having achieved the downright impossible. The Reverend Milner had told the truth. I grinned. What else should I have expected from a man of God?

I ambled down the High Street to Barclays Bank and walked inside. Less than an hour ago I'd passed through these same doors, in another time warp. A young man with a mass of curly hair stood behind a desk. The name plaque told me he was Kevin King. I turned down the urge to arrange an appointment with him in fourteen years' time, when he was the manager.

A calendar standing on the counter brought me down to earth. The 10th of December 1998 stared at me. It jolted me into the unpleasant reminder that the Reverend's daughter had been murdered today. Time was on my side. Carin wouldn't be at the church until at least four o'clock.

My next port of call was my favourite tea shop. Tea and toast were served by a younger version of the lady who had so readily looked after my needs on previous visits. I asked if my friend Julius Milner was still the rector of St Leonard's. She carried on with the habit of patting her hair whenever his name was mentioned.

"You're a fortunate young man to count him as a friend. Yes, he's still looking after his flock."

She walked away to serve another customer. As I relaxed with my tea and toast, time-trekking was foremost in my thoughts. Unwittingly, I had meddled with time in the auction-house car park, when Grodam had run me down. That saga threw up a few puzzling things. I was the only person who remembered what had happened before I changed the past. My feet were set in the fabled parallel worlds of time. The other puzzler was how had I managed to time-travel when I hadn't got the stones with me? And, if I'd travelled back in time, why hadn't I met myself? I took another sip of tea and checked my watch. It was nearly half past three, and time to go. An old lady took my money. I tipped the waitress and wished her well. I didn't tell her that she was destined to enjoy the good life, as the future owner of the tea shop.

I left the tea house and drove to St Leonard's Church.

CHAPTER EIGHT

Ten minutes later I was inside the church. A quick search satisfied me that Carin's murderer wasn't lurking in the shadows. I couldn't control my shivering. It was a combination of the temperature nudging the bottom end of the thermometer and what lay ahead of me. I settled down behind the pulpit, to the left of the chancel steps, and made myself as comfortable as the cold stone floor would allow.

Fifteen minutes passed. It seemed more like an hour. The only sounds intruding on the silence were the fluttering of bats and the occasional vehicle trundling by. The church door finally creaked open. Somebody switched the lights on. I craned my head, but couldn't see who it was. The door protested as it was closed. The unknown person walked into view. I wasn't surprised to see him. Reverend Milner had broken his God-given promise and had travelled back in time to save his daughter's life.

He didn't need my help. I'd only be watching a rerun of something that had already taken place. I prepared to return to my own time. It wasn't to be. I sneezed. Julius Milner came as near as possible to jumping out of his skin.

"Who's there?"

I stood up. "Sorry to frighten you, Rector. It's me. Kit Milner."

"What the hell are you doing here?" He scowled at me. "You'd better not get in my way."

"Don't worry. I won't. I only came back to find out why things had changed since I was last here. Now I know why, I'll be on my way."

He put his hand over my mouth as the door creaked open, then closed.

"My daughter's here. Get your head down. You're the last person I want her to see." He poked me in the chest and whispered, "Not a word out of you." He called to her as he hurried across to the main door. "It's only me, darling. I got back early from Ely, so I popped into church to put the heating on. Would you go to the village shop and get a bottle of milk for your mother? I'll see you back at the rectory."

A few moments later they walked up the central aisle, arm in arm. The rector hadn't exaggerated her beauty. Her face was outlined by a mass of auburn hair. I couldn't see, but I would have bet she had green eyes. For the second time in as many days, I lost my heart to her. The rector's daughter was a younger version of Anne Wood. I wondered again. Why the change of name?

The two of them chatted happily together before they disappeared up the chancel steps. I heard a bolt being drawn, then a door was slammed shut and bolted. Julius Milner hurried back and knelt beside me. The church door opened and closed. He shoved his hand over my mouth.

"My daughter's murderer has turned up."

The bolts on the door were drawn before an obese youth, wearing a base-ball cap and looking about seventeen, walked up the central aisle. He was the spitting image of a young Billy Grodam. His small piggy eyes were set in a washed-out face with a weak chin and a wide gash that masqueraded as his mouth. His looks weren't helped by a severe case of acne. He was clutching a knife in his hand.

He walked up the chancel steps and yelled out, "Are you there, Carin?"

The rector tapped my arm. "That's Joseph Grodam. He's going to get what he deserves for what he did to my daughter."

His whispered words scared me stiff. "What do you mean?

Your daughter's safe. That's what you wanted, isn't it? Hang around for a few minutes and he'll be gone."

The brutal look on his face worried me.

"He's not going home."

I couldn't believe what I was hearing, and put my mouth to his ear.

He pushed me away. "Stay here, and don't interfere." He got to his feet, and yelled out, "I'm afraid my daughter can't join you, Joseph. Don't do anything silly with that knife. I've got a gun."

I glanced around the pulpit. He wasn't bluffing. This was beyond belief. Priests are supposed to save souls, not take them.

"Put the knife on the altar. You won't be using it, like the last time you were here."

The gun didn't seem to worry the youngster, but he did as he was told.

"You don't scare me, vicar. Are you going to shoot me because I've come into your bleeding church?"

The rector wasn't impressed. "You're going to suffer like my daughter did."

"What are you on about, you wanker? I saw her come into church and thought I'd talk to her. Sod this. I'm going home."

The Reverend's voice carried a malicious edge. "Shut your mouth! Is that why you bolted the door and brought a knife with you – because you wanted to talk to her, you bloody liar?"

He pointed the gun at the youth's head. Joseph Grodam's mood changed.

His voice shook with fright. "Look, Mr Milner, nothing's happened, because she's not here. Honest."

"You wouldn't know honesty if it kicked you up the arse."

I got up and stood at the chancel steps.

"Hold on, Reverend. Put the gun away. Let's discuss things in a calm and rational way."

His eyes protruded from their sockets as he screamed at me in a high-pitched voice, "Did this little shit let my daughter discuss things rationally? If you'd seen what he did to her, you'd have put a bullet in his brain. I'm letting him off bloody lightly. I won't torture him, and I'm not going to stick a candle up his arse, like he did to my daughter. If you feel upset, then bugger off back where you belong."

Grodam was gobsmacked. "I ain't done any of those things to your daughter."

The rector swiped him across his head with the gun. He slumped to the floor. I was furious and moved towards him.

He pointed the gun at me. "Stay where you are. I won't tell you again. Bugger off."

"You'll get found out if you kill him. They'll put you away for the rest of your life. You can forget about spending quality time with your family."

"Nobody will find his body. It'll be hidden under one of these marble slabs."

"Oh, yeah. And how are you going to lift it?"

"You're not the only one with powers." He muttered a few words under his breath.

The effect was startling. A large marble slab in front of the altar raised itself off the floor until it was stood on one end.

He leered at me. "Nobody will smell his decomposing body. It's airtight." He kicked the youngster. "Get up, and stand in that hole."

In situations of grave danger, cowards as well as brave men have been known to take on the cloak of courage when their chips are well and truly down. Joseph was no exception. With malicious calmness, he kicked the rector in the groin. Julius cried out in agony and collapsed. The gun slipped from his fingers. The young man snuggled the gun in his right hand. I hoped the rector's stones were as good as they were made out to be.

Joseph's coarse laugh echoed through the church. "I don't know what you're on about, you twat, but I'd have given your daughter a good shagging." He looked thoughtful. "My dad says you've got a bag of stones that he's after." He eyeballed me. "Up here, you, where I can see you."

I had no option, and sat down in a choir pew.

He poked the rector in the ribs with his foot. "He says you wear them around your neck. Give 'em to me."

The rector's words were etched in pain. "They're in my desk, back at the rectory. You can search me if you like."

This was madness. He was slumped on the floor with a gun pointed at his head, and the life-protecting stones were lying in state, back in the rectory.

He put the gun against the rector's head and shouted at me, "Don't try anything or he gets it." He ripped the rector's dog collar off and made a frantic fruitless search of his clothing. He went spare. "Shit! I've had enough of this." From the look on his spotty face, I could tell he'd thought of something really nasty. "After I've shot you both, I'll call at the rectory and get the stones." A stupid grin appeared on his face. "I'll shag your wife and daughter." His thoughts were running riot. "I'll make them take their clothes off, then I'll tie them up. I've never shagged an older woman before. Thanks for telling me where the stones are, vicar."

The rector's voice took on an air of desperation. "Wait a minute, Joseph. There's no need to harm my family. Let me get the stones for you. My friend will stay here as hostage." He gave me a knowing look. "Don't worry, Kit, your stones will protect you."

His pain must have addled his brain; otherwise I'd have sworn he'd deliberately dropped me in it.

My words were laced with sarcasm. "Thanks for telling Joseph about my stones. I was about to give them to him."

That humourless grin covered the boy's face. "Your mate has got some stones, has he?"

The poor sod had no idea what he was about to spark off. In the next few minutes I became converted to the firm belief that the power to change life lay in my hands. My eyes focused on a brass altar candlestick. As a single consuming thought concentrated on it, the candlestick stirred from the altar and hovered in the air before turning into a horizontal position. I barely saw it as it hurtled towards Grodam. It caught him a sickening blow on the back of his head. He staggered across the floor with the gun still clutched in his hand.

Whatever power was guiding me hadn't finished with him. I pointed at the gun. A vivid flash of white light spewed from the tip of my finger. As it struck the youth's wrist, his severed hand dropped to the floor. The fingers slowly unfolded and let go of the gun.

He stared in disbelief at his twitching hand, lying on the floor. He shouted a string of profanities at me, then reached for the gun with his good hand and aimed it at me. His finger tightened around the trigger.

Lightning isn't supposed to strike twice in the same place. Take my word for it, it does. My forefinger lined up with his body. A violent bolt of blue light engulfed him. I could feel its crackling heat from where I stood. He screamed in agony as his clothes burned on his body. He dashed past me and ran down the central aisle, flames licking from every part of him. His naked burning body started to break up. His head exploded in a cloud of red smoke, then his arms, followed by his upper body. The only body parts left, as he reached the church door, were his legs and feet. They evaporated in one final flash of brilliant red light. The only proof that Joseph Grodam had ever been in church was the stench of burned flesh.

I hurried to the church door, expecting to find charred body parts littering the floor. There was nothing. No scraps of flesh, no blood, no clothing and no gun. My lightning bolt had vaporised him into nothingness.

I made my way back to the altar. Julius was on his knees, rubbing at his body. He showed no sign of surprise at what had happened.

"Are you all right, Reverend?"

There wasn't a hint of compassion in his voice. "Don't worry about me. That little sod got what he deserved, seeing what he did to Carin. Thanks for saving my life."

The full impact of the youth's death hit me. An unknown force had used me to kill him. Whether or not he deserved to die was beside the point. It only made me feel a little better, knowing that I'd saved Julius, as well as his wife and daughter. That aside, I felt used. If the rector had handled things differently, none of this need have happened.

"I've had enough of this! For a man of God, you're taking

this bloody calmly. What's going on? I didn't save your life. The stones did. They were using me. What other powers do they have?"

He spoke in a matter-of-fact way. "Don't concern yourself about their powers. They'll show themselves when the need arises, like when that car tried to run you down." He laughed. "Even if you hadn't time-travelled to change what happened, your injuries would have healed themselves by the next morning, thanks to the stones. Even though they were in my desk, in your saleroom, they were still protecting you. Don't feel badly about Grodam. The stones came to our rescue – end of story. Let's leave it at that, shall we?"

"Am I missing something? You're acting as if that boy's murder was an inconvenience. You deliberately dropped me in the mire when you told him about my stones. I'm really happy for your daughter, but I've had enough of this. I'm off."

He grabbed my arm. "Please, Kit. Sit down and hear me out."

I relented. "It had better be good. I'll need a lot of convincing."

He got on his high horse. "For a start, you shouldn't be here! Today's nonsense came about because you stuck your nose in." He shook his head. "I'm puzzled, Kit. I made notes of everything that happened when I went back in time and saved my daughter. They should have been passed to you by my solicitor. You needn't have turned up today if you'd bothered to read them."

"Don't you bloody well blame me. I've never seen these notes."

"I'm sorry, my boy. It took courage to come here. God only knows why my papers never reached you. In that case, I'll tell you why I've been so calm about Grodam's death. A few weeks ago I travelled back in time and saw what he did to my daughter. It brought on a manic hatred of him."

"I don't believe this! You watched him murder your daughter? All you achieved was self-inflicted torture."

"I don't go around killing people for the sake of it! I had to hate him enough to make me want to kill him." He laughed in a demented way. "See for yourself what he did to her. It'll mean tapping into another of your stone's powers." I must have looked startled. "Don't worry. You're going to bond with my memory cells. Put your hands on the top of my head, close your eyes and think about my daughter's murder."

I did as he asked. A sequence of moving pictures slotted into my mind's eye. I was repulsed at the sight of Grodam slashing at Carin's naked body with his knife as he sat astride her on the altar. The bastard slit her throat, then dropped his trousers and made love to her. As if he hadn't degraded her body enough, he got down from the altar, picked up an altar candle and rammed it between the top of her legs. He started humming an inane tune and made his way out through the chancel door. I was bloody glad the toerag was dead.

"I've seen enough. You're right. The little bastard deserved what he got, and I'm glad it was me that did it."

"It wasn't pretty, was it? I put a bullet in his head the first time round, and hid him under that marble slab. I'm thankful that Carin and Meg don't remember what happened in that other life."

"When your daughter gets home, won't the present-day rector find it strange when she mentions meeting up with you in church?"

"That wasn't a problem. I met up with my younger self a few days before I came back to save Carin. He'll be at home, waiting for her to return with that bottle of milk."

I was horrified. "I don't believe it! Two men of the cloth connived to kill Grodam." I thought about what I'd said. "That was a daft thing to say. Knowing what an arsehole he was, you did the right thing."

A satisfied look crossed his face. "I'm glad you agree. We'd better clear up what's left of Grodam." He sniffed the air. "I'll open the church door and let some air in. Then we'll get up to the chancel."

We hurried up there after he'd opened the door.

He pulled a face. "You can get rid of Grodam's hand while I sweep up his charred clothing."

I didn't touch his hand. The stones did it for me. A single

thought made his hand hover above the ground.

I guided it into the slab recess. Another thought closed the slab.

We were interrupted by a voice from the main door. I turned round, and found myself confronted by the rector's slightly younger self. He strode up the central aisle, totally ignoring me, and spoke to his twin.

"Carin's just returned home. Did you get rid of that little bastard, or have you let him go?"

Julius shook his younger self's hand. "He's been done away with." He pointed at me. "We have to thank Kit for doing away with Grodam."

I was rewarded with a hug from the younger Julius Milner. He wiped tears away from his eyes. "Thank you, Kit. You've taken a weight off our shoulders."

"I don't want your thanks. I didn't consciously do it, although I'm glad I did." I pointed at the older Julius Milner. "As I told him, something was controlling me. He says it was the stones that gave me the powers to do away with him."

"He's right, Kit." He shook the older Julius Milner's hand and hugged me again. "It's been a treat meeting up with you both. You'd better return to your own time."

He was rushing things, as far as I was concerned.

"Whoa! Hold on a minute. There's a few things I want to sort out with you two. Does your daughter know about the stones and their powers?"

The older rector smiled. "She wears one of the stones to protect her, after what Grodam did to her."

That explained why there were only three stones in my bag.

"I'll tell her about the stones when she's older. Is there anything else on your mind before you go?"

"There is. You two met up with each other when Julius travelled back in time. Why didn't I meet myself in the auction-house car park when I went back that second time?"

The older rector looked at his twin. "I'll tell him. There's a simple answer, Kit. You are unique. You can never meet up with yourself when you time-travel. You'll find out why one day. Is there anything else troubling you, because we ought to be on our way?"

"Just one thing. Does the name Anne Wood mean anything to you?"

Their shoulders moved in silent mirth.

The younger one spoke. "It should do. It's my wife's maiden name, but I've always called her Meg." He pulled a face. "Where did that thought come from?"

I laughed and lied at the same time. "I picked the name up when I was reading the rector's mind back in church."

"Good. I'm glad that's cleared up. Off you go, then."

I willed myself back to my car in my own time zone.

My adrenaline was still up and running. I'd just saved Carin from being murdered, so I wondered if I could prevent the rector's death. It didn't take long to find his grave. I ordered my mind to take me back to the day he had died. Nothing happened. I was stuck in my own time.

I wasn't surprised. Something had denied me meeting up with the rector. I knew why. Preventing his death would have aborted this mission. I wouldn't have bought his davenport, and the stones wouldn't be hanging around my neck. I had to accept that the questions buzzing around in my head would be answered one day.

A lot had happened these last few hours. Most of it was double Dutch to me. I had to smile at how little I really knew. My learning curve was only just beginning.

As I walked into my flat, the phone rang.

"Hello, Kit. How are you?" It was Billy Grodam.

I registered no hint of surprise. In fact, I felt a little sorry for him. I'd just killed his brother.

I humoured him. "What can I do for you, Billy?"

"You've got something I want. I'm willing to pay for the stones. Let me have them and you'll be richer by £10,000. That's enough to pay for the desk, with a lot of spending money left over." He was acting like my best friend, but came over as an evil, odious sod. "Listen, Kit. You and I got off on the wrong foot. Are you going to accept my offer? Tell you what, as it's you I'll make it twenty grand. That's what friends are for."

His new-found familiarity was getting up my nose. Why was I holding a conversation with this piece of shit?

My feelings spilled over. "Get stuffed, Fat-man."

There was a splutter on the other end of the line. "You've made the biggest mistake of your life, Milner. There are other ways of getting those stones."

I spiced up the verbals. "Bollocks. You don't scare me, Fat-man. Your hoodlums won't always be around to protect you, unless they wipe your arse and sleep in the same bed as you. Bugger off, you arsehole."

He hung up on me. I put him out of my mind. I'd promised to visit Anne in hospital. Before doing so, I counted out £1,150 of the rector's money and put it in an envelope.

I walked into Martin's office and threw the envelope on his desk. "There's the money for the davenport. I've included your commission."

He tore the envelope open. The disbelieving sod compared some of the numbers to satisfy himself they were real. With shaking hands, he tidied them into a neat pile. I left him counting the notes and drove to King's Lynn Hospital. I parked up, and within minutes was standing outside Anne's ward. She waved when she caught sight of me. I plucked up courage and planted a gentle lingering kiss on her cheek. She didn't object.

"Thanks for coming, Kit." Her hands clutched mine. "I've missed you."

"What has the doctor got to say about you?"

"There's no physical injury. I need to take it easy for a few days. I'm feeling better already. They're letting me out tomorrow." She looked at me with pleading eyes. "Would you pick me up?"

"Of course I will. Someone has to look after you."

"That's great. But don't spoil me too much."

It was a simple predictable conversation, but I was happy to flounder in the intoxication of the moment. Our cosy chatting came to an abrupt end when a nurse told me that visiting time had ended twenty minutes ago.

As I got up to leave, Anne pulled me towards her. She kissed me on the lips. "That's for being so caring."

I returned her kiss. "I'll ring the hospital tomorrow morning, to see when I can collect you."

As I floated away from the bed, she called me back. "Bring me some clothes, will you? Trousers, a blouse, a pair of shoes, socks, panties and a warm coat. You'll find them in my bedroom wardrobe and the chest of drawers. You'll need the security code to get into the flats."

I wrote the number down.

"Did you lock the flat before you came to see me in hospital?"

I kissed her again. "Don't worry. The flat key is in my pocket."

I unlocked Anne's pad. The smell of her perfume lingered in the bedroom. I raided her wardrobe for the clothes she'd asked for, then opened the chest of drawers. The socks and panties were there, and so was something else. Peeping out from beneath her smalls was a large brown envelope. I couldn't resist pulling it out when I recognised Julius Milner's handwriting. He'd written on it, 'Strictly Private and Confidential. To be passed to my solicitor after my death.' The envelope was torn open and empty. I put it back in the drawer. I knew why his notes on Carin's murder had never reached me. The puzzling thing was what were they doing in Anne's flat?

It was gone nine o'clock when I drove into the auction-house premises. Martin's car was parked outside his office. He was working late, even by his standards. After a nightcap I fell asleep on the sofa.

There's no telling where my dreams would have taken me. One minute I was asleep, the next moment I was awake, with my eyes stinging and tears running down my cheeks. The lounge was full of smoke. I heard a roaring sound behind the lounge door. The staircase was alight, and it was the only way out of the flat. I was calmness itself as I weighed up my only option. The one escape route was out of the lounge window. The idea of clambering down to the ground didn't appeal to me. The fresh air when I opened the window cleared my muddled thoughts. The stones would provide my escape route. I scrambled on to the window sill and stepped out into the night air, hoping the instructions that I'd fed into my mind would come to my rescue. It's impossible to describe the feeling of elation that swept through me as a latent power lowered me slowly to the ground.

I saw two figures running past Martin's office. A car started up and squealed off down the road. The strident sounds of a siren clamoured in the near distance. Was firing the flat Grodam's doing? If so, I wondered how he hoped to get his hands on my stones. Perhaps it was out of sheer spite. There was one way of finding out as well as saving my flat from being fired. I time-travelled to earlier in the evening, to a quarter past nine, and materialised on the other side of the car park. The stones revealed another of their hidden powers. Although it was pitch-black, I had a daylight view of everything.

Half an hour passed before I heard the crunching of feet on gravel. Two men sidled up to my front door. I recognised them as Grodam's henchmen, whom I'd come across at the viewing. One was carrying a petrol can. The other guy opened the letterbox so his mate could pour petrol through it. I sneaked up on them and made myself visible.

"Good evening, guys."

They jumped out of their skins.

"I've got a box of matches, in case you've forgotten to bring your own."

The goon holding the can put it down and showed his composure. "Well, look who it is, Reggie! It's Milner, and he's on his own. Billy says he wears the stones around his neck."

Reggie sniggered. "This will save us firing his flat. You know what to do, Alfie."

They each pulled a canister from their overcoat pockets and aimed them at my face.

The pink light that poured from my fingertips played over

their bodies with a muted crackling sound.

They were unconscious before they hit the ground.

I checked out the canisters. It was CS gas. I put my hands on Reggie's head and flipped through his memory cells. They told me what I wanted to know. They had followed me from the hospital. I picked up a phone call from Billy Grodam, telling Reggie to set my place on fire. He was to ring Billy back so he could alert a crony in the local fire brigade, who hoped to find my stones after the fire had been dampened. A picture in Reggie's mind sickened me. I chased across to Martin's office. He was lying on the floor in a pool of blood. I knew he was dead because I'd seen Alfie slit his throat.

He didn't deserve this. I willed myself back in time again, to twenty-five past nine that evening, and hid outside Martin's office. A few minutes later a car drove slowly down the road and stopped. The two goons got out and crept towards me. They had no idea what hit them as I zapped them with the pink beam. I pocketed their CS canisters and put their petrol can in the car before creeping up to Martin's office window. I peered in. He was sitting at his desk, writing furiously.

It took seconds to shut down Alfie's mind. I ordered him to do everything that Reggie told him to. As for Reggie, he was about to be reduced to the role of a robot, if the power of the stones allowed it. One thought later, I was inside his body. It was like standing in a dark room, but seeing everything through his eyes. I was in Reggie's driving seat, reading his memory cells, manipulating his brain and limbs and putting my words into his mouth. He was completely under my control. The element of elation at my new-found abilities quickly deserted me.

Reggie was my secret weapon in satisfying my Grodam hate complex. He'd done his best to blight my life, and I'd had my fill of him. Reggie's memory banks told me that Billy lived an hour's drive away. I got Reggie to ring him on his mobile.

Billy answered. He wasn't a happy bunny.

"It's about time you rang. Have you fired Milner's place? I want to get the bloody fire brigade down there pronto."

I put my words into Reggie's voice. "Sorry, Billy. Things

haven't worked out. Milner must have seen us following him. He's pulled into Grinton Police Station. What do you want us to do?"

"You bloody idiot. I don't want the police involved. Get back here, you twat. Make sure nobody follows you, especially Milner."

The line went dead.

My own mobile phone materialised in Reggie's hand. I got him to ring Grodam.

Billy sounded peeved. "Hello. Who's this?"

I used my own voice. "Good evening, William. Thought I'd give you a bell."

He swore at me. "Where did you get my number from? Listen to me—"

I interrupted him. "You listen to me, toerag. Your hoodlums have been following me since I left the hospital. I've had enough of your antics. I know where you live. It's time I called on you."

He laughed. "Come and join me for a cup of tea. I'll be waiting for you." He sniggered. "Do you want to be buried, or would you prefer a cremation?"

He slammed the phone down. His reaction was what I'd expected. He felt safe and secure surrounded by his guards. His cocky attitude made me even more determined to present him with my visiting card. I ordered Reggie to drive to Billy's house.

Billy Grodam's front door opened, and Craig, Billy's cousin, walked out. He scowled at the dozen or so men standing outside.

"Shut your mouths, you lot, and listen to me. The boss has had a phone call from some dickhead called Milner. He's on his way here. The boss wants you to hide around the grounds and catch this geezer when he turns up. Milner won't come in by the front gate. The boss thinks he'll try and reach the house from the back garden, through the graveyard." He pulled a canister from a bag he was carrying. "When you see him, spray him with this CS gas straight away – and I mean straight away.

There's one for everybody. Billy got them from a policeman friend."

They all laughed.

"The gas will stop him from thinking commands or pointing his fingers at us, so the boss says."

Everyone sniggered.

Craig wasn't impressed. "I'm only telling you what Billy said, so shut up. I know it sounds like a load of bollocks, but that's the way you're going to play it. Now listen. Once you've gassed Milner, the first thing you're going to do is cut away a pouch that he wears around his neck. Then gag him, tie his hands behind his back and keep spraying him with the gas. Spraying him is the important thing. Don't look inside the pouch or it'll be the last thing you ever do. Play it that way, or else. When you've got Milner, bring him to me, with the pouch, so I can take him to the boss man. There's £1,000 for everyone when you catch the twat." He barked out more orders. "Cover the boundary and the graveyard. Stay out of sight, and no talking or smoking. Now get out there. Find Milner and bring him back here."

An hour later, we were driving down a tree-lined road. I counted six palatial-looking houses, each standing in acres of open space. Sandwiched between two of them was a small cemetery. I wondered how many of Grodam's victims had been laid to rest there, unbeknown to the vicar.

Five of the houses were partially lit up. The other house was ablaze with light. We drove down a long drive and parked outside the well-lit house. Reggie, with me on board, walked up to the front door with Alfie. We were welcomed with a grunt from a man in the porch.

He opened the door and yelled inside, "Craig, Alfie and Reggie are here."

Craig appeared. "The boss wants a word with you, Reggie. You stay here, Alfie." We walked into a large hall and trod across a monstrous floral carpet.

Craig opened a door. "Reggie's here, boss."

Grodam yelled out, "Get him in here."

Billy was lounging on a groaning sofa, his grotesque body bathed in the light of a standard lamp. His ill-judged attempt at casual clothing ran to a pair of baggy trousers and an oversized jumper, while a pair of slippers struggled to hide his huge feet. A foul-smelling cigar hung from his lips. He stared at Reggie, his piggy eyes set in that fat ugly face. He didn't look happy.

"Have I got to do the bloody spadework myself? You're a waste of space, bollock-brain."

My loathing for him spilled over. I put words into Reggie's mouth. "If you want Milner's stones so bloody badly, sod off outside, you fat bastard, and get them yourself."

The cigar shot out of Grodam's mouth. He struggled to his feet. "You little shit. No one speaks to me like that." He waddled across to Reggie and whacked him on the jaw. Reggie grunted, but I willed him to stay on his feet. I exploded Reggie's fist into Grodam's face. He staggered backwards and slumped in an unconscious heap on the floor.

Reggie spoke my feelings. "That's for the trouble you've caused me."

Reggie would have some explaining to do when Grodam recovered consciousness, but that was his problem.

I willed myself back to my flat, undressed, curled up in bed and slept pleasant slumbers.

CHAPTER NINE

I phoned the hospital after breakfast. The ward nurse said I could pick Anne up at eleven o'clock. What with having to collect Anne, and not knowing when this mission would come about, I decided to take two weeks' holiday, so long as Martin was happy about it. I walked into his office. He was drinking his never-ending supply of coffee.

He smiled at me. "Good morning, Kit. I didn't get the chance to thank you for your client's cash for the davenport. What can I do for you?"

"Something has come up that needs my attention outside of work. I want to take two weeks' holiday. You can manage without me, can't you?"

His eyes blanked out for a few seconds. For one moment I thought he was ill. The smile on his face told me otherwise. He got up and put his arm on my shoulder. "You know I appreciate what you do for me. Take a couple of weeks off. You've earned it, Kit."

I drove to King's Lynn Hospital. When I arrived, Anne took her clothes and dressed behind the bed curtains. I couldn't stop fussing around her when I got her back to the flat, competing with myself to satisfy her every whim. She giggled as she enjoyed my attention.

Her mood suddenly changed. "As much as I love you waiting on me, there's something you should know about me." She took a deep breath then blurted her words out. "I've never had a boyfriend in the whole of my life." She looked me in the eyes. "But you're different. I feel at home with you around." She started fiddling with her fingers. "I'm not sure how to handle a one-to-one relationship. If you fancy me, I don't mind, but please don't rush me." She let out a sigh of relief. "There. That's off my chest." She put her hand over my mouth as I tried to speak. "There's something else you need to know. It might change your feelings for me." Tears welled up in those green eyes.

I rubbed her cheek with my fingers. "Don't worry. I know more about you than you think." I peddled my words. "For a start. Anne Wood isn't your real name. It's Carin Milner. You're the daughter of the late Rector of Lovington."

"How do you know? There's no—"

I butted in. "This isn't easy to explain." I was in unknown territory, walking on eggshells. "Some crazy things have happened to me these past few days. . . ."

She shouted over me. "You seem to know all about me, yet I don't know a bloody thing about you!"

"Would it make sense if I told you I've been chosen to carry out a mission?"

The hostility left her. "You're mixed up with the Merlin stones, aren't you? Now you're beginning to make sense, Mister."

We were on the same wavelength again.

"I bought your father's davenport at our auction. I didn't want to buy it, but something was working my bidding arm. His Merlin stones were hidden inside the desk, together with a letter from him. It told me about these stones and mentioned this mission. If you promise not to laugh, I'll tell you what I've been through these past few days and nights."

She listened patiently and didn't bat an eyelid as I recalled my experiences. I played safe and didn't mention meeting her father, or how I'd killed Joseph Grodam. Of course, I didn't tell her she'd been murdered in a past life.

"That's fascinating," was all she said.

"Now I've told you about my encounters, can you fill in some of the missing pieces?"

"First things first, Kit. Let me tell you about me. Daddy was a lovely man, and spoiled me rotten. I left school and got a brilliant job at the British Library in London." She pulled a face. "The only thing missing in my life was boyfriends." She laughed. "My friends kidded me that I was a female gender-bender. This woman you care for has never felt the need for an emotional bond with any man." She clasped my hands and looked me in the eyes. "That was until I met you." Her face coloured up. "I'm twenty-seven, for God's sake, and I'm still a virgin."

I couldn't help laughing. "What are you worried about? You're looking at the longest-serving member of the Hertfordshire Society of Over-Twenty-Five Virgins, and probably the only one."

She looked at me with doubt in her eyes.

"Honest to God, it's true. I'd never kissed a girl until I met you." I pushed the chat in another direction. "What do you know about this mission?"

"I came across it eighteen months ago, when Daddy went down with a bout of flu. I took a few days off work to nurse him. One morning he asked me to fetch his diary from his desk. Every drawer was stuffed full of papers. I didn't find the diary, but I chanced on a folder. My father had written 'Private and Confidential' on it. Don't ask me why, but I tore it open." She pulled a face. "I wish I hadn't. It changed my life completely." She tossed her mane of hair. "It was full of father's handwritten notes. I didn't have time to read them, so I put them back in the drawer. I couldn't sleep that night. My mind was full of that folder. I finally gave into temptation, and before I knew it I was sat in the dining room with the papers spread out on the table. I read about these Merlin stones and the powers they possess. His writings mentioned this mission, but there was no detail. When Daddy wrote that he'd time-travelled, I lost interest. I've never read so much crap in all my life. I thought he was jotting down some ideas for writing a fantasy novel.

"As I was putting the papers away, I came across a brown

envelope in the bottom of the drawer. My father had written on the envelope that the contents were confidential and were to be passed to his solicitor, after his death. The words were like a red rag to a bull. I ripped the envelope open and read the two sheets of paper inside."

Tears trickled down her face. I put my arm around her.

She pushed me away. "Not now, Kit." She took a deep breath. "He'd written an account of something that happened in his church back in 1998, and how he'd used the stones to travel back in time to put things right." She wiped more tears away. "Daddy's words didn't make pleasant reading, but they explained why I'm saddled with a hang-up against men."

My stomach tied up in knots at the sense of foreboding that raced through my body.

I tried to change the subject. "Why upset yourself? I don't care what was in those papers."

She snapped at me. "For Christ's sake, listen, will you! I have to get this out of my system. I've accepted that it really happened, and I can't do a bloody thing about it." Her fingers scrubbed at her lips. "If it wasn't for my father travelling back in time, I wouldn't be here. It's as simple as that." She waved an agitated hand at me. "I need a drink."

She got up and vanished into the kitchen before returning with a bottle of gin and a glass. I was ignored as she poured herself a generous measure. She downed it, poured another, then glared at me.

"Don't look at me like that. I need this to help me." She drank the second glass. "His words were like reading horror fiction, except it really happened. According to him, I was murdered, then raped. Daddy had put every last detail in his writings, as to how my body was violated only to be reborn by a trick of time." Her speech was beginning to slur. "I know his words were true, but because of him my life is an everlasting lie."

I said the first thing that came into my head. "Did you tell your father you'd found his papers?"

"Of course I didn't. I moved out of the rectory because I

needed space to get my head around things. I didn't tell him my real reason for going. His notes went with me when I moved into this flat."

I tried to steer her away from the subject. "You must be earning a good salary to live in a pad like this. You should see the pigsty I live in."

She slapped me down, as if I'd insulted her. "So what if I have got a nice flat! There's nothing wrong with that, is there? I rented and furnished this flat with money my father lent me."

"So, you didn't cut your ties with him?"

"No, but I never looked on him in the same way. Something died inside of me. The Milner moniker was dirty. That's why I changed my name. When Daddy passed away I couldn't bring myself to keep all of his possessions other than a few bits and pieces. I disposed of the rest." She put her head on my shoulder and cried.

I cursed Julius for what he'd done. Why had he put everything down in writing? I even began to doubt whether we'd been right in bringing Carin back to life.

"By rights, I should be lying at peace in my grave. I wish I was. This woman you profess to fancy is some kind of living-dead freak. Don't you understand? I was dead, dead, dead!"

As hard as I tried, I couldn't register any kind of bodily emotion. I was floundering in a bog of uncertainty.

Her forehead furrowed in a questioning way. "Why don't you say something?"

She was looking for the right signs in my face, together with words of comfort. Those words never came, and my looks finally gave me away. She shook her head and stared at me in disbelief. Revulsion covered her face. She slapped me across the face. I rubbed at the stinging pain.

Her eyes showed the anger raging inside of her. "You bloody bastard! You knew about this, didn't you? My father told you, didn't he?"

She realised the enormity of what she'd said and pulled away from me. The withering look on her face didn't suit her. She threw her glass across the room, then buried her face into mine.

Her gin-ridden breath caught at the back of my throat.

"So, you little arsehole, what's this all about, then? Do you get some kind of cheap thrill in touching someone who was murdered then brought back to life? Is that why you put me through the torture of telling you things you already knew? You were enjoying it, weren't you? Did you relish the thought of making love to someone who'd died, to give you that extra thrill? You're a sick man, and I hate your bloody guts."

I tried to reason with her. "Listen to me. Your father used his stones to right a tragic wrong. You deserved to live. He was only caring for the people he loved. He told me how your mother went through hell after you died. She suffered a mental breakdown. Can't you see? He did it for both of you."

She was totally unmoved.

I threw my last card on the table. "I don't care about the past. My feelings for you are real. I'd never hurt you." My words withered and died as they fell on barren ground. My trump card curled up at the edges.

She got up and looked down at me. Her loathing for me was written all over her face. "And I thought you were someone special." She walked across to the front door and opened it. "Get out of my life. Goodbye, and bloody good riddance."

I wasn't surprised by her behaviour. Her sanity had failed to suppress the seething mass of nightmares stewing in the psychotic cauldron in her mind. Sooner or later someone would have borne the brunt of her pent-up anger. It was me who'd opened Pandora's box, and lost the girl in the process.

I stuck my foot in the door as Carin shoved me out of the flat. Her unseeing eyes stared at me as I waved a hand in front of her face and brought her under my influence.

My words were soft, but firm. "Sit on the sofa and sleep until I get back."

As things were, my chances of retrieving Carin's affection were as likely as the Pope taking a wife. Thank goodness there was a way of sorting out this mess. I time-travelled back to late 1999 and knocked on the front door of Lovington Rectory.

Julius Milner answered my knock. "Kit. This is an unexpected surprise."

This was no time for small talk. "Something needs sorting, and quickly."

"You'd better come in."

We walked through the hall and into the room I'd seen in my dream. Everything was in its rightful place, including the davenport. I stared at it.

Julius gave me a knowing smile. "I'll make sure the envelope is in the hidey-hole when the time is right. What are you doing here?"

I had to smile. If someone had bothered to tell me that I was capable of time travel I could have collected the envelope today. But that wouldn't have followed the blueprint of what was expected of me.

"The good news is I've met your daughter. There's some bad news as well. She threw me out of her flat a few minutes ago. It's all your bloody fault. She found those notes you wrote about Grodam killing her, and how you brought her back to life. Did you need to write it all down? You're an idiot. Destroy those notes so Carin doesn't see them. If you don't, you can tell whoever's behind this mission to forget it."

His face dropped. "I'm sorry about that. I had no idea Carin knew what happened to her."

"Didn't you realise that you hadn't got those papers when you contacted your solicitor? Didn't you ever wonder why she left home and virtually cut her ties with you?"

His attempt to disarm me with a smile failed. "There was a lot going on at the time. At least I can put things right. As soon as you've gone, I'll destroy those papers."

Of course he'd known the papers had gone missing. He was beginning to annoy me.

"I want to make sure those papers are destroyed. Go and get them. I'll take them with me."

He hurried out of the room and returned clutching a brown envelope. "Here they are, my boy."

I snatched it from him. "I expect to see a different Carin

when I get back to my own time. Goodbye."

"Before you go, have you discussed the mission with my daughter."

"No, I haven't. Your oversight ruined that train of thought. I have to get back."

He began to sweat. His whole body shook and his face turned a deep red as he tried to speak to me. It took an effort for him to force a few words out: "Before . . . you . . . go . . . something . . . for . . . you."

He staggered across to the davenport, fumbled a drawer open and took out two small brown bottles and a crucifix. He clutched at his chest and got his breathing under control before thrusting the bottles and crucifix into my hands.

"Take . . . with you."

I put an arm around him. "You'd better sit down."

He pulled himself away. His shaking hand pointed at the bottles: "Holy . . . water . . . will . . . help . . . you. . . . Now . . . get . . . back . . . to . . . Carin."

I wasn't happy leaving him like this, but did as he asked. I willed myself back to my flat, ripped the brown envelope open and read his account of how he'd killed young Grodam. He'd spelt out in great detail what that lowlife had done to Carin. I put them in the fireplace and fired them with my finger ray, until they were charred embers.

I returned to Carin's flat, hoping she still lived there. I sighed with relief. She was asleep on the sofa. I looked around the room, admiring the new furnishings, including the whatnot and canterbury, as well as four splendid watercolours hanging on the walls. I'd last seen them at our fine-art auction when we'd sold her father's possessions.

I snapped my fingers in front of her face. She came to life. I was rewarded with a full-blooded kiss, and no smell of gin on her breath.

She spoke as if nothing had happened. "I'm glad we've got our non-existent love lives out into the open, Kit." Her face broke into a saucy grin. "So, we're both virgins."

I played along with her, in this new life of hers, and used her real name for the first time. "We're probably the only two virgins of our age in these parts, Carin. I meant to ask you, how long have you lived here?"

"After Daddy died I had to move out of the rectory, so I bought this place. It wasn't big enough to take all of Daddy's furniture. I put most of it into auction."

The pouch hanging around my neck proved she'd chosen Martin to sell her stuff.

"I was telling you about Daddy's papers. A few days later I owned up to him that I'd read them. He wasn't angry. That's when he told me about the Merlin stones. He mentioned a mission and said the stones would play a big part in my future life, whatever that means. He gave me this bracelet when I was fourteen. I didn't realise at the time, but it has a piece of a Merlin stone set in it. Daddy said I was to wear it day and night as a good-luck charm."

"So, why didn't the stone save you from those thugs the other night? And there's something else. You've got this fantastic job at the British Library, so what are you doing serving drinks in that pub?"

"I wasn't wearing my bracelet that evening. I took it off and couldn't remember where I'd put it. I found it in my dressing-table drawer when you brought me back home. The pub job has nothing to do with money. I thought it might be a way of finding a boyfriend." Her face lit up. "I wasn't wrong, was I? I found you. My car broke down that day, so I walked to the pub. The boss asked me if I wanted a lift home. I turned him down. I'll never know why I did that." Her green eyes bored into mine. "Do you have an answer, Mister?"

"Merlin arranged it, that's why. His stones are influencing our lives."

"How do you make that out?"

"The way we met was too contrived to be a case of bumping into each other by accident. Merlin arranged for our paths to cross. He made you mislay your bracelet. What really annoys me is you suffered in the process." I snorted. "Then the negative side of me kicks in. Why wait 1,400 years to get us together?"

She made no comment, so I changed the subject. "Does the name Billy Grodam mean anything to you?"

She nodded. "I remember him as a boy. He wasn't a charmer. His twin brother, Joseph, used to shout crude things at me. He disappeared one day and was never seen again."

"I'm pretty sure it was Grodam's yobs who attacked you the other evening. I've got a feeling he was responsible for your father's death as well."

"You can't be sure of that. Anyhow, Daddy didn't have the stones to protect him once he passed them to you, but that was his decision."

"No, it wasn't. Merlin made the decision for him."

"Whatever you say. Daddy once said that when he died it wouldn't be forever. I thought he meant meeting up in the afterlife. After he died I had my one and only shot at time travel, by using my stone. I had this quaint notion that I could save his life by travelling back to the day he died." She shrugged her shoulders. "Nothing happened. I obviously don't have the knack."

"You're not the only one who tried to go back in time to save him. I did the same, but nothing happened because Merlin stopped us. He didn't want us upsetting his plans for us. Do you really believe he could be alive after 1,400 years?"

"I don't know. Perhaps he's time-travelling from his time to ours."

"He can't be. He's imprisoned inside that rock I told you about."

In a split second her mood changed. She looked a trifle pissed off. "Does it matter?"

I changed tack. "Do you fancy going out for a meal?"

Her face lit up. "Why not? It'll get us away from your endless chit-chat about Merlin and this bloody mission."

We didn't paint the town red. To our fellow diners we would have seemed like two young people enjoying each other's company. Carin's earlier moodiness had gone by the time we returned to her pad.

She looked at her watch. "It's pretty late, Kit. There's no point in you driving back to Grinton. Why not stay the night?"

I didn't need convincing. "Great. It'll give us more time to talk about Merlin."

She let out a loud yawn. "Let's save him till tomorrow, shall we? I'm whacked. We'll have a nightcap, then I'll sort out your sleeping arrangements." She disappeared into the kitchen and returned with two glasses and a bottle of red wine. She poured two generous measures. "Here's to us and our future, whatever it holds."

I raised my glass. "I'll drink to that."

"It's time for shut-eye. You'll have to make yourself comfortable on the sofa. Sorry I can't offer you any pyjamas."

She found me a blanket, kissed me goodnight and slipped into her bedroom.

Merlin and Emeralda were watching the living images of Kit and Carin on a mirror in his castle. "They are close to returning to our time, even though my son is proving a stumbling block. For someone who has my blood flowing in his veins, he disappoints me. No matter. I will make sure he carries out my mission."

"I feel sorry for him, Merlin. He loves her and should have taken her body by now."

"Be patient, my dear. When our daughter's asleep we will pay her a visit. This is what I want you to do when we get there."

She shivered with excitement at the words he whispered in her ear.

A white light shimmered in Carin's bedroom as Merlin and Emeralda appeared.

He put a finger to his lips and whispered, "We must not waken my son. I want you to live in her body until they join us in our own time. You know what you have to do." He smirked. "Use your skills well."

She grinned and blew him a kiss before her body broke down into a white vapour, which slid up Carin's nose.

I stripped down to my underpants, turned the light out and made myself comfortable. I'd no sooner closed my eyes than the light was switched on. Carin stood in her bedroom doorway dressed in a flimsy nightdress.

She held her arms out to me. "I feel lost without you. Will you keep me company?" She waggled a finger at me. "Let's get one thing straight, Mister. I want no funny business."

She had laid the ground rules, and I didn't intend to break them. Anyhow, where would a novice male virgin have started?

"Whatever you say."

We settled down in bed. She let me kiss her, but there was no passion in the way she returned my kiss. I'd no sooner drifted off to sleep than I was woken by Carin stroking the hairs on my chest. My manhood stiffened. She ran her fingers through my beard.

"I couldn't sleep." She giggled and rolled her tongue across my lips. "I was thinking about Merlin and that woman you told me about." She giggled again. "I read about what went on between them, in a manuscript I found in the British Library. It was written by Merlin himself." She let out a throaty chuckle. "He bedded plenty of women in his time."

I couldn't believe my ears. "What! Why didn't you mention this manuscript when we were talking about Merlin?"

She pulled me down into the bed and shut me up with a lingering kiss. Her hands wandered down to my lower regions.

"I wanted to tell you when the time was right, like now. The woman's name was Emeralda. When she first walked into that clearing, she pretended to faint. Merlin had no idea who she was, and rushed to help her. He loosened her clothing at the neck to help with her breathing. The young woman's breasts flopped out. He couldn't stop himself from making love to her in her half-conscious state."

Carin's hand slipped into my underpants and gently stroked my manhood. I was jolted into disbelief. Why this sudden change of mind about sex? A deep lust, welling up inside of me, drove those thoughts away.

She whispered in my ear, "Who's a big boy, then? It's time

to lose our virginity, Kit. Get your pants off."

"Why the change of mind? I thought you wanted to wait."

"Do you want my body, or don't you?"

The uncertainty faded away as I savoured the pleasurable feelings coursing through my body. I yanked my underpants off. She guided my manhood in between her legs. I spoiled the moment as a sticky mess burst from my manhood.

I yelled out in anger, "Damn it!"

She laughed. "Don't worry about that. You can pleasure me as many times as you like by touching your stones."

I grasped the bag in my hand. Her fingers caressed my limp manhood. It bulged under her touch.

She whispered in my ear, "Make love to me, and this time do it for real."

I did as she asked. We managed to climax at the same time, and kissed a long, tender kiss.

She sighed with satisfaction. "That was wonderful, Mister."

"For someone who's a virgin, where did you learn to make love like that? And how did you know the stones would revive me?"

She hit me around the head with a pillow. "You've got to thank what I read in Merlin's manuscript for that. Come on, Romeo. Let's clean ourselves up in the bathroom."

We nestled down in bed again, where we lay side by side in our nakedness. She asked me to cuddle her. I shouldn't have. My manhood swelled, and we indulged ourselves in each other's bodies. We both fell into an exhausted sleep in the early hours of the morning.

She was asleep when I woke. I couldn't resist kissing her. She opened her eyes. There was no repetition of last night's behaviour. She slapped my behind and got out of bed.

"I'm going to the bathroom."

As she left the room, the wall started to flicker in shades of grey and white as it tried to form a picture. It didn't panic me. I'd been there before.

I yelled out to Carin, "Come in here, quick. There's

something you ought to see."

She ran into the room with a towel draped around her body. "What is it?"

"Look at what's happening on the wall."

Her face lit up. "It must be Merlin. He's trying to contact us."

"How do you know it's him?"

I got a glare from her. "Who else could it be?"

That was the very first time I got a gut feeling that there was more to Carin than she was letting on. The picture glimmered unsteadily on the wall. It kept fading away, leaving fuzzy images.

I made light of it. "Reception isn't very good tonight. I'd better go up on the roof and give the aerial a shake."

She wasn't amused, and thumped me in the ribs. "Stop arsing around, Mister. This is serious."

CHAPTER TEN

The images finally sorted themselves out. Merlin's face shimmered on the wall.

He smiled at us. "Welcome, my children. It pleases me that you have sealed your bodies in a token of love."

I took a fleeting glance at Carin. She showed no surprise. Merlin was a symbol of the sixth century, yet he'd been updated about our lovemaking. That knotted feeling of doubt niggled at me, that things weren't as they should be.

He droned on. "I have led your footsteps throughout your lives, and you are now ready to carry out my mission. You must travel to my time, and free me from my rock prison using the Merlin stones. I will tell you how to use them to rescue me, when you get here."

The picture broke up and slowly faded away.

A totally unfazed Carin looked at me. "We're going to help him, aren't we? Merlin's stones will protect us from harm, so why not?"

"Hold on. Can't you see there's something phoney going on? How did he know we'd made love? Is he really a prisoner in that rock? I'm not happy."

She threw a wobbly. "You bloody well annoy me with your endless doubts and questions! Pull yourself together, man! I know him better than you. He wouldn't mislead us. Try taking one step at a time, instead of jumping ahead of yourself and making bloody stupid comments."

"You're not thinking straight, woman! Can't you see he's feeding us a load of crap?"

"You're wrong, Mister. He has to be freed from his prison, and we're going to help him."

The wall lit up again. Merlin's face stared at us.

"You are right in what you say, my dear. As for you, Milner, your doubts about my mission anger me. Never speak that way again or you will be punished." His voice softened. "Time does not allow any further delay. Tell me that you will accept my mission."

Carin shouted at the wall, "We will help you, won't we, Kit?"

She looked at me with pleading eyes. This was the spider-and-fly syndrome, with me as the fly. I was in a no-win situation. This wasn't the same girl I'd met a few days ago, but I wasn't prepared to lose her. That had nearly happened yesterday. I was a prisoner of a situation that had been hand-moulded for me.

I nodded. "I'll go with her."

Merlin grinned. "Good. Now, listen to me. Two days from now you will travel to my castle in Llalogan. It lies in the country that you call Wales. On the third day, the two of you must stand within my castle walls just before the sun sets. From there you will be transported to my time. The clothes you need in my century will be provided for you. Do not bring any weapons with you, and wear my stones at all times." He pointed a finger at me. "Do not fail me, boy. I am watching you."

His face vanished from the bedroom wall.

Carin was so laid-back she was horizontal. "Well. That's that. I'll get back to the bathroom."

I had a sneaking admiration for the way she'd taken Merlin on board, even though she seemed to know more than she was letting on. She's not all beauty. There's a tough side to her.

Twenty minutes later she burst into the room looking radiantly beautiful, with that wonderful thatch of auburn hair bouncing around her shoulders.

She grabbed my face and planted a huge kiss on my lips.

"That's for last night." She sat down beside me. "I know you're not happy about rescuing Merlin. When this is over, you and I are going to start living. What do you say?"

"I have my doubts about this mission, but that's my problem. I'm going, but I'll keep my eyes peeled every step of the way. I want to get this nonsense over with and lead a normal life, where people don't get killed and our footsteps aren't manipulated."

She smiled meekly. "Whatever you say, darling."

Carin said she'd arrange some holiday while she was at work. She also promised to tell me more about Merlin's manuscript when she came home.

I spent the morning relaxing in her flat. It gave me time to think about this mission. I was getting more sceptical by the second. Something needed checking out. I willed myself back to Merlin's time, to the day he'd been banished to that rock. Nothing happened, so I tried again. It was a wasted effort. My powers of time travel had seemingly deserted me. What, or who, had stopped me? It only added fuel to my doubts about this whole saga.

I drove back to my place in the afternoon and put some clothes into a suitcase together with my toiletries, before travelling back to Lovington. I also took the holy water and crucifix that Julius had given me.

When Carin arrived home, she laid down the law. "Now that we're an item, you're moving in with me." She ruffled my hair. "Come on, lover-boy. Everything's going to be fine. I've arranged holiday for the next two weeks."

After dinner, we pored over a map of Wales to find where Llalogan was. There was no sign of it. Carin suggested checking the Internet. She led me into a small room at the back of the flat, which doubled as her study. She typed 'Llalogan' into the computer. We were quickly rewarded. Someone had researched what we wanted to know, by transposing Merlin's kingdom on to a modern-day map of Wales. His castle nestled off the old B5381 Roman road, south of Abergele.

Carin was full of herself. "We'll drive up tomorrow. We can book into a hotel when we get there."

"I think we ought to book before we go. I don't fancy sleeping in the car if all the hotels are full."

"There'll be plenty of room at this time of the year."

I didn't bother to argue. There were more important things to discuss. "Tell me about this manuscript you found."

"Why not? Have you ever felt you're not in control of your life?"

I laughed out loud. "Most of my life has been like that, especially these last few days."

"Take my job at the British Library. God only knows why I applied for the position. I'd always wanted to be a doctor. One lunchtime, on an impulse, I wandered down to the basement, where our rarer books are kept. I wouldn't have minded if I'd known why I was there. I felt this urge to clamber up the library steps to a particular shelf of books. One book grabbed my attention. On a whim I pulled it out. The damn thing was so heavy it slipped out of my hands. I climbed back down and opened it up to make sure it hadn't suffered any damage. Nestling inside were some delicate-looking sheets of parchment covered in animal skin. It came as a shock to discover that I was holding an account of Merlin's life, written by the man himself."

"That manuscript's worth a small fortune. Can I see it?"

"Sorry. It's locked away in my desk at work. Don't worry. I can recall every word."

I wasn't daft. She'd fobbed me off.

"His writings cover the last twelve months of his life before he was imprisoned in that rock. It's the last few weeks that make the most interesting reading." She squirmed with pleasure. "I told you about this Emeralda creature, and how Merlin fell in love with her. He's very explicit about their lovemaking. Giving him her body addled his brain." She laughed. "Just like you last night."

I grunted. "He gets himself trapped in a bloody great rock,

his magical powers can't release him, but he's able to lead our footsteps on this mission. Come on. It takes some swallowing. Let's forget this mission. We'll keep the stones and buy our happiness with them. We could even get married."

She looked down her nose at me. "There you go again with your endless uncertainties. You're forgetting one crucial thing. You and I are destined to live out the role that was chosen for us." She frowned. "You're shit-scared, aren't you?"

"I should be, but I'm not. Merlin doesn't frighten me one bit. Can't you get it into your head that I love you and I want to make you happy. Is that a sin? Sod Merlin! Can't we forget him?"

The face she pulled wasn't pretty. "Lovely sentiments, darling, but running away isn't an option. Your eagerness to make me happy has muddled your brain."

I kidded myself that her brainpower complemented my inner strength of character. She tended to accept things at face value, whereas I double-checked every facet. Without her doggedness I doubt if I would have gone on this mission.

She poked me in the chest. "I want no ifs or buts. We're going to help him, full stop." Her words were a threat.

I gave in, for the moment. "OK. Cut out the battle-cry speech. I'll go, but I'm doing it for our future life, not Merlin."

She sneered at me. "You've got an attitude problem, Mister. You're not thinking straight. Merlin's going to be disappointed with you."

"As if I care. I own up to being doubtful, but why have we been chosen? Didn't he have kids of his own?"

"No, he didn't, at least not with his wife." She chuckled. "In his manuscript he says he fathered a son with some maiden. He also prophesies that one of his descendants will give birth to a child who will rule the world." She banged the arm of the sofa. "Stop wittering, and accept that he needs our help."

This bickering had to stop. "OK. OK. I give in. Your father once told me that Merlin was guiding my footsteps, so he must still have some powers. That's where the negative side of me kicks in. How can he mastermind things from a prison in the sixth century?"

She rolled her eyes at me. "There you go again. We'll find out when we get there."

My questions were getting too near the mark, that was her problem. I gave up on my negative approach, and we spent the rest of the evening talking about the manuscript and speculating on what might happen when we met up with him.

I couldn't resist having a last dig. "If Merlin comes out on top, how will he reward us? Can you really see him letting us return to our own time, knowing what we know?"

Carin snapped, "Questions, questions and more bloody questions! Stop going on." She glanced at her watch. "I'm off to bed. Don't wake me when you come in."

The days were running out before we meet up with Merlin. We're journeying to Wales tomorrow, but Carin wants to see her father before we go – that's if the Merlin stones will allow it. If we do manage to drop in on Julius Milner, I have the feeling he won't be surprised to see us. A sixth sense was warning me that the only reason for visiting her father was so that he could convince me that everything about this mission was above board. We will see.

When I finally got to bed, I enjoyed unbroken sleep. My dreams seem to have dried up, thank God. That was just as well, because I was going to need all the sleep I could get.

CHAPTER ELEVEN

I couldn't contain Carin when we woke up. She was over the moon at the prospect of seeing her father. We'd both become blasé about time travel. To us, it was the norm, in the same way that people jump into a car to visit their relatives. It's also a damn sight cheaper and quicker.

I'd no sooner finished breakfast than she was at me. "I can't wait to see him, Kit. Let's be on our way."

I calmed her down. "How far back are you planning to go? I don't want a younger Carin opening the front door when we knock."

"That's no problem." She rummaged around in a drawer and found a small book. She shuffled through its pages. "This is my diary for 2004. We'll go back to the 19th of September."

"OK. Ready when you are. I'll concentrate on that date. What about eleven in the morning?"

She nodded and put her hand in mine. I thought the instructions, and seconds later we were standing in front of Lovington Rectory. I smiled to myself. How strange that time travel had kicked in today, yet it hadn't done so when I'd tried to travel to the day when Julius Milner had died, or when I'd wanted to visit Merlin. Carin rang the bell. Julius opened the door.

"Carin, my dear. It's so lovely to see you." There was no genuine trace of surprise in his voice. He embraced her and planted a kiss on her lips. He turned to me.

"Good to see you too, my boy." He shook my hand. "Come in, the pair of you." We were shepherded into the lounge. He grasped Carin's hand and grinned at her. "You're at work today."

Carin put her arms around him. "I've missed you so much. I do love you."

He planted a kiss on her head and stroked her hair, then whispered in her ear, "Don't forget your younger self shares my life. Come and sit on the sofa with me. Make yourself comfy in that armchair, Kit. Now, tell me about yourselves."

She told him how we had met, how Merlin had contacted us, and that we were setting off for Wales as soon as we got back to our own time. She made no mention that we were an item and had slept together.

Julius beamed at me. "I'm so happy that you've accepted the mission, my boy. There were times I thought you weren't up to it."

"I've accepted, but I'm not happy. I'm only going because your daughter is hell-bent on meeting up with Merlin. Someone has to look after her."

A look of displeasure crossed his face. He raised his voice. "You are an annoying person! Start believing in this mission! That's what you were put on this earth for! Get a grip of yourself!" He calmed down. "I'm sorry, but I meant what I said."

His whole attitude had changed since I'd last seen him. That's when he'd given me the crucifix and holy water. Carin stroked his face and planted a kiss on his lips. I cringed. Her affection for him was too intimate for my liking. She gazed into his eyes. "Ignore him, Daddy. I'm going because I trust Merlin. He can't escape from that rock unless we help him."

He looked at her lovingly before throwing me a dirty look. "Thank goodness someone trusts him!" He kissed the palm of her hand. "How can we knock some sense into his head?"

I put my oar in. "You can't blame me for the way I feel. Why have we been chosen for this so-called mission? I've been knocked from pillar to post, and pushed around the houses, not knowing what the hell was going on until I was told that all the fuss is about a trip into the past to supposedly save a sorcerer. I've suffered pain and mental agony as well as an attempt on my life. For Christ's sake! Your own daughter was nearly raped. There has to be a simpler way of finding out what this game is all about."

They both stared at me with the same condescending look on their faces, as if I was some kind of cretin.

It was Julius who spoke. "This isn't a game, young man. Why have you been chosen, you ask? You'll find out when the time is right. Merlin's peril is real. He's been tricked into imprisonment, and is waiting for his chosen people to help him. That's you two." He let out a sigh of exasperation. "You've got the wrong end of the stick, and not for the first time. Why you? you ask. You're the only person who's been gifted with the knowledge of how to use the magic of the stones, thanks to Merlin handing those stones to that young feller who was one of your forebears. You will have to use some of their powers when you go back in time; otherwise what's the point of having them?"

Carin nodded her head. "Daddy's right. Get real, and go along with the flow."

They smiled at me like a pair of Cheshire cats. I wasn't convinced, and I was getting confused by this over-cosy relationship that father and daughter were displaying.

"I hear what you say, but nothing gels with me. I'm trying to make sense of something that's beyond me, but all I've done is stumble from one problem to another. Why?"

Julius clicked his tongue. "You've been subjected to a period of training and adjustment, to make you use your brain and to encourage you to make decisions in preparation for accepting the powers of the Merlin stones. How would you have reacted if all your powers had been revealed to you in one fell swoop? What if I'd told you that you had killing powers at your fingertips and you could fly through the pages of time? Or that you had the knack of taking over people's bodies and slowing down time? Your mind wouldn't have coped with it. You'd have been shut away in a mental institution. The visions you saw are a backdrop of what you can expect when you travel to Merlin's time. His period was a time of man's inhumanity. He had to be satisfied that you were the right person for this life-changing mission. That's why obstacles were put in your way." He kissed his daughter. "Thank God Carin is around to hold you in check. Merlin must be wondering if he's chosen the right man."

I gritted my teeth and didn't pursue the argument any further. What was the point, with the judge and jury sitting opposite me? Julius Milner had changed, and Carin's behaviour was becoming weirder by the day.

I put on a placating show. "Don't worry. I'll see this thing through."

They both looked relieved. Julius nodded to his daughter, and the subject was dropped. After another ten minutes of chit-chat, Carin and I returned to our own time.

As soon as we appeared in her flat, Carin was snapping at my ankles like a Jack Russell terrier. Her enthusiasm knew no bounds. We were about to stray into uncharted territory, using the medium of time travel to consort with a magician and assorted bad guys, yet she was treating it as if we were planning a trip to the cinema. And how did I feel? I was not worried or scared. I was just bugged that everything was too timely, too opportune and working to a prearranged timetable.

Our journey to Wales was uneventful, and we reached the outskirts of Abergele at about half past five.

Carin pointed out a sign advertising the comforts of The Ffarm Country House. "That sounds nice, Kit. Let's see if they've got a room. It'll save us searching around."

I popped into the hotel while Carin sat in the car. The young female receptionist confirmed they had a room, and asked my name. She gave me a funny look when I told her.

"You're already booked in for the night." She checked her computer. "For two people. The booking was made weeks ago."

Someone was a step ahead of me. I blustered my way through, trying not to look like a complete idiot. Within minutes we were signing in. We were told dinner could be taken from six o'clock.

I unlocked the door to our room and, once inside, I let rip at her. "What's going on! I looked a right prick when I asked for a room. It's been booked for weeks. You know something about this – otherwise why did you choose this hotel? How about being upfront with me for once?"

She stood with her hands on her hips. "Don't you shout at me! I had a gut feeling we should use this hotel. For heaven's sake! You keep rattling on about us being guided, and that's what happened. Perhaps you'll believe me now. Let's unpack and get ready for dinner. I'm starving." She walked across to the wardrobe, flung the doors open and let out a surprised cry. "There's a parcel in here." She lifted out a bulky package. "Perhaps it's for us. Merlin said he'd provide some suitable clothing for our trip."

"For crying out loud! I suppose he got Eddie Stobart to deliver it."

She let out a sigh of frustration. "There you go again. For the great white chief, you're displaying all the naivety of a five-year-old. Even in his prison he's retained some influence. Our stones are probably acting as a catalyst, increasing what few powers he has left."

She was probably right. If he could communicate with us, then why shouldn't he control other things in our time? She threw the parcel on to the bed. I pored over the label. It was addressed to 'Kit and Carin Milner, c/o The Ffarm Country House, Abergele'.

Carin looked smug. "I told you so. You've got to start taking Merlin seriously."

"OK. OK. I give in. You'd better open it."

The duvet was quickly covered with shredded brown paper. Two sets of clothing were revealed. One long garment was designed, in the widest sense of the word, to be worn next to the skin. Made of a coarse woven material, it had three holes in it – one for the head, the other two for the arms. An animal-skin cloak was intended to be worn over this garment, with a rope belt to draw it together. A pair of makeshift leather-crafted footwear and a crude attempt at some form of headgear, fashioned from what looked like rabbit pelts, completed the outfit.

We packed the clothes away and wandered down for dinner. I asked the receptionist if she knew anything about a parcel being left in our room. She couldn't help. A young waitress showed us to our table. Three other couples were dining at candlelit tables. The food didn't disappoint us, and we managed to consume a bottle of wine between us. We finished our cheese and biscuits and decided to have coffee.

As I turned around to summon the waitress, my eyes settled on a table in the far corner of the room. A good-looking man, with a wickedly hooked nose, long hair and a beard, was sat there. I could have sworn it was Merlin. I closed my eyes to clear them. When I opened them the man had gone.

My fixation was broken by Carin. "What's wrong?"

I told her what I'd seen.

"That's impossible, and you know it." She got hoity-toity with me. "You've had too much to drink. Order yourself a coffee. I'm going up to our room."

I spoke to the waitress about the man who'd been sitting at the corner table. From the disdainful look on her face, she obviously thought I was drunk.

"I'm sorry, sir. Nobody has sat at that table all evening."

I pressed her further.

She stopped me in full flow. "I can't help you. Would you like to speak with the manager?"

I declined her offer. I'd made a complete fool of myself. I finished my coffee and returned to our room. Carin was asleep. I slipped into bed and fell asleep, hoping I wouldn't dream, but I did. It was a short dream about Julius Milner.

He put his hands together in a sign of prayer and spoke to me: "Use the holy water and crucifix."

I forced myself to wake up. A surge of doubt resurfaced in me about this mission. It didn't last for long. Julius Milner had given me the tools to help me if I found myself facing the occult.

Feeling happier in my mind, I nodded off into dreamless sleep.

CHAPTER TWELVE

The next morning, the receptionist gave us directions to Merlin's Castle. She said it was a popular tourist attraction, but was closed until next spring. That suited us fine. Carin showed no signs of concern.

She looked at me with those green eyes. "Are you still willing to go ahead with this, Kit?"

I parried the question. "What about you? Are you as committed as you make out?"

"I've never felt so sure about anything in my life."

I wasn't going to let my doubts come between us. She was hooked on the whole idea, no matter how I felt.

"If you're in, so am I."

She thumped me on the arm. "Let's be on our way, then."

We headed out of Abergele, until we reached the B5381. I turned left, and after five miles we came across a sign pointing out Merlin's Castle. I headed down a narrow track, which petered out into a car park. The castle ruins stood about 100 yards away, perched on a high mound of rock. A chain-link fence, with a tall hedge growing inside it, encircled the site. I told her that we could hide the car inside the fence, behind the hedge.

"Oh, yeah. And how do you propose to get through those locked gates?"

I laughed. "I came prepared."

It didn't take me long to cut through the padlock with the

bolt cutter that I'd brought along. I pushed the gates open.

Her voice was laced with suspicion. "What else have you got in that boot?"

"Don't worry. Just our sixth-century clothing, a spare wheel and my toolbox."

"What about the broken lock? It'll just be our luck for someone to spot it and call the police."

I laughed out loud. "You're asking all the right questions." I delved in the boot. "I have another padlock with me. Don't ask me why I brought the bolt cutter and padlock along. I had this feeling that we would need them."

I hid the car out of sight, shut the gates and replaced the broken lock. We made our way up a rock path towards the castle ruins. The roof and walls were virtually intact. We walked inside. Stones littered the floor and a chill wind blew through the openings that had once served as windows.

Carin's eyes glazed over. "This place reeks of history. Can you feel it?"

I closed my eyes. Centuries of history were being played out inside the walls. The smell of smoke and cooking, mingling with the voices of men and women, set about my senses. I opened my eyes. The sensations shrank away.

She held my hand. "I felt the happiness in this place, Kit, but look at it now."

"We've seen enough. Let's find somewhere to pass the time until sunset."

We retraced our steps along the B5381 and stopped at a roadside restaurant. We lunched and whiled the afternoon away, chatting about our mission, over numerous cups of coffee. Before we knew it, it was time to drive back to Merlin's Castle. I parked behind the hedge and locked the gates. Carin changed into her sixth-century gear, in the car. I dressed in the open air. I delved in the boot for the phials of holy water and the crucifix, and hid them in my pouch with the stones. I put the canisters of CS gas, which I'd taken from Grodam's hoodlums, underneath the car.

I didn't recognise Carin when she stepped out of the car.

All traces of femininity had gone. She'd removed her make-up, and her hair was tucked under the rabbit-skin hat, her body hidden beneath the animal skins. I glanced at my watch. Sunset was less than ten minutes away. I locked the car and hid the keys under a stone in the hedge. Minutes later we were inside the castle. The wind moaned as it tumbled through the window openings. It was talking to us. I held her hand.

"Can you hear what the wind is saying, Carin?"

She nodded her head.

"Do what it tells you."

The wind's whispered words were soothing: "Prepare to undertake your journey. I will guide you through the ether of time."

I felt my body break down into particles as we were swept through the centuries, down that familiar tunnel of bright light. Then the wind was gone. I opened my eyes. We were standing in the forest clearing that I'd seen in my dream.

I turned to Carin. "We've arrived. Merlin's shut away in that rock over there."

We walked across to it and I picked up a piece of wood. I threw it against the rock face.

"Let's see if there is a force field."

An intense surge of energy broke the wood into small pieces and hurled them through the air. A crackling white light played around the rock's surface.

Merlin spoke to us from inside the rock. "Welcome to my time. The force field you saw has caged me in this rock. My magic cannot undo it. Madrog is camped on the other side of the forest, waiting to snatch me from my prison and steal my magical powers. I have no idea how he plans to free me. That is the reason the two of you are here. You have to find out what he is planning for me, by journeying to his camp tomorrow. Use the power of your stones to capture the minds and bodies of two of his warriors. They visit the clearing every morning. Think the command and the stones will place you inside of them. Use their minds to discover what Madrog has planned for me. Sleep in the hut tonight. Is there anything you wish to ask me?"

I had something to ask. "There's a much simpler way of freeing you. Why don't I travel back in time, and stop that woman from casting you into the rock? That would save us a lot of trouble."

His voice purred at me. "Your idea is well thought out, but Madrog is a dangerous adversary and I want him out of my way forever. That is why my plan is best. Let him remove the force field, and once he releases me I will use my sorcery to kill him. It is vital that you learn of his plans. Do you understand?"

I'd never heard so much codswallop in all of my life.

"No, I don't. My way is the best way of solving your problem. Once I free you, you can do what you like with Madrog." I shrugged my shoulders. "Problem solved."

A bolt of lightning flew from the rock and hit the ground at my feet.

He screamed at me, "You will do things my way! Do you understand?"

It was the answer I'd expected.

I appeased him. "Whatever you say."

"Make sure you do."

The rock stood silent.

Carin flew at me. "What are you playing at with your stupid ideas? Get your act together." Her anger quickly vanished. "I'm sorry, darling, but we must do what he asks." She shivered. "Let's see what our sleeping quarters are like."

The inside of the hut was a fair size, but offered nothing in terms of luxury, only a makeshift bed, a sink, knives, various pots and pans, drinking containers, plates, two large stone pots, and a table and chairs. Animal skins were strewn over the floor.

Carin put her twopenny-worth in. "It's getting cold. What about making a fire?"

Five minutes later I'd gathered a pile of wood in front of the hut.

She stared at it. "Are you going to light it, then?"

I wasn't in the best of moods. I snapped at her, "I seem to be doing everything. You've got a Merlin stone. Use its powers and light it yourself."

She pointed a finger at the pile of wood. Nothing happened.

She shrugged her shoulders. "I don't seem to have your knack."

I hadn't time to argue. A searing flame leapt from my fingers and ignited the wood.

She wasn't impressed. "I'm feeling hungry, Kit." Her sarcasm showed itself. "If you can light a fire without matches, I'm sure you can rustle up some grub."

"I'll check the forest out for food."

I scouted around and killed two game birds with one of my killing rays. She was sat warming herself when I got back. I plucked and gutted the birds, stuck them on a branch and roasted them over the fire.

She scratched at her body after she'd finished her food. "I need a wash."

I checked out the pool. It wasn't exactly swimming-pool size, just an oval shaped fifteen feet by ten feet. I dipped a stick in the water to check its depth. It was about four feet deep. "If I heat the water, we can have a soak. Are you happy with that?"

She nodded eagerly. "Before we do, I'll put some of the water in those pots for drinking."

I floated the pots through the air and immersed them in the water before floating them back into the hut. My finger-induced flames licked the water's surface. It wasn't long before steam started to rise.

I put my hand in the water. "That's about right. Let's strip off."

I couldn't take my eyes off her body as her animal skins fell to the ground. She waggled her bottom at me before jumping into the water, closely followed by me.

She nestled against me. My manhood stiffened as she fondled it. This was the first time she'd shown any interest in my body since that first night when we'd made love.

She whispered in my ear, "I had a dream about Merlin last night. He said we have to bond our bodies in a sixth-century ritual as a sign of our love for each other. We must cut our thumbs and mingle our blood together." She looked me in the eye. "If you really love me, say you'll agree to the ritual."

She saw my uncertainty, and gently rubbed my manhood.

Blackmail came to mind. She guided my manhood in between her legs, then pulled it out.

"The ritual will strengthen our love for each other. Do it for me."

The feelings in my groin made my mind up. "Sod it. Let's do it. I'll get something to cut our thumbs with."

I scrambled out of the water and brought a knife back from the hut. We stood together in the pool in each other's arms.

"You know I love you. I don't need this nonsense to prove it." Her eyes pleaded with me.

"All right. Let's get it over with. You won't feel any pain."

I scraped the blade across our thumbs. As we squeezed our bloodied thumbs together, our blood dripped into the water.

She thrust my manhood into her body and whispered in my ear, "Do something else for me. Dip your stones in the water to mark our love ritual."

With my manhood caressing the inside of her body, who was I to argue? I did as she asked. After our lovemaking finished, I grabbed her thumb. Like mine, the wound had healed itself.

She kissed me passionately. "That was wonderful, darling."

Her enthusiasm quickly subsided as her feelings switched off. She yawned, got out of the water and picked up her clothes.

"I'm stuffed. Don't wake me when you come in."

Carin had changed. Her thoughts didn't gel with mine any more. Several things were beating me up. Why hadn't she bothered to show me Merlin's manuscript? Why had Merlin spoken to her in a dream? And what was all that twaddle about in the pool?

She was gently snoring when I settled down beside her. An idea flashed into my mind. She'd read the manuscript, so the images of his writings would be trapped in her memory banks. I placed my hands gently on her head and tried to read her mind. Nothing happened. Unsurprisingly, my gift of mind reading had deserted me. I turned over and fell asleep.

Michael and Azurina were watching Kit's antics. She looked grim.

"This isn't fair. Surely we can do something to help our son?"

Michael grunted. "I made the same point at yesterday's meeting with Magnus. He says we can give a helping hand so long as it doesn't upset his plans. What can we tell our son that will ease his mind?"

"That's easy. It would help if he knew the real reason he wears Merlin's stones. And it's about time he learned about his own supernatural powers."

"You're right. Our son's asleep at the moment. Go down and tell him what he needs to know, in one of his dreams. Don't give anything away about his mission."

She grinned. "Thank you, darling."

"Before you go, let's get one thing straight. By all means tell him about his own powers of sorcery, but make it clear that I won't allow him to use them until Merlin finally reveals what his mission is all about. He'll need his powers then to fend off Merlin's sorcery. Off you go."

I fell into a totally unplanned dream.

A petite lady, wearing a veil across her face, appeared and spoke to me. "I'm here to help you in your mission. I know what I'm about to tell you won't faze you. You have the depth of mind to accept my words without feeling intimidated. Now listen carefully. The Merlin stones that you wear around your neck have magical powers, and they protect you from harm. But that's not the real reason you have to wear them. Merlin is using the stones to control you. You don't need his stones to create magic. You have your own powers of sorcery. By placing a single thought in your mind, you are capable of magical powers that no one else in this world possesses, and that includes Merlin. He doesn't know about your powers and mustn't find out, so carry on wearing his stones.

"You have doubts about this mission, but you must follow it through and do whatever is asked of you. But, get this into your head. You will not be allowed to use your own sorcery unless the situation demands it. I don't want you upsetting Merlin's plans. There's something else you have to know. When you finally meet up with Merlin, he won't get on with you. Your behaviour will upset him, and he'll be ordered to kill you." She laughed scornfully. "That's a waste of time because you're the only person on earth who has the gift of immortality, so no one can kill you. Do not tell your woman what I have told you. I must be off."

"Hold on a minute. How do you know so much about Merlin and what the future holds for me? Is this some kind of trick?"

Her tinkling laughter made the hairs on the back of my neck tingle. "You must trust me. All your questions will be answered one day. Now I must go."

"I'll do as you ask. Before you go, who are you?"

She blew me a kiss. "You'll find out in good time."

I woke with a start. I didn't feel overawed or intimidated by my dream. In fact, I believed everything the lady had told me. The experience certainly wasn't a dream. The knowledge that I possessed powers of my own, as well as being immortal, didn't intimidate me one bit. So many strange things had happened these past few weeks, so why should I be cowed with this new twist in my life? I decided to check out my dream-lady's words. I concentrated on the two canisters of gas lying under my car, back in the twenty-first century. I can't describe the elation I felt when they appeared on the ground in front of me. I hid them in a corner of the hut. Sleep came easily, knowing I held magical gifts to thwart Merlin when the time was right.

While the two of them slept, Emeralda materialised out of Carin's body. She walked to the edge of the pool and muttered a few words of magic. The effect was startling. The water in the pool was sucked up in a swirling column, which disappeared beyond the heavens, leaving the pool empty. She whispered a few more words. The pool slowly filled up with water. She re-entered Carin's body.

I was woken by Carin stirring.

She sat up and stared at me. "I hope you've got rid of your

hang-ups about Merlin. Are you happier about him and our mission?"

Lying was becoming an easy habit. "I'm not worried any more. I'll be doing all I can to help him."

She smiled. We washed ourselves, before eating the last of the meat, in complete silence. I didn't trust her any more, but I needed a working bond with her.

I broke the silence. "I'm sorry for going on about Merlin. Can we be friends?"

She hugged me. "We're more than friends, you idiot."

"That's good to hear. We'd best be off to find Madrog's two men that Merlin mentioned." I put a hand on her arm and pointed to the edge of the clearing. "That's handy. They've found us."

Two warriors stood staring at us. They were dressed in animal-skin jackets covered in light chain mail. Hide trouser leggings were tucked into knee-length boots, while cloaks of a blue woven material hung from their shoulders. Their heads were protected by metal helmets. They weren't blessed with good looks. Long greasy hair hung down on to their shoulders, and each sported an untidy beard, sitting below a mouthful of missing or blackened teeth. One of them let out a blood-curdling yell and rushed across to where we stood. He shrieked as he raised his sword, intent on burying the blade in my skull, his eyes betraying the pleasure he was feeling at the thought of slaughtering me. I sensed myself being guided into using the stones' powers. I fixed my eyes on the blade as it sliced through the air towards the top of my head.

The blade should have taken a split second to slice my skull open. That split second spanned an eternity, as I slowed time down. I eyeballed my aggressor and waggled my tongue at him. In his state of confusion he chickened out. His weapon floated through the air as he threw it away. Movement returned to its normal pace as the warriors threw themselves down on the ground in homage of me.

Carin purred. "That was wonderful. I knew the stones would protect you."

I pointed at the ugliest-looking one. "Get inside of him. It's easy. I've done it once before. Give the instruction to your mind. Once you're inside, think your orders to him and he'll do whatever you ask. You can read his memory banks and feed on his knowledge."

Seconds later they were on their feet with us at their controls.

I looked at the other warrior and laughed. "To think I used to fancy you."

Her reply was deep and manly. "You don't look much better yourself."

"My one's called Barum. You must have worked out that you're his brother, Dugwump."

"I'm picking up Dugwump's thoughts. Madrog sent us out to search for Merlin's manuscript. It's hidden somewhere on the edge of the clearing."

"What good will it be to him if we find it?"

She didn't get the chance to answer. Two other warriors burst out of the forest. One was clutching something in his hand.

He shouted at us, "We have found the manuscript. Head back to camp."

We jogged towards Madrog's camp, and twenty minutes later ran into a clearing. A huge fire burned in front of four crudely built huts. Madrog and his two sons were seated at a long wooden table. Another warrior stood by the fire while a handful of women skulked in the background.

Madrog was an intimidating sight, with his missing eye and scarred face. He was dressed in leather garments of the finest quality.

The warrior waved the manuscript in the air. "I have found Merlin's writings, My Lord."

"Bring them to me."

The warrior did as he was told. Madrog read through the pages, then threw the manuscript on to the table. A satisfied smile creased his face.

"I now know how to draw the wizard from his prison by using one of his own spells. Prepare yourselves to march on Merlin's rock."

I sidled up to Dugwump and whispered in his ear, "You didn't mention that Merlin's spells were in the manuscript."

Her reply was predictable. "I must have forgotten."

Within minutes we were assembled. Madrog and his sons sat astride their horses, dressed in chain mail and metal helmets, each with a sword at his side and a shield on his left arm. We warriors stood behind them, each armed with a shield, broadsword and spear.

As we set off I sensed a mood of expectancy oozing from men and beasts. The sound of horses' hooves and men's feet beat an even rhythm on the forest floor. It was a living awareness that masked the stench of masculine and animal sweat. We arrived at the clearing. Madrog saw the ashes of the fire that I'd lit.

"We have visitors. Search the forest. If you find anyone, bring them to me."

Our inevitable fruitless search satisfied him that no one was lurking in the trees.

He barked out more orders. "Collect lots of firewood. I need heat to entice the magician from his prison."

The tongues of flame, leaping from the fire, sent layers of smoke through the clearing. Madrog pulled the manuscript from beneath his tunic and turned the pages until he found what he was looking for.

He shouted at the rock, "I have the means of freeing you from your prison, Merlin. One of your own magic spells will surrender your powers to me." He nodded to one of his sons. "Bring the drinking vessel that hangs on my saddle."

He threw the manuscript down, picked up a fragment of rock, then muttered a few words. The fragment moved around in his hand until it was a perfectly rounded stone. He held it against the rock's surface. The force field disintegrated in a brilliant flash of white light and the stone remained embedded in the rock face. Madrog took the vessel from his son. He removed the stopper and fumbled at his lower clothing before peeing into it.

His voice boomed out more words of magic. Everyone gasped as a cloud of vapour gushed from the rock face where Madrog had placed the stone. The vapour formed itself into a small rounded cloud, which he enticed into the vessel with his fingers. As the last trace of vapour vanished, he replaced the stopper, shook the contents and threw the vessel on to the blazing fire.

He barked out orders to one of his sons, who ran into the hut. He reappeared with a small container, which he filled with water from the pool. He used his sword to drag the vessel from the hot embers, then threw it into the container. Madrog picked it out of the water when it had cooled and drank the contents.

A brief wave of uncertainty swept through me. What if Merlin had lost his powers to Madrog? I brushed the thought aside. This was an almighty scam. I was being taken for a fool.

Madrog yelled at us, "Merlin's powers now flow in my blood. You are looking at the most powerful sorcerer in the land. If you pieces of dung need convincing, then I will show you."

He disappeared in front of our eyes, only to reappear on the opposite side of the clearing seconds later, where he hovered in the air. A burst of flame shot from his fingers and set a tree alight. Our reaction was mutual. Everyone prostrated themselves on the ground, shouting his name out loud as if he were some kind of god.

I crawled close to Dugwump and whispered in his ear, acting like the complete prat that Carin expected of me. "What's going on? We were supposed to rescue Merlin, not watch him die."

A stupid grin appeared on his face. "You worry too much. Wait and see."

I kidded her along. "You're not squaring with me. If you won't be upfront with me, I'm going to sort Madrog out. He can't harm me, because I'm wearing Merlin's stones."

She gripped my arm. "Shove your heroics. Get your act together and put your thinking cap on. Do you really think someone as great as Merlin would allow himself to be outdone by a cretin like Madrog? Don't do anything stupid or you'll regret it."

I placated her. "OK. I hope you're right."

She found it hard to hide the bite in Dugwump's voice. "I'm never wrong, and don't you ever forget it."

Madrog reappeared in front of the rock. "On your feet, vermin, and get more wood for the fire before I speak with you."

CHAPTER THIRTEEN

Madrog stood before us like a general surveying his battlefield of victory. His head nodded knowingly, a twisted smile on his face.

"In my moment of triumph, traitors stand in my midst. Two of you are plotting against me."

There were cries of disbelief from the other warriors. I couldn't believe that Madrog had managed to pick Carin and me out. I wasn't worried. Our stones would protect us. He yanked his sword from its sheath and walked towards me. I was completely taken by surprise as he whirled around with a quickness of foot that belied his size. Two blows from his sword killed his sons. Their severed heads rolled across the ground.

He shouted at us, "My traitor sons are no more. Set their heads on wooden stakes and plant them at the edge of the clearing to show what will befall anyone who plots against me. Now. Listen to me—"

He didn't finish his words. He clutched at his chest and slowly collapsed to the ground.

A plume of vapour trailed from Madrog's nose, and Merlin appeared. His black hair and beard had been trimmed, and he was clad in fine blue robes with a red cloak thrown across his shoulders. The other warriors drew their swords and made a beeline for him. His death ray cut them down. He walked across to us.

"We meet at last. Come out of those loathsome creatures' bodies and show yourselves."

We did as he asked. His death ray sent Barum and Dugwump into oblivion.

Carin ran across to him and planted a loving kiss on his lips. "I have missed you, My Lord."

He put an arm around her waist. "And, I have missed you too, my dear."

I stayed calm. This wasn't my Carin.

I looked him in the face. "You're good at inflicting pain on people. I suppose you were controlling Grodam as well, back in my time? Was it really necessary for him to kill people as a means of getting me here?"

He showed no concern. "Grodam was an evil man. He suited me well for the tasks I gave him." He clicked his tongue. "Unfortunately, life has turned its back on him. One of Madrog's sons was the beginning of the Grodam family lineage. He is dead, so Grodam will never be born." He pointed at Madrog. A blue ray enveloped him and he disappeared. "That buffoon is no more."

My strength of character was showing itself. I was completely unruffled by his butchery.

I pointed at Carin. "She isn't the girl that I used to know. What have you done to her?"

"She is not in charge of her mind, that is why." He turned to Carin. "Come out and join us, my dear."

A trail of vapour poured down Carin's nose. She slumped to the ground in an unconscious heap. The vapour swirled around before forming itself into a beautiful woman. The past came back to haunt me. This was the woman who had cast Merlin into his rock prison in my dream-vision.

She curtsied to me. "I am Emeralda. I enjoyed bonding with you whilst I was in your woman's body. Your lovemaking was breathtaking."

I felt dirty and used. My eyes lingered on Carin.

Emeralda laughed. "Your woman was under my spell. When we wake her, she will not remember you. I have removed every image of you from her mind. She never fell in love with you of her own free will. Merlin made her do that."

He butted in. "You should thank me. Because the Grodams were never born, no one will die at their hands in your time, including Carin's parents. They are both alive, and she will return to them to take up the reins of her new life without you."

I was hurting like mad, but didn't show it. "You're a cruel bastard, Merlin. So, why did you pick on me for this mission?"

He stared at me, keeping me in suspense before the two of them burst out laughing at the top of their voices.

He looked at Emeralda when they had quietened down. "Shall I put him out of his misery, My Lady?"

"Why not, My Lord? He will never guess why he is here."

Merlin waggled his head and smiled at me. "Have you not worked it out for yourself? I picked you for my mission because you are my son."

This bolt from the blue should have floored me, but it didn't.

"That's impossible. I had a father back in the twentieth century. You'll have to do better than that."

He reacted with a sneer. "You were born in my time. I had you snatched from your mother's arms when you were born. You remember, do you not? Your mother was singing a lullaby to you."

Of course I remembered.

My outward coolness forced a pleased smirk on his face. "I took you to your own time after you were born, and used my sorcery to place you in the body of the woman you called your mother. As my son, you were chosen to help a powerful ruler called Damnus to bring mankind to its knees one day, which will allow him to rule this world."

The thought that I was his son disgusted me. As for this Damnus person, he was a new twist in my life. I gave nothing away about my inner feelings, and stood in silence, just staring at him.

"You have taken my words well. So you should, seeing you are my son. Now listen. My gifts of sorcery flow in your body because of the stones you wear. I will allow you to use your powers freely, but only when you show a willingness to fight for Damnus." His face creased in anger. "You are a great disappointment to me in not wanting to further his plans." He shrugged his shoulders. "Never mind. It is of no concern to me. You have already given Damnus what was expected of you."

"What the hell are you on about? I've done nothing for him, and I don't intend to."

He roared at me, "Have some respect for Damnus, and listen to me! You and a woman of my bloodline have provided him with what he needs to conquer the world."

"What are you on about? What have we given you? And who is this woman? You can't be talking about Carin."

The two of them burst out laughing again.

"Oh, dear. It must have slipped my mind. The woman you profess to love is Emeralda's daughter, and I am her father."

I was poleaxed at the realisation that I'd fallen in love with my half-sister. I didn't give him the pleasure of showing my true feelings.

"Nothing's changed, then. You're still making my life a misery. Why?"

His lips twitched into a semblance of a smile. "I believed that a lack of love in your childhood would have moulded you into the son I wanted for this mission." He grunted. "I failed, but Emeralda and I enjoyed feeding on your misery. It has given us much amusement."

"I'm sure it has. Never mind that. What was all that nonsense about pretending to be shut away in that rock?"

He grinned at Emeralda. "He asks a lot of questions, does he not, my dear?"

She nodded her head and smiled back.

"The vision provided you with a good reason for my stones to come into your possession, so you would know what they were and where they had come from. It was the simplest way of getting you here."

I sneered at him. "I can't believe you waited twenty-seven years."

"Who said I waited twenty-seven years?"

"What do you mean?"

"I time-travelled into different parts of your future life to mould you as I wanted." He pointed across the clearing. "In my time, you were born twenty-eight days ago, in that hut over there."

I was gobsmacked and driven into silence.

He rubbed his hands together. "So, let me tell you why you are here. You have been the means of creating twelve male disciples, who will serve Damnus. And, before you ask, his disciples lie in your woman's body. She is pregnant."

I felt as if a thunderbolt had hit me.

"I don't believe you. Anyhow, she can't give birth to twelve children. That's impossible."

The two of them embraced each other as they roared with laughter.

He shook his head at me. "Your woman carries a fertilised egg, from which Emeralda will create twelve disciples by using her sorcery."

I was still lost for words.

"You have created something else which is vital to Damnus's plans. Emeralda coaxed your woman into carrying out a love ritual with you in that pool. Your love juices and blood turned the water into a powerful brew when you dipped my stones in it. A few drops of that magical brew, placed into a country's drinking water, will convert everyone to Damnus's beliefs after they have drunk of the water." He spoke to Emeralda. "It is time to remove our daughter's egg."

He waved his fingers in the air. The bottom of Carin's skins moved as a cloud of blood-red vapour drifted from beneath them. He enticed the vapour towards Emeralda. It crept under the bottom of her garment.

She sighed. "Her egg is safely in my womb, Merlin."

"Return our daughter to her own time."

She clapped her hands and Carin was gone.

He put his arms around Emeralda. "Our mission is complete. We are done in this place."

I rounded on him. "Hold on! Not so fast. What have you got planned for me?"

He grunted. "At last you are showing some interest. Lord Damnus wanted you to rule in his other worlds as his Lord Protector, to make sure his subjects, even after death, do not stray from the evil path he set for them on earth."

This was something new to me. "What do you mean by other worlds?"

"Of course, you know nothing about them. Let me explain. The spirits of the earthly dead travel to one of many parallel worlds. Those who have dabbled in evil on earth will end up on one of Damnus's worlds. They lie in another dimension of time, hidden behind the earthly veil of death."

"What if I don't like what I find and want to come back to earth?"

He went mental. "Yours is the highest honour that can be granted by Damnus! Once there, you will never set foot on earth again! Enough of this nonsense! Let us make preparations for your journey to his parallel worlds."

"If you think I'm being sent to some life hereafter, you can shove it! I belong here, and there's nothing you can do about it!"

He wasn't given the chance of answering me. The rock began to shake, and a voice of razor-sharp authority rang through the clearing. The two of them fell to the ground, in homage to the voice.

It screamed at me, "I am Damnus. Your negative words have angered me. Merlin has failed to convince you, so it falls on me to deal with you."

CHAPTER FOURTEEN

I struggled to get my muddled thoughts into some sort of working order. Damnus was from a faraway universe, so how was I to deal with him? I was jolted back to reality by a sense of self-assurance that flooded through my body. I snatched the pouch from around my neck and nestled the crucifix in my hand.

"If you are Damnus, then show yourself."

The rock trembled, and seconds later a monstrous six-foot creature with the head of a bull on a man's body stood by my side. Its unblinking blood-red eyes stared at me. Smoke curled from its nostrils. Licks of flame spurted from the matted red hair that covered its body. I couldn't believe what I was seeing. As it raised its head and roared, red flames erupted from its mouth. The creature's breath was rancid.

It spoke in a voice that shook the ground. "You have driven me to anger." Those red eyes bored into mine. "With Merlin's blood flowing in your veins, wickedness and you should be constant companions. But they are not. You are an irritating thorn in my side, and I have no further use for you." The beast yelled at Merlin, "On your feet. Bind this disbeliever with your sorcery."

Merlin scrambled to his feet and screamed a spell at me. It was meant to capture my mind and body, but it didn't. My own powers of sorcery, which the dream-lady had mentioned, overcame his magic. I played along with him and allowed my body to stiffen.

144

Merlin bowed to Damnus. "What would you have me do with my son?"

The beast looked me in the face. "I wanted you to rule my parallel worlds, instead of which I will have you killed." He turned to Merlin. "Off with his head."

My coolness surprised me, as my brain conjured up a thought that brought the gas canisters, from the hut, flying through the air towards the three of them. As the cans floated above their heads, I sent a mental command to the cans. The gas was released, which sprayed over the three of them. They screamed in agony and collapsed on the ground.

It took me a split second to hurl the crucifix at the beast. As it struck its body, it embedded itself in its flesh, where the skin and hair began to smoulder. I unscrewed the cap of one of the glass phials and sprinkled holy water over the beast's head. It screamed as it broke down into dust and disappeared.

I shouted some words at Merlin and Emeralda which came into my head. Their minds and bodies were shackled by my sorcery. I flew into the forest and took shelter behind a tree. My fingers sent a bolt of lightning speeding towards the rock, which exploded, sending hundreds of rock missiles whining through the air towards them.

I walked into the clearing and looked down at them. They were a bloodied mess. Their hate-filled eyes bored into mine. If Damnus's plans were to be aborted, I had to kill them. I paused for a moment, wondering where the courage to kill them would come from. My hesitancy vanished as quickly as it had come. I was about to shout the words that came into my mind, when I was distracted by a sound from the forest. An old stag and a fawn stood at the edge of the clearing, watching every move I made. The animals let out bellowing cries before turning their backs on me and scampering into the forest.

I ordered my mind to exterminate Merlin and Emeralda. My left hand pointed at them, sending twin bolts of crackling white light surging from my fingertips, which enveloped their necks. Their heads rolled across the ground, before exploding in a shower of intense red light.

The hairs on the back of my neck stood on end as I heard a child's voice call me. "Father, I'm afraid. Please help me."

I pulled back the hem of Emeralda's dress. A baby boy lay on the ground, looking up at me. I was confused. This couldn't be my son. He'd only been conceived a few days ago, yet this was a fully grown, talking baby.

The baby pushed itself into a sitting position and held his hands out to me. "Don't leave me here, Father. I'm your flesh and blood. We belong to each other." The baby's blood-red eyes were dull and lifeless. He clutched at my hand. His fingers felt like ice. "Take me back home with you, Father."

The baby changed in front of my eyes. Hair started to sprout on its bald head, and he was gaining in size. The colour of his eyes changed to a cornflower blue.

The child gripped my hand more tightly and smiled. "You must look after me. I've nobody else in the world. We need each other."

I twigged why he needed me. He was drawing strength from my body, through his fingers. In a matter of seconds, my son went through the phases of toddler, young child and teenager. He was the spitting image of me.

He sneered, "Surprised, are you? Grandfather Merlin is dead, but I intend to carry on with his cause, whether you like it or not. Are you with me or against me?"

The world wasn't prepared for my son. I had no hesitation in killing him, in the same way as I'd dealt with the other two. Some serious doubts surfaced in my mind. I'd murdered my father and his mistress, together with someone masquerading as my son. Should I have felt shock, sadness and a little pity? My mind accepted my bloodthirsty acts without any problem. I couldn't summon up one single grain of emotion for their deaths.

Memories of my miserable life flooded back into my mind. Merlin had woven a trail of misery during those years, and many people had suffered in the process. Killing him hadn't changed what he'd already forged in my century. If people's past lives were to be changed, it would mean time-travelling to the morning before Merlin had journeyed to the twentieth century, to influence so many lives, including mine. I ordered my mind to take me back to that time.

I materialised outside a small stone building. Two horses were tethered outside. I walked around the building and found its only window. Merlin and his mistress were inside.

Her words floated to my ears. "What about my husband?"

"Make an excuse to bring him here tomorrow. I will put him into a deep trance while we travel into the twentieth century to prepare our children's lives for this mission. I have something planned for him when they join us in the sixth century."

I captured their minds and bodies, and entered the room. Within seconds I had killed them in the same way as I had done in the clearing. As I walked outside, that same large stag and fawn stared at me. They turned tail and rushed into the forest. I time-travelled to the clearing that I'd left a few minutes earlier. My sorcery had worked. There was no sign of their bodies, and the rock was undamaged. I tugged the pouch from around my neck and threw the stones on the ground. I wouldn't be needing them any more. The blue light that burst from my fingers turned the stones into dust. I took a last look around me before willing myself back to my own century.

In that small stone building in the forest, Emeralda looked lovingly into Merlin's eyes. "You are the greatest sorcerer in this world. This is the second time you have outwitted your son. How did you know he was on his way here?"

"A hair that I planted in his scalp, when he was born, tells me of his movements. Knowing he was on his way gave me enough time to create living replicas of ourselves, and for the two of us to hide in the forest."

"Your replicas are wonderful. This is the second time they have saved us." She shrugged her shoulders. "What a pity we have lost our daughter's unborn son."

"Do not worry about that. She will produce another fertilised egg in a few days' time, when my son meets up with her again. At least, the magic water is safe on one of Damnus's parallel worlds, unaffected by what my son has done. My thoughts are still locked in both of their minds, which will prevent them from forming loving relationships with other people until they meet each other.

"You will take over our daughter's body when they meet each other. You must make sure that their lovemaking produces a fertilised egg." His shoulders rocked with silent laughter. "My son will make a third attempt to kill us when he discovers we are still alive, but that's in the future. When that happens, another of my planted thoughts will make itself known in his mind. That thought will tell him why his first two attempts to do away with us failed, or so he will think. He will kill our replicas for a third time, after which the idiot will finally believe we are no more. That will leave us free to fulfil the ambitions of Damnus without any further interference from him."

She looked puzzled. "Did your son not do away with Damnus?"

He roared with laughter. "Of course not. Damnus is an immortal. He pretended to die, for the benefit of my son. It was all part of our plan. Let us return to my castle."

As they held hands they disappeared.

CHAPTER FIFTEEN

I ended up inside the walls of my father's castle. The warm sunshine that streamed through the window openings made me feel like a human being again. My body wound down as my mind uncoiled. It was a relief to be back in my own time, away from Merlin's barbaric time. I smiled as I thought about the old Kit Milner. I'd been reborn, and with the new-found powers under my bonnet I bore no resemblance to the man I used to be. With Merlin dead, many lives had changed for the better. None of them would remember that other life, except me. My cheerfulness slipped away as I thought of Carin. I was gutted that she never fell in love with me of her own free will, and couldn't even remember me.

I trudged across the field to my car and changed into my modern-day gear. Minutes later I was speeding through the Welsh countryside. I toyed with the idea of contacting Carin and making her fall in love with me by using sorcery. That was rubbish thinking, and I knew it. How could I live an eternity with someone who says she loves me, knowing she's reading from a script that I've lodged in her mind?

There was also the little matter of the bloodline we share. Common sense flew out of the window as my heart overruled my head. Nobody knew we share Merlin's blood. I came to a dodgy compromise. I decided to call on her and take things from there.

The journey became more bearable. I stopped at a service

station, had a wash and shave, and managed to enjoy an overpriced meal. As I left the restaurant a crowd of people were milling around someone lying on the ground. Curiosity got the better of me. I eased myself to the front of the crowd. A paramedic was kneeling beside an elderly woman. Her face looked ashen and lifeless. He applied pressure to the woman's chest, then gave her mouth-to-mouth resuscitation. His face betrayed his thoughts. She was a goner.

I felt an immediate impulse to help her. First aid and me aren't bedfellows, but that didn't stop me from patting the medic on the back.

I looked him in the eyes. "Let me have a go."

He got up without protest. I copied everything he'd done. Nothing happened. My non-existent first-aid skills were crap.

I yelled out in sheer frustration, "For goodness' sake breathe, woman."

My stomach turned over when I felt her breath brush my cheek. Her eyes blinked rapidly, then opened. She took hold of my hand and kissed it.

The medic's mouth dropped open. "Bloody hell, mate. What have you done? She was . . ." He ran out of words and stood awestruck, shaking his head.

I was way out of my comfort zone. I pushed through the crowd and legged it into the car park. I made myself invisible and hurried to my car.

I switched the radio on as I drove down the motorway. It hadn't taken the BBC long to pick up on the service-station incident.

A breathless female was speaking to the nation. "I'm at Watford Gap Services on the M1 motorway." I heard the hubbub of excited voices in the background. "Everyone is talking about a young man who brought an elderly woman back to life. I've got the paramedic with me, who was attending her. Tell me what happened, Mike."

He grunted. "I'm still trying to get my head around it. I tried to revive a woman who'd collapsed, but she was already dead. That's when this chap stepped out of the crowd. He did everything I'd done, but it didn't help. The next thing I know, he's screaming at her to breathe." He paused, and lamely added, "And she came back to life."

The reporter caught her breath. "Thanks, Mike. Go and get yourself a coffee, or something stronger. Details are still sketchy, but eyewitnesses swear the man vanished in front of their eyes. Let's have a word with some of them."

I switched the radio off.

It was late afternoon when I parked in Lovington Marketplace. I strolled down the High Street to the tea shop I knew, and ordered a coffee. The shop emptied, and the grey-haired lady wandered over to me.

"Haven't seen you before. Visiting for the day, are we?"

She wouldn't have remembered that we'd met in her previous life.

"I have some business with the rector of St Leonard's Church. Do you know of him?"

Of course she knew him. She almost had a multiple orgasm when I mentioned his name.

Her eyes twinkled and she patted her hair. "Know him? I'm one of his congregation, bless him. He's a lovely man. A real darling." She snapped out of her self-induced trance and smiled saucily at me. "Are you arranging a wedding or something?"

I winced. "No, I'm not. Does his daughter still live with him?"

"Yes, she does." She pulled a puzzled-looking face. "She's a real beauty, that one. But there's something about her that I can't get my head around. She's never shown any interest in men, so the rector told me."

Relief swept through me.

"I hope she's not one of those strange women we hear about." She winked, and nudged me with her elbow. "You know what I mean, don't you?"

After more idle chit-chat, I bade her goodbye. Ten minutes later I was parked in St Leonard's car park. A car trundled by and turned into the rectory drive. A girl with vivid auburn hair got out. I locked the car and hurried after her. With a tad of nervousness I rang the bell. Carin opened the door. My mouth stopped working as I caught sight of her. She stared at me with no hint of recognition, sharing my tongue-tied state. This wasn't the first time I'd been blown away by her looks.

The awkward silence was broken by a familiar voice. "Who is it, Carin?"

Reverend Milner came to the door. He eyed me up and down. "Do I know you from somewhere?"

He couldn't possibly have remembered me.

I shook my head. "Not as far as I know." I put my well-rehearsed words into play. "I've called about your fundraising appeal. I can offer some help."

My words hit the bullseye. "Really? You'd better come in."

He shook my hand, then guided me into the lounge. I smiled when I saw his davenport, standing in its rightful place. The reverend gentleman couldn't hide his excitement.

"Would you care for a sherry, Mister . . . ?" He clicked his tongue. "I'm sorry. I didn't ask your name."

"I'm Kit Milner. Please call me Kit. I wouldn't say no to a sherry."

He laughed. "What a coincidence! We share the same moniker." He motioned to the girl. "This is my daughter, Carin."

I grabbed the hand she offered, and hastily let go when I realised I was stroking the back of it with my thumb.

She blushed, then grinned at me. "It's lovely to meet you."

Julius sat me down and poured the sherries. He knocked his back in a single gulp, then stood in front of the log fire.

He turned to the purpose of my visit. "The church has mega money problems, Kit. There's so much work needs doing, and so little money rolling in. We're barely crawling towards our financial target." He stopped and stared at me. "Are you from Lovington?"

"No. I live in Grinton, but Lovington holds memories for me. I used to know someone who lives in the town."

Carin was hanging on to my every word.

The time for idle chit-chat was over. It was time to make the rector's dreams come true.

"I can arrange a donation to your restoration fund. How much are we talking about?"

Julius's mouth dropped open. "Really? That's wonderful. The figure's rather daunting. We have to find £180,000, give or take a pound or two."

"That's no problem. I'll be upfront with you. It isn't coming out of my own pocket. I know some people who'd be more than willing to cough up that kind of money."

They weren't empty words. The lottery would be stumping up the cash. It was as simple as travelling forward in time and making a note of the winning numbers. "It'll take a few weeks to organise, but consider your problem solved."

Julius swept across the room and nearly shook my arm off. "Words fail me, my boy." His face twitched and he looked uneasy. "Is there a catch? I've been down this road before, and never did see any money."

"You'll get the cash. That's a promise."

He visibly relaxed. "How about staying for dinner? I can tell you how the money needs to be spent. What do you say, Carin?"

She put her hand on my arm. A tingle surged through my body.

"Please stay for dinner, Kit."

The Reverend hopped around like a beggar who's found a £50 note. "I'll get Meg to lay an extra place at the table."

Carin looked me in the eyes after he'd left the room. "You are for real, aren't you? I don't want Daddy getting hurt."

I ached to take her in my arms, but contented myself by joining her in front of the fire.

"Don't worry. Your father will get the money."

She grinned knowingly, "So, who's this person you knew in Lovington? I bet it was a woman."

"You don't beat about the bush, do you? Yes, it was a woman. We recently lost touch with each other. You reminded me of her. That's why I stared at you when you opened the door."

"I envy you, Kit. I'm a mature woman . . ." She became flustered and couldn't spit the right words out. "I'm nearly twenty-seven . . . and all my life . . . you won't believe this . . . what I mean is . . ." She got angry with herself. "This is stupid. What I'm trying to say is I've never been out with a man in the whole of my life." The colour in her cheeks matched her auburn locks. "God only knows why I'm telling you this. I've only known you for a few minutes."

A warm feeling flowed through me. We'd had this same conversation three weeks ago. "I wouldn't worry. I'm the same age as you and she was my first girlfriend." A necessary lie tripped from my lips. "We split up after three weeks. It wasn't a close relationship. You're looking at a fully paid-up member of the Hertfordshire Society of Adult Male Virgins."

She rocked with laughter. "I'm not the only one, then? My friends must think I'm a full-blown lesbian."

"Welcome to the adult virgins' club. I'm saving myself for someone special when she comes my way."

She slipped her hand into mine and gave me a saucy look. "I'm sure you'll find her soon."

Her father walked into the room with Mrs Milner. "Kit, this is my wife. She won't mind you calling her Meg. Please call me Julius."

Meg kissed me on the cheek. "Of course I don't mind."

She was a plumpish middle-aged lady, but attractive with it. Her dark-brown hair was showing the first signs of grey, and her natural good looks were set off by countless freckles and vivid sky-blue eyes. Meg clicked her tongue. "The man hasn't even taken your coat. I'll hang it up for you, Kit."

Most of the meal was taken up with Julius describing each repair that needed doing in the church. I wasn't bored; nor were the other two. Relief was written all over their faces, that a financial lifeline had been thrown to him. The weight on his mind had lifted. The Milner family could enjoy a lifestyle they deserved without the spectre of Merlin hanging over their heads. I knew they'd taken a shine to me, which had nothing to do with the monies I'd pledged to the church. I said my goodbyes to Carin at the front door. She said she'd like to see me again, and blushed. I agreed to make contact with her.

My feet barely touched the ground as I hurried down the road to where my car was parked. In my love-filled state I got careless. My foot caught the edge of the kerb. As I clattered to the ground, my forehead smacked against the top of the church wall. I felt no pain, but countless coloured lights danced in front of my eyes. I struggled to my feet, holding on to the wall for support.

I screwed my eyes up to see off the aurora borealis light show, then opened them. They focused on the church noticeboard, and soaked up words that had no right to be there:

'THIS HOUSE OF WORSHIP IS
DEDICATED TO LORD MERLIN.'

Lights shone out of every window. I staggered down the path and went inside. The air was polluted with the stench of death. Every religious trapping had been stripped out. Black sheets draped the pillars, and woven tapestries depicting scenes of an erotic nature hung from the walls. A soiled black carpet ran the length of the central nave and up into the chancel. I walked up to the altar. My stomach turned over. A knife, axe and black chalice lay on its bloodstained wooden surface.

A feeling of light-headedness came over me. I staggered back to the rectory and frantically rang the doorbell. Julius opened the door.

"Kit! What's happened to you?" He put an arm around me. "Let's get you inside. That cut needs looking at."

He bundled me into the kitchen and sat me down. Meg fussed around me while Carin bathed my wound, then wrapped a bandage around my head.

"That's a nasty cut you've got there. I'm taking you to the hospital."

She wasn't to know it would self-heal.

I slotted my words into their minds. "There's no need for that. I'm not in pain. See how it is in the morning."

155

Carin was the first to react to my planted words. "Have it your way. One thing's for certain, you're not driving back home tonight."

Meg said she'd make up the bed in the spare bedroom. Carin got me to swallow a couple of painkillers. I fell asleep as soon as my head hit the pillow.

Emeralda and Merlin materialised in Carin's bedroom as she slept.

He whispered in Emeralda's ear, "See that our daughter makes love to my son and produces a fertile egg." He smirked. "Enjoy yourself, my dear."

He kissed her, then vanished. Her body broke down into vapour, which flowed up Carin's nose.

CHAPTER SIXTEEN

I was woken by a soft tapping on the bedroom door. A worried-looking Carin sidled in. Her pyjamas did nothing to hide a figure that was worth going to prison for.

"It's only me. Mummy said I was to let you sleep in. How are you feeling this morning?"

"Much better. What time is it?"

"Just gone ten. Would you like a hot drink?"

"I could murder a coffee. I'll get dressed and come down."

"No, you won't. I'll bring it up to you."

I didn't argue. "If you say so. Where's the bathroom?"

"Second on the right, along the landing."

My face looked disgustingly healthy in the bathroom mirror. I undid the bandage. The skin on my forehead was as smooth as a baby's bottom, with no sign of a scar. I found a plaster in the bathroom cabinet and stuck it on my forehead, where the cut had been.

I'd just settled back into bed when there was another tap on the door. Carin came in. She was still wearing her pyjamas.

She put my mug of coffee on the bedside cabinet and pulled a face. "I see you've taken the bandage off. Let's get that plaster off, so I can have a look at your forehead."

As she leaned over me, I caught sight of her milk-white breasts nestling under the loose-fitting pyjama top.

I grabbed her hand. "There's no need. I've had a look at it. It's healing nicely."

157

"If you say so." She frowned. "You're a quick healer. There's no sign of swelling or bruising." She shrugged her shoulders. "Your shirt's in the airing cupboard, along the landing, when you're ready. It was covered in blood, so Mummy washed it. I'll fix breakfast for you when you come down."

Her cooking was as pleasing as her looks. She'd chosen not to change out of her pyjamas. I found it off-putting for all the right reasons. She sat with me at the breakfast bar.

"What happened, last night?"

I wasn't sure myself. Had I ventured into the future? That was crap thinking. Merlin was dead. The blow to my head had made me hallucinate.

Carin brought me back to reality. "Are you OK?"

"Yeah. Sorry. It's no big deal. I tripped over the kerb and smacked my head on the church wall."

She didn't press me further, and let me finish my breakfast.

We made ourselves at home in the lounge. Carin stood in front of the fire while I sat on the sofa. Those stunning eyes stared at me as her tongue licked nervously around her lips. I soon lost interest in her eyes. The flames, behind her, were outlining her naked body through the thin pyjama material.

I broke the silence. "Haven't you got a job to go to?"

"Not until this afternoon."

Without any warning, she plonked herself on my lap. Before I knew it, she was in my arms. The warmth of her perfumed body seeped into mine. I felt as mesmerised as a snake's prey as she looked me in the eyes. I knew she was gagging for me.

"The first moment I saw you, I fancied you like mad. I've never felt this way about a man before." She realised what she'd said and shook her head in frustration. "That's a hell of a thing to say, seeing I don't even know you. Call it intuition, call it what you bloody well like. What does it matter? I want you to make love to me." She blushed like mad. "There. I've said it."

Even at this late stage, I tried to stall her. "What if your parents come back?"

My feeble half-baked excuse was too late.

She laughed huskily. "They won't be home for hours."

The next moment she was unzipping my trousers. "Get them off, Mister."

She took her pyjamas off. Half-sister or not, my body was aching for her. Not a word was spoken as we stretched out on the carpet. She guided my manhood between her legs and sighed with pleasure. After a few minutes of foreplay, I took control of her body. She writhed and groaned as we climaxed together. We dressed, then sat on the sofa, draped in each other's arms. Our talk flowed as if we'd known each other a lifetime. I asked her where she worked, hoping she wouldn't say the British Library.

"I'm a full-blown doctor."

"What a coincidence! I keep getting this aching pain in my groin. The symptoms started when I met this gorgeous woman. Is there a cure for it?"

Carin reacted as I hoped she would. "I've never come across your condition before, but I know how to handle it." She fluttered her eyelashes at her risqué humour and thumped me playfully on the arm. "This woman had better be me, or you're in big trouble, Mister." She concocted a serious look. "I'll give you something to rub on it later."

We rolled about with laughter.

"How long have you been a doctor?"

"It's over three years since I graduated. I practise at the Brink Street surgery, in town. What do you do for a living?"

"I'm an auctioneer at an auction house in Grinton. My task is to extract as much paper money as I can from the punters." I knew I still worked there, even though I had changed time. My flat key was in my pocket.

She laughed. "That sounds fun. I'd love to come to one of your auctions."

"Why not? We have a Fine Art Sale this Saturday week. That's where we sell the best gear. You might even end up buying something."

"I'm not sure about that, but it's a date."

I looked at my watch. "I'd love to spend the rest of the day with you, but I have to get back to Grinton."

She nibbled my ear. "I'll let you go on one condition."

"What's that?"

"Take me out for a meal tonight. I'll book somewhere and ask Mummy if you can stay over."

The look on her face showed she had an ulterior motive for my sleeping over. The past came back to haunt me. She'd fallen for a baby when we'd made love. My face told its own story.

She frowned. "Don't you want to make love to me?"

"Of course I do. It's not that." I blurted my worry out. "What if you have a baby?"

She laughed her head off. "Haven't you heard of the morning-after pill?" She shook her head. "No. Of course you haven't, seeing you're a recent member of the male virgin's club." She waggled a finger at me. "Watch my lips. I won't get pregnant. Trust me, I'm a doctor. Now that I've put your mind at ease, you're going nowhere until we make love again." She laughed. "And I won't have a baby."

As I left the rectory my guilt complex resurfaced. What a bloody fool I was, conveniently forgetting we share the same bloodline.

As I opened the car door, a breath of wind tickled my face, then it spoke to me.

"Hello, Kit. Don't be afraid. I'm here to help you."

This was ridiculous, but no more out of the ordinary than the many other things I'd encountered. I certainly didn't panic.

"Who's there?"

The tinkling tones relaxed me. "Would you believe me if I told you I was your mother?"

"No, I wouldn't. That's damn well impossible. You're not even a human being."

"Don't let's worry about that. That's not why I'm here. You're troubled by the love you share with your woman." She giggled. "She's pretty, that one, isn't she? I want to put your mind at ease. Merlin called you his son, but he's not your father."

"This is ridiculous. What do you know about him? And who told you he wasn't my father?"

Her breath caressed my cheek as her laughter tinkled through the air. "There are a lot of questions that need answering. It's time you learned more about yourself. Let's sit in the back of your car."

I made myself comfortable on the back seat. A pretty blond lady with cornflower-blue eyes appeared beside me. This was the lady who had sung a lullaby to me when I was born.

I put my arms around her and kissed her. "This is incredible – you really are my mother."

She hugged me. "You're so relaxed. You take after your father. Nothing worries him. I wish I was the same." She looked me in the eyes. "Let's talk about your father. His name's Michael Seraphina. He's a very powerful man who governs several parallel worlds in another dimension of time. I told you in your dream, the other night, that his paranormal powers have passed to you, and you're an immortal. Before you were born, he planted some thoughts in your mind to make you accept whatever life threw at you without question, or fear." She grinned. "It's worked, hasn't it?"

"So that's why I've never been fazed by the strange things that have plagued me, like meeting up with you today and finding out that you are my mother. Talking about immortality, Carin is Merlin's daughter. Is she immortal like me?"

"That's easy to answer. Merlin does not possess immortality, so neither does Carin." She laughed out loud. "But you changed all that when you carried out your blood ritual with her back in Merlin's time. Because your blood mixed with hers, she's inherited immortality from you. That's enough about that. What do you want to know about yourself?"

"How about starting at the beginning."

"OK. Magnus, the leader of our parallel worlds, ordered Michael and me to have a baby. That's you. He was concerned that another powerful ruler from the parallel worlds was planning to take over earth. This man is called Damnus. You are our leader's weapon in ensuring that Damnus's plans for earth never succeed."

My built-in gift of never being ruffled kicked in. "I've met him. Go on."

"I know you have, but you didn't kill him. He's immortal. He ordered Merlin to sire a son to help him take over the world. Your father deceived him by creating living replicas of the two of us. Merlin raped my replica, and she bore a child in that hut where you and Carin stayed. Our replicas returned to our parallel world with their baby while Michael and I took their place. That's when Merlin had you snatched from me, in the mistaken belief that you were his son."

"You mentioned this Magnus person. So, I'm working for a top man, am I?"

She smiled and shook her head at how laid-back I was.

"I hope I'll meet up with him one day. Tell me something. Is my mission against Damnus completed?"

"You'll have to wait and see." She took me in her arms and kissed me. "I have to go now."

"Before you go, tell me, can I make replicas of anybody?"

She smiled. "You're capable of anything. Think the command, and you'll have a living, breathing, thinking replica, as perfect as the real thing, with a beating heart and blood running through its veins. I must be off." She kissed me, then the car door burst open and she was gone.

I drove back to Grinton with my mother's words ringing in my ears. I hadn't a care in the world. Why should I? Merlin isn't my father, so I could lavish as much love on Carin as I wanted, without any feelings of guilt.

CHAPTER SEVENTEEN

My plan was to crash out for a couple of hours. However, my brain couldn't cope with it. Differing trains of thought jostled around inside my head. My father's a powerful sorcerer, as well as governor of some parallel worlds. I surprised myself, again, at how I could coolly ponder on such mind-boggling matters. I had him to thank for that.

My mother's a spiritual being, yet she possesses a human body. So, where does that leave me? Am I a human being, some other-worldly cross-breed or an alien? I let that thought slip away.

I was still left with a niggling feeling that my destined path in life had a lot of mileage left in it. My thoughts were interrupted by a blast of wind that swept down the chimney and into the lounge. My mother took shape in front of me.

"Magnus has sent me. You have failed in your mission. Merlin and his woman are still alive. You must come with me."

"What! I don't believe it. Where are we going?"

"You'll believe it when you see where we're going. You are about to witness what awaits the human race in years to come."

I tumbled down that whirling tunnel of white light and found myself floating above St Leonard's Church.

"Why are we here?"

"You'll soon find out. Fly down, but stay invisible. Before you do, let's get one thing straight. These are visions of the future. Don't try and change what you see. The only way to make sure they don't become a reality is to go back in time and kill Merlin."

I touched down by the church porch. A gaggle of adults and children jostled to get into the building. I checked out the church noticeboard. Last night's fleeting vision came back to haunt me. The church was dedicated to Merlin.

I hurried to the south end of the church and peeked through the chancel window. The congregation started shouting: "Sammael, Sammael . . ." Their words threw me. Who was this Sammael person they were shouting about?

A man walked out from the side chapel. The people greeted him with noisy applause. This vision of the future had got wildly bizarre. What was Julius Milner doing here, wallowing in the adoration of the people? He quietened them with a wave of his hands.

"On your knees, brethren. We are honoured to have one of Lord Damnus's chosen disciples with us. Let us welcome the Master by showing him the love and respect he deserves." He bowed to someone standing in the shadows. "Reward us with your words of wisdom, Master."

A young man walked to the front of the altar. I shook my head in disbelief. This Master person was the spitting image of me, a throwback to the son I had killed in Merlin's time. He was dressed in a black cassock, his long curly hair held in place with a black bandanna. The rowdy crowd started shouting: "Master, Master . . ." over and over again. He raised his arms to quieten them.

"On your knees as we pray to our king-in-waiting." He knelt in front of the altar. "Lord Sammael, we give you thanks for leading the people of earth into your father's fold. You and Lord Damnus will reveal yourselves to your worldwide followers, for the very first time, in a few weeks from now, when you will be crowned King of the World. Lord Merlin, Lady Emeralda, Lord Milner and myself, together with your disciples, have worked to harvest mankind to your father's doctrines. Thank you for guiding and inspiring us to achieve his wishes."

My son got to his feet and shouted at the congregation, "You have recognised Lord Sammael as your king-in-waiting, so he expects your adulation. Never forget that all disbelievers will be sacrificed on his altar.

"Swear your everlasting allegiance to him, then bond your bodies in carnal passion."

The church was filled with cries of lustful pleasure as the congregation ravished each other in acts of wanton sexual depravity. The Master and Julius Milner selected willing young girls and took their bodies.

The Master clapped his hands and the congregation fell silent. My son walked into the side chapel, and returned pulling a naked woman by her hair. Those green eyes that I knew so well had lost their sparkle. In her drugged state, Carin made no protest as the Master lifted her on to the altar.

"My own mother will be sacrificed this evening, because she refused to recognise Lord Sammael as the absolute ruler of the world."

I felt sick at what I was seeing.

My mother blew around my head. "Fly with me to see more of what the future holds, and remain invisible."

I did as she asked, and plunged down that tunnel of light. Moments later I was standing in familiar surroundings in another segment of the future. New buildings had sprung up on Brine & Cherry's site. My jaw dropped as I spotted the burned-out shell of my flat. Another change had taken place. Hundreds of people were packed into a huge car park, which had replaced the old cattle pens. They sweltered in the hot sunshine.

I raised my eyebrows at a golden throne, standing on a stage at the far end of the car park. Four smaller thrones sat alongside it. Tiered stands were positioned on either side of the stage. The first stand was chock-a-block with mega-important people. I moved closer to make sure my eyes weren't deceiving me. They weren't. The British monarch was dressed in full royal regalia, chatting with officers of the armed forces and police. The Archbishop of Canterbury and the Pope relaxed in the balmy sunshine, in the company of leaders of other religious denominations and members of the royal family. A smattering of peers were seated with bishops and judges, all attired in their best finery. The Prime Minister and the leader of the opposition were in deep conversation.

Heads of the Commonwealth and other countries were sitting in the second stand. Their national flags flapped in the gentle breeze. The main road, fronting the car park, was packed with radio and television vans. Hundreds of yards of cable littered the ground, while hordes of media people were busily milling around. Two giant television screens were positioned on each side of the car park.

I flew into the sky to get a bird's-eye view of Grinton. The whole town was gridlocked with vehicles, every street jam-packed with people, all jostling to make sure they missed nothing on the television screens that were dotted throughout the town.

On an impulse I checked out the new auction-house buildings. My mouth dropped at the scale of vandalism that had taken place. Every pane of glass was smashed, and doors had been ripped off their hinges and taken. All of the display units, shelves, carpets and light fittings, as well as radiators, had been stripped out.

I opened the door of the main corridor. Some toerag had emptied their backside, leaving a foul stench in the air. A corpse was lying on the floor in the main office. I knew Martin was dead, from the smell of his decaying flesh. A knife was embedded in his chest. I flipped into his mind, and dragged out his last living images. Rick Adams came into the frame. His face was screwed up in manic anger as he pulled a knife from his belt and threw it at Martin. The mental picture show blanked out as the blade ended Martin's life.

A calendar lay on the floor. I picked it up. The 25th of December had been circled. I'd seen enough, and made my way down Grinton High Street, hovering above the milling crowds. Broken glass and other debris littered the road and pavements, where shops had suffered at the hands of looters. The United Reformed Church was a pile of rubble, and the police station was a ruined stack of fire-blackened bricks. I could have sworn some bodies lay partially buried in the rubble. The incessant sound of public loudspeakers ordered every citizen to be outside in the open at midday.

I'd seen enough. I returned to Brine & Cherry and sat on the main office roof.

One man in the crowd suffered a tantrum. He yelled out, "Bugger this for a lark. I've got better things to do than sit around on Christmas Day. The miracle was supposed to happen at midday. It's a bloody scam."

I glanced at my watch. Noon was still a minute away.

Another man shouted at him, "Don't knock Sammael, you twat, or you'll end up on his altar. Get a watch that keeps the right bloody time, arsehole."

The grumpy man was quickly forgotten as the crowd went wild. Their din drifted off the decibel scale as a shaft of intense white light burst from high up in the heavens, spotlighting the golden throne. People were drifting down within the shaft of light.

The crowd dropped to their knees and started chanting: "Sammael, Sammael, Sammael . . ."

The dark clouds that raced in from the west were stage-managed. Thunder reverberated around the sky as tongues of lightning vented their fury against the ground. Palls of smoke rose from the town centre, where buildings had been set on fire by the vicious lightning strikes. The thunder and lightning ceased as quickly as it had started. A crescendo of female voices burst into song from somewhere beyond the clouds. The menacing mass of dark cloud quickly dispersed, and the sun appeared.

The crowds were stunned into silence, overawed by the breathtaking impossibility of what they were witnessing. Five people floated down on to the stage while other figures hovered above them.

Merlin, Emeralda, Julius Milner, my son and a young man set foot on the stage. They were attired in flowing blue robes with red cloaks over their shoulders. A cold shiver passed through me. Was the young man Sammael, the spawn of Damnus?

A technician ran across to them. He bowed before pinning microphones on to their robes. The young man sat on the golden throne while the other four sat on the smaller thrones beside him.

The crowd stood in shocked silence, overwhelmed by the sorcery that had captured their minds. The singing voices stopped and Merlin got to his feet. His outflung arms embraced the crowd.

"Citizens of earth, this is the most momentous day in the history of civilisation."

The crowd came alive with their cheering, then fell silent.

A look of humility covered his face. "Today's celebrations are not about me. Save your adulation for the man who sits on the golden throne. He is Lord Sammael." He fell to his knees, kissed the young man's feet, then stood up. "This 25th day of December is the first time that the people of earth have looked upon his face before he is crowned King of the World. Sammael is the beloved son of Lord Damnus, whom we will meet later today. This very special day will forever be known as Damnus Day." He bowed to the young man. "Your subjects await you, My Lord."

The crowd went wild as he stepped forward. He was a slim man, standing over six feet tall. His long red hair matched the colour of his eyes. A small pair of horns sprouted from his forehead.

He smirked as he acknowledged the fervent passion being shown to him. "Thank you, Lord Merlin, for the words you have chosen. I acknowledge the debt I owe to you, as well as to Lady Emeralda, Lord Julius Milner and the Master for making this day possible." He pointed to the eleven men floating above him. "My grateful thanks to my loyal disciples for the manner in which they have spent the past five years converting the peoples of earth to my father's cause.

"Before the rituals begin on this festive day, my worldwide subjects will be witness to the unshakable belief that I am indeed the son of Damnus." Aggression masked his face as his shouted words boomed throughout the town. "Never doubt that the mighty Damnus fathered me and I was born as man."

His body stiffened and his eyes protruded from their sockets. An animal roar resonated in his throat as a stream of red smoke poured from his mouth. The smoke swirled about the stage before forming itself into the hairy body of a man with a bull's head. This was the second time I'd come across Damnus. The crowd cringed in terror at the sight of the beast as it grew in size until it towered thirty feet above the crowd. As he bellowed his defiance, red-hot lava cascaded from his mouth, which spewed on to the people standing at the front of the crowd. Hundreds of them collapsed as the lava touched their bodies, inflicting instant death upon them.

The rest of the crowd was terrified, and fell to their knees.

The creature roamed around the stage as it roared its words at them. "I am indeed Lord Damnus. My son was created when I took the body of a young woman. I live inside Sammael, to guide his thoughts. Surrender your loyalty to me for all time or you will suffer the consequences." His voice softened as he looked down on his son. "Sammael is my beloved one. I have granted him the mantle to reign over mankind on my behalf."

The Damnus beast exploded in a cloud of smoke and flames, which disappeared down Sammael's throat.

I'd witnessed scenes that made my blood boil. The huge crowds, as well as the billions of people watching this spectacle on television, were being sucked further into the Damnus fold by the stage-managed special effects, together with added dashes of sorcery thrown in for good measure. One thing was painfully clear. Sammael had proved to the people that he was the son of Damnus and was their ruler-in-waiting.

I'd seen enough, and willed myself back to my flat. I wasn't in the best of moods. How could I be, knowing my efforts in the sixth century had been a waste of time. It was bad enough that Merlin and his mob were alive. Now I had Sammael to contend with. By rights, I should have been checking into the nearest mental institution, but I won't be. I was not even scared. Why should I be? Time was on my side, because I knew when Sammael was to be crowned. I swore I'd rid this world of the likes of Damnus, Sammael and Merlin, as well as the Master, and I would make sure that his coronation would lead to a short period of monarchy.

I hadn't got time to give it more thought. I was taking Carin out for a meal this evening.

CHAPTER EIGHTEEN

Carin answered the door. She was one unhappy bunny.

"Where the hell have you been?"

She didn't realise how close to the truth she was.

"Sorry. Some unexpected business came up. I got here as quickly as I could."

She dragged me into the hall. "We're going out for dinner, in case you've forgotten. Wait while I get my coat."

Julius sauntered in from the lounge. "Good to see you, my boy."

I was baffled. Could this mild-mannered cleric really become a Damnus advocate? Being the suspicious sod I am, I flipped through his mind. Everything was normal.

Meg walked in, dressed up to the nines. She pecked me on the cheek.

"Julius is taking me out to celebrate your stumping up the restoration monies. I've made a bed up for you. You're not driving back to Grinton tonight."

Julius guided me into the lounge. "Fancy a sherry before you go?"

I wasn't given the chance.

Carin swept into the room. "Ready when you are." She blew a kiss at her parents. "Enjoy yourselves. See you later."

She put her hand against my back and pushed me out of the room.

Jude Carter lounged in his armchair. He lit a cigar and drew the smoke into his lungs. Jude hadn't a care in the world. His recently opened Mandies restaurant in Lovington's old marketplace had quickly gained the reputation of being the area's best eating house.

His eyes suddenly blanked out as he drifted into unconsciousness. A cloud of vapour tumbled down his nostrils and drifted to the ground. Merlin materialised in front of him. He sat himself down.

"Listen to me, Carter. My son and daughter are eating in your restaurant this evening. His name is Kit Milner. I have placed an image of him in your mind, as well as one of me. You are going to liven their evening up, and remind him that I am still around. You will hate Milner's guts from the moment you see him. I will arrange for four young men to get in touch with you, so they can help you make my son's evening miserable. Sit them at a table close to where Milner is sitting. This is what you are going to do." Merlin put his hands on Jude's head and forced his thoughts into his mind. He cackled to himself, "My son will read your mind to find out why you have ruined his evening. That is when he will see my image."

Merlin vanished and Jude woke up. He drew on his cigar as if nothing had happened.

Mandies was heaving. We eased our way to the bar and ordered drinks from a surly-looking man. He didn't say a word, contenting himself by throwing dirty looks at me. A young waitress showed us to our table.

I sat Carin down and nodded towards the man. "Look at that great lump of misery. Did you see the looks he was giving me? He doesn't seem to like me. Goodness knows why."

"Forget him. Nothing's going to spoil our evening." She gave me a full-blooded kiss and whispered in my ear, "He's probably jealous of the company you're keeping."

Even a blind man could see that she was head over heels in love with me. How does a fellow know? Is it the things she says, the words she uses, or the way she says them? Perhaps it's in her body language, the look in her eyes or the way she flaunts herself. My stunning girl ticked all of those boxes.

She stared into my eyes. As they sucked me in, my senses wallowed in a limpid pool of wanton happiness. The words she whispered made me tremble. "I can't wait to make love to you tonight." She realised what she had said, and shivered and blushed at the same time.

Some whispered words I wasn't supposed to hear floated over from a nearby table. My oversensitive hearing honed in on them as if they'd been shouted at me. "That's Milner, sitting with the red-headed bird."

I casually looked around me. A bald guy was talking to his three mates. Their eyes gave them away. They were as pissed as newts.

One of them stood up and muttered to the bald one, "The knobhead's staring at us. I'm going to stick one on him."

Baldy grabbed the guy's arm. "Sit down and shut up. He'll get what's coming to him when I'm ready."

Carin kicked me under the table. "Why can I hear everything they're whispering, as if they were shouting at me? Let's go. That lot mean trouble."

One of her latent powers had shown itself.

I made light of it. "I heard every word, too. They're drunk. Don't worry. I can handle them if they cause trouble."

I eyeballed them.

Baldy yelled at me, "What are you staring at, dickhead?"

The other diners looked uncomfortable. I muttered a few words to cast a calming effect over them. They visibly relaxed and carried on eating as if the shouting match was a normal part of their evening.

I stood up. "If you don't know what you are, Baldy, then I'd better tell you. You're a drunken cretin with a big mouth and no taste in friends."

I got a round of applause from the other diners.

Carin yelled at me, "Have you lost your marbles? We're getting out of here." She snatched her handbag and got up.

I pushed her gently back into her chair and whispered in

173

her ear, "Sit down, and enjoy yourself. Everything's under control."

My words had the desired effect. She waved at the four yobs.

That was too much for them. Baldy got up and lurched towards me, with the other three swaying in his wake. I stopped them in their tracks with a single thought, and trawled through their brain cells. The four of them were consumed with a manic desire to punch my head in. I picked up an image of the bar-slob chatting to them. Was he the sod who had put them up to this? If so, why?

Baldy reacted to another thought I threw into his mind.

He turned to his mates. "Sit down, lads. The fun's over. Milner's an OK guy." He shouted across to Carin. "Sorry for what I said, lady. It was the drink talking."

Carin raised her glass to him.

He walked over and shook my hand before making a mock bow to the other diners. "Sorry, guys. Hope we haven't spoilt your evening."

He obviously hadn't, because the diners clapped their hands.

The bar-slob hurried across to our table and glared at me with a beery, dirty look plastered across his face.

He leaned on the table and hissed at me, "I'm Jude Carter. I own this place. You and the cow, get out of here."

I forged a link with his mind. Like the four yobs, he was showing a manic dislike of me. A fleeting, smirking image of Merlin brought me out in a cold sweat. The sorcerer waved at me. What the hell was he doing in this guy's mind? I swore at myself for being so stupid. It was Merlin who had arranged what was happening. I recovered my composure and glowered at him.

"Why the hurry to get rid of us?"

"You're upsetting my customers, that's why."

I snapped back, "It wasn't us causing the problem. It was that lot over there. You put them up to this, didn't you?"

He was stressed out. It showed in his flinching eyes and the beads of perspiration running down his face. He was a stocky, medium-sized bloke, probably in his early forties. His body had gone to seed. The paunch hanging over the top of his trousers had been nurtured on a diet of too much fatty food and alcohol. He nestled his forehead against mine. His breath stank of cigars. I wasn't sure what to do with him. The poor sod was a blameless sucker.

He grinned at me. "What if I did put them up to it? Do you want to make something of it?"

Carin put in her twopenny-worth. "Don't take it out on us. You didn't hear what those yobs—"

The ratbag yelled at her, "Keep out of this, you stupid bitch. I'm talking to Milner, not his shagging machine."

Carin shoved her face into his. "Nobody speaks to me like that. Apologise, or else."

She got warm applause from the other diners.

The goon leered at her. "Or else what?"

Carin banged the table.

He smiled at her and kissed her hand. "I apologise for the misunderstanding." He walked over to where the four yobs were sitting. "Out of here, you lot. I'm not having you upsetting my customers."

They got up and left the restaurant without a word. I had been watching Carin's face. Her lips were mouthing every word that Jude Carter had said.

He returned to our table. "I'm sorry for what I said." She was still putting the words into his mouth. "Your meal's on me, as well as a free bottle of wine."

I couldn't help smiling. Another of her father's latent gifts had surfaced. She had a twitchy, self-satisfied look on her face.

She knocked back her drink, then whispered in my ear, "How did I manage that? He spoke the words I was mouthing. I saw you smile. You know what's going on, don't you?" She was reacting as I would have expected Merlin's daughter to have done, cool and calm.

"If I promise to tell you on the way home, can we get on and enjoy our evening?"

She nodded her head.

I had no intention of telling her. The time wasn't right to

175

wean her on her special gifts. I made the excuse that I was off to the little boy's room. In the shelter of a cubicle, I time-travelled to a few minutes before we'd arrived at Mandies. Jude was behind the bar. In my invisible state, I sidled up behind him and got into his mind. I removed Merlin's planted thoughts and threw in two of my own: 'You're going to lay on the entertainment that I've suggested, as well as a free bottle of wine for every table.'

I sidled over to where the four yobs were sitting. It took seconds to cleanse their minds and feed them a thought that they'd be entertaining the other diners later in the evening.

I returned to the present time and rejoined Carin.

As I sat down, Jude clapped his hands. "Can I have your attention, folks. I'm giving a free bottle of wine to each table, as a thank-you for coming this evening."

Everyone cheered the good news.

Jude picked up my mental prod and walked across to us.

"Good evening, guys. I'm Jude Carter. I own this place." He shook my hand and kissed Carin on the cheek. "Have you chosen your starters, and what wine would you like?"

We gave him our order.

Jude smiled at us. "Is there anything else?"

I asked if he'd got any entertainment arranged for the diners.

He tapped the side of his nose with a finger before speaking my mentally scripted words. "You'll have to wait and see, won't you?"

Carin and I jawed our way through a three-course meal, supping Jude's freebie wine. The food was good, the company even better.

Carin held my hands across the table and sighed. "I hope Mummy and Daddy are enjoying their evening as much as I'm enjoying mine." She frowned. "There won't be any problem in getting the monies for the church, will there?"

"Don't worry. Your father will get the loot. As a matter of interest, has he ever thought of playing the lottery?"

"He's not a betting man. End of story, Kit."

"Well, I feel lucky. I'm having a flutter next week. If I win, it means your father will get his money sooner."

She let out an expansive sigh. "You're an optimist."

Our coffees arrived, and the matter was dropped.

It was time for the cabaret to get under way. I threw my prepared words into Jude's mind, and the minds of the four lads.

Jude clapped his hands and yelled out, "Tonight is a first, folks. Not only are you drinking my profits away, but I've arranged some entertainment for you." He grinned. "The performers come at no expense, thank goodness. I hope you enjoy the routine."

He shouted at the four yobs, "Up on the stage, lads."

They waved their arms in the air before joining him. I hummed 'The Stripper' tune out loud, which was quickly taken up by the other diners.

The five of them reacted to the tune, and slowly took their clothes off, dancing in a larger-than-life comic manner. They stripped down to their underpants, then turned their backs on the diners, pulled their pants down and waggled a mixed bag of backsides. To tumultuous applause, they waved to their captive audience before picking up their clothes and running into a side room.

They appeared a few minutes later, to another round of applause. Jude bowed and made his way to our table.

He winked at Carin. "Did you enjoy the floor show?"

"It was a scream. Well done, you."

He looked chuffed. "I hope I'll see the pair of you again." He shook my hand and pecked Carin on the cheek before scuttling off.

Carin settled back in her chair, a contented look on her face. "What a nice guy! That was good of him to find the time to talk to us."

I teased her. "I think he fancies you."

She put her arms around me. "Whether he does or not doesn't matter. There's only room for one man in my life, and that's you." She grinned. "Mind you, if Daddy doesn't get his money, I might come back here on my own and get Jude to show me that dance routine in private."

CHAPTER NINETEEN

Carin's parents were still out when we arrived back at the rectory. I felt shattered.

"Do you mind if I hit the hay? I've had a hectic few days. I'm really pooped."

She cupped my face in her hands and gave me a mega-kiss. "You must be tired if you're turning down the chance of making love to me later on. You go up. I'll wait for Mummy and Daddy."

I winked at her. "Who said I didn't want to make love to you? Wake me when you come up. A nap will recharge my batteries."

My sleep pattern was disturbed by someone slipping into bed beside me. Her perfume hit my senses and drove all thoughts of sleep away.

She wrapped her legs around me and whispered in my ear, "I've come to cure that lingering pain in your groin. I'm convinced a massage will do the trick. If the symptoms come back, I'll give you a repeat prescription."

Our long sensual lovemaking satisfied our cravings. I cradled her in my arms, feeling the comforting warmth of her body against mine.

She gently pushed me away. "I'd better get back to my room – I don't want Daddy catching us in bed together. It won't always be like this, I promise."

Carin returned to her room and opened the drawer of her bedside cabinet. She took out a packet of morning-after pills, and smiled at Kit's concern that she might have a baby. Her body suddenly stiffened and she fell back on to the bed, into a deep sleep.

The bedroom door opened and Merlin walked in. A white vapour drifted from Carin's nose, and Emeralda appeared beside him.

She smiled at him. "Our daughter carries a fertilised egg in her womb, My Lord."

Merlin nodded. "Good. Damnus's plans are back on track. Place her egg in your womb."

A stream of red vapour poured from between Carin's legs and disappeared under Emeralda's dress.

He put his hands on Carin's head and muttered a few words. "I have wiped from her mind what just happened to her. Sit her on the bed, then we can return to our own time."

Their bodies shimmered and they were gone. Carin picked up the pack of pills and swallowed one. She turned the light off and went to sleep.

Michael and Azurina were watching Merlin's antics. She looked grim.

"This isn't fair. Can't we do anything to help our son?"

Michael grunted. "I made the same point at yesterday's meeting with Magnus. He's still insistent on letting Damnus dream the dream before he spoils his celebrations. Our son mustn't upset the leader's plans, especially as everything is nicely on course." He pulled a face. "What's our son's biggest worry?"

"That's easy. He can't work out why Merlin and Emeralda are still alive."

He allowed himself a smile. "Whatever he does, he'll never kill them, because the crafty sod is using replicas of himself and his woman. When our son was a baby, Merlin planted a thought in our son's mind which will tell our son how Merlin has tricked him out of being killed, or so he'll believe. Merlin will release that thought any time now. There is some good news. Magnus will speak to our son after his third failed attempt at doing away with Merlin and Emeralda. Magnus is going to come clean as to what's really going on and what he wants our son to do. Are you happy with that?"

She pulled a face. "As happy as I can be, I suppose."

"Don't worry. Our son will get a big helping hand from Magnus once Damnus rules the world. He'll give our son a book and a sealed scroll. The book contains every conversation that Merlin has ever had with Sammael, Emeralda and his fellow plotters, so he'll know what's been going on behind his back over the years. As for the scroll, it's a powerful weapon that will do away with Damnus and his lot. You needn't worry. Raphael will sort them out. So he should do, with his own sorcery and the powers in the scroll."

Merlin and Emeralda materialised in the main bedroom of his castle. He ran his fingers over her swollen stomach and smiled. "Your sorcery is working well. Are you ready to give birth to our daughter's children? I have two women waiting outside to help you."

She nodded. "Bring them in."

The two women slipped into the room, carrying towels and containers of hot water. They stripped her naked and laid her on the bed. Merlin knelt by her side.

"I will be back soon, my dear."

When he returned, a screaming baby boy lay on the bed. He ushered the two women out of the room. They held their hands out, expecting a few coins. Merlin grunted and clicked his fingers. Their bodies broke down into nothingness. He hurried into the bedroom and stood over Emeralda.

"I have done away with the women, to keep their mouths shut. I will help you give birth to the rest of our daughter's babies."

He pulled more babies from between her legs until twelve wailing baby boys lay on the bed. He looked unhappy at the noise they were making.

"Stop them crying, and age them to their eighteenth year. Make sure you fill their minds with the knowledge that lies in your mind, as to what Damnus expects of them."

A flurry of words spouted from her mouth. The babies vanished, and twelve men dressed in black cassocks stood around her. They bowed to Merlin.

He spoke to them. "You have been born on sixth-century earth. Our names, and details of who we are, are sealed in your minds. You will treat us as your parents until you meet your real mother and father one day. Which of you is the firstborn?"

One of them raised his hand.

"I name you Belial, but you will be called the Master. Before I name the rest of you, there is a ritual to perform."

He sliced his thumb open with a dagger, then, one by one, he cut the young men's thumbs and mingled his blood with theirs. The sorcerer held his bloodied thumb in the air. The cut healed in front of their eyes. They looked at their own thumbs and gasped in amazement.

Merlin smiled. "As you see, your wounds have also healed. You now share my blood, so my magical powers and beliefs lie rooted in your minds. Over the next few weeks, I will unlock your gifts of sorcery and teach you how to use them. We will shortly travel through time to a dwelling place in the twenty-first century. It is from there that we will launch Damnus's crusade into the world. Let us be on our way."

They appeared in a large room. The lighting failed to bring any cheer to the black-painted walls and ceiling. Furnishings were scant – just a long wooden table and chairs set down one side of the room. The table was laden with food and wine. A black-painted altar stood against the opposite wall.

Merlin seated himself at the head of the table with Emeralda by his side. He invited the young men to sit down.

"This is Dalbury Manor. Everything you need is here. You have beds, washrooms and food, and I will provide you with the clothes that people wear in this century." He pointed at the altar. "We also have the means of showing our loyalty and devotion to Damnus. You will venerate him twice a day. Once every month, a woman will be sacrificed on that altar, when you will drink her blood and swear your allegiance to Damnus. Before we eat and drink, I have a question to ask. Why are we here?"

The Master stood up. "I have the answer, Lord Merlin. We are here to bend the minds of mankind into worshipping Lord Damnus. Through our efforts, his as yet unborn son will be crowned King of the World. All other religions will wane as we use our sorcery to ensnare the minds of people, to ensure that Damnus's dream becomes a reality."

His brothers clapped his words and nodded their heads.

Merlin couldn't hide his pleasure. "Sit down, Master. The words you have spoken prove that all of you were born with my thoughts in your minds." He banged his fist on the table. "This is how we will achieve Lord Damnus's vision, with his son at our helm. We will travel the length and breadth of the world, befriending monarchs, presidents, tyrants and politicians, as well as the heads of the armed forces, the police and secret services. We will win them over to our cause, together with the leaders of every religious faction. There is an easy way for you to gather them into our beliefs, without fear of resistance." He smiled. "Words alone would never achieve this end. I will teach you how to use your sorcery to sow Damnus's desires into people's minds, where they will lie forever. It would take a lifetime for the twelve of you to harvest the whole of civilisation to his cause." He banged the table again. "We cannot wait that long. We will bring the people of earth to their knees in just five years from now. I will use my sorcery to produce tens of thousands of living replicas of you all, to help us in our work. If that number is not enough, then I will create even more."

The Master looked puzzled. "It would not be possible for us to meet every citizen on this planet and place Lord Damnus's thoughts in their minds. How do we convert them to his creed?"

"Your thoughts come easily, Master. There is a way of converting the lower orders of society to his creed. In the twenty-first century, mankind has the means of reaching the eyes and ears of people all over the world. Man has created something called television. We will use this device to capture people's minds by way of sorcery, to win them over to our cause. We also have another weapon in our armoury – a magical water which I have named the Damnus brew. A few drops of this brew, placed in the water that nations drink, will take over people's minds, and will force them to bend the knee to Damnus." Merlin picked up a goblet of wine. "Let us drink to our domination of the world, and the forthcoming birth of Damnus's son."

They quaffed their wine, then shouted, "Damnus!" at the tops of their voices.

"Whilst you eat your meal, I have a task to carry out, which involves my traitor son. He has decided to oppose our cause."

They all burst out laughing.

"I know why you are amused. You are picking up my thoughts. I will provide him with the answer as to why he twice failed to kill me and Lady Emeralda. When he tries to do away with us for a third time, I will trick him again. He will finally be convinced that he has succeeded in doing away with us, so we can carry on with our work without any further interference from him. Lady Emeralda and I will travel back to the sixth century. Once there, I will release a thought that has lain dormant in his mind since he was born. It will provide him with the answer as to why he hasn't killed us on two occasions."

They all laughed out loud.

Merlin quietened them. "Wait here until we return."

The two of them held hands and disappeared from the room.

Sleep eluded me after Carin had returned to her room. How could I sleep, knowing that Merlin was on the loose somewhere? How the hell had he and Emeralda twice escaped being killed by me? That's when an answer burst through the grey murkiness swirling around inside my head. It was so simple. If I was right, I had to admit to a tad of admiration at the simplicity of how the crafty sod had fooled me. I couldn't wait to put my thought to the test.

I launched myself back to the sixth century. Seconds later, I was stood inside that same stone building in a state of invisibility. Merlin and Emeralda were canoodling on the bed. I looked out of the window. The same stag and fawn that I'd seen before were standing outside. My thoughts came into play as to how he had tricked me. He had somehow known I was on my way, and had hidden their souls in the two animals moments before I'd killed them. It didn't take me long to carry out my sham killing of them. I made myself visible and walked outside. The stag bellowed at me. I trumped Merlin's game by shouting a spell that turned their souls into dust, before snuffing out the life of the two animals with my killing ray. The agonising sounds spewing from the animal's mouths proved my brainwave was right. They weren't animal sounds, but the screams of Merlin and Emeralda. The animals burst in a cloud of dust as a crackling white beam of light enveloped their bodies. I was delighted, knowing I'd done away with the evil pair forever.

I returned to the rectory and nestled down in my bed, delighted in the knowledge that Carin and I would be guiding our own footsteps from now on.

CHAPTER TWENTY

The three of us sat at the breakfast table, displaying varying degrees of body language. Meg scurried around, tending to the needs of our stomachs. Julius was immersed in silent thought, his blank eyes staring into space. Carin tackled her breakfast as if she hadn't eaten for a week. I felt shattered, and picked at my food. The traumatic exertions of the past weeks and the pleasing intrusion into my sleep pattern last night were responsible.

Julius coughed and returned to the land of the living. "You look tired, Kit. Didn't you sleep well?"

Carin gave me a warning look. "Don't worry about him, Daddy. He's fine."

He clicked his tongue. "Why do women take it on themselves to speak for everyone else? Let the boy tell me himself."

"She's right, Julius. I'm OK. Just a little crumpled around the edges. I've been burning the candle at both ends."

Julius grunted.

I changed tack. "What are you up to today?"

He rolled his eyes. "A day of awesome pleasure awaits me. I'm meeting up with the archdeacon. He's a nice fellow, and his wife makes a passable fruit cake. We'll be discussing which contractors to use for our restoration work once you stump up the money."

Carin giggled. "Kit has a second foolproof money plan, haven't you?" She poked her tongue out at me. "It's his quick fix to solving your money problems."

"Your daughter is taking the rise out of me. I thought we might have a shot at the lottery, if it doesn't offend your religious beliefs." A little lie tripped out. "This would be a quicker route than getting the money from my contacts. I don't hold out much hope, but what harm is there in trying?"

He had the courtesy not to laugh in my face.

"A fat chance you stand. The idea doesn't offend me. Do what you like, my boy." He couldn't resist a passing shot. "In case we should win, I don't want any publicity." He got up. "I'd best be off. Will we see you this evening?"

"No. I've got some catching up to do at work. I'll be burning the midnight oil."

"OK. I'll see you when I see you."

Meg gave me an old-fashioned look. "Not hungry, young man?" She shot a quick glance at Carin. "My mother would have said that you two are an item."

Carin blustered and blushed at the same time. "Mummy! What a thing to say!" She looked at her watch. "Time I was away. I've got a nine-thirty surgery." She kissed her mother, paused at the door, and beckoned me with her hand.

I got the message.

"I'd better be off as well."

We said our goodbyes on the drive with a full-blooded kiss. I asked if we could get together on Saturday evening. She squeezed me in the groin.

"It seems a long time to wait, but I'll get through."

I drove back to the auction premises. My first port of call was Martin Henderson. I knocked on his office door and walked in. He was sat behind his desk. A Cheshire-cat grin creased his face.

"Didn't expect to see you so soon. You're still on holiday, or so I thought."

"It didn't take as long as I thought to sort my business out."

"I'm glad you're here. I want you to take the auction in the posh-room on Saturday."

That caught me off guard. Martin had always looked on the posh-room as his sole domain.

"It'll be good experience for you. I want to find out what you're made of. It's a sod of a room to get the punter's money, especially at a general sale, so it'll be a real challenge. If you manage to take the kind of money I do, I'll have a serious think about where you're heading for in the business."

I couldn't disguise my feelings. "I'm a bit overwhelmed. Thanks for your trust. I won't let you down."

He smiled, then waved me away.

I took the hint. "See you later, Martin."

I collected the list of sale items from the main office and ambled across to the posh-room. The tables and shelves were groaning under an assortment of modern wares and collectables, with a few antiques thrown in. Several dealers were sorting through the spoils. I heard Traffy Evans airing his Welsh knowledge on ceramics to a very disinterested Doris Goring-Hart.

The sound of china being rung floated through the air. Ding-a-Ling Yates was doing his rounds, ringing every piece of china with a spoon, checking for cracks. He held an overriding mania that china had to be perfect, whether it was made last week or 200 years ago.

I spent the day checking out every sale item. It was late afternoon when I caught up with Martin.

"There's a smattering of good gear in the posh-room. Can't see any problem in getting the sellers' reserves, even though a lot of it is rubbish."

From the thoughtful look on his face, I could see he was bursting to open up to me.

"Listen, Kit. I'm getting too old for this game. I've been giving it some thought. It's taken me forty years to come to the conclusion that I'm a silly old sod. I work my bollocks off every day, and get home feeling knackered. My wife asked me what it was all about last night." He beamed at me. "She's right for once. I should have made this decision years ago. I'm stepping back from the front line while I've still got some strength left in my drinking arm. I need a capable young feller to run things for me until I decide to retire. There'll be more money for the right guy." He slapped me on the back. "I wanted you to be the first to know."

I must have looked disappointed that the right guy didn't seem to be me.

He grinned. "Don't look like that, you great goof. You're the man for the job. As of this moment, you're head auctioneer, starting with next week's Fine Art Sale. After that, you can take over the reins as deputy boss man. I won't take no for an answer."

I felt overwhelmed at the responsibility he was placing on my shoulders, but I knew I could do the job.

"Thanks for having faith in me. I'm sure I can run things for you."

He wiped his face. Was he crying? I didn't get the chance to find out.

He gave me the elbow. "Let's leave it there, Kit. I've got work to finish."

I understood him wanting to get rid of me. He'd just terminated his ritual way of life, in passing the reins of his self-built business to someone else. His decision to give up Brine & Cherry hadn't been easy. The auction house had been put together with his sweat and hard graft. He'd have nothing else left in life once he retired, other than an understanding wife and copious amounts of gin.

"I'll lock up at the end of the day, Martin. See you tomorrow."

He grunted, without bothering to look up.

I checked everyone had left, before locking the saleroom, then padlocked the car-park gates. The memory of Billy Grodam running me down in that other life was rekindled. Thank God he'd never been born.

I rang Carin. We chatted for about ten minutes.

"Can't wait to see you on Saturday" were her parting words.

My pangs of hunger were satisfied by takeaway fish and chips, swilled down with a can of lager. I made myself at home on the sofa and nodded off. My dreams seemed to have dried up, and I had to be content with a man's voice that invaded my sleep.

His words were gentle and reassuring: "I am Magnus. You know who I am, from what your mother has told you. You will not be alarmed in hearing from me, because you share your father's gift of accepting the unexpected. I chose you to carry out my mission against my arch-enemy, Damnus, who is using Merlin to capture the minds of the people so that his unborn son can rule the world one day. Your most recent attempt to do away with Merlin has failed. Don't be concerned. That is the way I planned it to be. You will do nothing to stop Damnus from achieving what he wants.

"I could have stopped him myself, but I will reap more pleasure in snatching away everything he has achieved when the time is right. When I am ready, I will call on you to cast Damnus and his son, as well as Merlin and his cohorts, into oblivion. I will provide you with a sealed scroll, which will be the means of destroying them. It is the most powerful weapon I have. You have to accept that in doing away with them the scroll will also destroy your world, but you have the powers to resurrect it. I will guide you when the time comes. You will encounter one or two hurdles before that day arrives, but you will overcome them. Until I call on you, lead a normal life with your woman, and do not concern yourself with what is going on behind your back."

He was right. I wasn't at all fazed by what he had said. "I understand, Magnus. I will do what you ask. There's just one thing. Did Merlin trick me by using replicas of himself and Emeralda?"

The dream voice laughed. "You are right. As you know, you can create replicas as well. There is one difference between your replicas and Merlin's. Yours have blood in their veins, and beating hearts. Merlin's do not. That is the key to finding out whether you are dealing with replicas or the real thing."

I woke with a start. The thought that Merlin was alive didn't go down well with me, but I vowed that I would do what Magnus had asked of me. That wouldn't stop me from watching out for signs of what they were doing. Magnus was right. I had inherited my father's gift of not letting anything in life worry me.

CHAPTER TWENTY-ONE

After a relaxed breakfast on Saturday morning, I collected my papers from the main office and walked into Martin's office. He was sat on his radiator, cup of coffee in hand.

"Everything ready in the posh-room, Kit?"

"No problems. There's not much quality stuff. I hope we've got better gear for the Fine Art Sale, seeing it's my first one."

"Don't worry about that. My solicitor friends have been over-kind to me. Clients' house clearances will be winging their way to us next week."

I looked at my watch. "I'd better be off. I've a few things to check out."

He raised his cup. "Best of luck, Kit."

I kept myself busy right up to the start of the auction. On the stroke of eleven I swept into the saleroom, mounted the rostrum and gave an exaggerated bow, to the deafening sound of cheers and applause.

"Thank you. It feels good to be taking my first auction in the posh-room. That doesn't mean you can take advantage of my good nature." I ignored their cries of shame. "Have you all got a bidding number? If you haven't, go and get one. I won't accept a bid without a number." Everyone frantically waved their bidding slips at me. "Well done. Let me remind you, if you pick your nose or scratch your face – or scratch anything else, for that matter – I'll take it as a bid."

This provoked good-humoured banter.

"I want no heckling, smoking, swearing or eating during the sale. Food and drink will be consumed outside. I'm the only person allowed to drink on the premises." I toasted them with my glass of water.

There were a few ribald cheers.

"Let's get the auction under way."

My feeling for auctions hasn't changed from the first day I got into the act as a porter. Auctions have a captivating quality, where everyone is transported on to another plane. The air becomes supercharged with frenetic particles of energy, released from the frenzy of bidding, as the punters do their utmost to outbid each other.

Most of today's goods fell into the 'junk' pigeonhole, with no reserve tag on them. That made no difference to the punters. As the sale went on, they were carried away, paying over-the-top prices for under-the-top goods. I sailed through the auction, and finally banged the gavel down for the last time.

Martin looked at me with expectation as I walked into his office. "How did it go, then?"

"Very good prices, bearing in mind how naff most of the stuff was."

The pound signs flickered in his eyes. He got up and patted me on the shoulder. "Well done, you. I'll be off, then. As the future boss, you can shut up shop." He poked me in the chest and grinned. "Don't forget to lock the safe after you put the takings away."

My staff had balanced the books by five o'clock. I put the monies in the safe and remembered to lock it. Arthur Horne was lurking in the posh-room when I went to lock up.

"I've locked the unsold lots in the storeroom, Kit." He took his flat cap off and scratched his head. "Don't know how you did it. All that crap, and only two lots didn't sell."

"Thanks, Arthur. The punters were behind me. I hope my first Fine Art Sale goes as well."

"So do I. See you Monday, Kit."

I rang Carin from the flat. "Hello, beautiful. It's me. Would your mother mind if I slept over, tonight?"

"Hold on. I'll ask her." She was soon back. "No problem."

"Thanks, darling. I'm on my way. See you soon."

I changed into my casual gear, threw my pyjamas and toiletries into a bag and sped off towards Lovington. Carin greeted me as if she hadn't seen me for years. A mischievous smile lit up her face.

"Mummy asked me, again, if you and I are an item. Are we?"

"What do you think?" I kissed the tip of her nose. "We're more than an item – we're inseparable."

"I feel the same way about you. Isn't it time we put Mummy out of her misery?"

"Good idea, so long as it stops her from giving me those funny looks."

Her parents were in the kitchen.

I took hold of Carin's hand and kept my words short and sweet. "We would like to get engaged. Do we have your blessing?"

Julius nearly shook my arm out of its socket. Meg pushed him out of the way and hugged me. Her finger was on the pulse of our relationship.

"When are you going to make an honest woman of her, Kit?"

I managed a rare blush. "All in good time."

She laughed. "I'm not pressing you. We're delighted to have you in the family." Meg frantically waved at Julius. "Dinner's on the table, man. Pour us a glass of wine, so we can toast the happy couple."

After dinner, we sat in the lounge, enjoying the warmth of the log fire. The memory of Carin seducing me in front of it stirred in my mind.

Julius drove those delicious thoughts away. "How did the auction go?"

"Very well, seeing it was mainly junk. We'll be selling the best gear at next Saturday's sale. I had one bit of unexpected news yesterday. The boss wants me to run the business when he retires."

Julius's eyes sparkled. "Congratulations. Carin tells me she's going to your next sale. Perhaps she'll buy something really valuable for a pittance. We could sell it on at Christie's and save you finding the money for the church restoration fund." He laughed. "I'm only joking."

With an overdone flourish, I pulled a lottery ticket out of my pocket. "Don't worry. I keep telling you. You'll get your money. In the meantime, I'm having a bash at next Wednesday's lottery with this Thunderball ticket."

My words went down like a lead balloon. They all groaned.

Carin hit me round the head with a cushion.

"What a waste of a pound!"

Julius finally controlled his laughter. "She's right. The odds are stacked against you."

"It won't do any harm to try. All I need is six numbers."

Julius threw his arms about in exasperation. "You're not going to win. You want six numbers, you say? Make it easy for yourself and use the numbers one to six. Let's forget it, shall we?"

The church restoration dominated the rest of the evening.

Meg finally clapped her hands. "I think we've had enough church chat for one evening. I'll make us a bedtime drink."

Bedtime rolled around. I slipped between the covers and waited. An hour later the door opened and Carin eased into bed beside me. Our lovemaking didn't disappoint.

She whispered in my ear, "How was it for you?"

"It gets better and better. I still hope you won't get pregnant."

"You worry too much. I told you I won't."

Monday was the beginning of five days' hard labour, preparing for Saturday's sale. The posh-room filled up with fine period furniture, smaller antiques and collectibles, as lorry after lorry unloaded its bounty. All the signs pointed to a bumper crop of mouth-watering temptations for our discerning buyers. More deliveries were due, adding a host of further riches for inclusion in the sale.

Martin was full of himself. "Have you seen what you're flogging on Saturday? The profits from that lot should help me through my retirement years." He waggled a finger at me. "If you want good tat, keep your solicitors happy. Drop the Queen's currency into their grubby little hands. If you don't, they'll take their chattels elsewhere. End of story."

"OK. OK. I get the message. Bribe them like buggery and they'll deliver."

He laughed. "You're a callous sod, but you're dead right."

I held my hand over my heart. "I swear I'll keep your supply lines open. I don't want you on the phone, complaining that your company pension doesn't cover your gin bill any more." I waved the sale catalogue at him. "This is terrific. Have you had any reaction from the punters?"

"It's been sent to everyone on our client list. I've had phone calls from all over the country. Even had two chaps phone me from America. They'll be bidding by phone, so have people standing by to take their phone bids. There's a lot riding on your shoulders."

"By the way, my girlfriend's coming to the auction."

"You're a bloody quiet one. Didn't know you had one. Where does she come from?"

"Lovington. It's taken me a long time to find the right girl, but she's the one."

"When are we going to hear the sound of wedding bells?"

"We haven't got that far. When we do, I won't need to look around for a church. Her father's got his own. He's the local rector."

He laughed. "I expect an invitation." Two vans trundled by the window. Martin rubbed his hands together. "More chattels from our solicitors. You'd better go and check them out."

Five o'clock came round and everyone disappeared. I was well satisfied with the day's work. Every item had been logged. The rest of the week would be spent putting every lot in its rightful place and preparing the paperwork.

I wandered into the local newsagent and took the Thunderball ticket out of my pocket. I couldn't help smiling. It would be one in the eye for the Milner doubters when it won. I took the rector at his word and used the numbers one to six. My thinking went one step further. She didn't know it, but Meg was going to win the Lotto jackpot.

I handed my Thunderball ticket to the shop assistant. She fed it into the machine and took my money.

I returned home and put my lottery ideas into motion. Winning the Lotto would be a doddle compared with getting my hands on the Thunderball top prize. It was too easy. I time-travelled forward in time to late Wednesday evening. It was child's play making a note of the winning Lotto numbers from the television results show. The voice-over revealed there had been no winning ticket for the £8-million rollover prize. Meg was on her way to becoming pigging rich.

My Thunderball numbers hadn't won; nor had anyone else's. I aimed to change that by applying my special talents on Wednesday evening. My time-travelling wasn't finished. I travelled back to Monday afternoon. Meg was in the rectory kitchen. In my invisible state, I planted my instructions in her mind. She was to buy a Lotto ticket for the coming Wednesday, using the winning numbers that I placed in her head, but she wasn't to tell Julius what she'd done until I prompted her on Wednesday evening. I time-travelled back to my flat.

I was the only customer in the fish-and-chip restaurant that Monday evening. My mobile phone rang. It was Carin. She asked me what I was up to.

"I'm eating haddock and chips, if you really want to know."

"Talk about the life of Riley. You haven't forgotten I'm coming to the auction on Saturday, have you?"

"No, I haven't. Would it be OK if I come over, Wednesday evening?"

"That'll be fine. I'll tell Mummy." She laughed. "Have you invested your pound on the Thunderball winning numbers?"

"Less of the cynicism, young lady."

"Is that a yes or a no?"

"You don't give up, do you? Yes, I have. I've used the numbers one to six, as your father suggested."

Her laughter almost deafened me. "What a hopeless failed optimist you are! Don't worry. Even when you lose, I'll still love you."

"Don't be so dismissive. As the rector's daughter, you must believe in miracles? You're going to have to eat your words. I'll expect an apology as well as your body."

"Bloody hell! You're for real, aren't you? I've never met anyone like you. That's why I love you."

"Thanks, darling. You were worth waiting twenty-seven years for."

We chatted for another five minutes before she rang off.

Back at the flat, the damned lottery wouldn't let go of my mind. I began to have serious doubts whether I had the ability to influence the lottery balls. I eventually dismissed any idea of failure. It would have been easier to have used the winning Thunderball numbers that I'd seen in the future. That wasn't on. I wanted to win the top prize by using the rector's numbers. That would teach him a lesson for poking fun at me.

CHAPTER TWENTY-TWO

I spent Tuesday and Wednesday finalising the preparation for the Fine Art Sale. Arthur Horne and his porters worked their socks off, putting each lot in its rightful place, under my watchful eyes.

My own brief was simple. It was to sell everything at the highest possible price and produce a healthy profit margin for Brine & Cherry, as well as realising the vendor's reserve price.

At five o'clock on Wednesday afternoon I locked up. The Milners were in for a shock this evening. Their lives, and the future of St Leonard's Church, would be changed forever.

It was gone seven when I drew up on the rectory drive. Carin opened the front door. I got a kiss and a hug.

Meg shouted from the kitchen, "Sit down, Kit. I'm ready to serve."

The rector poured me a glass of wine while Meg put the meal on the table. He asked if I'd had a good week.

"It's been a hectic one, getting myself ready for Saturday's auction."

He lowered his voice. "Don't let Carin spend all her money. Doctors are very poorly paid, you know."

Carin showed mock hurt. "I won't be spending any money. The thought of bidding against other people frightens me to death." She looked at her father and winked at me. "I'm more at home poking my finger up a patient's backside."

Julius pulled a face. "You wouldn't think she was the rector's daughter, would you?"

I played along with him. "She's put me off my dinner, for a start."

She kicked me under the table. "I was talking as a doctor, not the rector's daughter. It's best you know what you're saddling yourself with."

Meg roared with laughter. "You've been put in your place, young man."

Julius brought things back to reality. "When are you two planning to get married, Kit? I'd be delighted to offer my services."

"I know you want your daughter out of your hair, but there are other things to consider. Where are we going to live? Does Carin want a family? What about her future as a doctor? My job prospects are about to take off, so I'll need to spend more time in the business. If we don't get married yet, it's not because we don't love each other."

The conversation was getting overly serious.

I looked around the room. "We could live here, Carin. It's not a bad place, once we redecorate." I grimaced. "We'll have to change that wallpaper, for a start. Perhaps we could build a granny flat in the back garden for Julius and Meg. I might even be prepared to pay them a small gratuity to look after us."

The seriousness of the evening vanished as they all roared with laughter.

Julius excused himself at the end of the meal. "I'll catch you later. I'm meeting up in church with my churchwardens."

Meg busied herself in the kitchen while we sat in the lounge.

Carin dug me in the ribs with her elbow. "When are you planning to buy me an engagement ring, or doesn't your salary run to that?"

"If you must know, I've seen a ring in the auction that'll blow your mind away. It's a bit of a cheek, but could I borrow one of your own rings to make sure it will fit your finger?"

"On one condition – that you slip this ring on my finger in

a candlelit setting. That's if you can afford the price of a meal after splashing out on this very expensive ring."

"OK. Fetch the ring, and I'll think about the meal."

She came back with it. I put it in my wallet for safekeeping. Meg came in with a tray of tea. The conversation became light-hearted, and we ended up watching television. The National Lottery came on in a blaze of computer images and loud music.

Carin nudged me. "Here's your moment of glory, I don't think. Got your ticket ready?"

I fed a thought into their minds to get them out of the room.

Meg groaned. "I'll be in the kitchen. I can't handle the sight of him crying when he docsn't win."

"Nor can I, Mummy. I've got some paperwork to do. I'll be in my bedroom."

I waved the Thunderball ticket at her. She stuck two fingers up in the air and waved them around.

The time for frivolity was over. I had to get my grey matter into working order if I was to influence the Thunderball result. It's a doddle controlling human minds. Forcing a machine to follow my bidding was a different proposition. Could I really send my selected numbers hundreds of miles through the ether and expect a machine to meekly react to what I demanded of it?

The lights and music faded away, and Roger, the voice-over, regaled our ears. "We're live at Lottery HQ. Thousands of people are going to win tonight, and some lucky person could get their hands on the Lotto double rollover jackpot of £8 million." He paused for maximum effect. "That someone could be you."

Vanessa Dyke, the presenter, set things in motion. "It's time for the Thunderball draw. Good luck, everyone. The dour-looking Draw-Master set the machine rolling, and Vanessa laid the ground rules. "To win the top prize of £500,000 you must match the five main numbers with the correct Thunderball number."

I concentrated like mad as the balls began to whirl around inside the machine. I closed my eyes and pictured the balls spinning around in my head. I isolated ball number one, and allowed it to run down the chute in my mind. My hands clenched in a concerted effort to speed my thought on its journey.

Roger radiated frenetic joy. "That's a good start. It's ball number one."

My stomach turned over. Had I really done the business, or was it a fluke? My mind intensified its efforts on bringing out ball number two.

"The next ball is number twenty-two."

My heart sank. Had my concentration been at fault? There was one way to find out. I travelled a minute back in time and waited until ball number one showed itself. Then I concentrated like mad on ball number two and waited for Roger.

"We have ball number two."

A feeling of elation flowed through me at the realisation that I was definitely influencing the balls.

Roger's voice faltered as the next ball rolled down the chute. "Number three has popped out. This is unbelievable. The balls are coming out in ascending order."

As the draw carried on, Roger was in danger of losing his marbles. "This has never happened before. The machine has chosen the numbers one to five, in that order." He thought on his feet. "I would remind viewers that the machine picks each number at random, under the watchful eye of the Draw-Master. There is no outside influence on which numbers are drawn."

Vanessa and the Draw-Master looked shell-shocked.

She got her mouth into working order. "Are we ready to start the bonus-number machine, Draw-Master?"

He nodded his head and set the machine in motion. The balls bobbled about inside my head. I focused on number six. A ball plopped into the slot on the television screen. I breathed a sigh of relief. Number six was staring at me.

Roger seemed to have lost his voice.

Vanessa got her act together. "Yet another ascending number. It's ball number six. I'll be surprised if anyone has picked those numbers." She flashed another of her smiles. "It's certainly been an exciting evening, and the Lotto draw is still to come. Join us shortly, when some lucky person could win £8 million. In the meantime, it's back to our game show with Dale Winton. See you soon."

Meg was still in the kitchen. I crept upstairs to Carin's bedroom. She was asleep on the bed. Back in the lounge, the lottery music struck up again. Lotto-time had arrived. The voice-over reminded us that £8 million was at stake. As Vanessa and the Draw-Master set things in motion, I sat back and relaxed; as Meg's numbers were drawn out, I bathed in the warm glow of success.

My conscience suffered an uneasy turn. Was I right in depriving other people of the chance of winning, by what amounted to cheating? My personal reasons for wanting the money overrode any feelings of right or wrong. St Leonard's Church needed money, and I was comfortable with the notion that a good part of Meg's Lotto winnings would be spent on people-worthy causes.

Vanessa put the show to bed. "Whether we have winners of the Thunderball and Lotto rollover will be revealed in our lottery update, later in the evening." She took a deep breath. "What an evening! Goodbye, and thank you for watching."

I switched the set off and crept upstairs. Carin was still asleep. I planted a thought in her mind, to come downstairs in five minutes, and did the same with Meg, to leave the kitchen. They walked into the lounge at the same time.

Carin was the first to pull my leg. "He doesn't look very happy, Mummy. I told him he stood no chance of winning the lottery, but he wouldn't listen."

Meg was more scathing. "He was never going to win with the numbers that Julius suggested, silly boy."

I let their words slip over my head. A necessary fib rolled out. "If you must know, I didn't watch the lottery show. I thought we'd catch the results show later, when Julius is here. If I haven't won, I know he'll want to have his moment of glory."

CHAPTER TWENTY-THREE

We spent the rest of the evening watching television and engaging in small talk. The peace was shattered by a hammering on the front door. Carin and Meg rushed out of the room. I was one step behind them.

A flustered looking man stared at them as Meg opened the door.

She shouted at him, "What's the matter, Kevin?" She turned to me. "It's Kevin King. He's one of our churchwardens."

I looked into Kevin's eyes. It took a split second to read his mind. I saw Julius walking down the tower steps. He stumbled, lost his balance and plunged headlong into space. His body rolled down the steps until he landed at the bottom. His head was twisted at an unnatural angle. I knew he'd broken his neck.

Kevin finally found his voice. "Julius has fallen down the tower steps. Get an ambulance, quick."

I was ahead of the game. I clapped my hands. Three faces went blank.

"Carin and Meg, go and sit in the lounge. Wait there until I get back. As for you, Kevin, I'll see you back in the past, but you won't see me."

I willed myself ten minutes back in time and ended up at the bottom of the tower steps. Julius's voice drifted down from above. I made my way up the steps and stood in front of him in my invisible state. He looked distinctly unhappy.

"It's going to cost us thousands to put that bell right. Our money problems are getting a damn sight worse."

That's when the silly bugger lost his footing. As he pitched forward, I gently pushed him back. He grabbed the handrail to steady himself.

Kevin King sounded relieved. "I thought you were a goner there, Rector. Are you all right?"

"I'm fine, Kevin. I lost my footing for a moment."

Meg and Carin were still in my induced trance when I returned. I sat down beside Carin and coughed. They carried on talking as if nothing had happened. It was gone ten o'clock when Julius came in. He wasn't in the best of moods. He threw a folder on the coffee table and plonked himself into an armchair. Meg asked how his evening had gone.

"Don't ask. My churchwardens are nice guys, but they have this unfortunate knack of being the purveyors of bad tidings." He pointed at the folder. "Our architect carried out his five-yearly inspection three weeks ago. That's a copy of his report." His sigh filled the room. "It's bad news, followed by more bad news. The font is crumbling away and the beams in the nave ceiling are falling apart. On top of that, one of the bells is damaged. We can say goodbye to another 5,000 non-existent pounds." He grinned at me. "Did you win the lottery?"

"We're waiting for the results show to check your numbers."

He laughed in my face. "A fat lot of good that will do."

He'd be laughing on the other side of his face later on. It was time to set Meg's mind in motion. I threw my thought her way.

She looked sheepish. "I hope you don't mind, Julius, but I broke our rule of a lifetime and bought a Lotto ticket."

"Well done, you. If it's good enough for smarty-pants, it's good enough for you." He shooed her out of the room. "Get your ticket. Let's see if you've won anything. The results show will be on soon."

Julius turned the box on. Meg came back with her ticket, and we all settled down.

A female voice-over was ready to take the nation through the draw results. "The Thunderball draw this evening was unique.

Consecutive balls were drawn. The winning numbers are one, two, three, four and five, and the bonus number is six. There is one lucky winner, who will receive £500,000."

They were dumbfounded until Julius suddenly came alive. He got up and wrapped his arms about me. "My dear boy! I'm sorry for everything I said about the lottery. How the blazes did my numbers win? This is wonderful. We've got the monies for the church repairs, with a lot left over." He thought on his feet. "I'm not having all of that money. The church can have £250,000. The rest is yours."

The four of us danced around the room, yelling at the top of our voices.

Meg kissed me. "Thank you, Kit. His worries are over, thank God."

I brought them down to earth. "Hold on a minute. The Lotto results are coming. Let's see if Meg has won anything."

Julius sat down with her ticket in his hand as the female voice confirmed the Lotto numbers. She ended by saying there was one lucky winner, who would receive £8 million.

Julius shook his head.

Carin put her hands on his shoulders and laughed. "Mummy didn't win, then? Never mind. You've got the church monies. There's no way we could have won twice in one evening."

He scrambled to his feet, an inane grin on his face. "The lottery's a game of chance, but good fortune can't ever have worked its magic like it has tonight. It's Meg who has won the £8 million." He embraced her. "You wonderful, wonderful woman! We're rich."

The four of us bounced around the room, whooping with pleasure, before we joined in a group hug.

Julius motioned us to sit down. "The money mustn't go to our heads. It's going to secure our future. St Leonard's will get a quarter of a million pounds, thanks to Kit, but I'll tell everyone that it's from an anonymous donor. As for Meg's win, the money won't change my lifestyle, and I don't want anyone to know that she's won. I'd like to carry on with my calling."

She clutched his arm. "Julius is right. Now the church has

got its money, we can live without the constant worry of that blessed restoration fund." She looked at me. "£8 million is a lot of money to win. I want you and Carin to have half of it. Is that all right with you, Julius?"

"Of course it is. If it hadn't been for Kit's enthusiasm for the lottery, I'm sure you wouldn't have bought your ticket."

Carin was over the moon. She kissed and hugged her mother. "Mummy! That's wonderful. Thank you very much."

Meg smiled. "That's the least I could do, darling. What will you and Kit do with the money?"

"It will go into a joint account, with Kit. As for me, I've always dreamt of having my own practice. Some of the money could make that dream come true. How about you, Kit?"

"Like you, I'm thinking about my future business life. A part of the money would come in handy for some plans I've got for Brine & Cherry, when I become the head honcho."

Meg looked worried. "Does that mean the end of your wedding plans?"

I answered for Carin. "We're only putting them on hold. All the money in the world can't change how I feel about her. We'll get married when the time is right. It's not far away, I'm sure. In the meantime, we might even buy a nice house and live together, if that doesn't offend the two of you."

They both smiled and nodded their heads.

Julius grinned. "Of course it doesn't, so long as you get married at some point in the future."

Carin purred her words out. "Kit's right. We've got the kind of relationship that could wait a lifetime. This money will strengthen our love, as well as helping us achieve our dreams."

We sat talking into the early hours before finally staggering off to our beds. Carin decided that we should sleep together all night.

Her last words before going to sleep were "Our future's made, Kit. You and I are going to enjoy a lifetime of happiness together." I muttered my agreement, even though I knew we only had a few years to go before I would be called upon to rid the world of the likes of Damnus, Sammael and Merlin. That didn't bug me. I'd put them to the back of my mind until that day arrived. The next few years would be all about achieving the dreams that Carin and I had, and I'd be keeping a close eye on Julius.

CHAPTER TWENTY-FOUR

It was back to work on Thursday morning. The office staff should have been thinking, and talking, Fine Art Sale. They weren't. The one topic of conversation revolved around the lucky bleeder who'd won the £8 million, and the jammy sod who'd scooped the Thunderball using bloody stupid numbers. The general feeling was that the money would be wasted on fast cars, holidays, designer gear and new houses. I took silent exception to their remarks. I wasn't intending to waste my share; a lot of it would be spent on the business, for their benefit. They were bloody lucky I was an honest guy. With my powers, I could have won the lottery week in and week out.

I pushed the lottery win to the back of my mind. Saturday's Fine Art Sale was my number-one priority.

Friday evening was manic at Mandies. A smiling Jude Carter stood behind the bar, barely keeping pace with diners' drink orders. A vacant expression suddenly covered his face.

He spoke to one of his staff. "Look after the bar. I'll be back in a minute."

He walked into his office, locked the door and sat down. Merlin appeared out of nowhere.

"Listen to me, Carter. I want you to travel to Grinton tomorrow, and attend an auction. Make sure you get there before it starts. The place is called Brine & Cherry. I have placed two items in the auction. All you have to do is to remember lot 159. That number is very important. It is a box of assorted trinkets. Kit Milner and his woman will be there. You will remember them from when they dined here recently. I have placed a picture of them in your mind, in case you have forgotten them. I want to make sure that she buys lot 159. Before she does, I will give you something to place inside that box. I will be guiding you on the day, inside your body."

Jude came to life after Merlin had gone, and returned to the bar.

No one was around when I unlocked the posh-room on Saturday morning. I walked across to the jewellery cabinet and took out a Victorian twenty-two-carat gold ring encrusted with diamonds. It had caught my eye when I'd first seen it. It would make a perfect engagement ring. I had already compared Carin's ring with the Victorian one, but it had been too large for her ring finger. It had been a simple matter to cradle both rings in the palm of my hand, then shake them like mad before thinking a mental instruction. The Victorian ring was now the same size as Carin's ring. It offends all the rules of auctioneering for an auctioneer to make a bid from the rostrum for his personal benefit. Someone would have to bid for me.

Arthur Horne strolled in. "Morning, Kit. Hope it'll be a humdinger of an auction. It needs to be, seeing it's your first Fine Art Sale."

"I'm glad you're here, Arthur. Are you free during the sale?"

He looked thoughtful. "I can be. Why?"

I took him across to the jewellery cabinet. "I want you to bid for that ring."

"Blimey. It's a stunner." The cheeky sod winked at me. "Who's the lucky girl, then?" He jotted the lot number down. "No problem, boss."

"Bid whatever it takes. I must have it."

"Will do. Listen. I didn't come in for pleasant conversation. Martin wants you in his office." He grinned. "A gorgeous girl with red hair is with him. I don't suppose the ring's for her, is it?"

He'd caught me on the hop. "I don't know what you're

talking about. I'll see you at the auction." I poked him in the chest. "Make sure you get that ring for me."

My feet couldn't get to Martin's office quickly enough. What the heck was Carin doing there? Martin's secretary winked at me and fluttered her eyelashes. Carin's voice floated though his office door as I pushed it open. Martin was slumped in his chair, hanging on to her every word.

She looked a million dollars, with her auburn locks tumbling over the collar of her red coat. Red shoes and cerise-coloured tights complemented the coat.

She turned around as the door squeaked open. "Hello, darling. We sent Arthur to find you. Martin has made me at home." She was behaving as if she'd known him for years.

Martin sighed at the mention of his name. "You're a secretive sod, Kit. You told me you had a girlfriend, but you didn't say how stunning she is."

Carin blushed.

I brought things back to normality. "I didn't think you wanted a full-blown description of what she looks like. If you'd asked me, I'd have told you what a stunner she is. When it comes to women, or work, I thought it was work that grabs your attention." I put my hand on her shoulder. "I'll show you around before the auction starts."

Martin waved us away. "I'll catch you later, Kit. Make plenty of money. Don't let Carin leave without saying goodbye to me."

I gave her an in-depth tour of the auction house. Martin contrived to cross our path three times, greeting her as if he hadn't seen her before. The daft bugger had even combed his untidy locks into place since we'd left his office.

We bumped into someone else we hadn't expected to see.

Carin gripped my arm. "Look, Kit. There's Jude Carter."

"So it is. We'd better say hello."

He looked genuinely pleased to see us. "Fancy seeing you here. It's good to meet you again. When are you coming back to Mandies for another meal?"

Carin looked thrilled. "We'd love to, wouldn't we, Kit?"

"We'll be along in the next couple of weeks, Jude. I didn't know you were interested in antiques. What are you looking for?"

"This is my first-ever auction. Someone told me you have some good furniture." He grinned. "I didn't realise you were the auctioneer."

"Listen, Jude. This is Carin's first auction as well. Why don't the pair of you sit together? I'll reserve a couple of seats in the front row, so you'll get a good close-up of me."

He laughed. "That'll be great. I'll catch up with you later."

I told Carin to have a nose around while I put 'Reserved' notices on their seats. When I came back she was peeking over Jude's shoulder as he picked up a lidded wooden box and delved into it. He made a note in his catalogue and moved away. Carin picked the box up and nosed around inside.

I joined her. She was looking at lot 159. I knew it was stuffed full of odds and sods that wouldn't appeal to many people.

I whispered in her ear, "Is there anything in the box you fancy?"

She put it down and shrugged her shoulders. "I don't think so."

The posh-room was filling up.

I showed Carin and Jude to their seats and excused myself. "I must get ready for my big entrance. I want no heckling from you two. As for you, Carin, don't spend all our money, there's a good girl."

Right on the dot of eleven I stepped on to the rostrum. A surge of excitement hit me. My adrenaline levels rose at the prospect of the cut-and-thrust bidding from the punters as they competed to buy quality goods. The door at the back of the room opened and Rick Adams walked in. He wandered around the shelves and picked up the box that Jude and Carin had poked around in. He shuffled the contents around, then put it back.

I thumped my gavel down. "Good morning, ladies and gentlemen, and anyone else." I treated them to my usual banter before offering the first lot.

Bidding didn't take long to warm up, and I was well satisfied with the money I was extracting from them. Lot 159 came under the hammer.

"I have an old wooden box full of assorted bits and pieces. Do I hear £20?"

The response was a sea of blank faces.

"£10, anybody?"

Rick stuck his arm up. "Yes, sir."

"Do I hear £12? If not, make no mistake, I'm selling it to Rick for £10."

I was about to knock it down when a female voice raised the stake to £12. Carin smiled at me, her hand held high in the air. Rick threw her a snotty look before bidding £15. Every time Rick pushed the price up, she countered it. The punters were enjoying the sight of Rick being outsmarted, especially by a young woman. After a few minutes of cut and thrust, he gave up. Goodness only knows why Carin was happy to pay £90 for a box of tat.

Rick suffered a tantrum. The prat muttered something under his breath and stormed out of the room, slamming the door behind him.

I ended the charade. "Well, folks, we have a winner, and we have a very bad loser."

Some of them voiced their agreement.

"In the absence of any other bid, I'm selling the box to the young lady for £90."

She earned a round of applause. All I got was a saucy wink and a blown kiss.

I nodded at her. "What's your bidding number?"

Carin pouted. "Sorry, darling. I haven't got one."

The punters who knew we were an item smiled sweetly. The rest wondered what kind of woman had the brass neck to call the auctioneer darling.

I took pity on her. "I can vouch for you, so I'll give you a number. If you decide to buy anything else, your number is 999, in case you need it in an emergency."

That brought the house down. Those who didn't know she

was my girlfriend smiled smugly, in the belief that this female smart-arse had been put firmly in her place. All I got from Carin was her tongue stuck out at me.

The rest of the auction went smoothly. Carin made no further bids, which helped. Arthur did the business, and bought the Victorian ring for me. It cost me 300 quid. Jude bought several items, paying a handsome price for the privilege. At the end of the day, I was well chuffed with the level of monies I'd taken. Even the few doubtful lots had fallen under the hammer. Everyone left the room to pay for their bits and pieces.

I still couldn't fathom out why Carin had lobbed out that kind of money for a load of tat. I emptied the contents of the box on to a table. In fairness, it was best-quality crap, except for a gentleman's gold signet ring. I looked at it under my magnifying glass. For what she'd coughed up, the Victorian eighteen-carat gold ring was very much underpriced.

I wasn't sure what the ring was doing in the box. I certainly hadn't come across it when I checked the box, but, in fairness, I hadn't checked the contents very thoroughly, thinking it was a load of tat. For a beginner, Carin wasn't as daft as I thought. Well done her. She'd got more than her money's worth.

I put the box back and strolled into the main office to make sure my staff were extracting money from the punters. Rick put in an appearance and paid for the couple of cheap items he'd bought.

That's when he let rip at my girl. "Who's the sodding bint who bought lot 159? I want words with her. Has she paid for it yet?"

My staff were well used to handling difficult people. "You know I can't give you that kind of info, Rick. If you've got a gripe, take it up with Kit Milner."

He gave her the evil eye. "Who do you think you're talking to, you stupid cow?"

She ignored him and turned to the next customer in the queue.

Rick pushed him back. "I'm not finished with her yet." He

grabbed hold of the girl's wrists. "Tell me the woman's name, you bitch."

I rushed outside and twisted his arm behind his back before frogmarching him to the main gate.

He ended up on the pavement with the rough edge of my tongue ringing in his ears. "I'm not having twats like you threatening my staff. You're banned from coming here. Do you understand?" I fished a £10 note out of my pocket and stuck it in his hand. "That's for what you paid out today. Now bugger off."

He got up. "I won't forget this, Milner. You made me look a right prick." He swore, then walked off down the road.

I was puzzled. Rick had always been a pain in the arse, but today's behaviour surprised me. With all his failings, he had never once shown violence.

I walked back to the main office. My girl was all right. She winked at me and mouthed a thank you. Martin was my next port of call. I told him about Rick, and what I'd done.

"You're the boss. I'd have banned him as well. We're not having our staff abused." He soon lost interest. "How did the sale go?"

"It went well." I cussed myself. Why was I embroidering the truth? "It went better than well. I worked my bollocks off to get good prices that weren't always there. Everything got sold. The commission I made will pay everyone's salary for the month and all our other overheads, and that includes the large payment into your pension pot, and there will still be money left over. When do I get that salary increase for the extra work I've taken on?"

He was gobsmacked. "Uhm! I'm glad you mentioned it. I was going to have a chat with you about it."

What a liar he was, but a good one!

"Until I retire, you'll get another 5,000 a year. When you take over, in a few months, you can set your own salary. What do you say?"

If he'd said, "Sod off," I'd have been happy.

"That's very generous, Martin. I accept."

He looked relieved. "I'll put it in place next week."

"I'll get back to the posh-room and leave you in peace."

Carin's voice floated in from the next room. "Hello, Arthur. Lot 159, please."

Arthur Horne walked in and winked at me. "Have you given her the ring yet?"

"Not a word to her, Arthur. Tell her I'll see her in the coffee shop in about ten minutes' time."

She was being chatted up by three of our regular male dealers when I walked into the coffee shop. Talk about bees buzzing around a honeypot. They said their goodbyes and I sat down with her. We were the only ones left.

She grinned at me. "I enjoyed the auction. You were superb."

"I'm really pleased you came. You lit the place up. And that's not all. You bought something. Wasn't £90 a bit over the top for that box of rubbish?"

"I just felt I had to buy it, no matter what the cost."

"With £4 million on the way, you can afford it. You were showing all the symptoms of a first-time buyer. You all tend to let your mouth run away with your brain. Have you looked at what you bought?"

She picked up a carrier bag, and took the box out. "Not yet, I haven't. I bet you've had a gander at it."

I shouldn't have felt guilty, but I did.

"Part of my job is to check any lot that attracts a higher bid than it deserves. I like to think you noticed the gold ring when you raked the contents around."

"Of course I knew it was there. That's why I bid for it." She took on a cagey look. "What's it worth?"

"Do you really want to know?"

She nodded.

I played her along. "It's not worth what you might think."

She looked disappointed.

"What if I said between £100 and £150?"

She was over the moon. "Are you kidding me?"

"I'm afraid I am."

Her face dropped.

"It's worth between £250 and £300."

"Wow! That's fantastic."

I kidded her. "What are you going to do with it? Why don't you put it in my next Fine Art Sale and make a profit?"

She played me along. "While I'm thinking about it, how about a coffee and a piece of sponge cake?"

I ordered the coffee and cake. "I'll be back in a couple of minutes. I need to see Arthur before he signs off."

Carin sat drinking her coffee, when Rick Adams walked in. He rushed over to her.

"I want that bloody box, you cow. Give it to me."

He made a grab at the carrier bag. She was too quick for him, and pushed it under the table. He pulled her out of her chair and pinned her against the wall. As he raised his fist to hit her, she mumbled some words under her breath. Rick's body froze. She brought her knee up and exploded it between his legs. He groaned and rolled around the floor, his body doubled up in pain. He somehow managed to drag himself up and staggered across to the serving counter, where he picked up a knife.

"You bloody bitch. You're going to pay for that."

He lurched towards her, brandishing the knife in the air. That's when Jude Carter appeared in the doorway. He hurled himself on to Rick's back, knocking him to the ground. The knife slid across the floor. When I walked in, Jude was sat on top of Rick, and Carin was coolly eating her sponge cake.

She smiled at me. "That bastard tried to snatch my box. He was threatening me with a knife until Jude walked in and knocked him down. If he wanted the box that badly, why didn't he carry on bidding?"

I patted Jude on the back. "I owe you. Thanks a lot for what you did."

He was as calm as Carin. "No probs. What are you going to do with this toerag?"

"I should call the police, by rights, but my boss wouldn't thank me. It could impact on the business, from the bad publicity. Leave him to me. I'll see him off the premises."

"So long as you're sure he won't come back."

"I promise you he won't."

I pulled Rick off the floor. For the second time that day, I frogmarched him to the main gates with his arm twisted behind his back. I let go of him and put his mind under my control. It was in overdrive turmoil, every thought driven by a manic desire to get his hands on that box of tat.

I spoke my orders into his brain. "Listen, Rick. Get that bloody box out of your system. I've had enough of you today. You're never going to set foot on these premises again. Do we understand each other?"

I released him from my influence.

He shook my hand. "Glad I bumped into you, Kit. You won't be seeing me any more. I'm giving up on this place. I can get better gear from the Middle Road Auctions, in Bakehamsted." He waved a hand and sauntered off down the road.

Jude and Carin were drinking coffee when I joined them. "I've got rid of the scumbag. He won't be turning up to any more of my auctions. Let's forget him, shall we? Speaking about more pleasant things, you mentioned having a meal at your restaurant. We'd love to, wouldn't we, Carin?"

She nodded excitedly.

"When do you suggest, Jude?"

"That's great. What about next Saturday, say seven o'clock?"

Carin put her twopenny-worth in. "We'll be there, Jude."

He looked at his watch. "I'd better be on my way. Tonight's a busy one. Look forward to seeing you next Saturday. I'll reserve a table for you." With a wave of his hand he left us.

We finished our coffees. "I've got to lock up. Here's the key to my flat. Make yourself at home. I'll only be about twenty minutes."

CHAPTER TWENTY-FIVE

True to my word, I was back in twenty minutes. Carin was sat in the lounge, supping a glass of my favourite Merlot. She poured me a glass. We toasted each other – to a day that had brought both excitement and profit for her. I had arranged another surprise to make her day even more memorable.

"How about giving your mother a bell and telling her you're sleeping over? There's a good reason. I've booked a meal for us at a local restaurant."

"That's wonderful, Kit. I hope it's a candlelit dinner."

"You'll have to wait and see."

Half past six rolled round.

I chivvied her along. "The restaurant isn't far away. We can walk there in ten minutes. Let's be off."

A quarter of an hour later, we were being shown to our table in the plush restaurant of The Rose and Crown Hotel. I smiled as I caught sight of the candelabrum that I'd borrowed from our next sale, standing in the middle of our table, with its seven candles burning cheerfully in the subdued lighting of the restaurant.

She was bowled over. "This is fantastic, Kit."

We ordered starters and I excused myself. She thought I'd gone to answer the call of nature. I collared the head waiter and fed him my instructions. He nodded his head and pocketed the £5 note I proffered. I sat down and winked at him. He took his cue and sauntered across to our table.

He followed my script. "This package has just been delivered for the young lady."

It looked outrageously expensive in its designer wrapping paper. He was proving good value for my £5, as he handed the package to her with a flourish. Job done, he left us.

She was lost for words, but not for long. "Who could have left this for me?"

I showed a touch of false jealousy. "Don't ask me. You've obviously got an admirer. Perhaps Martin or Jude sent it. I told them we were dining here tonight. Put me out of my misery. Open it and find out."

It didn't take her long to tear the expensive wrapping away. A small box was revealed. Her fingers shook as she opened it. The light from the candles glistened in the diamond setting of my expensive Victorian ring.

She shouted out, "Oh, my God. It's an engagement ring."

The lady diners sighed. One wag insisted I should get down on my knees and propose to her. I duly obliged, and formally asked her if she would marry me. Her silent answer was to hand me the ring and hold her hand out. I slipped it on her ring finger. The dust settled, and we were forgotten as the diners carried on eating. Carin's eyes shone with happiness.

"Thanks for making my dream come true."

After an enjoyable main course, she slipped off to the little girls' room. No sooner had she returned than the head waiter appeared with an envelope in his hand.

He popped it on the table in front of me. "This is for you, sir."

The handwriting meant nothing to me. Carin grinned in anticipation.

"We all seem to be getting special deliveries this evening."

The envelope wasn't stuck down. I took out a blank sheet of paper. The signet ring that she'd bought at auction was taped to the bottom of it.

She pulled the ring away from the paper and kneeled at my feet. "This is a bit unusual, but why shouldn't I propose to you?"

Another flurry of sighs floated from the lady diners.

Carin slipped the ring on my finger. She looked me in the eye. "I love you, Kit Milner. Will you marry me?"

"I love you too, Carin Milner. The answer is yes."

Surely there won't be another evening like that? Our love bond had been sealed forever. Tying the knot at our wedding would only be a religious formality.

The lights dimmed, and more sighs broke out as a waitress wheeled in a candlelit cake on a trolley.

Carin leaned across and grasped my hands. Her eyes twinkled. "I'll never forget tonight, Kit."

It was nearly nine o'clock when we left. We walked back to the flat, two happy lovers who were destined to spend an eternity together.

Merlin materialised in the main hall of Dalbury Manor. Emeralda and the disciples were eating.

She smiled at him. "I can tell from the look on your face that your scheme worked."

He nodded. "My son and daughter are wearing the rings they bought at my son's sale. I persuaded our daughter to buy one of them, and my son bought the other one. By wearing the rings, it tells me of their whereabouts."

She looked puzzled. "Your son has no need for a ring for you to know where he is. You planted one of your hairs in his scalp when he was born, which tells you of his whereabouts."

"I can't chance my son finding out about the hair. If he does, he will stop me from using its powers." He banged the table. "Enough of this. Listen to me, everyone. The main reason he wears the ring is to stop him from using a powerful weapon to topple us once he finds we have conquered the world. Damnus tells me that my son will be ordered to seek out a sealed scroll, by his brother, Magnus. If he gets his hands on that scroll, and opens it in our presence, it will spell the end for all of us. That's why we must know of his whereabouts, so we can be on hand to stop him from finding the scroll.

"There is something else you should know. The people of

the world will not see Damnus's son until he is crowned King of the World. He will need to live in someone else's body so he may guide us in our quest without being seen. I have found that person. His name is Jude Carter." He smiled. "I got him to hide my son's ring in a wooden box at his auction." He roared with laughter. "And that is not all. I got a man called Rick Adams to try and take the wooden box from my daughter after the sale. She rose to the occasion by muttering a spell under her breath, which disabled Adams. She does not realise I am her father, but what happened proves that she has taken on my powers of sorcery."

He clapped his hands. Two young wenches appeared with bottles of wine. They filled everyone's glass, then left the room.

Merlin stood up. "Let us toast Lord Damnus as we start our crusade to capture the hearts and minds of mankind. We also pray for eternal damnation on my son. Your days are numbered, Kit Milner." He looked at the Master. "Tell my guards to bring in the young girl. We have to sacrifice her to Lord Damnus."

Azurina wiped the images of Merlin from the mirror and turned to Michael. "Our son's going to be up against it with that lot. Are you sure he'll win through in the end?"

"Of course he will. With the help of the sealed scroll, he'll have the beating of anyone, including those bastards. Our leader reminded me that he'll be passing a book to our son when Damnus has gained control of the world. I told you that it will contain every conversation that Merlin has ever had, be it with whoever. It will fill him in with some vital facts, like the hair that Merlin planted in his scalp. It's all in the book. It won't mention the rings they both wear, because that would upset our leader's plans. I'm confident our son will find out about the rings in good time."

"How will Magnus get the book to him?"

"He'll lead our son to it. The book will also give him a clue as to how he can find the scroll."

She managed a smile. "You seem pretty certain that our son will come through this with flying colours."

"Of course I am. With his powers, and the scroll, he can't lose, especially as he knows about Merlin's use of replicas. Roll on the day when he faces Sammael and Damnus for the last time."

CHAPTER TWENTY-SIX

We settled down on the sofa, drinking our wine and talking about the engagement meal we'd just enjoyed.

Carin put her glass down and touched my arm. "There's something I must tell you, Kit." She shivered. "It's about what happened in the coffee shop this afternoon."

A feeling of concern hit me. "That's OK. Spit it out."

"Something bizarre happened that I can't get my head around. That sod was going to hit me, when I found myself mouthing strange words at him. They had a weird effect on him. The bastard couldn't move, as much as he tried, which gave me the chance to kick him between the legs. And that's not the only thing. When we were at Mandies and Jude told us to bugger off I muttered some words at him. His attitude changed straight away, and he apologised for his behaviour. The words that he spoke were being fed into his mouth by me. He was saying what I wanted him to say. And that's not all. Suddenly everything changed. It was as if someone had waved a magic wand. There was no nastiness, and the four young men who had caused all the trouble were as nice as pie. Jude was a different person – he gave us his personal brand of service, and even provided a free bottle of wine to all the diners, as well as performing a striptease act with those four lads. You told me that you'd explain what had happened, but you never did. That was deliberate, wasn't it?" She stared into my eyes. "So, what's going on, Mister?"

Talk about being put on the spot. I made a quick decision.

There was no going back. I had to be truthful about her special gifts, knowing that she would accept the truth without having a mental breakdown. After all, she was Merlin's daughter, but I wouldn't be telling her that. Thank goodness she couldn't remember that I had gone back in time to change what had already happened.

"Are you sure? There's the chance you might not believe me."

I was treated to a piercing stare. "Let me be the judge of that. And don't try and fob me off. Tell me everything, and I mean *everything*."

Where the hell was I to start?

"OK. Out-of-the-ordinary talents lurk inside that body of yours." I shook my head in frustration. "For Christ's sake! Why am I beating about the bush? You possess powers of sorcery. I don't mean like a witch. Your skills are more subtle. Those words you muttered at Rick Adams automatically popped up from your subconscious to protect you from harm. Any questions so far?"

She coolly poured herself another glass of wine. "Don't worry about me. I won't be throwing any tantrums. You seem to know a lot about these powers of" – she spluttered, as if she found it hard to say the word – "sorcery. I suppose you share the same gifts?"

I was pleased with myself. She hadn't overreacted so far.

"The answer is yes. You and I are poles apart from other people. We're stuffed full of sorcery."

She giggled. "You make it sound so dramatic. Don't worry. Don't ask me why, but I'm happy to live with what you're telling me. What kind of magic are we capable of? How about showing me some sorcery?"

"Hold on. You're way ahead of me. I didn't discover my skills in five minutes, so I'll take the same approach with you. Let's try something simple."

I pointed at a framed painting hanging on the wall. The artist had painted a swathe of bluebells growing on the banks of a woodland stream.

"See that painting? It's a bit dull. It needs livening up."

223

I fed the thought into my mind. The bluebells started nodding in the breeze.

"There's still something missing."

The sound of birdsong filled the room. I was rewarded with a round of applause from her.

"Hold on. I'm not finished yet."

A trickle of water from the stream dribbled out of the painting and ran down the wall. A small puddle started to collect on the floor.

"I'd better stop the flow before we get flooded out."

A single thought restored the painting to how the artist had intended. The water on the floor surged back up the wall and into the picture. The bluebells stopped nodding and the birdsong ceased.

Carin was stunned. The hero worship on her face made my efforts worthwhile.

She finally managed to put her looks into words. "You've blown me away. That's real magic."

"I'm a bit of a fraud. It's not as hard as it looks, but it will take you some time to find out what you're really capable of. Anyway, enough of that. Now it's your turn to perform; but before you do anything, let's get one thing straight. I'm playing games with our sorcery, but our powers aren't intended to impress people. Don't ever use them to disadvantage anyone unless, like Rick, they're giving you a problem. No one must ever know what we're capable of. One last thing. Use your gifts for good, not evil. I mean every word of that. Understood?"

Her nostrils flared. "Don't paint me as a complete idiot. I'm a cleric's daughter, remember. I know the difference between good and evil."

She wasn't Julius Milner's daughter, but thank God a lot of him had rubbed off on her. She simmered down as quickly as she'd flared up.

"What do you want me to do?"

I pointed at a bottle of wine and glasses standing on the table. "I could murder a glass of wine. Pour me one without using your hands. The power lies in your mind. Tell it what you want it to do, and don't let your attention waver."

Her face creased in concentration. The wine bottle floated in the air, then hovered above a glass. She managed to pour me a drink. The bottle drifted gently back down on to the table. She went spare, dashing around the room with all the enthusiasm of a small child. She'd passed her first hurdle. The glass of Merlot didn't go to waste. I enticed the glass through the air and tipped the wine into my mouth. She quietened down and joined me on the sofa. I set about telling her some more home truths while she was in the right frame of mind.

"Welcome to the sorcerer's club. Does it really worry you that you're poles apart from everyone else? Be honest with me. Can you handle it?"

"I should be off my rocker, but I'm not." She started to shake her head. "You used your powers to rig the lottery results, didn't you? Am I right or am I right?" She wasn't slow in coming forward.

"I hold my hand up. Yes. I fixed the results, for all the right reasons."

I told her how I had done it. She accepted it without question.

"What are you going to show me next?" Her mind was ready to be stretched.

"There's nothing else to show you, but I am going to tell you about one of our other powers – time travel."

She looked at me as if I'd gone barking mad. "Did I hear you right?"

"You did. We both have the gift of travelling through time. It was me who changed what was happening at Mandies, by going back in time and getting Jude and the lads to behave themselves."

The barking-mad look changed to deep concern. "Wow! That's incredible, but you won't catch me time-travelling, end of story."

"I'm glad to hear that, but I'm still going to tell you a few things about time travel. Trust me. When it comes to time-travelling, we have to understand that as well as a past and present life, we also have a future life that is already mapped out for us. There are two things to remember if we time-travel.

We will always be invisible when we arrive at our location. The second thing is this. If we decide to go back in time, you and I will never meet up with ourselves in another time frame. Don't ask me why, because I don't know. Time travel is one of our greatest gifts, but, like everything, it carries its own set of rules. It's not a game, and must only be used when the occasion demands it. There's one overriding rule. Never change what has already happened unless there's a bloody good reason for doing so, like I did at Mandies.

She shivered. "As I said, I don't intend to time-travel; and if I did, I certainly wouldn't want to change what had already happened."

"Quite right. We don't have the divine right to rework the past, present or future. Things are meant to be. Can you imagine people's reaction if you told them that a volcano was going to erupt the next day? Why should they believe you, and how would you explain how you knew, after it had happened?"

The combination of wine and the excitement of the evening had had its effect on us. We were whacked.

As we lay in bed, Carin whispered in my ear, "Thanks for being honest with me. I won't ever do anything silly with these powers, I promise."

We kissed, and fell into a deep sleep.

She drove back to Lovington the next morning.

CHAPTER TWENTY-SEVEN

Merlin and Emeralda were sat in their bedroom at Dalbury Manor. He pulled her to her feet.

"Whilst I love your company, you have another task to perform for Lord Damnus. The time has arrived for his son to be born. We will use our daughter's body to produce his son. I want you to visit her and place yourself inside her body. I have ordered the Master to be present at the birth." He kissed her. "You had better be on your way."

Carin sat brushing her hair at her dressing table. Her mind wasn't on what she was doing. She was focused on the powers that Kit had told her about. She put the hairbrush on the dressing table, made it hover in the air, then looked at herself in the mirror and sighed. Her new-found sorcery had done wonders for her confidence. She wondered where her new-found abilities could take her. The thought of helping to treat sick people made her smile. Perhaps hands-on healing was about to make a comeback. She shivered at the thought of creating life-saving medicines with her new-found abilities.

Her thinking was disturbed by a man's face in the mirror.

"Kit? What are you doing here?"

She turned around. No one was there. She stared into the mirror. The man's face smiled back at her before vanishing. The new confident Carin didn't panic. She thought her mind was playing tricks on her.

She lay on her bed, amusing herself with her new-found talents. Every moveable object in the bedroom floated in the air as if attached by wires from the ceiling. She soon bored of this and picked up a magazine. Her train of thought was broken by a rustling sound in the bedroom corner. She gaped at a young man standing by the far wall. He smiled at her. She could have sworn it was Kit, except he wasn't wearing the clothes that Kit wore. His flowing black cassock testified to this. Strangely, she felt no fear of him.

"Who are you? You look like someone I know."

He bowed to her. "I am the Master, one of the leaders of the Church of Atonement. And you are my mother."

Carin remained upbeat, which surprised her. How had this strange man got into her bedroom? He looked like Kit Milner, even spoke like him, but, most alarmingly, had welcomed her as his mother.

"What the hell are you talking about? That's impossible. I'm twenty-seven, and you look my age." She let her words sink in. "I don't know how you got in here, but if you cause me any problems I'm more than capable of dealing with you."

He shook his head and clicked his tongue. "Your mind has grown stronger these past few days. So has your confidence. That is good. But your powers are no match for mine." He ran his fingers through his beard and laughed. "No matter what you think, you are my mother and Milner is my father. That is why I look like him."

A few days ago Carin would have screamed blue murder at the sight of a strange man in her bedroom. She'd changed, and wasn't alarmed at his intrusion.

"You don't scare me. I've had enough of you." She pointed a hand at him.

His shoulders shook with silent mirth. "If you are thinking of incinerating me, forget it."

Carin looked frantically at her fingers as no killing ray appeared. The Master had heard enough. He snapped his fingers. Carin fell back on to the bed in a deep trance, her chest rising and falling in a regular rhythm.

He showed his impatience. "You can stop pulling my mother's strings. Come out and show yourself, My Lady."

A trail of vapour flowed from Carin's mouth. It floated above the bedroom floor, slowly forming itself into a human form. A stunning woman, with auburn hair and vibrant green eyes, bowed to the Master. She wore a low-cut green dress, showing a generous cleavage. Lady Emeralda had made her entrance.

She looked down at Carin. "You are an attractive girl, my dear, but not as beautiful as your mother." She stared at the Master. "I suppose you have come to collect my daughter?"

"I have, My Lady. Lord Merlin has asked me to take my mother to Dalbury Manor, and has ordered you to leave a replica of her behind so her parents will not miss her."

"Very well. Pick your mother up."

The Master took his mother into his arms. Emeralda whispered a few words. The next moment, a replica of Carin lay on the bed.

The Master looked a little concerned. "Will your replica remember what has happened during the last few minutes?"

She looked at him and shook her head in derision. "Never underestimate my powers. As soon as we leave she will wake up and act as if nothing has happened. When this business is over we will return my daughter. Let us go."

Emeralda and the Master appeared in the main hall of Dalbury Manor. Merlin was waiting for them.

"Take my daughter upstairs to our bedroom and lay her on the bed."

The three of them trooped upstairs.

Merlin gave his instructions to Emeralda. "Prepare our daughter in readiness for Lord Damnus."

She stripped Carin naked and laid her face down on the bed, with her legs kneeling on the floor at the end of the bed.

"Get back inside our daughter, and make sure Lord Damnus fertilises her egg." Merlin raised his arms in the air. "Lord Damnus, my daughter's body is ready for you, so we may look upon the face of your son."

A stream of red smoke spewed from out of Merlin's mouth,

which formed itself into Damnus. Smoke curled from the creature's nostrils, and flames flickered in his eyes. The bedroom was cloaked in a repellent choking smell of decaying flesh. The creature caught sight of Carin and licked her bottom.

Sparks flew from the beast's mouth as he spoke. "From my granddaughter's spawned seed I will create my son."

The beast kneeled behind Carin. With deceptive gentleness, he spread his arms on the bed and covered her body from behind. The back end of the beast moved backwards and forwards as he pleasured Carin's body. He grunted as his semen exploded inside her.

The creature roared. "Is the woman's egg fertilised, woman?"

Emeralda appeared beside him. "Yes, My Lord."

The beast roared with delight. "Lay my granddaughter on the bed and let my son's birth begin." He muttered a spell.

Carin's stomach swelled. She groaned as the baby pushed itself free of her body, before falling back into a silent trance. Merlin picked the baby up and held him out to Damnus, who took him in his arms.

He placed his son on the floor, then waved his fingers at the screaming child. "Grow to your twenty-fifth year."

Within seconds, a young man, dressed in flowing red robes, stood before him. He bowed to Damnus.

The beast spoke to him. "It pleases me that you know I am your father. My thoughts of the past, the present and the future are planted in your mind. I name you Sammael. You will oversee the task of converting the minds and hearts of mankind to worship me, with the help of Merlin and your disciples. I will live inside your body to guide you until the day you are crowned King of the World. That is when you and I will reveal ourselves to the people of Earth for the very first time."

Sammael bowed to him. "I am proud to have you as my father, and I swear I will carry out your wishes."

The beast smiled, then vanished in a cloud of red smoke, which poured down Sammael's throat.

He turned to Emeralda. "Clothe the woman and use your sorcery to heal her mind and body, so she will not remember giving birth to me, or seeing the Master in her bedroom." He spoke to Merlin. "Get the Master to return her to her home and dispose of her replica. But before he does that we will go downstairs and meet my disciples."

They walked into the main hall. The disciples were seated at the long table.

Merlin frantically waved his hand at them. "You are looking upon Lord Sammael, the son of Lord Damnus."

They sprang to their feet and bowed to him.

Sammael motioned them to sit down. "Without you my father's plans cannot come to fruition. So, what lies ahead of us? Merlin has already told you that our first task is the need to ensnare the minds of monarchs, dictators and politicians, together with the heads of the armed services, secret services and police in every country of the world. My father does not crave a perfect world. The more mankind suffers, the happier my father will be. Using our sorcery to manipulate people's minds is the easy part. Merlin has told you about mankind's invention of television. We will use this device to mesmerise people's minds into joining our new religion. Sadly, some people will not be affected by our sorcery and will oppose us. Those people will die. We will promote ourselves as a new religious movement, to be known as the Church of Atonement. We will take over churches, and other places of worship, as they become empty because nobody attends them any more. These buildings will be used by the Church of Atonement to introduce our followers to our own brand of religion. Lord Merlin has given me the name of someone who can help in winning over the minds of religious leaders. His name is Julius Milner. I intend to bring him with us. We will leave a replica of him at home.

"Sorcery is our greatest weapon, but you are aware of the magic brew which is stored on one of my father's worlds. A few drops of this water, placed in rivers, oceans and lakes, will produce a potent potion. If it is drunk, or if people eat fish from these waters, they will immediately become avid followers of my father's creed.

"We must not lose sight of our objective. My father has

decreed that there is only room on this planet for one worldwide government, and I am to be crowned King of the World when we achieve his aims. He has chosen England as the country in which I will be crowned, and it is from there that I will conduct my duties as the worldwide ruler.

"It would take a lifetime for us to subjugate the people of earth to our cause. Merlin has spoken about creating replicas of yourselves. He is right. For a start, each of you will be replicated 10,000 times, but every replica of you will look different. I do not want people wondering why there are so many people who look alike. Merlin and the Master will bring the United Kingdom to its knees in readiness for my coronation, but their replicas will travel the world with you. As for me, I must keep myself hidden from people's eyes. I will travel the world in the body of a man called Jude Carter, to check on your progress and to give you orders." He turned to the Master. "Fill our glasses with wine, so we may drink to our success and the final demise of Kit Milner."

CHAPTER TWENTY-EIGHT

My first chore on a Monday morning was to meet up with Martin Henderson. He was sat behind his desk when I walked in.

"Morning, Kit. Had a good weekend?"

"Yeah. How about you?"

He purred. "Fine. Your Fine Art Sale was nothing short of brilliant." He was displaying all the signs of being demob-happy. "I've chosen the right guy to take over, if your first sale is anything to go by. My pension is safe in your hands."

I helped myself to a mug of coffee. "You're not getting your gilt-edged pension for nothing. If you expect me to carry on delivering the goods, I'll be awarding myself a decent salary. I might even introduce a bonus scheme for myself."

He spluttered on his coffee. "As long as my annual pension goes up by two points above the rate of inflation, you can do what you like." The subject was quickly forgotten. A goofy look covered his face. "How's that lovely woman of yours?"

I probably looked doe-eyed as well. "She's great. We're officially engaged now."

"Hope you both have a long and happy life together."

"We will. Things can't get better than this. You and the wife will get an invite to the wedding when we arrange it – which reminds me, I've got a favour to ask of you. Will you be my best man?"

He was lost for words, and satisfied himself by getting up and shaking my hand before finding his tongue. "I'd be delighted to. Thanks for asking me."

I left him before he broke down in tears.

Carin rang early on Monday evening. She sounded excited. "Kit, Jude Carter rang me. He reminded me that we're eating at his restaurant on Saturday evening. He's having us picked up, as well as the meal being on him."

Jude had restored my faith in human nature. He'd been a right bastard the first time round, but had come over as a nice guy at the auction. We'd seen the worst side of him because of Merlin's influence over him. I looked forward to meeting up with him.

It was a run-of-the-mill evening at Lovington Rectory. The Milners settled down in the lounge after dinner. Julius switched the television on, and Meg caught up with her knitting.

A voice bawled out from the television, "Listen to this message from the Church of Atonement."

The two of them stiffened, their lifeless eyes gaping at the screen.

The loud, eager voice spewed out his words. "We are a new religious movement, and at some point in the future we'll be opening a church near you. Prepare yourselves for the religious liberation of the world, and give your support to the Church of Atonement. We'll keep you updated."

The two of them sprang back to life as the transmission came to an end. Nothing was said. Ten minutes later they both showed signs of tiredness and made their way to their bedrooms. Julius removed the crucifix from around his neck and placed it on the Bible lying on his bedside cabinet. Acrid smoke curled into the air as the crucifix burned its way through the pages.

He picked the crucifix up and smiled. Meg nodded her head in approval.

The Saturday auction swung into gear. A larger than usual crowd had turned up, which helped the bidding to reach higher levels than even I had anticipated.

The auction ended, and by four thirty the books were balanced, monies counted, safe locked, and everyone had gone home.

Martin hadn't turned out for the sale. I telephoned him to let him know how things had gone. He said well done before ringing off. A 'well done' from Martin was equivalent to receiving a knighthood from the Queen.

I locked up, had a wash and brush-up, then headed for Lovington. Carin was waiting at the rectory door. After a huge hug and a kiss she pushed me into the lounge.

Julius rushed across and shook my hand. "Before you young things dash out, let's toast our luck in the lottery. Meg's had a visit from Camelot." He rubbed his hands together. "The cheque is clearing in our bank account. Julius filled four glasses and toasted what they thought was a stroke of luck.

Carin and I winked at each other.

Carin brought the revelry to a close. "We're off to Mandies this evening. A car is picking us up at seven fifteen. It'll be here any minute."

Right on cue, the doorbell rang. We said our goodbyes and left.

Julius and Meg poured themselves another glass of wine.

Julius raised his glass in the air. "Never mind them. More importantly, here's to us and our future in the Church of Atonement."

They fell about in fits of laughter. Wisps of vapour trickled from their mouths. The Master and Merlin gazed at the frozen features of the Milners.

The Master allowed himself a broad smile. "The money that the woman has won will help us fund Lord Sammael's plans."

"You are right." Merlin grinned. "It would be foolish to let that wine go to waste. Will you join me in a glass?"

"Why not, My Lord. We have much to celebrate."

Merlin raised his glass. "To Lord Sammael and Damnus Day. Also, a toast to us and your disciple brothers back at Dalbury Manor." Merlin wiped wine from his beard. "Sammael has ordered me to bring Julius Milner with us."

He waggled his hand at Julius. His replica appeared by his side.

Merlin looked at it. "You will remain here and lead Julius Milner's normal life. His thoughts are set out in your mind."

The replica bowed to him. "I understand, and will do as you ask."

Merlin pointed at Meg. "She will wake up when we have gone, and will act as if nothing has happened to her."

The driver told us that Jude had put his own car at our disposal. His restaurant must have been doing well to pay for the plush Mercedes that sped us to Mandies.

Jude was waiting to welcome us. "Good to see the pair of you." He guided us to the bar, and spoke to the head waiter. "Kit and Carin are my special guests this evening. Look after their every need." He winked at me. "I'll leave you in Richard's good hands and catch up with you later."

Richard led us to our table. "Jude says order whatever you want. He'll take care of the bill. I'll leave the menu with you and come back."

This was so different from the last time we'd been here. Carin looked stunning in her green dress. She was in her element. The male diners couldn't take their eyes off her. Neither could I.

She reached across the table for my hands. "This is wonderful, Kit."

I picked up my glass of wine. "Here's to our future."

She emptied her glass and patted my arm. "I'm glad we agreed not to get married, in the short term. I know Mummy and Daddy were disappointed."

I ignored the other diners and gave her a long lingering kiss. "We're doing things the way they should be done. We'll end up getting married when the time is right. That's not to say we can't start planning for the future. Shall we buy a nice house, ready for our big day?"

She kicked me under the table. "You want to get me in bed every night, don't you?"

"What's wrong with that?"

"Nothing. I quite like the idea."

The evening passed quickly. The company was good, the food

couldn't be faulted and the two bottles of wine we consumed completed our enjoyment. The evening had all the trappings of a party, without quite being sure what we were celebrating. Jude was the perfect host. He almost came over as a kid brother – a much older kid brother. Our desserts turned up, together with two more glasses of wine.

Jude joined us at the end of the meal.

"It's been great meeting up with you guys. We'll do the same thing again, but it won't be for some time. I'll be travelling around the world for the next few years. I've landed a top-notch job, doing some important work for a large retail catering organisation. It's what I've always wanted to do. I wish I could tell you more about it, but my lips are sealed. Richard will be running the restaurant in my absence. You're always welcome to pop in." He poured himself a glass of wine. "Here's to the pair of you. Your good health, until we meet again."

I shook his hand. "Thanks for your hospitality, Jude. We're not getting married just yet. You'll probably be back by the time that happens. You'll get a special invitation."

Jude smiled. "Look forward to seeing you spliced. Would you like coffee?"

We finished our coffee and bade goodbye to him, with the promise that he'd look us up when he took over the restaurant reins again. His chauffeur-driven Mercedes whisked us back to the rectory.

Julius fussed around us while Meg provided some strong coffee to drown the wine we had drunk. The evening ended with more laughter and conversation.

Half an hour after I'd gone to bed, my bedroom door opened. Carin climbed into bed.

"I've come to prove how much I love you. I wouldn't let you have my body if I didn't."

I took her in my arms and nuzzled her. "That makes two of us."

CHAPTER TWENTY-NINE

Where had the last five years flown to? Christmas was only weeks away. The acceleration factor depends on how you spend your time. Carin and I had crammed two lifetimes into the last five years.

Yours truly now headed three auction houses in the south of England. They were the biggest in the world, and that included Christie's and the other once-mighty auction houses. None of them could hold a candle to my businesses. In the process I'd become a self-made multimillionaire, with every pound honestly made, without using any of my powers. I bought up the surrounding land at Grinton and increased the size of the business, including doing away with the cattle pens and making a large car park, which I'd seen in my second premonition of the future. It now boasted seven auction rooms, plus an upmarket restaurant. Carin and I had set up a charitable trust fund using most of the lottery money that Meg gave us. The fund had already benefited many worthy causes, with more waiting in the wings.

My own achievements paled into insignificance compared with Carin's watch. She had taken on the role of senior partner in her practice, giving her the chance to spread her wings. She was very keen to help people with their health problems, but not in the conventional National Health Service way.

I'll never forget one particular evening. She couldn't contain herself. I sat her down, put a glass of wine in her hand and asked what her state of flummox was all about. She swallowed the wine in one gulp and patted the sofa for me to sit down.

"I was treating a patient today. She's got cancer, bless her. Thank God it's in remission. After she'd gone, I had this crazy thought. You and I have got these special powers, but they're locked away doing sod all. Wouldn't it be great if we could channel some of our abilities into producing a tablet that would cure cancer and other life-threatening diseases? Think of the millions of people we could help. You've always said we mustn't use our powers to change what has already happened, but you weren't talking about illnesses, were you?" She cocked her head on one side and stared at me with questioning eyes. "Am I talking through my backside, or does this idea strike a chord with you?" Her eyes pleaded with me. "What do you think?"

I scrubbed at my forehead. "I've always believed we mustn't change what has already happened. By that I meant natural disasters or man-made circumstances."

The more I thought about it, the more sense her idea made. Why shouldn't she help people by bringing a little magic into their lives? She wasn't changing the past. We were talking of changing the present and, more importantly, the future. What harm was there in creating happiness for people instead of them facing premature death?

She knew what I was about to say, from the look on my face. "I've no objection to helping sick people. We need to think carefully as to how we introduce your magic tablets. Are we talking of helping people who use your surgery, or do you go national and international? Personally, I think you've got to go for the latter."

Carin grinned. "Thanks for your support. I want us to have our own company, manufacturing a cheap multi-healing tablet. It can't be copied by anyone else, because our tablet would have a magic ingredient that no one else can command."

I liked her idea. "Why don't you take a sabbatical from work? As head of practice, I'm sure you can arrange that, so you can work things through with no outside distractions."

She hugged me. "Thanks, darling. I'll do that."

That's where we stood. Carin was on her sabbatical and I'd got a few more auctions to arrange before Christmas was upon us. We'd started planning the manufacture of our life-saving drugs. Carin was to have talks with the NHS so they could run an eye over her tablets, with a view to giving their blessing for their distribution. With her special powers, there was no doubt that permission would be given. Once we had overcome that hurdle, she would look for an industrial unit and find suitable machinery to manufacture and package our tablets.

The happiest guy around was Martin. With the pension I paid him, he must have been close to becoming a millionaire himself.

You've heard the plus side. With every good side there's a down side. Crime was on the increase – not just in this country, but throughout the world. Every day I read about murder, terrorism, warring factions, racism, mindless vandalism and the antisocial effects of drugs and alcohol, not forgetting the frauds and scams that were going on in this world, at both the top and the bottom of society. The latest crime to raise its head was the hundreds of suicide bombers, who were killing thousands upon thousands of innocent victims in this country and throughout the world.

I knew what was causing it. Correction: I knew *who* was causing it. Sammael and Merlin were making it happen so that Damnus could feed on the misery as the world moved closer to his absolute control. I'd kept my word to Magnus, and hadn't interfered with what the two of them were weaving behind my back. I'd seen the Church of Atonement advertising their wares on television. The voices and eyes of the presenters were full of mesmerism, which must have weaned billions of people to their cause. They were also advertising their wares in the national press, which was readily embracing the changing face of religion, as if it was the best thing since sliced bread. I'm no fool. I knew the Church of Atonement was Sammael's flagship, to gather the people into his father's hands.

What sickened me was that suicide bombers were targeting synagogues, churches, chapels and mosques, as well as some of the Atonement churches. I smelt a rat. Merlin and Sammael were behind the bombings, including their own churches to throw me off their scent. I could have gone back in time to stop these attacks, and see who was carrying them out, but my promise to Magnus stopped me from doing that.

Reports in the national press talked about the congregations of all religions being in sharp decline. Their congregations were flocking to the Church of Atonement. Other churches, synagogues and mosques stood empty – but not for long. The Church of Atonement had taken over thousands of empty places of worship to accommodate the millions of people who were attracted to their style of religion, and the other religions hadn't raised a finger in protest. A few churches were still hanging on to much smaller congregations. Strangely, it hadn't led to any of the religious bodies taking steps to find out why their followers had abandoned them and what could be done about it.

It was not only this country that was showing these signs. Television reports implied that all countries of the world were experiencing the same state of affairs, where established religions were joining up with the international Church of Atonement.

I spoke with Julius about what was happening. He shrugged his shoulders, and said there was nothing he could do about it. His congregation had insisted that his church should commit to the Church of Atonement, and he'd spoken with the Bishop of Ely, who had told him it was in order to go down that road. I hadn't forgotten that I saw Julius in my first vision of the future welcoming the Master into his church.

Being the suspicious sod that I am, I checked out Julius's mind. I found nothing untoward, except for one disturbing thing. He hadn't got a heartbeat. That didn't surprise me. This Julius was a replica, while the man himself was out in the world somewhere, helping the Damnus cause. I could only sit back and wait for Sammael and Merlin to show their final hand, when Magnus would call on me.

Sammael was sat in a hotel room in Paris in the company of Merlin, the Master and Julius Milner. Jude Carter was slumped on a sofa in an unconscious state.

Sammael raised his glass and invited them to join him in a toast. "Let us raise our glasses to how we have very nearly achieved my father's aims. We can add the people of France to the countries who will show us their loyalty on Damnus Day." He looked at Merlin. "It only remains for the United Kingdom to be brought completely to heel. How close to succeeding are you?"

Merlin glanced at Julius and the Master, and smiled. "The three of us have spent the last few years drawing the population into your net, but we couldn't have done it without the replica disciples that I created. The armed services, secret services and police are under our control. We also control the banking system and the Stock Exchange, as well as the national press and all television services. Julius and the Master have been busy making sure the Church of Atonement ensnares the followers of all the other religions that used to practise in the United Kingdom. Do you wish to say anything, Julius?"

"Thank you, Lord Merlin. Our mesmerising television commercials have attracted the majority of people to our religion. On top of that, the magic brew which has been added to the nation's drinking water has also been a great success. A few of the old Churches are still functioning, but we know who they are and we'll be putting a stop to them. We have ensured that every school is now teaching the principles of our Church as a part of their curriculum."

Sammael looked delighted. "Splendid. What about Parliament and the royal family, Lord Merlin?"

"No problem there, My Lord. They are putty in our hands. The monarch has agreed to give up her sovereignty of the nation. She and all the royals will move out of their palaces and mansions, and will reside with her on her Sandringham Estate." He smirked. "They had no other choice. We have followed your orders, and Buckingham Palace, together with all other royal properties, will be home to you and your chosen bishops. We have also removed the grace-and-favour people from their mansions and country houses. These properties will come under your control, for you to decide who should live in them. As for the Members of Parliament and the House of Lords, they will do whatever I ask of them. The Master will be visiting them during the next few days to tell them that both institutions are to be done away with. My disciples and I will have finished our work in the next few weeks. The country will then be ready for your coronation."

Sammael applauded them. "Refill our glasses, Master, and let's toast what you have all accomplished."

Merlin stood up. "Gentlemen, let us also toast Lord Sammael for the guidance he has given us. We look forward to the day when he is crowned King of the World."

Carin rang on Saturday, just before the auction. She was on a high. "It's me, darling. Jude Carter just rang me. He's back in the country, and has invited us to his restaurant for a meal tonight. I know it's short notice, but I said yes. Is that OK with you?"

"That's fine. Anything to get away from this madhouse. What time?"

"He said about half seven. His car will pick us up at the rectory. I've got to go. See you at the rectory."

CHAPTER THIRTY

At seven fifteen, a chauffeur-driven Mercedes rolled up. Ten minutes later we were jawing with Jude. We spent half an hour catching up on the last five years. Over the meal, Carin and I were able to relax, with the outside world forgotten. We managed to drink our fair share of Merlot before our desserts turned up.

Carin had a smug look on her face. "There's one thing missing from our lives. Isn't it time we thought about getting married? It's five years since you proposed to me."

"Why not? We've got the house and the money. What about next spring?"

She held my hand. "Mummy and Daddy will be over the moon."

Jude Carter made his way to a side room. The Master was waiting for him. He motioned Jude to come in.

"Fill three glasses with red wine and bring them to me."

Jude returned with the filled glasses on a tray. The Master pulled a glass phial from out of his pocket.

"You are going to toast them." He poured a liquid from the phial into two of the glasses. "They must drink from these two glasses. The other one is for you. Do not mix them up." He placed a finger on Jude's forehead. "Serve them the dosed drinks. When they become sleepy, you will drive them back to Lovington Rectory."

Jude brought drinks to the table. "We must toast your wedding next year. Here's to your future happiness."

We quaffed the wine. I stood up, somewhat unsteadily, looked around the room and regretted it. Everything was swimming in front of my eyes. A queasy feeling of giddiness was swiftly followed by a sensation of tiredness that flowed through every limb. My brain ceased working. I slumped into my chair. It wasn't an unpleasant feeling. I felt on a high, but knackered with it. I looked at Carin. She was asleep. I tried to get up, but the effort was too much for me.

Jude put a hand on my shoulder. "Are you all right, Kit?" His words echoed inside my head.

I managed to whisper in his ear, "I feel pleasantly tired." I attempted a joke. "Must have been something you put in the wine."

Jude laughed. "Nothing like that. I'd better get the two of you home."

Jude pulled up on the rectory drive. The front door opened. Julius came out and helped carry the comatose pair into the lounge.

Julius grunted. "Everything went to plan, then?"

Jude nodded. "Exactly as the Master ordered."

"We'll wait for them to come round."

I opened my eyes and tried to get up. Nothing happened. My damned legs wouldn't budge. As for my brain, it felt like a dried-out sponge, full of holes and lifeless. I tried to speak, but nothing came out. Out of the corner of my eye I saw Carin lying next to me on the sofa. She was asleep. Sammael, Merlin, the Master and Julius Milner stood staring at me.

Sammael sniggered. "What have we here, then? How the mighty are fallen!" He turned to the other three. "I will put him in the picture before we kill the pair of them."

"Why not?" said Merlin. "He deserves an explanation."

"You cannot move or use your powers, Milner. I arranged for Carter to drug you. In a few minutes' time you will not have a care in the world, because you will be dead. We are close to fulfilling my father's desires for this world." He beckoned to the

Master. "Do you have anything to say to Milner before you kill him?"

I tried to conjure up my powers, but my fumbling thoughts wouldn't allow it. My only body parts in any kind of working order were my eyes and ears.

The Master scowled. "He has betrayed our line. I would sooner see him dead."

Merlin's face softened. "My feelings for my daughter are different. I am proud of her, but she must die as well."

Sammael stared down at me. "Listen, Milner. In a few weeks we celebrate Damnus Day, when the citizens of earth will worship my father because all other religious faiths have been wiped out." He looked at the other three. "Before we kill them, I think Milner should see the next television screening of the Church of Atonement."

They nodded their agreement.

"It is a pity that Merlin's daughter is not awake to see it. At least it will prove to Milner, once and for all, that there is no way back for any other religion. Once people have seen this bulletin, when it goes out, mankind will be indoctrinated into my father's beliefs forever."

He waggled a finger and the television screen burst into life.

A voice bawled out, "This is the last update from the Church of Atonement. Store what you hear in your minds." The voice-over spouted on. "On the coming 25th of December you will witness the crowning of Lord Sammael in the presence of his father, the mighty Lord Damnus. That day will forever be known as Damnus Day. Declare your belief in them, and show your undying faith as Sammael is crowned King of the World."

A young man's face filled the screen, his hypnotic eyes staring out at the viewers. "Your freedom from the false gods starts from today. You are free to practise Lord Damnus's religious beliefs. If you know of anyone who is not a believer in Lord Damnus, then kill them. That is your right, as of today. Long live Damnus and Sammael."

The picture faded away. The four of them looked down at me, inane grins on their faces. I closed my eyes and concentrated harder than I'd ever done before. Nothing happened. My attention span was still eluding me.

"Their time is up," said Sammael. "Let us finish our business."

Merlin ripped my shirt collar off, and the Master returned to the room with a knife and cleaver in his hands. The sight of the knife brought back the memory of what William Grodam had done to his wife years ago. My heart raced. A fleeting recollection had shown itself. My brain was starting to work again.

The Master moved behind me. "Goodbye, Milner."

As the knife caressed my neck, I mustered some strength from somewhere and grabbed Carin's hand. A random thought broke through the misty barriers in my mind. We vanished into thin air.

Sammael showed no anger at their escape. He rubbed his hands together and looked smugly at the other three. They all burst into fits of laughter. He motioned them to sit on the sofa.

The Master mopped his brow and sighed. "There were moments I had misgivings that your scheme was not going to work. My father came very close to having his throat cut."

Merlin spoke. "I had no doubts. My son did not realise that Lord Sammael was controlling his powers through the ring that he wears. It was he who arranged for the two of them to escape."

The Master shook his head and looked puzzled. "Will Lord Damnus's scheme work?"

Sammael glared at him. "Of course it will. We have let Milner go, deliberately. My father knows that Magnus wants Milner to find a sealed scroll, which has the power of wiping us out forever, as well as bringing the world to an end."

The Master wasn't happy. "You should have killed him while he was under our control. That way he would never have needed to find this scroll." He thought about what he had said. "Perhaps not. If we had killed Milner, Magnus would have opened the scroll himself, so we could not win."

Sammael sneered at him. "That is where you are wrong. You know nothing about this scroll. Magnus cannot open it. Only a human being can. If we had killed Milner, Magnus would have recruited someone else to open it. Milner is the chosen one, and we can track his whereabouts from the ring that he wears."

The Master carried on with his doubts. "I take it, My Lord, that your father has no knowledge of where the scroll is hidden?" He scratched his beard. "You said the world would be wiped out if the scroll is opened. Why would Magnus be prepared to destroy something that they both created?"

"That is the reason Magnus cannot break the seal himself. When Damnus and Magnus finished moulding the earth, Magnus swore that he would never raise his own hand to destroy what he and my father had created. If the need for this situation ever arose, Magnus said he would engage someone else to do his dirty work. A word of warning to you all. Milner is a very clever man. Not only has he inherited awesome powers, but he is a great thinker. Although we can control his powers through the ring, I will not take them away from him until he unearths the scroll. Otherwise he would smell a rat." He laughed out loud. "As for the ring, he will not have any suspicions about it. Why should he? He has worn it for five years."

Merlin had misgivings. "What if he travels back in time and tries to change what we have achieved? How can we stop him?"

"You disappoint me, Merlin. He will not travel back into the past to undermine my plans. Magnus will have told him that the answer to changing what we have done lies in finding the scroll, and not in undoing the past. As well as that, my father tells me that Magnus would most definitely destroy the world if he was ever to do away with us. We must leave Milner alone. That way he will never suspect we are manipulating him and his woman."

The Master was still not convinced. "Could you not get inside Milner's body, when the time is right, and let him lead you to where the scroll is hidden? That would save us a lot of trouble."

Merlin smiled and shook his head. "That is a reasonable suggestion, but it would not work. I tried several times to enter his body when he was a young boy, but I was never able to. That did not surprise me. He is my son, and the powers he inherited from me prevent me from taking over his body."

Sammael turned to Merlin. "I believe you are in touch with someone who will help us bring together the criminal gangs in the United Kingdom, to carry out our bidding."

"That is right, My Lord. We need someone who is entrenched in villainy, and Vinny Gunn is our man. I rang him the other day and gave him my instructions. He is waiting to hear from me."

"Excellent. I will force Milner into finding the scroll by raising the stakes. You will meet up with Gunn and impress on him what I want him to do. While you are doing that, I will be busying myself in setting up some devastating catastrophes. I intend to bring more carnage and suffering to humanity. I know Magnus too well. The more evil that shows its face, the more likely his hand will be forced to bring about our end. That is when Milner will fulfil his destiny, with the help of the scroll." He licked his lips. "I too will enjoy feeding off the suffering of the victims."

Merlin pointed to Jude Carter. "Do you have any further use for him?"

"No. He has done all that I wanted of him." Sammael muttered a few words in Jude's ear. "He knows what he has to do."

Jude regained consciousness, and without a word he left the room. He drove into Lovington town centre and turned into a supermarket garage. He parked at a petrol pump, unhooked the hose, pushed the nozzle through his car's open window and saturated the interior with petrol. He pulled the nozzle out of the car and splattered petrol on the ground before dropping the hose. Jude got back into the car and casually put a cigarette between his lips. As he struck a match, the car blew apart, setting the garage alight.

A single dark cloud scuttled across the moonlit sky. It came to rest over the garage. A bolt of lightning launched itself from the cloud and smashed into the supermarket complex, obliterating it in an almighty firestorm.

CHAPTER THIRTY-ONE

Merlin tapped away at his mobile phone keypad.

A gruff voice answered, "Vinny Gunn here. Who's this?"

"This is Merlin, Gunn. When I rang you the other evening, I ordered you to get some hand-picked men together. Have you arranged what I asked of you?"

"I have. I've signed up over 200 willing criminal gang members, with more on the way. You didn't say what you wanted them for, but they'll do anything you ask – and I mean *anything*." His voice took on a questioning tone. "They're more than willing to work for you because I've told them there's money in it for them. They will be rewarded, won't they? Their work will be of the highest standard."

Merlin was surprisingly composed. "My incentives are generous, so long as they carry out their work to my complete satisfaction. Do I make myself clear, Gunn?"

"They won't let you down."

"Let us talk business. I have drawn up my plans. I will meet up with you at your home next Wednesday at one o'clock. Make sure your contacts are there. Tell them there is £10,000 for everyone who turns up. You will get £20,000 for what you have done."

Vinny gasped. "That's very generous. I'll arrange it."

Merlin cut him off. He poured a glass of wine for himself and Lord Sammael, and told him what Gunn had said.

He wasn't at all happy, and snarled at Merlin, "Who gave you the right to splash my money around?"

"Do not worry, My Lord. I have promised them money, but they will not be getting any. It is only an inducement to make sure everyone turns up."

Sammael raised his glass to Merlin. "I have taught you well."

Carin and I raced down a tunnel of light and ended up sitting on a cold stone floor in complete darkness. The ring on my finger glowed for a split second before fading away. I wondered what the light was all about, before putting my thought on hold and using my finger light to see where we were. The walls of a windowless room were covered in shelves, each stacked with a plethora of books. I located a switch and turned the lights on. The only furniture consisted of a solitary table and two chairs.

I knew where we were. A random thought had slotted into my mind back at the rectory, and had brought us to the British Library. Carin hadn't said a word. Her face showed her unhappiness.

I put my arm around her. "Sorry you had to go through what happened back there. Are you all right?"

She threw a strop. "That's a bloody stupid question. What do you think? I heard all of what was going on. Those scumbags tried to kill us. Other than that, everything's hunky-dory."

I couldn't control my sarcasm. "Thanks for accepting our dinner date from your mate Jude. Some friend he turned out to be. The scumbag drugged us before setting us up." I backtracked. "It's not his fault. He was under Merlin's influence."

She eyeballed me. "Cut the crap. Merlin called me his daughter." She pulled a face. "Why didn't you bother to tell me that he was my father?" I wasn't given the chance to concoct an answer. She screamed at me, "Don't tell me any more sodding lies! I know why you conveniently forgot to tell me. If Merlin's my father, that makes you my half-brother," she snorted. "You thought if I knew, it would put a stop to getting your leg over. You've got some explaining to do, and I don't want any more bullshit."

"OK! OK! You've made your point. Let's get Merlin out of your hair. OK. I've been economical with the truth for a bloody good reason. I didn't know how you would take it if I had told you that Merlin was your father. Let's get one thing straight. I've already told you that Merlin isn't my father, no matter what he thinks. I know who my real father is, but his identity is so preposterous that I'm saying no more than that. I repeat: Merlin is not my father." I let my words sink in. "It's not only your body that I'm in love with. If our sex life worries you, I'll keep my trousers zipped up."

She still wasn't pleased with me, as her questioning sarcasm showed. "You told me that you'd killed Merlin. Oh, dear. What went wrong with your powers of sorcery?"

"He tricked me by using a replica of himself. I killed his replica, not him. Never mind about Merlin. Did you hear that television advert, back at the rectory?"

She still wasn't happy. "Of course I did. What chance do we stand against that lot? They must have hypnotised most of the population into converting to the Church of Atonement. Merlin and his lot must be laughing their heads off at you. Why don't you admit it? They've been too clever for you."

With my self-esteem rapidly draining away, I took the conversation in another direction. "I'm intrigued as to why we managed to get away from them. It was all too pat, too easy. They wanted us to escape, but why?"

Carin's mind was still elsewhere. "Is Merlin really my father?"

"I'm afraid so. You were born in the sixth century, like me. Julius and Meg are your surrogate parents. Merlin influenced them into bringing you up as he wanted. Don't change the habit of a lifetime. Look on them as your real parents."

She went for my jugular. "Cut the patronising, Mister! It's all very well for you to talk like that. You can't begin to understand how I feel inside." She had a rush of conscience. "Sorry. That wasn't fair. I know you meant well."

"Listen to me. We mustn't squabble. Whatever happens in the world, you and I are fated to be two of the big players. We're still a partnership, aren't we?"

She grabbed my hand. "Of course we are."

I felt relief. The demons had left her.

"I've not been very nice to you, have I? I'm sorry, but I'm worried about Mummy and Daddy. What's going to happen to them?"

I scrubbed at my beard. "They'll be converted to this new religion, whether they want to or not."

Carin sighed. "What a mess! Where do we go from here?"

"Things aren't as bad as they might seem. There is a way of defeating them."

She managed a laugh. "That sounds high and mighty. What do you mean?"

"I'm harping back to my dreams again. A voice once told me what I must do when evil gets out of hand. It was the same voice that told me about Merlin's replica, and the fact he is still alive."

She shook her head. "You're so bloody cool and calm about everything. My cynical side thinks you're talking a load of crap." She looked disdainful. "And what else did this voice tell you?"

"I've got to find a sealed scroll and use it to destroy Damnus and his son, as well as Merlin and his cohorts."

Carin spluttered, yet managed another laugh. "Six months ago I'd have crapped my knickers. You're talking way above my head, and everything you're saying is too incredible to be true. Yet I know it is true." She managed to relax. "I'm sorry I've been rough on you. Don't ask me how, but I've accepted that I'm Merlin's daughter and there's nothing I can do about it." She hung herself around my neck. "I do love you. Normal services are resumed." She looked around the room. "Where are we?"

"First things first. You've accepted Merlin as your father, because, like me, you have a strong mental state. Where are we? you ask. Welcome to the British Library. This place slotted into my mind just before we left the rectory. My brain told me that there is something here which will help me understand what Merlin's mob are up to."

Her sarcasm returned. "Perhaps it's a book, or hadn't you thought of that?"

I returned the sarcasm. "Thanks for telling me. I'd never

have guessed. Until it shows itself, let's find the answer as to why they let us go. Think about it rationally. My glimpse of the future showed me that Damnus will do away with every religious movement in the world. They've got that cut and dried already, yet something is worrying them. There's a blip on the horizon which worries them." The answer settled in my mind. "Of course. It's all about this sealed scroll. Damnus obviously knows about the scroll. He wants me to find it, and when I do he'll stop me from breaking the seal."

"Hold on. How will they know that you've found this scroll?" She was asking the right questions.

The answer clattered into my brain. "It's to do with the ring you gave me."

She frowned. "Whoa! Hold on. What are you on about?"

"I was never happy about that stupid box of trinkets that you bought. I knew every lot in the auction room backwards, and I'm convinced that ring wasn't in the box when I first checked it. You bought it for no obvious reason, and – blow me down – a valuable gentleman's ring is nestling amongst the rubbish. To cap it all, it ends up on my finger. Be honest. You didn't know there was a ring in that box, did you?"

She shrugged her shoulders. "No, I didn't."

I didn't press the matter further. "Merlin arranged for someone to put that ring in the box. It was either Jude or Rick Adams. It doesn't matter."

She looked doubtful. "That's a fanciful story based on very dodgy evidence."

I smiled like a Cheshire cat. "It sounds dodgy, except that my ring holds one peculiar property. This room was pitch-black when we arrived. Any ring bought from a reputable jeweller doesn't do what mine did. They don't shine in the dark for a split second. Suppose my ring provides Sammael with the means of keeping in touch with us. What could be simpler? Merlin puts a spell on the ring, and Carin gives the ring to Kit. Bingo. They'll know where we are when I find that sealed scroll."

I flaunted my ring in her face. "To them, this is magical radar. I bet your ring's been doctored as well."

Carin laughed her head off. "What nonsense! Prove it to me if you're so sure."

She was right. It's one thing having a theory, and a completely different ball game to prove you're not a complete dickhead.

"I'm putting my neck on the line; but if my thinking is right, I wouldn't be surprised if they can restrict my powers with this ring."

"You've got to be more convincing than that."

"We've got to be careful. If I'm right, I don't want them to know that we've rumbled them." I thought like mad. "There's a simple way to convince you. Sit as close to me as you can."

She obliged by sitting on my lap.

"I'll turn the light off before transporting us back to our house. Keep your eyes on our rings."

We put our ring fingers together and I switched the light off with a thought wave. Both rings gave out a minute glow as I thought the command to time-travel. It would have been so easy to have missed the glow if we hadn't been looking for it. Seconds later we were stood in our lounge.

I didn't push the 'I told you so' line. I contented myself with a shrug of my shoulders. "See what I mean?"

She shook her head. "The great master is proved right again. What happens when it glows?"

"If my guesswork is right, they pick up a signal which tells them where we are. If we time-travel to a destination that worries them, they can be with us within seconds, in case we should be chasing down the scroll. Lesson number one: we leave our rings at home when we're told to find the scroll."

"Something else worries me, Kit, and it's a big worry."

"What's that, darling?"

"We're not getting any help from this Magnus person. With his powers, he must know everything that Merlin's been up to over the years, yet he's prepared to sit back and let you sort things out. That's not fair, and I'm not impressed one bit."

Her bluntness took me aback momentarily. "Good question. I'm sorry to keep harping back to my dream-voice, but Magnus's answer to your concern is simple. He told me that when the earth's population is eating out of Damnus's hands, only then will Magnus snatch the glory away from Damnus, in what he has achieved. That's when the scroll will come into play. He'll get more pleasure out of playing things his way."

She started to strip her clothes off. For a moment I thought my luck had changed.

"I'm taking a shower and changing my clothes."

"Go and have your shower." I laughed out loud. "Thinking of your body reminds me of something I should have done years ago. I'm going to stop Sammael and his crew from being able to take over your mind and body."

She smiled knowingly and shook her head. "I bet it means you having my body."

"Nothing as pleasant as that. It's as simple as casting a spell on you." I held both her hands and chanted a few words at her. "That's it. I've placed a force field around every opening in your body, so no one can get inside you and control you." I laughed. "It won't affect the call of nature or our lovemaking."

She was so bloody laid-back. "Thank God for that. I didn't feel a thing. I'll have that shower now."

Merlin, the Master, Emeralda and the disciples were sat round the long table in Dalbury Manor. The youthful Sammael sat at its head. He thumped the table to gain their attention.

"Our task is nearly completed, thanks to your endeavours. I intend to control the affairs of man, as well as being the sole sovereign of the world. Every government, in every country, will be ruled under my supervision. Under my rule, mankind will be encouraged to use drugs. They will become a recreational pleasure. The monies they raise will go into our coffers. As of now, we control every drug producer in the world. The drugs they produce will be sold to the Church of Atonement, and no one else. We will decide who sells and distributes them. The existing drug networks will have to work for me, because they can't get their drugs anywhere else. I will not tolerate renegade dealers. They will be killed as a lesson to anyone who might be tempted to follow their lead.

"As regards the United Kingdom, Merlin is in talks with a villain called Vinny Gunn, who is arranging a meeting with the bosses of all the major criminal gangs in this country. Merlin will meet up with them to ensure their minds come under our control. Once this is achieved it will bring Great Britain's criminals in line with the rest of the world.

"My rules for mankind are simple. Work hard, have complete veneration for me and my father, and I want a constant supply of female virgins for my amusement and their ultimate sacrifice. Anyone who cannot work, through illness or old age, or does not have the will to work, or where there is no work available, will have to take their chance in life. They'll get no financial help from my governments. Every country in the world is completely in our pocket, except for the United Kingdom. Merlin and the Master will soon be putting that matter right. They know what I expect of them."

An hour later, Carin and I were back in the basement room of the British Library. I sat her down.

"Make yourself comfortable. I'm getting a feeling that a special book will somehow find me. I'll check them out to see if I get some kind of inspiration." A mosey along the shelves revealed nothing that remotely seemed of any use to me. I shrugged my shoulders and spoke to myself. "Be patient, Milner."

My patience reaped its reward. A book on one of the top shelves made a scrabbling noise as it shifted around in a manic way. It teetered on the edge of the shelf before dropping into my hands. I opened it. The words were written in a language I'd never seen before. That didn't stop me from understanding every word.

"This is what I've been waiting for."

I handed it to Carin. She flicked through the pages, then pulled a face.

"What a strange language! It doesn't mean a thing to me. I can't understand a word. Does it tell you what you have to do next?"

My casualness was so overplayed it belied what was happening. How often does a factual written account of your past and future life land in your hands? Within a few minutes I speed-read the last twenty-odd pages. They set out what would happen in the world during the next few weeks. I closed the book.

"Thankfully, I understand this language. This book answers your question about getting help from Magnus. He's mapped out my past and future in this book. In a sentence, it's all down to finding this sealed scroll, wherever it is."

She snorted. "Didn't know your boss man was in the publishing business. What's the book all about?"

"It maps out my past and what the future holds for us. Every conversation that Sammael, Merlin and his cohorts, have had within their group since the day I was born is in the book, as well as setting out what will happen in the next few weeks. Don't ask me how it found its way here. By the way, I was right about our rings. The book says they are tracking devices that can also interfere with our powers. I'll read all of it when we get back home."

Her sarcasm showed itself again. "Oh, goody. Does it tell you how to destroy Damnus and his lot when we find the scroll?"

"It goes further than that. Once Damnus and his lot are no more, the scroll will bring about the end of the world, which in turn will create a new world."

She made her position clear. "If mankind gets to the point when evil becomes over-rampant, and there's no turning back, I'd gladly bring the world to an end. I hope we won't be twiddling our thumbs until it happens."

"In a word, no. The book says we've got to find this scroll before Sammael is crowned King of the World. His coronation will take place on the 25th of December this year. We are to spend the next few weeks seeing what is going to happen out there."

At long last, Carin got into the spirit of things. "It's beginning to make sense. Any guilt we feel in punishing civilisation will be tempered by our changing things for the better again."

Our conversation was proof of our state of mind. We spoke as if we were planning a summer holiday.

"You're right. The book says that the Damnus mob will be cast into a lake of burning sulphur and never be seen again."

"Does the book tell you where to find this scroll?"

"That's the easy part. It does. Magnus has provided me with the answer?"

"You make everything sound so simple. What does the book say about the scroll?"

I opened the book and read out the last paragraph to her:

> The fate of the world lies in your hands. I have always sworn I could never personally destroy the world that I created. That is why I chose you to carry my wishes through. Spend the next few weeks finding out what a world under the domination of Damnus is like. His form of rule must never be allowed to flourish without end. He holds no feeling for people, only a deep-rooted desire to nourish himself on their pain and suffering. When I am ready, I will take you to meet your parents. My sealed scroll is in their hands. Let me give you a word of warning. Take heed of Damnus's trickery. Make sure he doesn't lead you into a world of unreality. From what I have previously told you, you know all about unreality.

I shut the book. "That's it."

"What does he mean by a world of unreality?"

"That's easy. Merlin has fooled me all along by using replicas of himself and Emeralda. That's what Magnus means. In other words, when they make an appearance on the day I find the scroll I have to check whether they are replicas or not."

She contented herself with a nod of her head. "As long as you know what we have got to do, I'm happy to be a part of it."

She wasn't to know, but the book made it clear that I alone would bring about Damnus's downfall.

I put my arms around her. "No point in staying here. Let's get back home. I can read more of the book to make sure I've missed nothing."

Sammael stared at himself in the mirror. The ring on his finger glowed briefly, sending a thought wave into his mind. He smiled to himself. Keeping a check on Milner's whereabouts was as easy as he'd expected.

He spoke to his reflection. "Milner dropped into the British Library before he went home." He smirked. "Perhaps he is seeking out how to find the sealed scroll. It will not be long before Magnus leads him to the scroll."

His reflection winked and answered him. "By the time we have finished with the world, Magnus will be begging Milner to use the scroll so he can do away with us. That is never going to happen. With the scroll in your hands, you will rule the universe without fear of your reign being undone by Magnus, or Milner."

His reflection was replaced by a scowling Damnus. His red eyes glared at Sammael. "We may be on the verge of taking over the world, but I am getting bored. Get out amongst the people and show me what misery and evil you can provide for me to feast upon."

He bowed to the mirror. "I will do as you ask, Father."

CHAPTER THIRTY-TWO

Carin and I materialised in our house. We didn't have a great deal to say to each other. Tiredness had taken its toll. She crashed out on the sofa, which gave me the chance of reading the story of my life in more detail. Word for word, it narrated how Merlin had guided my life, and what had happened behind my back. One particular passage hit me like a ton of bricks. The book recorded, in sordid detail, how Damnus had raped Carin and she'd given birth to Sammael. I filed that passage away in my mind. It would serve as my biggest reason for enjoying doing away with Damnus and his crew. The book revealed another essential piece of information. Merlin had planted a hair in my scalp, as a baby, which told him of my whereabouts.

As I finished reading the last page, the book moved about in my hands before it flipped into the air and burst in a cloud of dust. I was disappointed at the loss of such a priceless volume, but at least it wouldn't fall into the wrong hands.

Carin shouted to me from the lounge, "Come in here. You've got to see this. Hurry."

The television was chuntering away. The newsreader was the conveyor of bad tidings. "We are now able to bring you an updated report of a serious fire in Lovington."

An airborne camera showed a burned-out building.

The newsreader carried on. "More than 100 people have died in an explosion at the local Tesco store. Eyewitnesses speak about a bolt of lightning striking the supermarket garage just after a man was seen spraying petrol into his car. Police have reason to believe that the man in question was the owner of a well-known restaurant in Lovington, called Mandies."

I turned the television off as I saw tears trickling down Carin's face. I put my arm around her. "We'll put this right one day, and bring Jude back into our new world. The bastards didn't need him any more. It's bad enough that Jude died, but the other people didn't deserve to die. This shows what we are up against."

Tiredness caught up with us. We went to bed, totally exhausted by what the day had produced for us.

It was late on Sunday morning when we woke up. I made coffee and knocked up a late breakfast for us. I'm in danger of becoming the most boring, repetitive individual, but it has to be said, one last time, that Carin is the coolest, most composed person I've ever come across, barring me. She'd been put through the wringer this last twenty-four hours, but you wouldn't have thought so.

She poured herself another coffee. "You could make the world a better place without all that rigmarole with the scroll. You know, and I know, that you could solve the problem right here and now."

I knew what she was thinking, because I had read her mind. I knew what she was on about.

"If we played things your way, I'd lose the most precious thing in my life. Forget it."

"That's not a good enough reason. At least talk it through with me."

I grunted. "OK. I could be a right bastard and stop that lot dead in their tracks today, without needing to find the scroll. It's as simple as travelling back in time and killing Merlin while he's in his mother's womb. Problem solved. No Merlin, no Master, no plot" – I pulled a face and clutched at her hand – "and no Carin. Is that what you really want? because I don't." I didn't give her time to answer. "Forget what you're thinking, because it wouldn't solve anything. Even if I killed Merlin, Damnus would still be alive, and he'd find a replacement for Merlin to carry out his dirty work. And, before you ask, I couldn't get rid of Damnus. He's immortal, like us, and that book told me that I need the scroll to take his immortality away.

"Why should I sacrifice you to appease billions of people who have allowed themselves to fall in with Sammael, whether by hypnosis or not? Millions of people were already treading his footpath before this hypnotic nonsense started. I'm not sacrificing you for their mistakes, and that's final. The only answer is to destroy Damnus, Sammael and the others, by using the powers of the scroll.

"Now, listen to me. Give some thought to my plan B. It says that Kit finds the sealed scroll. The book of my life made it clear that if I break the scroll's seal, in the presence of Sammael and the rest of his crew, they would be cast into a lake of fire and done away with forever." I was getting into my stride. "On top of that, the world will be destroyed by the scroll as well. You and I would survive, because we're immortal. So, after doing away with that lot we return to our own time, where we left it, and what do we find? The world is still the same as Damnus left it."

Carin nodded her head. "Of course. The legacy he left still carries on." She frowned. "You mentioned killing Sammael and the others with the scroll, but how do you find Damnus, to do away with him?"

"That's simple. The book told me that Damnus lives in Sammael's body; so when Sammael dies, Damnus dies. We would then travel back in time to kill Damnus and Merlin in their past lives before they brought the world to its knees. I would use the scroll to kill them, after which the world religions would be back to normal, your mother and father would be their old selves, and I would fast-forward myself to meet up with you again. Damnus would be permanently out of everyone's lives. Plan B will have worked. Problem solved."

She wrapped herself around me. "I'm lost for words." She looked at her watch. "I don't know about you, but I'm still whacked. Do you fancy going to bed?"

"Good idea. I need some rest. I've got an auction to arrange next week. Tell you what, come and work for me. It'll keep your feet on the ground and take your mind off our problems. I'll arrange something tomorrow – which reminds me, I meant to tell you that Merlin planted one of his hairs in my scalp when I was born, which tells him where I am. I've got to get rid of it."

I placed a thought in my mind to remove it. My sorcery obliged me, as a hair floated down on to the table.

She showed no surprise. "I'm glad you've got that sorted, Kit." She grinned at me. "Shall we go to bed?"

Merlin and Emeralda were lying in bed together. He kissed her, then whispered in her ear, "I have a task for you. We should have done this before. I want you to get inside our daughter's body and read her mind. She could be carrying some information which will give a clue as to what Milner is up to. It is no good trying to read Milner's mind. No one can enter his body."

"You want me to do it now?"

"Yes. It will not take you long."

She shrugged her shoulders and disappeared in front of his eyes.

Ten minutes later Emeralda returned. She didn't look at all happy.

Merlin's face dropped. "From the look on your face, things have not worked out as I hoped."

"I tried to enter her body, but found my passage was blocked."

Merlin swore. "Milner has been too clever for us. He has used his sorcery on her. I am not surprised. I expect nothing less from my son. He is a clever man, and is making our job harder. Thank goodness they are wearing my rings. He will not catch us unawares when he goes in search of the scroll."

Bishop John of Hereward stood in his pulpit, delivering a hard-hitting sermon to his congregation. He was a very worried bishop. His Sunday congregation had noticeably dwindled. This was borne out by the half-dozen or so people scattered over the wide expanses of the cathedral.

His worries weren't only confined to the reducing numbers.

His concern also lay in the evil revolution that was sweeping the country. He had spent the last few weeks denouncing this evil trend from the pulpit. His words had fallen on barren ground.

He was deeply troubled by a long string of television commercials, playing up the merits of a new religious order calling itself the Church of Atonement. It purported to be a new-style Church. He'd found its message sinister and disturbing. Bishop John was convinced that the Church of Atonement wasn't pushing God's wares.

The Sunday service ended and the last of his flock bade him goodbye. The Bishop disrobed and left the cathedral by the back entrance. As he closed the door he was accosted by a young man dressed in a black cassock. The man placed a hand on Bishop John's chest. He felt every muscle in his body tighten up. He could neither move nor speak.

The man spoke to him. "Let me introduce myself. I am the Master, a disciple of the Church of Atonement. I am concerned that you are canvassing for the wrong kind of religion. If you changed your allegiance to the Church of Atonement, you would fill your house of worship every Sunday. That is not going to happen under your ministry, is it? What a pity! You are a menace, an irritating nuisance, and you are getting under my skin. We have had our fill of you. But there is an answer. Why not come and join us?"

The Master laid his hands on the Bishop's head and muttered a few words.

Bishop John smiled as he looked the young man in the face and spoke to him. "It's a pleasure to meet you. I will be visiting the local newspaper tomorrow to tell them to print the news that this religious building is now a cathedral which houses the Church of Atonement."

Merlin appeared from nowhere, in front of Vinny Gunn's grand country house. He grimaced at the expensive cars parked on the front drive and down the road. Merlin passed through the locked front door and found himself in the hall. The house and the back garden were bursting at the seams with hundreds of men, all speaking with the volume button on loud. Those closest to Merlin stopped their verbal diarrhoea at the sight of his unusual entrance. Vinny was talking to three particularly evil-looking bastards. He dropped them as if they weren't there, and hurried across to Merlin.

"Welcome to my humble abode."

Merlin wasn't amused. "Your ill-gotten gains have stood you in good stead, Gunn."

Vinny felt flattered. "Thank you. Would you like to speak to my associates now?"

Merlin grunted. "That is why I am here."

Vinny yelled out in an attempt to impress Merlin, "Shut your faces, you lot. I want you in the back garden with the others – like now."

The hum of conversation ceased as they trooped into the wide expanse of Gunn's garden. Merlin followed them. He knew from reading their evil thought waves that Vinny had chosen well.

A particularly ugly villain, standing at the front, shouted at him, "When are we getting the money you promised?"

Merlin stopped him with a stare and yelled at him, "There is no money for turning up today. Your real reward is working for me."

Sounds of discontent filled the air.

Merlin snapped his fingers. Everyone stiffened, their dead eyes showing they were under his hex.

"When you leave this place, you will do all that I am about to ask of you, without question and without money. Do you understand?"

Their roared their agreement.

"Good. This is your first task. The gangs that you control are going to take on the role of criminal bashers. You will go back home and seek out all known criminals in your area. Once you have found them, order them to work for me. If they refuse, kill them. The purpose of this exercise is to show them that through you the Church of Atonement runs things now. You do not need to worry about the police. They will be more than willing to lend a hand. Forget your past relationship with them, and work alongside them. I have spent years nurturing the police to do what I expect from them. Make contact with your county police forces as soon as you get back home. They will be delighted to join up with you in your assault on small-time crooks who do not join our cause." Merlin's face creased into a semblance of a smile. "That should be a novel experience – you and the police fighting on the same side."

He walked towards a table, which was crammed with glasses of wine that he had asked Vinny to provide. He pulled a bottle of the magic Damnus brew from his pocket, opened it and stood it on the table. As he muttered under his breath, droplets of the liquid floated through the air, and drop by single drop they fell into every glass of wine.

He ran his eyes over the hoodlums. "Come and help yourselves to a glass of wine and drink it. It will clear your minds, and give you extra strength and powers to carry my task through. I am delegating Vinny Gunn as your commander-in-chief. He will answer directly to me. Do what I have ordered, and only then will your success be well rewarded. Do you understand?"

They cheered and clapped him, and after they had drunk the wine they bowed to him and left the garden.

Merlin grabbed Vinny. "Stay here, you." His eyes glared into Gunn's face. "Do not fail me in carrying out my instructions. If you do, I will take your worthless life."

Vinny's voice showed the fear he felt. "I will not fail you."

Merlin snarled, "Make sure you do not. You will be hearing from me."

CHAPTER THIRTY-THREE

The twenty children walking up Akeman Street, in Grinton, found it hard to curb their excitement. They had been given Monday afternoon off from school as an end-of-term treat. Their teachers were taking them to Grinton Natural History Museum. They gathered in front of the magnificent Victorian building. The head teacher called the children to order. They fell silent. She pulled her coat tightly around her in an effort to keep out the chill breeze blowing off the downs.

"When we get inside, you will be on your best behaviour. There are other visitors, and I don't want their visit spoilt by any unruliness from you lot."

The head teacher led her charges up the steps and into the museum. They were met by Glynn Jones, the head curator. The children listened patiently as he gave them a brief account of the museum's history.

"Welcome to Grinton Natural History Museum. The founder, Walter Rothschild, was a well-known Victorian zoologist, who travelled the world collecting animals. He brought many live animals back to this country and had them released into Grinton Park. The last one died many years ago.

"Walter was keen to put the many animal skins he had collected on display. He had them stuffed, so they could be shown off in this wonderful building. You will also find fish, birds and reptiles on display, as well as collections of insects and birds' eggs." He brought a smile to the children's faces, with a rare display of humour. "Do not be frightened of the animals. Some of them look really fierce – a bit like your teachers. The difference is that the animals are dead, so they cannot hurt you. We will look around the ground floor first." He nodded to the head teacher. "Ready when you are."

The children were thrilled at the sight of the hundreds of stuffed animals imprisoned in their glass cabinets. The curator ushered them into the gorilla and monkey display area. Six angry-looking gorillas stared at the children through their menacing glass eyes. They were posed in fighting mode, their arms raised in an intimidating manner. Several children hid their faces, and two started to cry.

The head teacher reacted to their fears. "Don't be frightened. Remember what Mr Jones said. They can't harm you. They've been dead for years."

She frantically waved at the curator, to move further down the corridor. They trooped past the gorillas and listened to what Mr Jones had to say about the deer exhibits. His words were cut short by the sound of breaking glass. The children screamed in terror at the sight of the six gorillas standing in the corridor, saliva running from their mouths. The animals roared and beat at their chests before ambling towards the children and the many other visitors. Mr Jones smiled and quickly made his way out of the building. He locked the front door behind him.

Everyone panicked and ran towards the main entrance. Several children were pushed to the floor in the mad scramble to escape. The gorillas swooped on them. The children's cries of pain fell on deaf ears.

The teachers shepherded the other children into the comparative safety of the front entrance. The head teacher felt a surge of relief as she turned the knob on the front door. Her feelings soon changed. Naked fear and hopelessness replaced it. Not only was the front door locked, but four lions were bounding down the staircase towards them. In that moment of desperation she gave up the will to live, knowing that death was a matter of moments away for all of them.

Mr Jones walked down the outside steps and disappeared behind some bushes before collapsing. A trickle of vapour spilled from his nose. A smiling Sammael became visible for a moment. He listened with relish to the screaming on the other side of the main door, before disappearing.

I introduced Carin to my staff on Monday morning. I told them she'd be joining the team as a temporary worker. She was accepted without question. Finding her a worthwhile job hadn't proved difficult. One of my porters was away sick. She would fill his role. Saturday's auction was to be Carin's baptism of fire.

She excused herself, saying she was going to ring the surgery from the flat. That's when Martin turned up out of the blue.

He grinned at me and looked around the office. "Hello, my boy. Carin not here, then? I heard she's joined the team."

"She's on a sabbatical. I thought I'd give her some work experience. We're living in the flat for a few days."

A daft look covered his face. "I hope you're putting her on the payroll. If she's worth employing, she's worth paying." He looked embarrassed. Martin had forgotten he no longer held the business reins. "Sorry, Kit. I'm out of order. What you do with Carin is your business."

Poor old Martin. He didn't realise she was worth millions. He was in a sentimental stupor.

"Do you mind if I have a nose around the premises? Who knows, I might bump into Carin!"

"If you find her, she won't mind a peck on the cheek."

He grinned, and doffed his hat to me. "See you, Kit. Keep up the good work."

I rang Carin's mobile. She answered and blew me a kiss.

"Save your kisses for Martin. Someone told him you're here. The silly old sod is out there looking for you. Make sure you bump into him. It'll make his day."

She laughed and rang off.

Sammael strode down Dorkingham High Street. Nobody gave

him a second glance. That was hardly surprising, seeing he'd made himself invisible. He stopped in front of the Terracotta Warriors Museum and went inside. He headed to the Warriors' Room. The clay fighters stared through unseeing eyes, their bodies destined to spend an eternity of lifelessness. He looked intently at them and muttered a few words.

A few minutes later a guide walked into the room followed by some eager-looking visitors. He did his best to ignore a young girl who'd whined incessantly from the moment she'd stepped into the museum.

He enthused about the warriors. "They are unique. Their life-size bodies are modelled in clay. Each head is individual, as are the thousands of warriors still being dug up in China."

The terracotta soldiers were oblivious of the gawking eyes and gaping mouths in front of them.

The stressed guide glared at the troublesome girl and carried on with his spiel. "The figures are so lifelike in the skilful manner of their moulding. If you look at the crossbowmen—"

His words were cut short by splintering sounds that filled the room.

One lady pointed at the warriors. "What's happening, for God's sake? Is this part of the tour?"

The fretful child stopped whining and clapped her hands in glee. Eleven pairs of unbelieving eyes stared at the warriors as they tore their feet from their concrete plinths. They flexed their arms and legs. The warrior general pointed to the visitors and yelled orders in a gabbled high-pitched voice. The crossbowmen and longbow men charged their weapons, then let fly their bolts and arrows. Seven visitors clutched at the missiles sticking out of their chests. They were dead before they hit the floor. The child whooped with delight as the general urged his warriors to advance on the rest of the intruders.

The smell of unbridled fear filled the air. The remaining visitors fled towards the exit, leaving the child behind them. Every door in the museum slammed shut, with the sound of locks and bolts falling into place echoing through the building. The tourists were left at the mercy of the warriors. The child drooled at the lips at the sight of the slaughter before she was snatched from the room by an invisible force.

Sammael tore his thoughts away from the pleasure he was garnering, and materialised from inside the girl. He patted her head, but showed her no sympathy.

He waved a hand at her. "You can go back in that room. Goodbye."

In her trance-like state she reappeared in the Warriors' Room. Sammael roared with laughter at the sound of her hysterical screams, which were quickly silenced. He clicked his fingers and vanished.

We were drinking coffee in the lounge, watching television. The programme was suddenly interrupted by a newsflash. The newsreader confirmed that sketchy reports were being received of mass deaths at Grinton Natural History Museum and the Dorkingham Terracotta Warriors Museum.

A news correspondent speculated on the reports. "In the Grinton Natural History Museum massacre, it appears the victims, mainly children, were torn to pieces by animals. A search of the museum revealed stuffed gorillas and lions covered in what appears to be human blood. Even more baffling, the animals were inside their undamaged glass cabinets.

"The terracotta killings are just as mystifying. Twelve people, including a small child, lost their lives. Most of the victims died from wounds inflicted on them by bolts and arrows. There was no sign of weapons inside the locked premises, other than those held by the model warriors on their display stands."

Carin looked me in the eyes. "Did you see the correspondent's face? She didn't appear to care a toss about what had happened. There was no trace of shock or compassion in her voice. I know they have to cope with bad news, but her reactions weren't credible. She was smiling half of the time, and licking her lips."

I got up and switched the set off. "We've seen enough of that. You know what this means, don't you?"

She spoke the words in my mind. "We're being pushed into looking for the scroll, aren't we?"

"Exactly. It won't be long now."

Lovington Marketplace was awash with people, chanting Sammael's name and brandishing placards in the air, written in blood-red letters. Most placards carried the message 'SAMMAEL IS OUR KING. LONG LIVE SAMMAEL.' Other placards carried a more chilling message: 'KILL THE NON-BELIEVERS.'

The door of the Methodist church, standing on the edge of the marketplace, was locked. Half a dozen people huddled inside.

The minister did his best to put their minds at ease. "These are worrying times for us non-believers of Sammael, which is why I arranged this meeting. As you can hear from the noise outside, Sammael's followers are on the streets. Our brand of religion is being stripped from people's minds. If only they realised that they've been mesmerised into submission. Thank God none of us have been influenced by those television programmes."

The shouting from the marketplace filtered into the church.

"I'm concerned for your safety. If those thugs find us here, you know what will happen to us. Return to your homes. Leave by the back door, and make sure no one sees you. Don't come here again. I'll try and arrange some services in your homes." He clasped his hands in prayer. "Let us spend a few moments in silent contemplation of the true God before we go."

The worshippers bowed their heads, except for eighty-year-old Doreen Welby. She had always been the butt of everyone's humour because of the way she dressed. She had worn the same garb to church for the past fifteen years. Her black dress, black tights, black coat and straw hat had long outstayed their welcome in the eyes of the congregation.

Doreen struggled to her feet and leaned heavily on the front pew. "Sod being silent. I've got something to say, and not before time."

Everyone looked startled.

The minister managed a smile. "What is it, Doreen?"

"For fifteen years you lot have ridiculed how I dress. God wasn't worried, but you lot were. I never had the courage to

273

say anything, until today. That's all in the past, because today is payback day." She averted her eyes to the ceiling and yelled out, "Hallelujah! Sammael rules! Your God is the false God!"

They gasped at her heresy. It was the last sound they ever made. The aggrieved Doreen Welby waved her hand in the air. There was an almighty explosion and the church was blown apart.

The marketplace crowd gathered outside the ruins of the church. Doreen Welby walked out of the rubble. The throng opened up to let her through. She turned towards the church and mumbled a few words. A violent sheet of flame erupted through the smashed windows. Doreen clapped her hands together. What was left of the building imploded and collapsed in a pile of smoking debris. The old woman vanished in front of their eyes.

Sammael, masked in his cloak of invisibility, yelled to the crowd, "This is what will happen to those who do not worship Lord Damnus and his son, Sammael."

The crowd sank to their knees and praised his name.

CHAPTER THIRTY-FOUR

The Wednesday parochial church council meeting provided an ongoing problem for the Reverend Nigel Smith. Nobody had bothered to turn up. Twelve months ago six committee members would have attended. His old congregation of some 100 souls had plummeted in the same way.

The Reverend had received a letter from Bishop John of Hereward some weeks ago, warning him that the Christian faith was being submerged by a newfangled body calling itself the Church of Atonement, and saying they had to do something about it. Nigel had caught a couple of their television commercials. He hadn't been moved by the experience.

Bishop John hadn't held back in his choice of words. He referred to this new movement as an upstart Church, probably leaning towards the dark forces. Bishop John considered this new religious faction to be the most dangerous adversary to all religions since the turmoil caused by Henry VIII and Thomas Cromwell.

Having described the Church of Atonement in such terms, Nigel had been absolutely amazed to receive another letter from Bishop John that morning, in which he confirmed that all cathedrals in the country, including Ely, had now turned to the Church of Atonement, and all Anglican churches which hadn't already done so were to welcome the new Church with open arms. Nigel wasn't prepared to go down that road.

As he opened the main door to lock up, the Reverend found

his way barred by four young men. One of them was the Master. He shouted a spell at the Reverend, who collapsed to the floor. The Master floated Nigel's unconscious body inside the church and dumped him on top of the altar.

During the next ten minutes, the four of them vandalised every Christian artefact. Crucifixes were torn down and broken into pieces, and ancient monuments were prised off the walls. The stained-glass windows didn't escape the desecration. Every stained-glass window was covered in paint.

They piled hymn books and Bibles under the altar. A fierce flame exploded from the Master's fingers, and the books and the altar were immersed in a fiery inferno.

He nodded to the other three. "This is what will happen to the remaining few churches who do not follow Lord Sammael's religious views."

He turned the lights out, and the four of them melted into the night on their way to deal with another Church of England priest who hadn't allowed his church to join the growing ranks of the Atonement movement.

We sat watching television on Wednesday evening, and were totally immersed in what was going on, but not relishing what was unfolding on the screen. A newsreader reported the murder of a clergyman in his vandalised church. His charred body had been found among the burned remains of the altar. Mobile-phone footage showed images of four men cornering another clergyman in his churchyard. The cleric was beaten to death.

We'd seen enough, and I switched the set off. I knew what was happening. Sammael was doing his utmost to force my hand into seeking out the scroll.

Carin showed her frustration. "When's it all going to stop? I'm getting a guilt complex about these killings. Every day we delay finding that bloody scroll, more and more people are going to die. Their blood is on our hands."

How do you counter something that you can't disagree with? I tried. "Listen. Saturday's auction is my last one this year. Get that out of the way, and we'll get things sorted. It's not all bad.

As soon as the scroll does its business, and I put the world right, none of what we're seeing will have ever happened. Every person who dies in the apocalypse will be restored to life, in the same way your parents were the last time I meddled with time."

"Point taken." She punched me playfully. "One thing hasn't gone unnoticed this week. You drive your staff too hard, including me. I'm knackered." I couldn't miss her larger-than-life wink. "Shall we go to bed?"

Who was I to argue with such a veiled invitation?

The week seemed to pass quicker than it normally would have done. Carin's boundless energy and personality infected my staff. There's nothing she can't do. I even caught her using her powers to move a heavy wardrobe while no one was looking.

By Thursday afternoon everything was up and running for Saturday's auction. As a special treat, I took her out to dinner at The Rose and Crown.

I switched the television on when we got back. We'd not become avid viewers. It was our chosen way of keeping abreast of what was happening in the outside world. The news was full of unbelievable reports. It was disturbing to see televised pictures, from all around the world, of thousands of people carrying placards declaring death to the infidels who did not believe in the Church of Atonement.

Someone, off-screen, handed a piece of paper to the newscaster.

He scanned it quickly before revealing more violence. "A large explosion has demolished the Statue of Liberty, and the Eiffel Tower has been toppled by explosives, as have the Tower of Pisa and Nelson's Column. Reports are sketchy, but many other such atrocities have been carried out throughout the world with a great loss of life."

Another piece of paper was passed to the overworked newscaster.

Unbelievably, he allowed himself a smile. "Vast swathes of Africa, Asia and the Middle East are covered in floodwater. Millions of people have been displaced from their homes, and casualties are expected to be high. No warning was given. The deep waters appeared within minutes, which explains the high number of deaths. Deserts are under many feet of water. It's the first time in centuries that water has been found in these areas."

We hadn't got much to say to each other when I turned the television off.

I gazed into her green eyes. "I know what you're thinking, and you're right. A lot of what's happening can only be down to sorcery. Damnus is feeding on the misery that's being created. This won't go on much longer, once I find that scroll. Thank God all the people who are dying will be resurrected one day.

She didn't need to say anything. Her eyes spoke the relief she felt.

It was Friday morning when the Master slipped into the House of Commons chamber. The members were taking their seats as he took over Mr Speaker's body.

He stood up and spoke the thoughts that had been placed into his mind by the Master. "Order. Order. I have the floor. There are important issues which require the approval of the House. I will leave the Prime Minister to bring the matters before you that require your approval."

The Prime Minister got to his feet. The Master, who had taken over his body, spoke his words. "You will pass all the measures unanimously, without the need for debate. I will have your approval, won't I?"

A positive roar met his words. That was no surprise, because every MP's body had been taken over by a replica disciple.

"Before I give details of the bills to be set down and ratified, there is one overriding matter that needs resolving. This particular subject has been discussed with the monarch. She has given her full support and approval." He read from the paper in his hands. "On the 25th of December of this year the religious movement known to you as the Church of Atonement will assume the role of the only permitted religious body in this country. All other religions will become non-existent, and the people of the United Kingdom will be subject to the laws of the Church of

Atonement." He took a sip of water. "Representatives of the Church of Atonement will be taking on the role of Members in this House, and will become responsible for lawmaking with immediate effect. As from today, you will all become surplus to requirements, and the Church of Atonement will appoint its own members to serve in the House. General elections are now defunct.

"The House of Lords will also be abolished. I have asked peers to convene in half an hour, when I will break the news to them. The leaders of the Church of Atonement will be presented to the world at midday on the 25th of December in Grinton, Hertfordshire. My cabinet members, together with the opposition's shadow cabinet, will attend the day of celebration. Be there in good time.

"As I have intimated, you will accept what I've told you without the need for discussion. Raise your hands to show your agreement."

A forest of hands shot up into the air.

The Prime Minister smiled. "Today's measures will be aired on television this evening. The legislation you have agreed today cannot be rescinded, and will be passed on to the statute book. There are other matters that I have to put before you."

On Friday evening we cooked a meal for ourselves and switched the BBC News channel on. Our timing was good, or bad, whichever way you look at it.

A newscaster appeared on screen. "This programme is being broadcast on all television and radio channels. In a sitting of the House of Commons this afternoon, Members of Parliament unanimously approved a raft of new measures, which have been passed on to the statute book. They include a ruling that all illegal drugs will be declassified, from the 1st of January next year. From that date, drugs will legally be sold through one approved agency. More detail will be made available nearer the time. The death penalty has been introduced for crimes against the state, including anyone caught selling drugs who is not a part of the approved agency.

"New commanders-in-chief have been appointed for the armed forces and the police. Details of the new appointments, and other changes, will be forthcoming." The surprises didn't stop there. "The Prime Minister has announced that, with immediate effect, Parliament and the House of Lords will be abolished, and members appointed by the Church of Atonement will run the country's affairs. A further measure, approved by Parliament, is the nationalisation of the United Kingdom's banking system, together with the Stock Exchange. All banks are to be merged into one banking corporation, which, together with the Stock Exchange, will be run by an approved body appointed by the Church of Atonement. The country's legal system is to be restructured. Precise details will be clarified in due course. As I have mentioned already, the selling of drugs is now legal, but they will only be sold through a supplier authorised by the Church of Atonement. An operation was mounted this morning against small-time criminal elements, including individual drug dealers, who refused to work with the newly appointed supplier. Early reports suggest that the operation has proved successful, and many small-time criminals, including drug dealers, have been killed in the process.

"This operation was masterminded by the Church of Atonement, backed up by the police. The Church's leaders are anxious to ensure that people do not have to suffer the pain and misery caused by small-time criminal elements operating in their neighbourhoods."

A smirk appeared on the newscaster's face as he confirmed that Parliament had installed the Church of Atonement as the only recognised religion in the United Kingdom. Any person acting against the Church of Atonement would suffer death by hanging.

The newscaster's face faded from the screen. Someone we knew well took his place. He looked as happy as a sandboy.

"Good evening. My words are being transmitted throughout the world. Let me introduce myself. I am Belial, but you will come to address me as the Master. I speak for the Church of Atonement this evening. You are already aware of the new laws which the British Parliament has approved. These laws grant my Church overriding powers in this country. The same decrees have been passed in every other country of the world. There is no need for concern. The role of the Church of Atonement will benefit every citizen in the world.

"The supreme leader of our church, Lord Sammael, will be presented to the world for the first time on the coming 25th of December. His father, Lord Damnus, will also be present. The monarch will personally crown Lord Sammael as King of the World at midday on that day. The crowning will be broadcast live on television throughout the world. Your monarch has agreed to abdicate, and will be moving to her Sandringham Estate together with all other members of the royal family.

"What is taking place in this country has already spread to every corner of the earth. Our Church holds sway throughout the world. No longer will there be tensions or conflicts arising from religious differences. I guarantee this." The camera panned in on the Master's face. A pair of staring, evil eyes filled the screen. "Listen to my words and store them in your minds. You will obey everything I tell you."

I had to fight hard to keep my mind open.

I squeezed Carin's hand. "Are you still in the land of the living?"

"Only just. The bugger's hypnotising everyone."

The Master's voice droned on. "You will all become followers of the Church of Atonement. Your nearest church will soon offer you our own style of religious service. The wearing, or displaying, of other religious emblems, such as the crucifix, will no longer be tolerated. The death penalty awaits anyone who breaks this law.

"You will all watch the coronation on your television screens. Give your full support to the leaders and chapter of the Church of Atonement, and do everything they tell you.

"As of today, every television channel is under the control of my Church, as is the national press. The new name for your television company is the Belial Broadcasting Company, or BBC. Do not switch your sets off. There is more to see and hear."

He snapped his fingers and faded from the screen. A six-part multi-screen appeared, showing crowds of people in different parts of the country. They were worked up to a frenzy, waving placards and chanting Church of Atonement slogans. The television cameras highlighted one of the gatherings in close-up. An agitated crowd gave vent to their manic support for the Church of Atonement. Their placards bore frightening predictions of what would befall anyone stupid enough not to support the Church.

As these scenes faded away, a male voice bawled out.

I nudged Carin. "This is what we saw at the rectory before we managed to escape."

The voice carried on with its message. "This is the last update from the Church of Atonement. Store what you hear in your minds. On the coming 25th of December you will witness the crowning of Lord Sammael in the presence of his father, the mighty Lord Damnus. That day will forever be known as Damnus Day. Declare your belief in them, and show them your undying faith, as Sammael is crowned King of the World.

"Your freedom from the false God starts from today. You are free to practise Lord Damnus's black arts. If you know of anyone who is not a believer in Lord Damnus, then hunt them down and kill them. That is your right, as of today. Long live Damnus and Sammael."

I'd seen enough, and switched the set off.

"The Damnus movement is motoring along in the fast lane."

Her eyes flashed. "The Master is an evil bastard. I'd throttle him if I got my hands on him." She quickly composed herself. "Everything's happening too quickly."

"That's where you're wrong. Their grand scheme has been nurtured during the last five years or so, ever since Jude left us for what he called his new job."

She gave me a withering look. "How can they have achieved what they've done in five years?"

For once her thinking processes had let her down.

"Merlin has created many thousands of replicas of his twelve disciples. They've spent the last five years travelling the world, taking over the minds of everyone in positions of power."

She shook her head and clicked her tongue. "Yeah, yeah, yeah! So all these replicas have developed special powers, have they?"

It was my turn to snarl. "And why not? Merlin will have made sure they all have powers of sorcery."

Her back was up. She stamped her feet on the carpet. "I'm so annoyed that thousands of innocent people are going to suffer, and the Damnus bunch couldn't care a toss. Our hypnotised idiot population are dipping their feet in the water and liking the feel of it. If people want to practise induced evil, that's up to them, whether they like it or not. I feel sorry for those folk who have a natural defence against hypnotism. They'll have to pretend to be under the Damnus influence if they've got any sense. You are getting this mess sorted out next week, aren't you?"

"That's a promise. We can't let things run out of control much longer." I looked at my watch. "We've got a busy day tomorrow. Shall we get some shut-eye?"

"So long as I have a cuddle, I don't mind."

I playfully smacked her behind. "So long as the cuddle leads to something else, I don't mind."

"I'm glad this business hasn't put you off my body. Come on, before I change my mind."

CHAPTER THIRTY-FIVE

Rick Adams lay snoring in his bed. His bedroom light switched itself on as the Master appeared at his bedside.

He knelt down and whispered in Rick's ear, "I have a job for you, Adams. You are going to put in an appearance at Milner's auction later today. I have planted a little trinket in one of his jewellery lots. Your job is to stir things up when I tell you. I will be guiding you. Get dressed."

He did as he was told, and stood at the Master's side.

The Master managed a grin. "You are the key man in leading Milner into what we planned for him years ago. He is about to come face-to-face with his destiny. Grab your overcoat. It is cold out there."

I lay in bed, with Carin sleeping by my side. Something had been niggling at my mind during the past few days. This coming Sunday was the date of that first premonition that I'd witnessed when Carin had been offered up for sacrifice by the Master. The book of my life had primed me with the knowledge that Sammael's lot would show their hand at the auction, and I knew how it would happen. I wasn't to change things, but I had no intention of letting them get their hands on Carin.

At this late hour of the night I had to prepare myself. I eased myself out of bed without waking Carin, and placed my hand on her head before muttering the words that sent her into a deep sleep, until I was ready to waken her. The next step was new ground for me. I was about to create my first human replica. I mumbled the words to get the process going. Within seconds, a dead ringer of Carin lay asleep on my side of the bed. I read the replica's mind. It contained Carin's memories of her lifetime. I slipped Carin's ring on to the replica's finger, then put my hand on her chest. Her heart was beating as she slept, sending blood coursing through her living flesh.

It didn't take me long to dress my Carin and sit her in a chair. I put her nightdress on her replica. My new-found replica skills came into play a second time. Within seconds a naked replica of me stood at my side.

I smiled at him. "I'm going to check your memory cells."

He raised an eyebrow. "You made me, so be my guest."

"OK. So what has the Master been up to this week?"

"Is that the best you can do? The smug swine made a televised broadcast this evening. That was followed by the last bulletin from the Church of Atonement. I'll go a bit further. You're preparing for a replica Carin to be snatched at the auction." He nodded at the chair. "That's why she's sitting over there. Her twin will take her place."

I had to smile. His mind was a mirror image of my own.

"I'm taking Carin home. I want you to stay here so that Merlin won't twig what I'm up to." I gave him my ring, and picked Carin up in my arms. "Wear this until I get back. I'll see you soon." I looked him up and down. "You'd better put some clothes on before I come back."

I sat her on the sofa, back at our house, then made her invisible and placed a force field around her. She was safe from anyone until I was ready to revive her. I willed myself back to the flat. My twin had dressed himself and was waiting for me.

He handed me a cup of coffee and winked. "I've picked up your thought wave. My job's done for now, but you'll be needing me in a few days from now. Am I right?"

"Sure thing. You've got a busy couple of days ahead of you. It's time for you to go."

He finished his coffee and put the mug down on the table. "Understood, boss. I'll see you soon. You'd better have your ring back."

I mumbled a few words and he broke down into a fine mist.

We were early risers on Saturday morning.

Even with the country's problems swimming around inside her head, my replica Carin couldn't contain herself. "Are you sure you've told me everything I need to know?"

Winding her up was the remedy for her condition. "Your job's simple. I announce the lot number. You pick the item up, or point to it if it's too heavy. Then I encourage the punters to spend their hard-earned cash. You push the price up higher by stripping your clothes off. Make sure you're not holding anything before you strip. I don't want you dropping things, except your clothes."

She roared with laughter and pointed at the fruit bowl. A banana winged its way through the air and slapped me around the ear.

I sent the banana flying back into the bowl.

"I'm very impressed – which reminds me, I don't want you using your hypnotic powers to get the prices up. Leave that to my natural means of persuasion."

She grinned. "As if I would."

"Let's go. Martin's invited himself to the auction. I said we'd meet him in my office. He's very anxious to see you in action. So, you'd better not strip. It wouldn't do his blood pressure any good."

Martin was waiting for us. It wasn't the Martin I knew. He was tossing a bread knife from hand to hand, and wearing a glazed look on his redder than usual face. Even the sight of Carin didn't melt his grim looks.

He pointed the knife at me. "Ah! There you are! About time too! Did you see the Church of Atonement pushing their wares on television last night?" He momentarily relaxed. "Sammael is the future of this country and the world." His face twitched;

so did the knife. "Do you two support him?"

I threw a thought wave at Carin, telling her to agree with whatever he said.

"We've been believers of him for years," I said. "I've even met the bloke who's running the outfit."

I could see he was impressed. The tension in his body dispersed like a deflating balloon.

"Just making sure. You'd have been a big loss to the company if you hadn't been a believer." He put the knife down on my desk and poked me in the chest with his finger. "I've checked your staff out while I was waiting, to make sure Sammael is their man." He attempted a smile and failed. "Only Joanne wasn't certain if she was one of us."

I wasn't surprised. Joanne had never owned a television set in her whole life.

Martin stared at me with those dead eyes. "With a little bit of gentle persuasion she came round to my way of thinking."

I took exception to his clumsy, unveiled threats, to me and my staff.

I pushed his resolve. "What would you have done if we hadn't been believers?"

He grunted. "Simple. If you don't believe, you die, no matter who you are."

I picked the knife up. "I'm bigger and fitter than you."

The sneer on his face answered my question. "Bollocks. Look behind you."

I turned round. The dour, dead-eyed faces of my staff stared back at us. Each was armed with anything from scissors to kitchen knives. Arthur Horne fondled a samurai sword, which I recognised as one of my sale lots.

Martin coughed. "This is all academic, Kit. We're all believers together." His voice rose several decibels. "Who are we followers of?"

My staff vented their feelings at the top of their voices. "Damnus and Sammael, and the Church of Atonement!"

Martin was filling my slot as boss man. I didn't like it one bit. I re-established my authority by snapping my fingers at

287

them. Their heads dropped on to their chests.

"Listen, you lot – and that includes you, Martin. I'm in charge here, and I've got a business to run. Put that bloody sword back where you found it, Arthur. The rest of you, get rid of those weapons and forget about the Church of Atonement. Cut out the bullshit and get back to work, all of you. Has everybody got that?" They nodded their agreement. "Bugger off, then. We've an auction to get up and running."

I grabbed Carin's arm and steered her towards the coffee shop, where I got my girl assistant to bring us a pot of coffee.

Carin's cup shook in her hand. "Things are getting worse, Kit. That television slot is their best weapon yet. I didn't recognise the new-look Martin, or your staff." She whispered, and nodded at the girl assistant, "She's got dead eyes as well. When is it all going to end?"

"When I find the scroll, that's when."

The saleroom was bursting at the seams when I made my entrance. I took the punters through the trustworthy ritual that has become my trademark. It earned me the usual ribald cheers, even though all of them had dead codfish eyes.

"Thank you, everyone. Before we start, let me introduce a new member of staff." I caught Carin's eye and winked. "Our porter today is Carin. It's her first auction, so handle her gently – metaphorically speaking, of course."

This produced hoots of laughter and a sprinkling of wolf whistles. Carin waved, as she basked in the public gaze. Her porter's smock had lost its battle to hide her hourglass figure and shapely legs.

As the sale sped along, there was no sign of trouble from the dead-eyed punters, but I knew the trouble would show itself very shortly.

I started selling from the jewellery cabinet. "The first lot is a Victorian lidded wooden box, containing interesting trinkets, including some silver pieces. Who'll start me off at £25?"

The door at the back of the room creaked open, and Rick Adams sauntered in. Everything was following the book's plot. He caught my stare and waved. I knew that he was the key to this lidded box of jewellery causing me mega-trouble.

I focused my mind on selling the trinkets, and starting a riot. "Open the box, Carin. Show them what they're missing."

She emptied the contents on to the top of the cabinet.

I appealed to their wallets. "There's some good gear, including a decent collection of silver charms mounted on a 1930s silver bracelet, as well as costume jewellery dating back to the 1920s. Hold some of the things up, Carin."

She did as I asked. I threw a thought into her mind, and she held up some necklaces and a silver crucifix. I felt the mood in the posh-room change, and already knew that this was the moment when trouble would click in.

Rick Adams followed the script, and shattered the calm by bellowing out, "What's that bitch doing, waving a sodding crucifix in our faces? They're sodding well forbidden. Milner's taking the piss. Stuff his bloody auction. Grab Milner and the ginger bitch, then help yourselves to his overpriced gear."

Pandemonium broke out. The crowd went mad, rifling bits and pieces from the shelves and carrying furniture out of the main door.

Rick Adams stirred them like mad. "Sort Milner and the bitch out first. They're bloody Christians. Kill them."

Martin grabbed the samurai sword and pushed his way towards Carin. She vanished from sight, and I knew she'd been taken. Rick Adams was under the Master's control. I drew back from using my powers against them, as Magnus had ordered. I'd seen enough, and took off to the flat. A frantic hammering on the front door, and the clamouring of people in the courtyard, brought me back to reality. I heard something plop on to the floor at the bottom of the stairs. The smell of smoke and petrol, and the sound of roaring flames, drifted up the stairs. I willed myself out of the flat, and travelled home.

Martin watched the hungry flames consuming Kit's flat as he made his way into the main auction office. Rick Adams saw him.

He pointed at Martin, then foamed at the mouth as he screamed the Master's words at the mob. "There's Martin Henderson. He's a close buddy of Kit Milner. Get him."

The rabble swarmed into the office behind Rick.

He pointed at the open safe. "There's the cash cow. Help yourselves."

Martin moved in front of the open safe, arms outstretched as if he was trying to protect it. He was a very confused man. Most of his brain was running with the Church of Atonement hounds while the other part had been thrown back to the old days, when he'd run the show.

The silly bugger made a big mistake. He closed the safe door and appealed to Rick's better nature. "You wouldn't hurt me, Rick, would you? We've known each other for years. I worship Damnus, like you do. He wouldn't want you to hurt me. Forget the safe and let's go home, eh?"

His words found some fertile ground. A few of the mob started to leave.

Rick yelled at them, "Hold on, you lot. I make the decisions here." He pointed at Martin. "That bastard never did like me. Forget all that bollocks about Damnus not wanting him hurt. Damnus thrives on death and violence."

Rick pulled a flick knife from his overcoat pocket. He opened it, then hurled it at Martin. The knife embedded itself in Martin's chest. As he sank to his knees, he unbuttoned his coat. He stared in disbelief at the sight of his lifeblood seeping through his white shirt. He moaned gently before his body pitched on to the floor.

Adams licked his lips. "Sling that twat into the corner, then help yourself to what's in the safe. When you have finished, I want you lot down the High Street. Some of the local police are refusing to join up with the Atonement movement. We are going to kill them, then burn the station down. Have you got that?"

The mob gabbled their support. Most of them followed Adams to the police station while their mates rifled the safe. They took their spite out on the police station, pulling up paving slabs and hurling them through the station windows.

Rick Adams shouted to the policemen inside, "Come out or we will smoke you out."

A lone voice drifted from inside. "Do you think we're mad? We're dead men whether we come out or not."

Small arms fire crackled from inside the station. Three of the mob screamed with pain and fell to the ground. The rest ran for cover, including Rick.

He yelled out, "It's your decision. You won't come out alive, that's for sure." He spat his orders out to the mob. "You and you, get down to the garage. Bring back as many cans of petrol as you can carry. As for you, Traffy and Doris, go to the newsagents and bring back plenty of newspapers."

They were back within five minutes with four cans of petrol and a stack of papers. Rick unscrewed one of the cans and threw it through a window. He soaked a newspaper in petrol, lit it, then tossed it through the same window. The inside of the police station ignited with a ferocious whoosh.

Adams became animated. "Don't just stand there, you morons. I want this place burning."

The other cans of petrol rained into the police station, followed by lighted petrol-soaked newspapers. Within minutes the station was a raging inferno. A couple of passers-by were stupid enough to try and stop the carnage. They were knocked out for their trouble and flung through the station windows into the raging flames. The roof of the building gave up the ghost. It creaked in protest before collapsing.

The destruction bug took hold of the crowd. The High Street shops attracted their attention. Shops were looted, then set alight. The spiteful hand of Damnus was creating destruction on a large scale.

Hundreds of people milled around inside Ely Cathedral. They weren't Christian worshippers. They were busily stripping the building of Christian artefacts. The beautiful, lofty Octagon Lantern was getting a makeover as paint was thrown on to the hand-painted religious panels.

Anything that would burn was taken outside and thrown on to a bonfire. Flames leapt high into the sky, lighting up the gloom of a frosty winter evening. Hundreds of local people were attracted to the blaze. Some of them linked hands and danced around the fire, raising a cheer as each Christian relic was thrown into the flames.

Inside the cathedral, extension ladders were raised to the level of the nineteenth-century stained-glass windows. Anyone with a head for heights scaled the ladders and busily slapped black paint over the religious figures in the finely crafted stained glass.

The strident sound of engines ripped through the building. Three cherry pickers chugged their way down the aisle before stopping. Three men were hoisted up on each platform. They busied themselves by spraying black paint over the ceiling paintings.

Raucous sounds of shouting and laughter came from the chancel. The magnificent golden altar was covered in paint, and the wooden altar was taken outside and thrown on the fire. A bunch of hoodlums whooped their heads off as they drank the Communion wine.

I materialised in my lounge at home. The peace and quiet was broken by the television set switching itself on.

A voice spoke to me. "This is Magnus speaking. My brother has gone too far. The time for waiting is nearly over. I will lead you to my scroll soon, then you will destroy Damnus and his evil followers." The voice sighed. "With the powers you possess, and with my scroll in your hands, you are stronger than any of them. Think whatever you want to happen, and the scroll will ensure that your needs will come about. Free the world of evil, and make sure you do not fail me."

I made myself a coffee and relaxed in an armchair. An image of Carin's twin winged into my head. Her replica was doing the job that I expected of her. I saw her lying on a bed, with the Master looking down at her.

His words rang in my mind. "You are my mother and I hate

you. It pleases me that you and Milner will soon be dead."

I laughed at what he had said, knowing his days were numbered. I popped upstairs and checked out the real Carin. I removed her invisibility. She was breathing normally in her induced sleep. I woke her, but kept her under my control. As she sat in the kitchen, in a stupor, I cooked us a meal and fed her. I got her to take some liquid refreshment, then returned her upstairs, where I made her invisible and placed a force field around her. As for me, I settled down on the sofa and snatched the sleep I needed. The next couple of days were crucial to me, as well as the world.

I had a late breakfast when I awoke, then got myself ready for the trip to St Leonard's Church via my auction house. I deliberately wore my ring and willed myself to Grinton.

CHAPTER THIRTY-SIX

I arrived in the auction-house car park with my invisible cloak on, and looked around me. Devastation was the name of the game. My flat was a burned-out shell, and every saleroom had suffered from the hand of destruction. The mob had filched anything that might earn them a shekel or two. I had made a conscious decision to drive to Lovington. It would give me some idea as to what was going on in the countryside. There wasn't much left of my car. It had been trashed, like every other vehicle. The Damnus mob had quickly acquired the knack of vandalism.

I scouted around the streets looking for a car. On the outskirts of town I found what I wanted. An old Ford Fiesta had somehow managed to escape the hands of the rabble. As long as it got me to Lovington I didn't care a toss what it looked like. Breaking into the car was easy. I passed through the door and sat behind the wheel. I willed the engine to start. It purred into life.

There wasn't much traffic on the roads. That was a contradiction of words. Plenty of cars were around, most of them burned-out wrecks, littering the roadside. I stopped and looked inside one of them. A charred body was slumped over what was left of the steering wheel. Two more bodies reclined on a non-existent back seat. It wasn't a pretty sight.

If things hadn't been so sordidly horrifying, I'd have grudgingly admired the way the Church of Atonement had brought the country, indeed the world, to its knees. Life and death were walking hand in hand, and Damnus was feasting on a sumptuous banquet of misery and suffering.

As I approached the outskirts of Lovington, I noticed two cars parked in a lay-by ahead of me. One car sped out in front of me, while the other swung out behind me. The car following me accelerated and drew level with me. The front-seat passenger signalled for me to wind my window down. I did as he asked. He grinned inanely as he pointed a handgun at me through his open window.

He mouthed a couple of expletives before shouting his orders at me. "Pull over, arsehole, or I'll blow you away."

This was no time for games. I waved back and smiled. He visibly relaxed. My bolt of blue lightning burst through his open window. The car and its passengers vanished from the face of the earth. The car upfront screeched to a halt, blocking my path. Two youngsters hopped out and pointed handguns at me. I blew them and the car away with another bolt of lightning.

I felt no twinge of conscience for what I'd done. These scumbags were probably responsible for the burned-out cars that dotted the roadside. One reoccurring thought cheered me up. When I open the scroll, and do away with evil, all this mayhem and misery would be undone, and the dead would live again on the day I resurrect the world.

I parked in the Old Marketplace, opposite Mandies restaurant. Mob rule had reached the town. Mandies had been fired, and other shops broken into and ransacked. In my invisible state I walked to St Leonard's Church. My ring would have tipped off the Master that I was around. Instinctively, I felt safe in the knowledge they wouldn't harm me until I had found the scroll. I played along with their game, and stood across the road, waiting for what I'd seen in my first premonition to roll out.

A gaggle of people wearing hooded cloaks entered the church. For the next half-hour I kicked my heels, knowing the Master was conducting a service dedicated to Sammael. The church door opened and the noisy rabble filed out. They were followed by Julius Milner and a laughing Master. They hurried away to the rectory.

I slipped into church and walked up the nave. My replica Carin lay dead on the altar. Her throat had been slit. The skill of my craftsmanship showed itself. This was proven by the blood that seeped across the surface of the altar from the replica's throat. What I saw didn't horrify me, knowing my replica carried the gift of immortality. I looked around me and managed to laugh.

"OK. Stop messing around, Carin. I know you're here somewhere."

A bat flew around the chancel, and Carin's laughter echoed through the church. The bat landed at my feet and broke down into a cloud of white vapour, which flowed up the nose of the replica. I was rewarded with the sound of a sigh from the replica as her heart started to beat. Her wound healed itself. My thought wave ordered her to sleep. Her clothes had been tossed into a corner of the chancel. I made her hover above the altar, then dressed her before cradling her in my arms. My mental instruction willed us back to our house. I laid the replica next to the sleeping Carin and mouthed a few words. Her twin disappeared in a fine mist.

I woke Carin from her long sleep. Her body shook as her eyes slowly opened. She stared around her and smiled as she held my hand.

"Good to see you, darling," I said.

She shivered. "What happened? I remember the punters going mental, but after that my mind's a complete blank."

I used the skills that my first-class degree in lying had taught me. "Do you remember holding up a crucifix?"

She nodded.

"The punters went ballistic and turned the place upside down. You were knocked out. I brought you back home and let you sleep. You've been out for a long time. It's Sunday afternoon. The punters weren't content with knocking you about. They ransacked the premises and burned my flat down."

She looked guilty. "Sorry about the crucifix business. I should have known better."

It wasn't her fault.

"Don't blame yourself. The Master was behind all the trouble. He put Rick Adams up to disrupting the auction. That's all over now. I don't know about you, but I'm starving. I'll get the frying pan on the go."

Twenty minutes later we were knocking back one of my cholesterol-laden mixed grills. It didn't take long for our talk to return to our favourite topic.

"If this is what the Church of Atonement is all about, then it sucks," she said. "Damnus isn't interested in a world where people live in harmony, and governments get on with the business of governing."

"You're right. He doesn't aspire to a self-regulating world. All the governing will be done by Damnus, through his son and his evil minions. They've got no feeling for people." I swallowed what I was eating. "Things are about to change. We're going to find that scroll."

She held her hands up. "I know I'm a boring fart, but are you sure you can stop their game?"

"Definitely. Before we do anything, I want you to see for yourself what we're going to put a stop to. You heard the Master spouting on about Damnus Day. It's a full-blown carnival day, to honour the crowning of King Sammael. We're not kicking our heels until the 25th of December. We'll time-travel into the future, to the 25th of December, tomorrow. After you've seen the shenanigans, we'll get our hands on the sealed scroll."

The unfazed Carin waved a crust of bread at me. "Sounds fine to me."

We settled down on the sofa. I put an arm around her. "When we get through this—"

She put her hand over my mouth, "*If* we get through this."

I ignored her. "When we get through this we're getting hitched. And I'm not waiting till next spring."

She kissed me, big time. "Let's make it happen, then."

We hadn't much to say to each other when we woke up next

morning. Our minds had been taken over by what had to be done. The future was clear – perhaps too clear. The stakes were high, but they were stacked in my favour.

Carin broke the silence. "What makes you tick? You're talking about killing people in cold blood, yet you're so bloody cool. It's too unreal. Is there something you're holding back from me?"

"If it's a crime to feel confident, then I plead guilty. I want our old world back. I'm not having every man, woman and child living the rest of their lives trapped in Damnus's straitjackets. I'll be more than happy to kill for that kind of dream. That's how it's got to be played, and it won't be pretty. You've been through enough trauma already, even though you don't remember what happened in that other life of yours. You've forgotten one thing. I remember everything. I've seen enough killing to last me a lifetime. You have to trust me if you want us to live a normal life again."

"Sorry. I'm being negative. Of course I trust you."

"When you're ready we're going to watch the coming of Damnus and Sammael."

She contented herself with a nod of her head.

"I know it's winter, but you won't need warm clothing. Damnus has made sure that December the 25th will be fine, and very hot, for his big day. I'm ready when you are."

She nuzzled my cheek. "The sooner we find that scroll, the better. Let's get our life back on track."

I had to smile. She still believed that she was involved. I wouldn't spoil things by telling her she didn't figure in my final plans.

"We won't wear our rings and, before you ask, I don't intend to try and change what we see. I'll leave the scroll to do that in a few days' time."

CHAPTER THIRTY-SEVEN

Five minutes later we were ready.

"Let's be on our way," I said. "No one will see us when we arrive. We'll be invisible."

I slotted the time-travel order into place. We ended up sitting on the roof of Brine & Cherry's main office.

Carin gasped. "Look at what the bastards have done to your flat."

"Never mind. One day it will look how it used to be. Have a gander at the tiered seating on either side of that stage. There are some mighty important people sitting over there."

"Hell's bells. I see what you mean. What's the monarch doing here? And that looks like the Archbishop of Canterbury and his bishops. Who else is there, for God's sake?"

"I had a closer look the last time I was here. The chiefs of the armed services are there, with assorted chief constables, leaders of the other obsolete religious faiths, the Prime Minister and Members of Parliament, plus a few defunct peers and judges. On the other side we've got the leaders of every country in the world."

The day panned out as it had done in my portent. Right on cue, dark clouds rolled in and claps of thunder resounded around the sky. Bolts of lightning set fire to some of the High Street shops. The rowdy crowd were silenced by the sight of five minute specks floating down from the heavens, picked out in a beam of bright light and backed up by hundreds of singing voices, while other figures hovered above them. Merlin, Emeralda, Julius Milner, the Master and another young man set foot on the stage.

I nudged her. "Don't worry about your father being here. They've taken over his mind. What do you make of the young man standing next to your father?"

"He's not like a normal human being, is he? He can't be, with those hideous red eyes and goat's horns on his forehead." She faltered. "He's a strapping six-footer, but he's definitely not the offspring of two normal human beings." The penny dropped. "Oh, my God. He's Sammael, isn't he?"

"Yeah. You're looking at the future King of the World, in the flesh. Sit back and watch what goes on. Some of it doesn't make nice viewing."

As their feet touched down, the dark clouds were blown away by a strong wind. The heavenly choir ceased their revelry. Sammael made himself at home on the golden throne, and waved a hand at his adoring fans. The other four sat on the thrones on either side of Sammael. The crowd stood in shocked silence, overwhelmed by what they had seen. Merlin got to his feet and spoke the words I had heard in my previous sighting of this premonition. He welcomed the crowds to this special day, which he said would be forever known as Damnus Day. He bowed to the young man and introduced him as Sammael, the son of Damnus. Sammael made the speech that I had heard before, and thanked Merlin and the others for helping him secure the world to his father's beliefs. They followed the script that I'd seen, including the part when Damnus had made his presence known, killing hundreds of people in the process.

Sammael's deep voice echoed through the town. "You now have no doubt as to who I am. My father, the spiritual Damnus, lives inside of me." He looked down at the hundreds of bodies covering the ground. "On this day of celebration, no one will be forced to suffer pain or death at my father's hands. I will take compassion on those innocent wretches who were overcome by his fire."

He stepped down from the throne, stared at the burned bodies of the dead and suffering, then moved his arms about. As they clambered to their feet, their bodies were dressed in their clothing. His powerful sorcery had the desired effect. The crowd rose to their feet and went wild in their affection for him.

Carin whispered in my ear. "He's nastier and scarier than Merlin. Are you sure you can handle him?"

"I'm quietly confident. It's the billions of people watching this charade that I'm worried about. If they're not converts now, they soon will be. He's scaring the shit out of them."

Sammael turned towards the battery of television cameras, which were greedily filming every action and every word of what was unfolding. "The whole world is witness to what I am capable of. I have a simple message for the people of earth. Celebrate this Damnus Day, and use it to make your belief in my father and me stronger." He hovered a few inches above the stage. "Now, swear your allegience to me and my father."

The crowd raised their fists in the air and bellowed out their commitment to him. He landed back on the stage and smiled in his approval of the affection they had shown him. He nodded at Merlin, then sat himself on his throne. Merlin beckoned to some of the special guests. The former leaders of the earthly religions left their seats and stood on the front of the stage. The former Archbishop of Canterbury was amongst them.

Sammael raised his hands towards the heavens. Flames crackled at his fingertips. "As leaders of the religious movements who once dominated the world, I have called you together so you may swear your loyalty to me. Do you renounce your false gods and prophets, and do you swear that you will worship me and my father, as your only gods?"

They shouted their agreement; then, one by one, they kissed Sammael's feet before moving to the side of the stage. He waggled a finger towards more of the special guests. A gaggle of them left their seats and stood before him. They bowed their heads to him.

Sammael stared into the television camera that was trained on him. "For the benefit of the billions of viewers who are not familiar with these people, I commend to you the former representatives of Parliament, the House of Lords, the police and armed forces, the judiciary, the Stock Exchange and the banking services, amongst others. The duties and dealings of these establishments will be carried out by chosen members of the Church of Atonement in future. The citizens of this country were made aware of this in a broadcast made by the Master some days ago.

"The matter of the Church of Atonement wielding overall power has already become law in all other countries of the world. I will be visiting every country during the next few months so that their peoples may swear their allegiance to me in person."

The former world leaders, sitting in the tiered stand, rose to their feet and clapped their hands. He ushered everyone back to their seats, with a wave of his hand, then waggled a finger at someone else. The monarch got to her feet and made her way towards him. Noisy booing ran through the crowd. She stood in front of Sammael and bowed to him. A technician placed a microphone in front of her.

Sammael shouted at the crowd. "Your heckling of my invited guest will not be tolerated. The monarch is here to swear her loyalty to me." He nodded to the Queen.

Her words were spoken in a monotone voice, totally lacking any kind of feeling, reading from papers which she held in her hand. "I am here today to renounce my position as head of the Church. My archbishop, his bishops and the clergy will relinquish their positions in the defunct Anglican Church with immediate effect, as will the leaders of every other faith."

The religious leaders vigorously nodded their agreement.

The monarch continued. "My prime minister has resigned, as have all Members of Parliament. A new House of Commons, appointed by the Church of Atonement, will be set up to replace that ancient institution. My House of Lords has been abolished." She turned a page of her notes. "As for myself, I relinquish my role as monarch with immediate effect. I will be giving up my official residence at Buckingham Palace, together with my many other properties and those of my relatives. They will pass into the hands of the Church of Atonement. I can reveal that Buckingham Palace will become the official residence of Lord Sammael. Westminster Abbey, together with the other fine cathedrals and churches in this country, have become major places of worship for the Church of Atonement. Lord Sammael has kindly given his permission for me and my extended family to live in my Norfolk home, at Sandringham." She smiled at him. "Thank you, My Lord, for giving me the opportunity to speak to your people."

Her duty wasn't finished. She moved towards Sammael, who was seated on the golden throne, and took something out of a wooden box standing by the throne. She raised a golden crown into the air, and turned around to face the crowd.

"It falls on me to surrender my rule of the people, and to crown Lord Sammael as the rightful King of England, the Commonwealth and the World."

Sammael stepped down from the throne and knelt before her. She placed the crown on his head. The crowd went wild, yelling at the top of their voices and applauding.

Sammael nodded his head and ushered the monarch away. "Thank you, Majesty. This is the last time you will be called by that title. As you have said, many things will change in this country and the wider world, under my guidance." He spoke to Merlin. "Speak to the media for me."

Merlin addressed the journalists. "Lord Sammael commands that one of you will have the opportunity to ask a question of him."

A gaggle of journalists raced across to the front of the stage. Sammael waggled a finger at a young female reporter. She ran on to the stage and thrust her microphone into his face.

"You have been accepted by every nation on earth as their one definitive ruler. Your powers are immense, and—"

Sammael showed his annoyance. "Instead of spouting out what everyone already knows, do you have a question to ask of me?"

She coloured up. "I'm sorry, Your Majesty. My question is in two parts. Why did you choose this back-of-beyond market town to show yourself to the world for the first time? Wouldn't London have been a more fitting place to demonstrate your powers, and for putting over your message to the world?"

He reacted tetchily. "It makes no difference. The world would have seen what is happening today, wherever I had shown myself. Why Grinton? you ask."

He waved his hands around in the air.

"A vile man called Milner used to own these premises. He is an avid follower of the false God, and will suffer the oblivion that awaits all unbelievers. I thought it fitting to honour Grinton with my presence, to pour scorn on Milner's beliefs."

I nudged Carin. "It's not every day you hear your own demise being announced on television."

A shaft of courage flowed through the female correspondent. She was hell-bent on furthering her reputation, and posed a risky question. "Why are you so sure that the whole of civilisation has bent its knee to you, Your Majesty?"

For a moment I could see that he was tempted to strike her down. His face twitched and his hands clenched and unclenched. He contained himself, and even managed to switch on a semblance of a smile.

"I take exception to your question. The whole world has already accepted my beliefs. Even as I speak, every building that was used for prayer, throughout the world, has been converted to my own temples, in which peoples of every nation will venerate me. Look around you. See with your own eyes how people idolise me. The rest of mankind has followed their lead. My disciples have spent years travelling the world, and they tell me that all the people of earth are showing me their absolute devotion." His bully-boy side showed through. "It will not be necessary, but I have the means of compelling all of mankind to accept my father as their only god." Dribble trickled down his chin. "The fate of those few who are not prepared to show him their devotion is simple. They will perish under my heel."

His words gleaned a reaction from a part of the crowd, but not the one he expected. Three men pushed their way to the front and pulled their robes off. Gasps of anger rent the air at the sight of their clerical collars and crucifixes. The priests were quickly bundled to the ground, where they were beaten and kicked.

Sammael froze the mob with a wave of his hand. "Enough. Disbelievers have the right to speak before they die."

One clergyman rose unsteadily to his feet. He wiped blood from his face. His words were slurred through his toothless gums. "Your miracles are spectacular, but your sorcery helps no one except yourself and your father, the false god. There's only one God, and He will return to punish you and your followers one day."

The clergyman pulled a gun from beneath his clothing. He fired off six quick rounds at Sammael. The bullets didn't reach their intended target, as they bounced harmlessly off the force field that protected him. His face showed his naked hatred for these followers of God.

"You have signed your own death warrants." He nodded to Merlin and passed a finger across his throat.

The blue ray spewing from Merlin's fingers wrapped itself around the clergymen. They disintegrated into nothingness.

Sammael couldn't hide his anger. He screamed at the crowd, "Forget these misguided believers of the false God. If there are people watching who have not yet taken me into their hearts, it is time for them to be converted to my cause."

He closed his eyes and raised his arms, allowing his fingers to move backwards and forwards. The crowd stood in soundless ranks, blank eyes fixed on him, their heads following the movement of his fingers. This was powerful sorcery of the first order. He was peddling his evil by mass hypnotism.

I whispered to Carin, "Are you still with me?"

"Only just. Anyone watching him on television doesn't stand a chance."

Sammael opened his eyes. His words were spellbindingly smooth. "Nothing can sway you from the road you are about to tread. Your footsteps will lead you along the highway to Damnus's fulfilment. Take my father and me into your lives, and worship him in his temples. Seek out those who still do not believe in me and convert them to my religion. If they disobey you, then kill them." He wasn't finished. "Many people have died in the past few days, from your old God's scheming. He deliberately flooded parts of the world, as well as destroying ancient buildings and monuments." He waved his hands and muttered a few words under his breath. "I have now put right the wrongs that were committed by Him. Innocent people will be raised from the dead, including those lives that were lost in your own natural-history museum recently, and the victims of the killings at Dorkingham. Your false God was responsible for these happenings."

I shook my head in admiration. He was clever. Very clever. What better way to impress your converts, and non-converts, than by using powerful magic to put his own atrocities to rights. The crowd went wild, shouting their acclaim of him. He accepted their hero worship with smiles and much bowing. The milling crowds simmered down.

"I now have a pleasant task to carry out. I am called upon to appoint an archbishop to oversee this part of my kingdom on behalf of the Church of Atonement. The man I have selected is very much committed to my cause."

I whispered in Carin's ear, "This is where your father becomes a television personality. Don't blame him for what's going on. His mind's been got at. It's pretty obvious that a replica of him was left in Lovington after he went on his worldwide jaunt with Sammael."

Sammael gestured to Julius Milner, who ambled towards him and knelt on the ground, where he kissed Sammael's feet.

He looked up at Sammael. "I pledge my mind and soul to your cause, Your Majesty. I will indoctrinate your followers with your teachings, and I will destroy any unbelievers. I swear this with my heart and soul."

Sammael turned to the crowd. "Julius Milner is my proven servant. From this day forth he will be known as the Lord Bishop, Julius of Canterbury. I have something else to tell you. During the last five years, my message has been spread throughout the world by the words and deeds of my eleven disciples. They are the Master's brothers. They have been guided in their task by their mentor, Lord Merlin."

He pointed towards the sky. A curtain of voices burst from

behind the clouds. The crowd were hushed into silence as eleven men, dressed in flowing black robes, floated down from the sky. As their feet touched the stage, they placed their right arms across their chests and shouted their loyalty to Sammael.

Sammael bowed to them before addressing the crowd. "I am proud of what these people have achieved for my father's cause. I am conferring on each of them the title of saint. They will be venerated by mankind forever."

A distant booming noise silenced the crowd's cheering. A whistling sound rang through the air and an explosive weapon exploded among the world leaders. The cries of the wounded were masked by a second explosion in the other stand.

I told Carin to stay where she was as I flew above the crowds to see what was going on. The cause of the bloodletting was a solitary tank, standing in a woodland clearing outside the town. Smoke and flames belched from its barrel as a third shell whistled through the air, before detonating among the crowd.

Sammael frantically waved towards the source of the gunfire. The Master and the disciples soared into the sky. They hovered like malevolent birds of prey, their eyes licking over Grinton to discover the source of the explosions. They spotted the tank. The tank crew felt no pain as they were blown to smithereens by the red rays spurting from the disciples' fingertips.

The crowd seemed unconcerned at the hundreds of dead and dying bodies lying around them. The Master and the disciples landed to cheers and applause.

Sammael brought the rabble under control with a spellbinding wave of his hands. "We have to thank my saints for preventing further death and bloodshed." He hung his head. "I pay homage to these brave people who have laid down their lives for me." He then burst out laughing. "We must not forget that today is a day of celebration. For that reason, nobody will have died in vain. Those people are not dead, they are sleeping. I will resurrect them to show the compassion I hold for my people. As for the injured, their wounds will be healed."

During the next few minutes Sammael manipulated the time zone. The crowd, including the people in the two tiered stands, were thrown back in time. The first shell didn't get the chance to kill people. Sammael's sorcery made it speed back into the tank's barrel. An explosion shook the ground as the tank blew up in spectacular fashion.

I flew back down to where Carin was sitting and found her hand.

She whispered to me, "Like everything else we've seen, that was stage-managed. He's clever is that one."

"That's what I thought. He's being compassionate today, but that will all change in the future. Sympathy and Sammael don't go hand in hand."

He was the centre of everyone's attention as he strutted across the stage from side to side, delighting in the affection that was being thrown at him.

He ceased his theatrics and raised his hands to quieten the crowd. "This day of celebration is not only about religion. I have been born to walk the earth for another reason. It isn't by chance that the former leaders of the world and the former representatives of the Commonwealth countries are here. Today I was crowned King of the United Kingdom. Tomorrow I will be crowned King of the World in what was formerly known as Westminster Abbey, but which will now be known as Damnus Abbey."

There was a few seconds of stunned silence before the crowd went off their rockers. They yelled with one accord at what he'd said. The former leaders of the world left their seats and walked on to the stage, one by one, and kissed his feet.

Carin tugged at my arm. "Can we go? I've seen enough of these arseholes. Let's get out of here, please."

I didn't need convincing, and fumbled around for her hand. "Let's go."

CHAPTER THIRTY-EIGHT

We arrived back in the sanctuary of our house. I sat her on the sofa.

"It wasn't pretty, was it? You can see why we have got to put that evil lot away for good. They'd be worth dying for, except we're not going to die."

She gripped my hand. "I know I'm immortal, but if what I've seen is the future, I'd sooner not be. People can have my share of life if they want to live that way." She wasn't making sense.

"That's not fair," I said. "Folk haven't chosen what we saw. Sammael's seeds have been set in their minds. They haven't seen the real side of Sammael. He was too busy showing everyone what a great compassionate guy he is. His bullshit was a bit rich – putting evil things right that were his work in the first place."

I detected a touch of moodiness in her voice. "Whatever. I don't particularly care. When do we start looking for the scroll?"

"Tomorrow, that's when."

We ran out of conversation. Carin couldn't get her head around her father becoming Sammael's archbishop. She seemed reluctant to accept my premise that he'd been brainwashed. After a cooked meal we sat on the sofa for the rest of the evening. She didn't want to talk about what we'd seen. She didn't need persuading when I suggested we should hit the hay.

Tomorrow would be the most critical day in the history of our planet. I was taking my first steps towards saving the world. My one aim was to ensure that Sammael and his evil garbage were no longer part of the human race.

I was the first to wake. It was barely five o'clock. Carin lay on her back, her chest rising and falling in deep sleep.

I put a hand on her head and whispered in her ear, "Sorry to disappoint you, but I'm going on this mission on my own. You're staying here. What I have to do won't be very pleasant, and I don't want you to see your father die. Sleep until I've finished with Sammael's crew, then I'll come back for you."

After a quick breakfast I conjured up a replica of myself. I sent him up to the bedroom to get dressed. He came back down and sat at the breakfast table with me.

He smiled knowingly. "Today's the day, then. I'm picking up your thoughts. It's a great idea of using me as a decoy when you get your hands on the scroll."

"I'm pleased you think so. Let's both be sure that we're on the same wavelength. You're going to wear my ring and stay here while I get the scroll."

I walked into the lounge and sat down. I closed my eyes and concentrated like mad.

I spoke the words that my mind was thinking: "I'm ready to find the scroll, Magnus, and carry through your task. Please take me to where the scroll can be found."

My words were quickly answered. I hurtled down a tunnel of light and ended up lying on the ground. What I saw when I opened my eyes shook me rigid. I was lying on the floor in Brine & Cherry's posh-room in the middle of an auction. Thankfully, no one noticed my presence because I was invisible. Martin Henderson was taking the auction, with Arthur Horne doing the porter duties. What threw me was how young the two of them were. So were all of the regular punters that I remembered. Every one of them looked in their mid-twenties.

A woman whispered in my ear as she slipped her hand in mine. I recognised my mother's voice. "I know you're puzzled at how young everyone looks. You are in another time dimension, many years ahead of your earth time. This is the parallel world of earth, where nobody ages more than twenty-five years. When people die on earth, who have earned the right to live on this planet of goodness, their spirit finds its home in their parallel body, which is living on this world. Enough of this. You are here to meet your father. Come with me."

I was swept out of the saleroom and found myself standing in a beautiful sunlit garden, where flowers nodded in the warm, gentle breeze. A stately mansion towered over my head. I stepped out of my invisible state. I recognised it as the grand mansion that stood in Grinton Park, back on earth. A petite blond lady appeared at my side and threw her arms around me. 1 hugged my mother and smothered her in kisses.

She looked me in the eyes. "Welcome to our world. I have waited years for this day. My name is Azurina, and you are my son, Raphael."

I must have looked slightly confused.

Her tinkling laughter put me at ease. "Kit is the name you were given when Merlin took you from me. Come and meet your father. As you already know, he is the governor of this world and some of the other parallel worlds." She clutched my arm. "Before we do, I have a surprise for you. I didn't tell you that you have a twin brother called Sariel. He can't wait to meet you; neither can your father."

Should I have been surprised that I had a brother? The answer is no. I'd become used to having bolts from the blue thrown at me. Two figures burst out of the back door of the mansion. One of them was the spitting image of me. I knew the other man was my father, because I could see where my brother and I had got our looks from.

They managed to calm down, and contented themselves by shaking my hand and gently hugging me. My father drew the four of us into a group hug. He couldn't hide his happiness.

"Raphael, this is the day I have long waited for. Welcome home. I know I speak for your brother as well."

My brother nodded his head. "Me too." A saucy smile

creased his face. "Having seen you for the first time, I now know how good-looking I am."

We all laughed, then trooped into the house. Our conversation, before and during the meal, was catching up on family talk, and telling me more about this parallel world. We then sat in a beautifully furnished lounge, where our talk became more serious. My head was full of questions.

"I'm pleased to be with my family at long last, but I think I deserve an explanation from you as to what the people of earth are being put through." I thought about what I had said, and smiled. "That's not to say I haven't enjoyed the last few years, and I don't regret possessing the powers that were passed to me."

My father nodded his head and grinned. "You inherited them from me, as you know. Before I tell you more, let's talk about where you are. This planet is an exact replica of your world in another dimension of time. How many times have you heard someone jokingly say that they lead another life in a parallel world? They didn't realise how right they were. The spirits of the people of earth who reach my planet are destined to lead a happy life for the rest of eternity. This planet is one of many that I govern. Our leader, Lord Magnus, chose you to undo the evil plans that his brother has lavished on your earth. As he has already told you, you will have completed your mission when you destroy your world and recreate it how it used to be, before Damnus used his evil ways to create a hell on earth."

I thought that was a bit over the top.

"What has happened isn't the people's fault. They've only accepted Damnus because of the sorcery he's used on them. If Magnus is so mighty, why is he getting me to carry out his own kind of evil? I've been put through a lot of misery in my life, and now he expects me to do his dirty work."

The look on my father's face didn't augur well for me. He didn't get the chance to say anything, as a stream of red smoke poured from his mouth. To say I was shocked at what materialised out of the smoke is putting it mildly. A young man in his mid-twenties stood in front of me. My parents and my brother dropped to their knees with their arms held out to this young man. I could tell he wasn't happy with me.

"I am Magnus. Do not dare to speak about me in that way. It was always decreed that I could not destroy my brother. You are the only person who is capable of carrying out my mission. Damn it, boy! Do you know who you are?" He allowed himself a smile, and wagged a finger at me. "You are my grandson."

This was the third time in my life that I'd been confronted with a relationship that was way beyond my reasoning. The previous two relationships hadn't fazed me, so why should this latest time bomb have a negative effect on me?

I managed a laugh. "I find that incredible, seeing you look younger than me."

I could tell he was impressed at my lack of surprise.

"That is a silly thing to say, seeing you have already been told that no one on my world looks older than me, no matter how many years they have lived here. Do you want to see what I would really look like if I lived on your planet?"

A shrunken old hunchback of a man, with hanging loose skin and furrows of wrinkles on his face, replaced him. The old man disappeared and the youthful Magnus replaced him.

"Enough of this. You are my chosen one, who will do away with my brother and his band of evil villains. Only you have been gifted to use the powers of my sealed scroll."

I could see there was no way of wriggling out of what Magnus had planned for me, but there was still one question I had to ask of him. "OK. Explain something else to me. If Damnus is your brother, why is he covered in hair, with a bullock's head?"

His shoulders moved in silent mirth. "He takes on that guise when he wishes to frighten people. In reality we are identical twins. Enough of these questions. Let us get on with this mission." He turned to my father. "Give him the ring."

My father removed a ring from his finger and gave it to me.

Magnus pointed to the ring. "Put it on one of your fingers. With that ring you are now ready to find the scroll. Concentrate on finding the scroll, and the ring will take you there."

I did as he asked, and found myself hurtling down the tunnel of white light.

I touched down on solid ground and looked around me. The breathtaking beauty of the sunlit garden was too sumptuous, and beautiful, to take in with one glance. An abundance of flowering and fruiting trees flourished among a profusion of flowers and vegetation.

All manner of animals foraged for food, while flocks of birds swirled noisily in the air. A thought surfaced in my head, telling me that this was the Garden of Philus, the fabled Garden of Paradise. I caught sight of what my brain told me I was looking for. The tallest and grandest tree stood smack in the middle of the garden. A narrow beam of light shone down from the heavens, picking out its rosy-red fruits.

I walked into the shade of the tree. Its sheer height, and the girth of its trunk, took my breath away. Without warning, the grass beneath the tree caught fire.

A voice spoke to me from the centre of the flames. "Welcome to my garden. Are you prepared for your mission?"

My words came easily. "I've never been more ready. Let's get it over with, so that my life can return to normal."

The sound of gentle laughter filled the air. "You have much work ahead of you before that happens. The scroll is concealed somewhere beneath this tree. Throw the ring that I gave you up into the air. It will guide you to where the scroll is hidden. Guard my scroll with your life."

I didn't get the chance to ask any questions. The fire vanished. The green grass belied the fact that the flames had ever existed. I threw the ring into the air. It floated to the ground like a feather and landed on the grass. A bolt of lightning leapt from a tree branch and struck the ring. It burst into brilliant light, which slowly faded away. A small wooden box hovered above a hole in the ground, then moved through the air towards me before coming to rest in my hands.

I opened the box and stared inside. A scroll lay in the bottom. Its tan-coloured animal skin was rolled up, and tied together with a piece of animal fur. I gently tugged at the fur seal without breaking it. I smiled. When the time comes, it wouldn't take much effort to break open the scroll.

I created a copy of the scroll and popped it into the box, before placing it back in the hole. The hole filled itself in, leaving a covering of undisturbed grass over it. I put the real scroll in my pocket and placed the ring back on my finger.

My replica was waiting for me when I returned home.

I put my arms around his shoulders. "OK. Your fun time is over. You're going to find my replica of the scroll."

I put Magnus's ring on his finger and spent a few moments giving him my instructions, about how to get to the Garden of Philus and find my scroll. "Keep my own ring on and, whatever happens to you, don't worry. Like me, your immortality can't be taken away. Let's hope things go the way I've planned."

CHAPTER THIRTY-NINE

My replica turned up in the Garden of Philus. I was right behind him, in my invisible state, with the real scroll tucked away in my trouser pocket. I hid behind a bush and waited to see what would happen. My replica threw Magnus's ring into the air. Events followed the same pattern as before, until the box floated above the ground. He opened it and took the scroll out.

His words were intentionally loud. "At last I've found the scroll. It's goodbye to Damnus and his crew when they show up."

Five crows flew out of a tree and settled on the ground behind him. They pecked away at the ground as if they were feeding, before flying behind a large shrub. A shaft of brilliant white light shot across the clearing from where the crows had disappeared. The light struck my replica at his kneecaps, taking his legs off. He was dumped to the ground like a sack of potatoes. The scroll flew out of his hands and disappeared behind the shrub, where the crows had gone. Five human figures walked out into the open. A cruel smile played around Sammael's face. He was in evil company. Merlin stood behind him, together with the Master, Lady Emeralda and Julius Milner.

I closed my eyes in concentration and sent out a mental probe of their bodies. Their hearts weren't beating. Merlin was up to his favourite trick of using replica bodies. The five of them walked over to where my twin lay. He followed my script, and attempted to summon up a ray to disable them. It came as no surprise that the ray failed to show. He allowed a look of total confusion and fear to cover his face.

Sammael spoke with added sarcasm. "Could you not summon your ray, Milner? What a shame!" His face showed mock surprise. He turned to Merlin. "Did you not bother to tell him that we control his powers through that ring he wears?"

They laughed at his pathetic attempt at humour.

He silenced them. "Welcome to the Garden of Philus, Milner." He made a mock bow. "My father pleasured your woman's body, and I was born." He shook his head. "You still disappoint me. What an ally you would have made in my new order. Magnus made certain that would not happen. Never mind. I have the scroll, and you have failed in your mission."

The false shock on my replica's face would have won him an Oscar nomination.

He tripped out trite words of desperation. "You evil bastard, you won't get away with this."

The Master butted in. "Shut up, Milner. Make the most of your last few moments of life."

Sammael rebuked him. "Quiet. I will tell him what his destiny is. This scroll is the means of taking your life away, so you will never walk this earth again." He pointed at a distant volcano. "That smoking pile of rock will be the way of ensuring your death."

He shouted a few words at the heavens. The volcano erupted in an ear-splitting explosion, and started to spew out fiery fountains of lava. Plumes of smoke and ash spilled across the sky, shutting out the sunlight. The ground groaned and shuddered as a wide fissure split open, from the foot of the volcano into the middle of the garden. Molten lava poured like a waterfall from the volcano, and sloshed along the fissure until it was filled to the brim with a bubbling lake of sulphurous molten rock. The leaves on the surrounding trees shrivelled in the heat and fell to the ground, as if autumn had arrived early.

Sammael smiled at the exhilaration he felt. He blew on the scroll. It soared effortlessly through the air before splashing into the molten lake. Lightning spiralled down from the heavens as the scroll burned fiercely. A cloud of dark smoke, smelling of incense, spiralled from the spot where the scroll had been consumed.

"Now it is your turn, Milner," said Sammael. He grunted. "Good riddance to you."

He flicked his finger at my replica. He was plucked into the air and fed to the fiery molten rock. The lava feasted greedily on his body, and then he was gone.

An eerie silence filled the gloom. The acrid stench of sulphur blew across the garden on the wings of a gentle breeze. The air felt heavy, almost too dense to breathe. Forked lightning etched spectacular patterns across the horizon, while threads of blue static electricity crackled around Sammael and his cronies.

He broke the brooding silence. "Let us rid ourselves of Merlin's sorcery. Our replica bodies have carried out their task."

Their bodies broke down into a fine vapour, which glided through the air towards five crows sitting on the branch of a nearby tree. The vapour was sucked into the mouths of the birds, who vanished in a flash of red light. Sammael and the other four stood beneath the tree. I scanned their bodies for heartbeats, and found them. They were living, breathing humans again.

Sammael's mouth dropped open when I stepped out from behind the shrub that had hidden me.

Merlin shouted at him, "We have been tricked, My Lord. He is not wearing your ring."

Their reactions were immediate. I countered their death rays by holding the scroll in front of me. It absorbed the deadly beams. A harsh red shaft of light leapt from the scroll. It completely enveloped them, imprisoning them inside a clear bubble of light. They were left paralysed. Five pairs of fear-filled eyes stared at me.

Red smoke began to filter from Sammael's mouth. The words that I shrieked put a stop to Damnus escaping from his son's body as a layer of flesh grew over Sammael's nose, eyes and ears, and every other orifice in his body. Damnus was trapped inside his son's body.

It was my turn to smile. My words were coated with sarcasm. "Fine superheroes you lot turned out to be. I'm surprised at you, Merlin. You're supposedly clued up in generating make-believe situations, involving people that are not what they seem to be. There's one difference between your inferior replicas and my own. Mine are living people, with beating hearts and feelings. Yours are physically dead replicas. Oh! There's one other thing. I'm immortal. Simple, isn't it? I'm relieved it was my replica that you consigned to the lava. That scroll wasn't real either. Let me introduce you to my kith and kin."

I snapped my fingers. My replica stepped out from behind a shrub. A smile stretched across his face. He bowed to them.

I joked with him. "OK, you've had your fun. Make your way back home. I'll catch up with you later."

He mockingly waved goodbye to them and vanished. Things were leading up to a blood-curdling ending, but I was enjoying myself.

I held the scroll in the air. "This is the real scroll. It will bring Damnus's dreams to an end."

They watched as I broke the seal open. A great wind swept down from the heavens and struck the huge tree, beneath which the seal had been hidden. It burst into flame, sending sparks and smoke flying into the sky. The flames gradually detached themselves from the tree and moulded themselves into a skeleton of a man, dressed in a flowing black robe and sitting astride a sickly-pale horse. The hooded, skeletal face of Death showed no emotion as he stared at them.

The horseman pointed his sword at them. His toneless words showed no trace of pity. "This sword is the instrument of death for those who dare to plot against Magnus. My sword will strip your heads from your bodies; and should you be immortal, beheading you will take away your immortality. My sword will also deny you a life after death."

The horseman shouted towards the heavens. The clouds changed shape and swirled around like a giant whirlpool until a gaping hole appeared in its centre. The words that came from the horseman's mouth were tinged with loathing. "Your evil influence on the world will be ended. Before I condemn your souls into oblivion, I shall pluck your real, and replica, disciples from wherever they may be. You shall watch them meet their end."

The sound of screaming echoed from beyond the clouds, before the swirling mouth of the manic whirlpool started to disgorge thousands of bodies. They shrieked in terror as they were pitched into the molten lake.

The horseman roared with chilling laughter as he stared at Sammael and the others. "Now it is your turn."

He threw his sword at them. It flew through the air and entered the bubble of light that imprisoned them, where it sliced through their necks before returning to his hand. Their bodies collapsed to the ground, and their severed heads exploded as red-hot flames poured from their mouths and eyes.

The horseman spoke to me. "Point the scroll at their bodies."

I did as he asked. A vivid red ray of light flowed from it, which filled the bubble and set their bodies alight before hurling them into the fissure of molten lava. As their souls burned away into nothingness, a column of black smoke rose into the air. The horseman broke down into a gaseous vapour, which glided towards me and seeped into the scroll.

Magnus's voice boomed through the garden. "Damnus and his evil legions are defeated. They will play no part in your present and future life, but they still survive in the past. Damnus has created a world of evil, which I cannot tolerate. You will bring about an apocalypse in your world, then create a new one by travelling back in time and doing away with Damnus and Merlin before they started to put their evil plans into place. Before you do, it is time for you to meet your father again in my parallel world. My tunnel of light will take you to him."

CHAPTER FORTY

He was true to his word. I stuffed the scroll into my pocket before I found myself hurtling upwards through that tunnel of white light. I found myself in my parents' lounge. The two of them were waiting for me. They rushed across to me and put their arms around me. After a few moments my father gently pushed me away. There was a look of pure hero worship on his face.

"Welcome back, Raphael. We were watching what you did down there. Your mother and I are very proud of you."

They didn't have the chance to say anything else. Magnus appeared out of nowhere.

"Enough of this. There is not a moment to waste. We must be on our way to destroy Planet Earth."

He was rushing things too quickly for my liking.

"Before I go, I want my woman, Carin, here on this planet. OK, she's immortal, but I don't intend to let her go through the horror of an apocalypse when I destroy the world. She's in our bedroom, at our house. I've put her into a coma while I am away."

My father looked at Magnus. "Is that all right with you, Father? Azurina can bring her here."

Magnus nodded. "Very well. Do as he asks, but hurry."

My mother disappeared, and minutes later she was standing in front of us with a silent, motionless Carin at her side.

My father put his hand on my shoulder. "She'll be safe with us until you return."

Magnus clapped his hands together. "It is time for us to go."

I shook my head. "Just a minute. How am I supposed to destroy the earth without harming myself?"

"Do not concern yourself about that. We will hover above the earth in a tunnel of light. Hold my scroll in your hand at all times. It will protect us."

My mother blew me a kiss and my father shook my hand. "We'll await your return."

Before I knew it I was hurling down that familiar tunnel, until my body came to rest at the bottom of it. I found myself looking down on Great Britain and the continental countries of Europe as they basked in the sun.

Magnus spoke to me: "Whatever happens, we will be safe. Point my scroll at your world."

I did as he asked. Streams of red light burst from the scroll and travelled deep into the heavens. Outer space was lit up in a fiery red glow, which encircled the world. Thousands upon thousands of huge flaming objects sped on their way towards the earth. As they impacted on every part of the planet, fiery explosions filled the atmosphere with flames and smoke. The whole of earth was clothed in a burning mass of destruction.

Magnus spoke to me. "I am not finished yet. Point my scroll at your world again."

Further streams of red light flowed from the scroll. The light hit the North and South Poles, then spread itself over the whole surface of the world.

Magnus's voice was full of the pleasure he was feeling. "Those fireballs will set off thousands of dormant volcanoes, beneath the oceans and under the land, as well as melting the frozen wastes of earth's two poles. The melting ice, together with the underwater volcanic explosions, will cause the oceans to rise and sweep across every continent on your world. We can say goodbye to mankind. Let us take a closer look at what is happening down there."

The tunnel of light carried me closer to earth's surface and moved me around the planet. Magnus's words were true. The oceans erupted in a fiery mix of water and lava, and every country was quickly covered by giant surges of water that moved swiftly across the whole of earth, killing and destroying everything that lay in their path.

He patted me on the back. "You have one more thing to do before your task here is completed, Raphael. Point my scroll at your planet for the last time."

I did as he asked. A deep-blue light spewed from out of the scroll, and it quickly covered the surface. The effect of the blue light made itself evident after a couple of minutes. The water, covering the whole of earth, turned into ice, and blizzards raged where every continent had been.

Magnus laughed with delight. "You have done well. Anyone who escapes the flood will soon die of the cold or starvation." A huge smile covered his face. "The evil that you created, Damnus, is no more. My dream has been achieved. It now remains for you, Raphael, to seek out Merlin and his woman. My scroll will lead you to them. After you have dealt with them, the scroll will take you hundreds of centuries back in time to the Garden of Philus, where Damnus is about to carry out the first stage of his evil plot to conquer your world. I will meet up with you there. In the meantime, it is time to return you to my world."

I was blasted up the tunnel of light and into my parents' house. They were waiting for me.

My father slapped me on the shoulder. "Well done again. It took a lot of courage to destroy your planet. Don't be upset about what you have done down there. It was the scroll's work, not you. You will soon bring the earth back to life again." He pointed to some clothes lying on the sofa. "Change into those for your journey into Merlin's time, so that you will blend in with the fashion of his century."

I did as he asked, and glanced at Carin, who was sleeping in an armchair. "Look after her while I'm away. When I return for her we'll travel back to a calm and peaceful earth, where I can pick up on being an auctioneer again, and Carin can get on with her doctoring."

My father tapped the side of my head. "Never mind that. Have you got the scroll?"

"Don't worry. It's in my jacket pocket, under this fancy-dress outfit. I'll be off, then. See you soon."

CHAPTER FORTY-ONE

The forest, where I materialised, gave me cover from prying eyes as I discarded my invisibility. I aged myself by forty years using simple sorcery. My disguise was perfect. Even Merlin wouldn't have recognised me. It took me five minutes to reach the town from where Merlin ruled his kingdom.

People walking along the dirt track that ran beneath Merlin's imposing castle didn't take a blind bit of notice of me. Some were selling produce and live animals. The hustle and bustle was silenced as three mounted men, wearing metal helmets, galloped through the town. Everyone bowed as they passed by. I asked a bystander who they were.

The man became agitated. "You are not from these parts, are you? We do not ask that kind of question here." He waggled a thumb at the departing riders and lowered his voice. "That was Merlin with his bodyguards." The poor chap was terrified. "Do not ask any more questions or you could end up a dead man. Merlin's spies are everywhere."

I set off down the track, where the three riders had ridden. During the next ten minutes I didn't meet a soul, until I rounded a bend in the track. Merlin's two bodyguards were loitering outside a stone building that I immediately recognised. As soon as they saw me they drew their swords and scampered down the track towards me. I scarpered back around the bend, then stood my ground, facing them. As they rounded the bend, their faces lit up with glee at the prospect of killing me. They weren't given the chance. As they raised their swords to kill me, I threw my hands out at them and muttered a spell. It stopped them in their tracks before they fell to the ground in an unconscious heap. I dragged their bodies into the forest.

I crept up to the building, as I had done several times before, and peered through a window. My timing was perfect. A worried-looking Merlin watched as an elderly woman delivered a baby from between Emeralda's legs. She slapped the baby's back. Carin's cries let rip. The woman cut the umbilical cord, then washed and dressed the screaming child before nestling her in Emeralda's arms. Merlin hustled the woman outside.

Emeralda held her hand out to Merlin when he returned. He knelt down by her side and kissed her on the lips.

His words carried through the window. "I have killed the woman. My wife must never find out about us and our child."

She looked worried. "Lord Madrog must never learn of our love for each other."

The sorcerer shook his head in disbelief. "Your magic has proved me wrong. It was only yesterday that I took your body. You promised me a daughter today, and I did not believe you. We must hurry. Feed the child, then I will take her to the twentieth century and place her in the care of the people I have chosen to be her parents."

Merlin placed a hand on the child's head and muttered a spell. He smiled at Emeralda. "She will not give her body to any man until she meets my son." He watched the baby sucking at her mother's breast. "Not only have we fathered a daughter, but my son already lives in the twentieth century. Our daughter will one day bear the son of Lord Damnus."

Emeralda pulled my Carin from her nipple and gave her to Merlin. "Take her. When will I see you again?"

"I will be back within the hour. Wait here for me. We have plans to make for the future."

Merlin returned and walked into the building. As I looked through the window, the two of them were canoodling in each other's arms. I took the scroll from under my animal skins and drifted through the wall of the building. Merlin nearly had a heart attack when I revealed myself.

He shouted at me. "Who are you, and what—?"

I didn't give him the chance to say any more. A brilliant yellow light flowed from the scroll and gorged itself on their bodies. They turned to dust, which drifted across the floor and into the scroll. I felt good, and why shouldn't I? The future of the world had already changed, by doing away with Merlin, and so had my own life. Merlin won't be controlling me or Carin in our future life, and Sammael won't be born. My next task was to do away with Damnus before he had the chance to spread his evil in the world.

The scroll took me back in time to the Garden of Philus. My time-shifting was spot on, thanks to the scroll. I spotted people buying produce from a few traders. I was surprised to see Damnus standing among them in his human form. A large lidded wooden box lay on the ground in front of him. I felt Magnus materialise beside me.

"You are looking at some of the first citizens to inhabit your world. My brother will shortly ask a young woman to open that box which you can see. The box contains many of his evil spells, in spirit form. He wants a human being to open that box, which will have the effect of spreading some of his evil throughout the world. With all the skills that he possesses, he is a coward in these early days of earth's existence. He will feel happier if someone else begins the contamination of the world with his evil." I could feel him shaking with silent laughter. "On your world the people talk of Pandora's box being opened, and spreading its evil wares. They are right. You are looking at that very box." He clicked his tongue. "His conscience will not worry him in years to come. Thankfully, I have removed his evil spells from the box. I want you to break your body down and hide yourself in that box. When the box is opened, you will come out and reveal yourself to my brother. That is the moment when the scroll will rid the world of his evil presence. Think the command, and get into that box, then point my scroll at him as soon as the box is opened."

I did as he asked, and didn't have to wait long.

I heard Damnus speak to someone. "Young lady, I wish to make a present of this box to you. Open it up and see what is inside."

I heard her squeal with delight; then she opened the box. That was my cue to make myself visible. The young woman, and the other folk, shrieked in terror and ran off into the forest.

Damnus turned on me. "Who are you? Where did you come from?" He started to mouth a spell at me.

I pointed the scroll at him. He screamed as he was shackled by the powerful yellow light that shone from it. An earthquake shook the ground, and day was turned into night. A blood-red moon hung in the sky. Two lightning bolts surged towards earth from out of the heavens. The first bolt struck Damnus on his neck. His screaming head fell to the ground, where it burned itself out, together with his body. All that remained of him was a pile of ashes. The other bolt buried itself in the ground, splitting it wide open. A lake of bubbling lava was drawn from the depths of the fissure.

A tongue of fire leapt from the scroll and licked at the burned remains of Damnus. A spiritual force leapt from his ashes in the shape of a winged bullock, which was drawn into the scroll. It moved about in my hands as the burned remnants of Damnus were enticed into it, to join what was left of Merlin and Emeralda.

Magnus spoke to me. "Throw the scroll into the lava. Damnus and Merlin have perished forever. Earth is free from their evil. Make a new life with your woman, and return to your father's planet. My thanks go with you."

He disappeared, and I tossed the scroll into the lava. As it burned away, I heard screams coming from it. Moments later, no trace remained of what had taken place. The fissure of lava, the dark sky and the blood-red moon had gone. The Garden of Philus flourished in all its beauty. I willed myself back to my father's world, where my parents were waiting for me. The three of us hugged each other, knowing that Damnus had gone forever. I returned to earth, with Carin, promising my parents that we would return to see them in the near future.

We ended up in our house, where I laid Carin on our bed. Being the suspicious sod that I am, I wanted proof that I'd really done away with Damnus and Merlin. I spirited myself forward in time to the Damnus Day celebrations that I'd witnessed. Brine & Cherry's premises lay silent. The crowds, the media and the hundreds of celebrities who'd gathered for his big day were conspicuous by their absence. My flat wasn't burned out, nor had the offices and showrooms been ransacked. I smiled at the sight of Martin Henderson taking a steady walk down the road. I can't describe the feeling of elation that flowed through me.

I travelled forward in time, back to our house. I kneeled by Carin and held her hand. Two things will change in our lives. I intend to walk her down the aisle during the next few months, and I will wipe the memories from her mind, of what happened in her previous life. She will never remember that Merlin was her father, but she will recall the powers of sorcery that we share. I still want her to produce her life-saving medicines by using our sorcery, to cure the diseases that ravage our world. I kissed my beautiful green-eyed woman and thanked Magnus, in my mind, for ensuring that the Damnus apocalypse had never taken place.